Intrepid

Intrepid

Gord Francis

iUniverse, Inc.
Bloomington

Intrepid

iUniverse books may be ordered through booksellers or by contacting:

iUniverse
1663 Liberty Drive
Bloomington, IN 47403
www.iuniverse.com
1-800-Authors (1-800-288-4677)

ISBN: 978-1-4620-6219-5 (sc)
ISBN: 978-1-4620-6221-8 (hc)
ISBN: 978-1-4620-6220-1 (e)

Printed in the United States of America

iUniverse rev. date: 11/01/2011

Chapter 1

"Babes in chain mail bikinis?" The voice was female and strong, authoritarian, with a touch of an exotic accent, and loud enough that it cut right through the rapid click clack of steel wheels on rails. Don looked up to see a real babe, in an officer's uniform. He dropped the paperback and was halfway to his feet, his right hand going for a salute even before he remembered to look for her rank. He glanced at her collar tabs, and though he was unfamiliar with the uniform, he guessed her rank was the same as his. Total bottom of the totem pole.

Olive skinned and very pretty, with jet-black hair drawn back into a tight bun, she had ebony eyes and stood at least a hundred and ninety centimeters to his two ten. She was wide in the shoulders, but slim in the waist and hips. An athlete. He caught the lightest scent of perfume and talcum, contrasting with the smell of unwashed bodies, grease and ozone that seemed to cling to every passenger car on every railroad everywhere. Her mouth was, he searched for a word and found it. Kissable. Definitely kissable. "Lieutenant?" he asked, catching the headrest of the seat in front of him. She, he decided, would look great in anything, including chain mail.

"Subteniente," she said, and smiled. Don felt something go flip-flop in his gut and he forced himself to swallow.

He noticed her shoulder tabs with the purple stripe and guessed, "Mexico?"

"Estado Libre y Soberano de Oaxaca." She held out her hand. "Juanita Concepcion Hernandez y Romero, with the air arm, the Fuerza Aérea Mexicana. You're not American."

Don had been enjoying listening to her accent and it took a moment for him to remember to reply. "Don Fields, Canada. From Saskatoon, or there a-bouts.

"Acting Sub-Lieutenant."

Her handshake was dry, firm and friendly, not too prolonged, not to short.

"There a-bouts?"

"Did you ever hear of a town called Prince Albert?"

"No, I think not. Is there a-bouts your state?"

He shook his head with a grin. "No, it means nearby. The province is Saskatchewan, Saskatoon is the capital, and Prince Albert is my hometown." He glanced at his seatmate, an old man muffled in a long gray overcoat in spite of the heat. He knew he couldn't ask her to sit down, so he said, "You know, there's a dining car on this train. Could we perhaps have a coffee, maybe talk shop for a while?"

She smiled. "I thought you'd never ask."

In the dinning car, with fresh coffee and Danish, they grinned at each other again.

"So, what are a Canadian acting sub-lieutenant, fresh out of college, and a beautiful, decorated, Mexican Subteniente doing deep in the American southwest?"

She took the beautiful part totally in stride, as was her due. "Decorated?"

"You have two ribbons below your wings."

"You've been looking at my chest," she deadpanned, though there was a devious glimmer in her eye.

"Professional curiosity only," he said, though he knew he had been caught looking.

"My foot," she said. "You were wondering what I would look like in a chain mail bikini." She didn't give him time to rebut the obvious, which was more than fortunate; Don was lousy with small talk. Usually he just babbled until he shoved at least one foot in his mouth, sometimes both feet, instantly losing whatever credibility he had. He just hoped she was a bit more sophisticated than the girls he was used to. Then he sighed. What girls? All he had done for the last four years had been school and the military. When he went home on leave, which was rare, all he did was study for the next term. There had been no time for girls.

No, that wasn't true either. The truth was, he was just too shy, and most girls thought he was a geek, which was why he had joined the armed forces anyway. Wasn't it? To become more of a man and less a living breathing calculator.

"The ribbons are the Mérito Técnico Militar, and the Condecoración al Mérito Facultativo, both prima class. I can't tell you about the Mérito Técnico Militar because that's top secret, but the Condecoración al Mérito Facultativo is for academic excellence."

"First class," he said.

"Si, prima class. I assume you did well in school also?"

"Very high honors. Physics, space sciences and math."

"You have wings as well."

"I did a summer with 4 Wing, Cold Lake. General Parkinson decided four months was long enough for me to qualify, so he sent me to flight school, even though that wasn't supposed to be part of my program. I ended up doing about three hundred hours in a CF-18A. I got hooked on it and I applied to be assigned to one of the Wings as a pilot when I graduated, but I got sent here instead." No hoof in mouth yet. He started to hope against hope.

"You didn't want to be a pilot when you started school? I can't believe that!"

Don laughed and his eyes lit up. "Well, I've gotta admit I love flying, but I also want to design the next generation of birds. Can you imagine being part of a team that designed a working sub-orbital strike-craft? Wow! Or maybe the next vertical takeoff and landing jet to be deployed from a submarine?"

He saw the look on her face and he took a sip of his coffee. "Sorry, I get carried away. What did you qualify in?"

"I trained in a Pilatus PC-7, and then moved to a Northrop F-5."

"I know the F-5. We call it the CF-5. It's a pretty old airframe. I took one for a spin around the base once, but I'd already qualified in the 18A, so, even though it's a good ride I wasn't terribly impressed."

"Honestly, I was, until I tried something faster."

Don was about to ask her what she had tried that was faster, but a smooth, deep masculine voice interrupted him.

"What is this, an invasion?"

Both Juanita and Don looked up and saw a tall, handsome young black man in a tailored, dark blue American naval officer's uniform. Don 's first thought was that he was another athlete, perhaps football, or maybe wresting. He carried his cover under his arm and a friendly smile on his lips. Don glanced at his sleeve and saw the single stripe. "Lieutenant?"

"Ensign. Ensign Robert White. Not a word. Not a single word."

Don decided on the spot that he liked Ensign White. "Which word? Bobwhite?" Juanita looked bewildered, but both young men ignored her.

"You, are asking for it." The threat carried no vehemence, so Don ignored it.

"Yeah. Siddown, Mr. Ensign White. My name's Don, and this is Juanita." He held out a hand to be shaken. The grip that answered his own was both strong and firm, but not boastful.

Rob put his cover on the table and slid in beside Don. "Don't mind if I do. Lemme guess. You two have got orders to Dreamland?"

"US Air Force Flight Test Center, Detachment 3," said Juanita. "Groom Lake, Nevada."

"Same here, Bob," said Don. "My orders say to come on this train, and I'll be met at the terminal in Kingman, Arizona."

"También las minas."

"Mine three," said Robert. "So, listen, call me Rob, not Bob. Looks like we're all going to the same place. Now my question is, what does Area 51 want with a newly minted naval ensign and a couple of foreign pilots, out in the middle of a desert?"

"Area 51?" asked Juanita.

"It's slang terminology for the base we're going to," explained Don. "It's got several other names, like, the Skunk Works and Dreamland, but Area 51 is the name it's known by. Believe it or not, the official government line is that the base doesn't even exist. Lots of chain link fence, no trespassing signs, lots of heavily armed guards with orders that say to shoot to kill, vicious dogs, spotlights and stuff, but you're not supposed to notice that. Officially, area 51 doesn't exist."

"Like the President's mistress, she doesn't exist either," said Rob. "Only, the whole country knows her name, and just about everything else about her, including her shoe size. So my question was, what does the good ol' US of A want with me, a traditional deep water sailor if there ever was one, and you, a couple of wet behind the ears foreigners, out here in the arid and dry desert?"

"We were just asking ourselves that," admitted Juanita. "I know my orders came directly from El Presidente."

"The president?" There was a hushed awe in Rob's voice. Don saw him sit up straighter, his jaw drop a little and his eyes open wide.

"Julio Mendez Salazar." Juanita looked at his face and laughed. "El Presidente de México. You Estadounidense! You can't see past your own borders."

"Of course," Rob said, closing his mouth and relaxing.

"Mine were signed by the Chief of the Defense Staff," said Don.

"He is important to your country?" asked Juanita.

"He's the chief military honcho of Canada. I'm surprised he even knows I exist. Actually, he probably doesn't. My working hypothesis is that somebody else drew up my orders and put them in front of him for a signature."

"Humph," sniffed Rob. "And I was pretty impressed when I saw mine were signed by Vice Admiral Shane."

Don glanced at his wristwatch. "Whoops! It's 23:35. We should be getting to Kingman any minute now. Let's get back to our seats and gather our stuff." Even as he spoke he could feel the train start to decelerate, and by the time he had made it back to his seat and gathered his laptop and duffel, he could see the local Amtrak station slowly roll into view. The porter was just opening the doors to the desert night as he reached them. He quickly stepped down the three steps to the tarmac and slipped on his cover.

The air was much cooler than it had been during the day. The last time Don had been outside was in Chicago, where he had changed trains from the Buffalo to Chicago run on the Lake Shore Limited, to the Southwest Chief. The day had been cool then, but by the time they had reached Kansas City at 07:45, the weather had become much warmer. Later, when they had rolled through Dodge City at 12:34, it had become a scorcher and he had chosen to stay in the somewhat air-conditioned comfort of the passenger car. Now however, the cool desert night had fallen and he was thankful for his uniform jacket and cover. Looking around for his new friends, he thought he saw uniformed figures over by the terminal building, but immediately he saw that it wasn't Rob and Juanita, but a middle aged police officer and a young, female American Army second lieutenant.

Even as he realized they weren't his friends, he saw her hand the policeman something, and the police officer hand her what looked like a small red box in return.

Turning, she noticed him and quickly stuffed the box into her pocket. Taking in his uniform at a glance she carefully put a smile on her face and held out her hand. "Acting Sub-Lieutenant Fields?" she asked.

"Got me on the first try," Don admitted, shaking her hand.

"I," she said, "am very good at what I do. Besides, you're the only Canadian in the lot.

"I'm Second Lieutenant Anna Fleet, and I'm here to drive you out to the base. You have checked luggage?"

"I do." He took a moment to look her over and decided that while she wasn't as tall or curvaceous as Subteniente Hernandez y Romero, she would still look great in chain mail. Maybe silver chain mail, as opposed to the gold he had picked for Juanita. She did make a good first impression though, medium length dark blond hair and a trim figure, a starched uniform shirt, neatly pressed trousers and gleaming combat boots. A second look showed him bags under her eyes and a weary expression. He filed the information away. This assignment, he decided, is looking better by the minute, though he preferred Juanita's uniform skirt, nylons and heels to Anna's trousers and boots.

"Why don't you grab it, and I'll look for the others. There's a Hummer in the parking lot; you can't miss it. It's light blue and it's got, 'US Air Force,' printed in huge black letters on the side."

"Well, if it's no problem, I'll just wait for them. I met Ensign White and Subteniente Hernandez y Romero on the train and we agreed to meet here on the platform." He looked over the small crowd of passengers and almost instantly spotted his new friends in the crowd. Fleet frowned and started to say something, but Don cut her off. "There they are now." He waived and the two grabbed their bags, trotting over. "Guys," he introduced them to Fleet. "Second Lieutenant Anna Fleet. Ensign White, Subteniente Hernandez y Romero."

"Pleased to meet you," said Fleet, but she didn't look pleased. For a moment Don wondered if he had done something wrong, but then he forgot about it. After waiting for a few minutes while the Amtrak baggage handlers unloaded their luggage from the train, they busied themselves gathering their various totes and carrying them out to the Hummer. Then Don and Rob climbed into the back, letting Juanita ride shotgun up front.

"Ok," said Fleet, when they were ready to go. "It's about two hours to Vegas, and another couple of hours to base, so we should get there about 03:30 or 04:00 hours. Sleep if you can, because reveille is at 06:30. Anybody who snores gets to walk. Got it?

"Let's go."

One moment Don was having a very pleasant dream, and the next thing he knew, the Hummer was sliding sideways on the shoulder of the road in a rude awakening. "What the?" he shouted, but the question was moot when a huge semi trailer blasted past them on the right side of the vehicle, going the opposite direction, it's air horn wide open. With a shudder of bakes, Fleet finally skidded the truck to a stop.

"What happened?" Rob demanded, even while Juanita spieled off a dozen questions in excited Spanish.

"I think somebody fell asleep at the wheel." Don said, and checked his wristwatch. "02:10 hours. Is everybody all right? Anna?"

The army lieutenant had her arms crossed across the wheel and her head down resting on them. She muttered something, but Don couldn't hear her. "Anna, are you all right?" he tried again.

"Yes, I'm all right," she said, raising her voice, but Don could see that she wasn't.

"I'll tell you what," replied the Canadian. "We've all been resting except you, so why don't you let me drive for a while, while you get some shuteye. It's not like we're going to be able to sleep anymore."

"And what's that supposed to mean?" Fleet demanded loudly.

"It means you fell asleep at the wheel and nearly killed us. We are now officially wide awake, and I'd like to take over for a while to let you rest," said Don.

"I think having Don drive for a while might be a good idea," said Rob, trying to soothe Fleet's bristle. "Besides, his grunting is keeping me awake."

Glaring at Don, Fleet got out and changed places with him. "We've just left Las Vegas. Keep going up US ninety-five until you reach a sign that says, 'Mercury Highway.' It's more of a Y than a turn. Follow that till you reach Short Pole Road. That should be about forty-five minutes. Mercury Highway will rejoin Short Pole about thirty minutes later and they run simultaneous for a while. When they split up, stay on Mercury Highway until you hit Groom Lake Road. Turn right on Groom Lake and drive until you see a heavily guarded entrance on the right. Pull in there, and you better have your orders with you, or you're dead meat."

"Got it. Take 95 to Mercury, Mercury to Short Pole, and Short Pole to Mercury Rd to Groom Lake. There will be guards on the entrance to the left. Are there any Tim Horton's around here?" Don replied. "You know, for coffee, eh?"

"I don't know what a Tim Horton's is," said Fleet.

"Then you ain't livin'," said Don, and threw the Hummer into gear. One and a half hours later he pulled up on the shoulder of the road, just as the lights on the gates ahead came into sight. "Hey, Lieutenant Anna," he called over his shoulder, waking her up. "Do you want to drive from here on in?"

"No," she snapped, suddenly sitting up straight and rubbing her eyes. As a tribute to her exhaustion she had actually fallen asleep, though the others were still wide-awake. "And get moving! You don't want to be found here, stopped on the road in the middle of the night, right beside a high security military facility!"

"Whoops," Don said, laughing, and quickly pulled onto the highway again, turning right onto the gravel road and driving right up to the closed, steel mesh gates that blocked it a hundred feet from the highway. The reception committee was about what he expected, two enlisted airmen with body armor and Kevlar helmets, what looked like machine pistols, a bomb-sniffing dog and a clipboard. There had to be a clipboard, just to make it official. Don could see what looked like a couple more men through the smoked glass window of a guard shack and guestimated that there might be at least two more standing to one side, unseen in the dark.

The airmen were courteous but thorough, having them step out of the truck while they went over it and examining all their papers with quick professional care. Ten minutes later the sergeant stepped back, gave Don a quick salute, and had his companion open the gate. Following Fleet's mumbled directions, Don drove five miles down the gravel road and then followed a deserted maze through the several buildings. Twenty minutes later he finally pulled the Hummer up to their billet, a low bungalow on a quiet side street, where they unloaded their luggage. Then he drove the truck through the camp over to the motor pool, grateful that the sergeant at the gate had given him detailed directions instead of Anna. A helpful airman on the midnight shift offered, and Don gratefully accepted, a lift back to the billet. By the time he stumbled inside the other three had already gone to bed, so he brushed his teeth in the communal bathroom, located a room with an empty bed and fell into it.

"Get up, and move," For a moment, Don didn't recognize the voice, but he instantly recognized the meaning of the words. "We've got a meeting with the Comandante in quince minutos." Reacting instantly, he rolled from his bed and charged into the bathroom, jumping into the shower while the water was still ice cold. Exactly fifteen minutes later, scrubbed, shaved and polished in his number ones, he walked into the General's anteroom with his new friends.

The base offices were all located in a group of three two story buildings a five-minute walk from the airstrip. They were smaller than the hangers, but all seemed to be built from the same plans, roughly twenty meters wide by forty long, the offices arranged on both sides of wide central hallways that ran the length of the buildings. The outsides were covered in white painted clapboards and they all had dark green metal roofs. The floors inside were hardwood, and the walls were generally wainscoted to about one meter high. General Hines occupied a two-room suite on the second floor at the north end of the first building, which Don noticed also held the base library and a small museum. He made a note to himself to come back and get a library card, even as he and his friends raced past.

The female sergeant at the desk was in her forties, trim and fit, with darkly dyed hair and pleasantly ugly in an old fashioned way. The sign on her desk said Sergeant McCowan. "Take a seat with the others," she said, pointing to where two young men in unfamiliar uniforms sat perfectly straight in ancient wooden chairs.

"Sargento, gracias," said Juanita, and they took seats.

Don had just pried his eyes from Juanita's legs, and was about to introduce himself to the two strangers when the phone on the Sergeant's desk rang and she answered it with a brisk, "Yes, sir?" A moment and another quick, "Yes, sir," later, the six were on their feet and moving into the general's office, automatically coming to a straight line and standing at attention before his desk. Fleet, the last one in, took a position at the end of the line, stepped forward, saluted and said, "Reporting as ordered, Sir." Then she stepped back into line.

The office wasn't large, but not small either, a desk, an assortment of chairs, a credenza behind the desk, under a large window, a dozen pictures on the walls, mostly of the general with other people. Don recognized the last President as one. The walls were light blue, there was an American Flag in one corner and both the desk and the credenza were clear of clutter. One wall was covered in books, but they were at the opposite side of the room from him and he didn't get to see the titles, which he regretted. He thought he could probably get a better picture of the officer behind the desk from the books he read than the people he had his picture taken with.

The General didn't rise; he just looked them over for a moment with sharp green eyes. Abruptly he snapped, "Stand easy." Don chanced a glance, but only a brief one. The man looked to be in his late fifties, or possibly early sixty's, bald and sunburned, slightly overweight, clean-shaven, strong and tough looking. Those were the two words that burned themselves into Don's memory. Strong and tough.

"My name is Major General Hines, and you report to me. To me, and only to me, nobody else.

"I assume that none of you have any clue whatsoever why you are here.

"For your information, you are part of Project Mountain Bluebird. I could call it an officer exchange, but I won't. For the two Americans among you, you are the brightest and best we have in your fields, and you have been assigned here to work on an ultra secret project that you may never discuss in a public place, with anyone else other than maybe the president himself. And then only if I tell you that you can. As for the four others, even your existence here is secret.

"The reason you are here is not because we wanted to have an officer exchange with your countries, though highly qualified officers have been sent to your respective lands in exchange for your services. The reason you are here is because you are the best. If I say that, within the project's parameters, Subteniente Hernandez is the best pilot, I don't mean the best pilot from Mexico. I mean that there's only one other pilot in the world that comes close to her, and that's acting Sub-Lieutenant Don Fields, from Canada.

"We could easily have filled our team with Americans and still had incredible talent, but we have a project here that is bigger than you, bigger than me, and certainly bigger than my pride as an American, so we decided to go for the absolute best people we could get, period. Flying Officer William Post of the New Zealand Air Force is uniquely qualified as a navigator; Lieutenant Doctor Tyrone Shackle of Australia is about six years older than the rest of you. He is presently an intern and will be completing his studies here at the base hospital. That's not going to leave him much time, but he will be liaising with you on certain parts of the project. He will also be reviewing your knowledge of first aid and medicine in general.

"Pay attention, he's more than good at what he does."

"Ensign Robert White, nicknamed Bobwhite, is also known as navy running back number twenty seven. I saw your moves in the Army Navy game last year, young man. You've got amazing hands on you, and astonishing footwork. You can really move those size twelve's."

"Ah, thirteen's, sir. Thank you, sir."

"Where was I? Oh, yes, Ensign White graduated from Annapolis with the highest mark ever awarded in the Nuclear Studies Program, and I hear he's a pretty good lawyer as well. Second Lieutenant Anna Fleet probably knows more about ordnance and electronics than anybody else alive.

"There were supposed to be two other members of this team, a Brit named Sarah Franks, and a Frenchie named Andre Dupuis. Unfortunately there was an accident late last night and their aircraft went down in the North Atlantic. There's a search team out looking for them of course, but our hopes are slim. Flying Officer Post, what's the problem?"

"Sir, I, ah, dated Sarah Franks when we were at Cranwell, sir.

We are actually quite close," William said. "We're not engaged, but I plan to ask her to marry me. Sir."

"I see." The General paused for a moment before he continued, and Don thought he detected a real note of concern in the man's voice. "Son, I will do everything I can to make sure you are kept up to date on the search. I'd forgotten you New Zealanders go to the RAF College Cranwell. I can see that things will be pretty difficult for you, but concentrating on your work might help. If things become too much, I'd suggest you report to the Chaplain's office. Dr. Slone is a trained councilor and can probably help you. Meanwhile, I'm shipping you off to study astronomy at the Kitt Peak National Observatory. It's near Tucson Arizona. You leave at 10:00 hours. An airman will pick you up at your barracks and take you there. I don't have to remind you that you will be representing me while you are there and I expect you to act like the supposed American officer you are. The airman who drives you over will have your papers and drill you on US Air Force protocols on the way.

"Which brings me to a couple of housekeeping items we have to consider. I can't keep calling you Acting Sub-Lieutenant, or Flying Officer, or Subteniente. For the next year you will be called, and respond to, in private, Ensign, and in public, Lieutenant. For the first while the uniforms that you wear will be US Air Force, with second lieutenant's bars. As far as the world is concerned, that's what you are, low class US officers. You can pick up appropriate uniforms at stores. There will be other uniforms for you later, but not yet. You may wear civilian clothing when you are not on duty. You will live on base in the housing assigned to you. You may leave the base, but only with a proper pass, obtainable by applying through the personnel office.

"You will not discuss the base or anything about it with anyone, including military officers when you are off base.

"Obviously, you will have no visitors.

"You will not send letters home telling your folks where you are. A forwarding address will be given to you, and you will use it.

"Lieutenant Fleet has already been here for a week. She can fill you in on the rest of the rules.

"You will return to your quarters and get yourselves properly squared away. I'll be sending someone over with further instructions.

"Dismissed."

All six had saluted and were turning to leave when he said, "Oh, and by the way. At the end of one year you will each be promoted one rank by your respective services. If you continue with us for a second year, at my discretion, you may again be promoted at the end of that year. Dismissed."

"And, we're still in the dark," said Rob as they exited the building. "Though I do like the idea about making full Lieutenant in two years! Nobody told me about that!

"So you two guys are from the other side of the world?" he held out his hand to Lieutenant Doctor Shackle. "I'm called Rob, not Bobwhite, and this here's Anna, Juanita and Don."

"Well, you all look normal enough," the Doctor said, his accent directly out of a Mad Max movie. He was perhaps 195 centimeters tall, thin, with a bit of a protruding Adam's apple and a neatly trimmed mustache. His voice was a rich baritone "Considering how the General was praising you in there, I thought you might all glow in the dark or something."

"You might want to wait until the sun goes down before you decide that," said Don. "So, do we call you, Doc, or Tyrone, or Ty, or what?"

"I prefer Sacks."

"You've got it. William, what do you prefer?" the New Zealander was a handsome man, strongly built with an intelligent face. Just a little shorter than the Doctor he had dark hair, darker eyes and a square jaw. Post looked at him for a moment and Don thought he was going to be verbally horsewhipped. The man had a reason to be upset and was. Then he gave a tight smile and said, "Personally, I'd prefer to be called general, or sir, in informal situations and just saluted in public ones, but in your case I'll make a special concession. Call me Will. I do not like, I do hate, and I will not respond to, Bill."

"You've got it, General," said Rob with a laugh that broke the tension. "I think you is a man after mine own heart," and even Will laughed a little.

"So," asked Sacks. "Where are we living, and is there a Starbucks nearby?"

"Obviously you don't properly appreciate a good cup of coffee," said Don.

"¿Qué, usted no quiere Starbucks?" demanded Juanita, more than a tinge of disapointment in her voice. "And all along I thought you were perfect!"

"A good cup of Navy Shaft Lube will convert the lot of you," said Rob. "If it don't kill you that its."

"You'll all probably have to live on overcooked cafeteria juice," said Anna.

"Does it have chicory in it?" Rob asked. "I hate chicory."

"I'll tell you what," said Sacks. "First guy who gets a pass runs into town, if there is one near here, which I doubt, he picks up a coffee pot and some decent coffee."

"Drip?"

"Duh."

"With salt?"

"You put salt in your coffee?" asked Anna, with a grimace.

"Well, yeah," said Don and Sacks together. "Doesn't everybody?"

Chapter 2

B ack at their barracks, Don got his first chance to look around. The barracks was a low square white clapboard building, a smaller version of the offices, with one long corridor dividing it in two, running right through the middle from front to back. On one side of the corridor were three bedrooms, each with three beds, and each of those with a battered bedside table, a lamp and a desk. One wall had three numbered closets and every bedroom had a small sink in one corner. On the other side of the corridor were a sitting room and a kitchenette, both open to the hall, and a communal bath separating them. There were two large covered porches, one at the front of the building, and one at the rear, each with a few chairs on them for sitting in the shade. Someone had tried to put in lawns, but obviously forgotten to water them.

There was an excellent view from both porches, but only of other barracks buildings, of which there were several. Off in the distance were some large buildings, marked with large numbers painted neatly on their sides so from their size and shape, Don assumed they were hangers. Every few minutes he could hear the roar of an aircraft taking off, though he couldn't actually see them from the porch. From the sounds there were many different types and sizes.

Further off, there was desert full of sun burned soil, scrub brush and nothing else.

Juanita and Anna had grabbed the middle room the night before, and Don had crashed in the first bedroom inside the front door, while Rob had snagged the back bedroom. Now, Will moved his gear in with Rob, and Sacks dumped his bags on one of the beds in Don's room.

"Welcome to my humble home," said Don, and grabbed one of his own bags to unload it.

"You haven't been here long?" the doctor asked, busy unpacking his own stuff. "Wow, nice sword."

Don grinned and hung the weapon above his bed. "I was in the color guard at Kingston. The sword was a requirement for the uniform. I sort of got hooked on it and I studied fencing for a year and a half. Got pretty good too, even though there was no requirement to know how to use the thing. Of course, I haven't had time to go home and drop it off since I graduated."

"I went to the Australian Defense Force School in Canberra for my B Sc. Then I went over to New South Wales for my MD in space medicine," Sacks said.

Don stripped off his dress uniform and pulled on civvies. Sacks did the same. "Physics, Math and Space Sciences. We got in here so late last night it wasn't last night anymore, it was early morning. I think I got maybe two hours snooze before Juanita called me. Which was fifteen minutes before we met you. Did you fly in?" he put his dress uniform on a hanger and covering it with a travel bag, hung it in the closet.

"Yeah. Seven forty-seven from Hawaii to Las Angles International, and then a short hop from there to Las Vegas. We were met in Vegas and transported here this morning by copter. It's actually been quite the six months."

"Six months?"

"Sure mate, six months. I graduated at the end of November, and I've spent the last six months in flight school. Course, soon as they taught me how to fly a plane, they go and try to teach me to jump outta one. Blooming generals all gotta have a real, full-size screw loose, I tell you."

"It's a pity about the Brit and the Frenchie," said Don.

"It's awful. I met Will on the plane from LA to Vegas. We weren't sitting together, didn't even know we were going to the same place, but he seems a nice bloke. I hope he's all right."

"Me too." They finished their unpacking and then went to meet the others on the front porch. Even while they were discussing walking back to offices so that they could all get library cards, a large white Ford van pulled up and Sergeant McCowan jumped out, walked up the steps and saluted.

"Sirs, General Hines said I should give you a lift to stores to pick up your uniforms."

"Thank you, Sergeant," said Rob. "Lead on."

It turned out that stores was a fifteen-minute drive away, and quite an extensive operation. Surprisingly, the clerk had also heard from General Hines, knew their names and rank. He guided them efficiently through the selection of uniforms and equipment, taking no more than an hour and a half to have them completely outfitted. Having McCowan drive them back to their billet, they each changed into air force uniforms and met again on the porch. "Wow," said Juanita, "qué buen aspecto o qué?"

"Don't we ever," agreed Will. "Though I'd rather be in my own uniform. Oh, and you might just want to take off some of those price tags. They make you stick out like a sore thumb."

"¿Qué?" Juanita yelped, checking her uniform.

"Not nice," said Anna, but she laughed along with the rest of them. Don thought she had a nice laugh. Not as nice as Juan's, but nice.

"General, we all stick out like sore thumbs," said Sacks. "Right now I just want to sleep, maybe right here on this chair." He slumped down on the chair and most of his new friends snorted their agreement. It had been a hard couple of days for all of them.

"Officer on deck," snapped Rob, springing from his chair and coming to a rigid attention. Instantly all five of the others followed suit.

"Officer on deck? You think you're in the navy Mister? This is the air force! Are you lost? Who are Hernandez and Fields?" the voice snapped the last question with a sound like a lion deprived of its prey. Don stepped forward to see an angry marine captain, flanked by a pair of grim looking first Lieutenants.

"Sir, I'm Lieutenant Fields. This is Lieutenant Hernandez," Don said.

"Oh you are," said the Captain, his voice dripping sarcasm. "What's your unit, Lieutenant? You're not wearing a patch, and that means you're out of uniform. That means you too Hernandez. And no name tags, though I see you're both wearing wings. What did you qualify in Mister, a Cessna?"

Don thought of telling him, but at the last moment decided against it. If he said CF-18A it would tell the man that he wasn't an American officer at all. "Sir, with all due respect, sir, I am not allowed to divulge that information. Sir."

"You're not going to tell me your unit? Not a smart move Mr. Fields. Hernandez, what unit are you with? What are you doing here?"

"Sir," Juanita said, "I am not at liberty to divulge that information to you. Sir."

"And what are you, sixteen years old? Are we sending teenagers to flight school these days? And just who do you two think you are?"

"Sir," said Juanita, "I don't understand your point. Sir."

"Flight school," said the captain. "I've got two good officers who've been disqualified from flight school tomorrow so that you two can be parachuted in."

"If I may ask, sir," said Juanita. "What airframe? Neither Lieutenant Fields, nor I, have orders to, nor have we applied to, flight school."

"Excuse me, ma'am, sirs," Sergeant McCowan was back with a small folder. "The Lieutenants are ordered to flight school at 08:00 hours tomorrow. The orders are signed by General Hines."

"Lemme see those orders," the Captain, whose uniform jacket bore the name Golden, reached for the packet, but McCowan refused to give it to him, or back down.

"Sir, These orders are stamped top secret, and I am under orders to give them directly to Lieutenants Fields and Hernandez. With all due respect sir, as you can see, I am armed and authorized to use extreme measures to maintain the security level stamped on these orders. Also, sir, General Hines is taking a personal interest in the Lieutenants. I strongly suggest that he would prefer to answer your questions himself. Sir."

"Are you trying to intimidate me, Sergeant?"

"Sir, no sir. I am giving you some respectful advice. Sir."

"Then you're just being subordinate?" demanded Golden.

"I think you are, Captain." Don risked a glance over Golden's head to see that several men and officers had gathered in the graveled front yard of the bungalow. Chief among them was a full Colonel.

"Sir." Captain Golden, as well as his two lieutenants, came to attention, saluting.

"Captain," said the Colonel, "I think you're new here, so I'm going to give you some quick advice. The rest of you, except for Fields and Hernandez, get lost." He waited a moment while the onlookers left and the other Lieutenants filed inside the cottage. Then he pointed at the chairs and said, "Please, all of you, sit down."

"First, Lieutenants, do you have a reason for refusing the Captain's orders?"

Don said, "Sir, we have direct orders from General Hines to maintain a certain level of security, sir."

The colonel nodded. "That's good enough for me. General Hines is my superior officer, and I respect the chain of command. Do you respect the chain of command, Captain?"

"Sir, with all due respect," began Golden, but the Colonel interrupted him.

"The question was fairly simple Captain. Do you respect the chain of command? A simple yes or no will do."

"Yes. Sir."

"Lieutenants," he was looking at the marines, who looked to Don like they both wished they were somewhere else. "Do you respect the chain of command?"

"Sir, yes, sir," they answered in chorus, with no hesitation.

"Good. You two are dismissed. Sergeant, please give the orders you have to their respective recipients and leave."

"Yes, sir," said McCowan, handed over the orders to the two ensigns and had them sign receipts. Poker faced, she turned back to the Colonel, gave him a parade ground salute and left.

"You two may now leave as well," he said to Don and Juanita. "I will send over unit patches for you later today. Please don't go anywhere without them."

Both Don and Juanita saluted and went inside, only to hurry into the dark bedroom shared by Don and Sacks, where they joined the other lieutenants listening at the windows to the conversation just outside.

"Captain," they heard the Colonel say in a conversational voice. "You know that this base is rumored to have more than a passing acquaintance with secret operations and protocols, right?"

"Yes, sir." It was clear from his tone of voice that the Captain was waiting for the other shoe to fall. He had made a mistake and knew it. And he didn't like where it had gotten him. The colonel, however, seemed to have decided not to be angry.

"Well, I'm not going to confirm, or deny that, but I think a wise officer might understand that old saying about smoke and fire. You know, where there's smoke, there's likely to be a fire? And I think a wise officer might want to avoid the fire, to keep from burning his fingers, you know what I mean? Especially if he's not only aware of, but signed the official secrets act. Right? You have signed the official secrets act haven't you? Because if you haven't signed it, then you shouldn't be here!

"I mean, I don't know you, or why you're here, but I do know that there is a specific marine captain, and a group of lieutenants who are here to train on and test a modified helicopter airframe, a secret super stealth modification I think. A captain who, if he made too much of a fuss might just find the whole exercise canceled and his group sent back to Texas without ever even laying eyes on the helicopter, disappointing both himself, his lieutenants, and maybe even the people who sent him here. Do you understand, Captain?"

"Ah, yes, sir."

"I see we understand each other. You see, I don't know much more about these youngsters than you do, but General Hines has asked me to keep an eye out for them. So, later today I'm going to send over shoulder patches from the twenty-third air force. I've done it before, and I don't worry too much about the commander of the twenty-third finding out. I do him favors and he does me favors. As far as you are concerned, all of these officers belong to the twenty-third. As a matter of fact, if you run into anybody here who does not wear a unit patch, and it will happen from time to time, you will assume that they belong to the twenty-third and you will never again mention it, either here, or after you leave this base.

"Also, I know this. General Hines is in charge of special operations here on this base, and he can be one vicious son of a gun. Well, that's putting it politely. When my General gives an order to a Lieutenant, and somebody, like a Marine Captain for instance, tries to interfere in the Lieutenant's execution of that order, then that Captain is making a very big mistake. Right? Because, the way I see it, he's defying the authority of the general in question. I'll tell you an open secret, Captain. General Hines has stepped on a lot of officers over the years, and they really, really, regretted it. You don't want to be one of them, do you?"

"Yes, sir, I mean, no, sir."

"Ok then, we're done here. Oh, and when you see those lieutenants again, not one word, ok? Not one word." He raised his voice only slightly. "Nor from you either, Lieutenants," and as the six lieutenants stared at each other in shock, there came the sound of two men getting to their feet and walking away from the front porch.

The orders were to helicopter training school. For some reason known only to him, Hines had decided that Juanita and Don were going to bump two marines, take an accelerated course and learn to fly the Army AH-64 Apache attack helicopter, from Marine instructors, on a non-existent Air Force Base. It was a very rough four weeks. Then they were assigned to a Chinook. Six weeks later they were taking instruction in flying the C-130.

"You've got to be kidding me," Sacks protested. "A Hercules? First you qualified on jet fighters, then on Apache attack helicopters, then the Chinook, and now you're qualifying on the C-130J, with Bobwhite as your flight engineer, Anna as load master and of course the General as navigator? Why? Bobwhite is a nuclear engineer for pity's sake! Anna is an electronics whiz! What do those four aircraft have in common, except that they fly?" It was late one Saturday night and Sacks had just finished a thirty-six hour shift. All he wanted to do was sleep, and all he could do was wonder, sitting with the other members of the team on the back step of their cottage, studiously avoiding the brass that seemed to stream by in the street out front.

"The only thing the General would admit to us was that the Hercules was the biggest plane he's got. He said, and I quote, if I had something bigger, like those modified 130s Lockheed sold to the UK, or even a guppy, or a C-17, then I'd have you flying one of those," said Juanita. "At least Mexico and Canada both fly this plane. Neither one of us will ever need to know how to fly the Apache. Neither Canada, nor Mexico even owns any of those! Let alone he forced us to take the paratrooper course on our days off!"

"Mind you," threw in Don. "At nearly thirty meters long by forty wide, this plane is more than plenty big. When you're sitting in that cockpit, ten meters above the runway, it's like you're already flying, and you haven't even lit off the engines!"

"Yeah," said Rob. "And with all the cramming they've been doing, shoving info on aircraft engines down my throat, this nuclear sailor is about to drown."

"You're full of it," Anna said, but with no rancor. She still seemed to be angry with Don, but she got along well with the rest of the six.

"I'll agree with Don," said Will. "You're sitting up there before they start the engines, and from where I'm sitting, all you can see is deep blue sky. There are no landmarks for a man to refer to. You can't see anything!" He started to say something else and stopped. Then he made a decision and went on. "I just wish Sarah was here to see it. She was trained as a flight engineer you know. This plane would be right up her alley."

They didn't know. Will had disappeared to the Arizona State observatory for a full four weeks and then had come back, sad and tired, but resigned to his girlfriend's death. "If they haven't found her body by now, they never will," was all he had said when Juanita had asked him, and he hadn't spoken of Sarah since.

"So, you never did tell us what they taught you at that school over in Arizona," said Sacks, in an effort to change the subject.

"It's secret," said Will. "Just like everything else around here." He got up from his seat on the back steps and turned to go inside. "But I will tell you this. It confused me good, it really did. It's got absolutely nothing, and I mean nothing, to do with flying a plane.

"Somebody tell me where the spare rolls of toilet paper are hidden?" he asked. "Or is that secret too?"

"Under the sink, in the can," called Don to Will's retreating back, "there's a requisition on the clipboard hanging on the back of the door. Sign it beside the X and initial your signature so that we know it's yours. Press hard, you're making three copies! Initial each copy beside your initial, and sign and date it at the bottom, and don't forget to initial the date!"

Fortunately, the closing door cut off Will's reply, though everybody else on the porch laughed. Sacks looked at his watch. "Man, I've got another shift starting in six hours! I gotta hit the sack."

"Yeah, well the rest of us are wheels up in eight, so we all better get some shut eye," said Don. "G'nite, yall," he said and followed his roommate down the hall.

"So, you think Will's all right?" he asked the doctor, when their door to the hall had been closed.

"Yeah, I think so," said Sacks, setting his alarm clock. "He spends hours at that telescope he set up in the back, but I think that's good. He's working on getting better at what he does. He's even invited me to take a look a couple of times. I'm no shrink, but I think he's going to be all right. Just give him a chance to heal, ok?"

"You got it, Doc."

When they arrived at the aircraft that was their assigned trainer one morning three weeks later, Colonel Urban, their usual instructor was not there. Instead, General Hines met them at the ramp, trailed by Sacks. Anna saw him first and snapped an instant, "Attention!"

Which command was followed just as quickly by the General's languid, "As you were."

"Sir," said Don, even as he noticed that the officer wore a flight suit much like his own. "Are you to be flying with us today?"

Hines nodded. "In a manor of speaking." He slapped the side of the ship. "I'm a certified instructor on this baby, and every now and then I feel the need to take the escalator up into her cockpit and go for a ride.

"The rest of you jump aboard and check out your stations." He nodded at Juanita and Don. "I'm going to check on these two while they do their pre-flight."

Both pilots expected the general to pepper them with questions during the process, but he said nothing as they quickly walked around the plane, checking that everything was ready for take off. Inside, he waited until they had buckled themselves in, Juanita to the pilot's seat, and Don to the co-pilot's before he asked his first question. "How much fuel have you got, son?"

"Thirty four thousand liters, sir," Don replied.

"Does that give you enough to reach, oh, say, Seattle? Lieutenant Hernandez?"

"I'm not aware of the distance to Seattle, sir," said Juanita.

Hines glanced at Don, who replied, "Approximately fourteen hundred kilometers, sir."

"Lieutenant Hernandez?"

"Sir, our range with the gas tanks full, but the hold empty, is three thousand, eight hundred kilometers. Yes, we could fly to Seattle, but I would suggest refueling before we start back. A full load would cut our range almost in half."

"Lieutenant Post?"

"Yes, sir?" Will replied.

"I understand your friends call you General Kiwi in private?"

"Sir, yes, sir. No disrespect intended, sir."

"None taken. I respect healthy ambition. I've filed a preliminary flight plan, but you'll have to update it as we go. You will establish a course for Nanoose Bay, British Columbia. The co-ordinates are approximately 48° 23.31'N by 123° 25.21'W. Meanwhile, Lieutenant

Fields, obtain clearance from the tower for runway fourteen thirty-two. Take her up, and if the general hasn't given you a heading yet, establish a course of three hundred and fifty degrees, true. The tower will tell you to take the plane up to sixteen thousand feet until you clear the box. Then I'm thinking they'll send you up to cruising altitude. Five sixty knots should put us there just before noon. The tower will give you further directions. You can modify your course when the General gives you your heading. When you reach the border the Canadians will challenge you. Identify yourself as flight SAM eighteen ninety-nine, from KXTA, Nellis Air Force Base. Your official destination is Victoria Airport. After you clear the border, the Victoria tower will divert you to Nanoose Bay. Lieutenant Hernandez, stay in the left hand seat, but act as co-pilot." Then Hines leaned back in his jump seat and closed his eyes. A moment later he started to snore softly.

Don and Juanita stared at each other, and then Don shrugged and pulled a binder from the pocket beside his seat, flipped to the first page and turned to Rob, who was sitting at the engineer's console. "Battery switch?" he asked.

Rob threw a switch on his overhead console. "On."

"Gas turbine?"

"On."

"ATM?"

"On."

"Cabin lights?"

"On."

"Avionics power switch?"

"On."

"Radios?"

Juanita leaned forward and flipped several switches on the forward console. "Radios set."

"Nose wheel steering?"

"Centered, brakes are set."

"Lights?"

"Set."

"Lieutenant Hernandez, please obtain engine start clearance from the ATC."

Juanita had already spoken to the tower. "Engine start approved," she said.

"Bleed valves?"

"Open."

"Propellers clear?" Don looked out his window. "Starboard propellers clear."

"Port propellers clear," Juanita echoed his call.

"Lieutenant, please start your engines."

Relieved for the moment while the flight engineer started his four engines and warmed them up, Don took a moment to wonder exactly what was going on. Neither he nor Juanita had seen enough training to start doing international flights. It just didn't make sense. But then none of this did. When Rob was done with his part of the checklist, Don took back the command and taxied the craft out to the flight line. A few minutes later he advanced the throttles and the bird lifted smoothly from the earth. Almost immediately, General Hines opened his eyes.

"Course?" He asked.

"Three fifty degrees true for the next hour, sir," Will answered him.

"Altitude?"

"Just coming up to sixteen thousand feet, sir. Autopilot engaged."

"Fields, get Fleet up here." Don called Anna on the intercom and she came racing up the stairs. "Ok, everybody give me one ear. Keep your other headphone on. Question, Lieutenant Hernandez, does the size of this aircraft intimidate you?"

Juanita flushed and looked angry, but bit her lip. "Señor, no, Sir."

Hines ignored her anger. "Lieutenant Fields, does the size of this ship intimidate you?"

Don had more of an opportunity to control his anger than Juanita did. "Sir, no, sir. We're both nervous because we haven't yet officially qualified in this craft, but we can both fly it. It doesn't scare me."

Hines nodded. "Lieutenant White, are you comfortable with the engineering seat?"

"Sir, I'd rather be babysitting an SG naval reactor, sir, but I can handle this."

Hines glanced at him. "An SG? Why submarines son?"

"Honest answer, sir?"

"Honest answer."

"Sir, any nuclear specialist is going to be locked away below decks for most of his life, so it doesn't matter if it's a sub or a flattop he's on, truth is he's not going to see much daylight. Therefore, I want to be on a ship where I get to see just as much sun as the captain does, and wearing dolphins on your uniform gets you a lot more respect, sir."

"Very good. You may get that opportunity Mr. White, you may not."

"For the next two years, you six, plus a couple of replacements coming in from Europe and Israel, one as flight engineer, and one as a back up pilot, will be working together as a team. You will be working with some fairly important scientists, people that you may have never heard of, but who have done incredibly important work on behalf of all mankind."

"Am I being melodramatic? Well, yes, I am, but it's an old man's privilege and I'm taking it."

"I can't explain it to you yet, but we're going to pick up some equipment in British Columbia. This equipment that was developed at Simon Fraser University by a group of Canadian scientists, working in the utmost secrecy. This technology should not belong to any one country, like Canada or the United States, but to the world at large. Unfortunately, until it is proven, it cannot be released to the public just yet, and, well I am a military man and it does give us a serious military advantage.

"Lieutenant Shackle, by all reports you've an incredible mind. Have you figured out what's going on?"

Sacks sat and chewed his lip for only a moment. "My best guess is that you've developed some sort of large, and I do mean large, helicopter of some sort, though, for the life of me, I can't guess why that would justify this type of security."

Hines nodded. "Close, but no cigar. Lieutenant Fleet, can you guess why this, ah, helicopter would require an officer as ordinance supervisor?"

"Sir, it would have to be one incredible helicopter to require my services as gunner, especially if I stay with it for two years and make it to Captain. I mean, well, a couple of competent NCOs can handle the guns on any normal airship. Sir, even more important than having a lieutenant as gunny, I mean, I've got a Pathfinder, and an International Shooter Badge. And then, even worse, to assign an MD to a single plane, and a nuclear specialist? Is this, helicopter, nuclear powered?"

"Intriguing, isn't it? Did you notice the armory installed on the forward bulkhead?"

"Yes sir. There's some very impressive firepower stored down there."

"Before we reach Nanoose Bay you will issue side arms to all personnel, and make sure they know what they're doing with them. You will set up a watch rotation aboard the ship, a minimum of two armed officers at all times, two hours on, two off. Anybody, and I mean anybody who steps aboard this craft without having authorization gets either arrested, or shot." Hines reached into a pocket of his jumpsuit and pulled out a pair of envelopes, handing one to Anna and the second to Don. "These are your written orders to this effect.

"For the duration of this mission, Lieutenant Fields is in charge, with Lieutenant Fleet as security officer. Try not to shoot anybody, but nobody gets on this plane."

"Sir," asked Don, "I've never been stationed at Nanoose Bay, it's a Naval Base, but I've been there for an exercise, flying cap. There is no runway equipped to handle a plane of this size. We were flying CF-16s sir, and we had to fly over from Vancouver every day."

"You know, I just knew you would say that," said the General, pointedly ignoring the question. "Hold the fort people, I'm going down to the cargo hold to stretch my legs."

The side arms Anna came up with were not standard US military issue. "These," she said, when she handed each of the crew a web belt with holster attached, "Are Glock 18s." Don noticed that she already wore her firearm, and he shifted around in his seat in order to fasten the belt around his waist. He had to adjust it twice, and didn't like the feel of the weight. It made the notion of having to actually fire the gun at another human being far too real for comfort.

Anna waited until they had each settled their weapons before she continued. Then she took her own pistol from its holster, popped out the large magazine and cleared the chamber. Then she held the weapon up in front of her. "The Glock 18 is a fully automatic machine pistol. It fires a 9mm round. Call it about just under a pound and a half, unloaded. This lever on the side controls the rate of fire. Be sure you adjust the lever to the top position, which is single shot. One trigger pull is equal to one bullet. In a pinch, push the lever down and the weapon will switch to fully automatic mode. A quick pull and release will give you several shots, depending on how quickly you release. The standard rate of fire is about eleven hundred rounds per minute, or, one, two, my weapon is empty, now what do I do? If for some reason we get involved in a firefight, you do not want to have an empty weapon.

"The standard magazine is thirty-three rounds, but because we're all trying to work here, and I appreciate the fact that some of you are actually trying to drive this plane, I've given you each three magazines of seventeen rounds each, one loaded in the weapon, two spares. When you are standing on guard duty, as the general has ordered, I'll give you a couple of extra magazines with standard loads.

"I assume most of you have trained with automatic pistols? I know that Don, Juanita and General Kiwi have all qualified as expert with both long and short weapons, but Sacks and Rob, do you know what you're doing?"

"I passed qualification," said Rob, "but I'm not a good shot."

"Don't worry about it," said Anna. "Rule number one, in peace time, using your weapon is a last resort. It will be up to your discretion if and when you pull it, but you don't want to. Remember, if push comes to shove, you point the weapon at the middle of your opponent's body and pull the trigger, but don't point it at anybody unless you have to. Once somebody is dead they're dead and there is no going back. I repeat, don't shoot unless you absolutely have to, but always shoot to the center of the body mass. Shoot to kill, not to wound. A wounded enemy can still kill you, a dead one can not.

"Sacks, what about you? Are you qualified to use this weapon?"

"I had to qualify, so I did." It was obvious from the doctor's tone of voice that he was not happy about having to carry a gun. He alone had not strapped his gun on, but stood there looking at it as though he was holding a puffer fish in his hands.

"Fine. Will and Juanita, Sacks and Don, Rob and me. These are your team assignments, in order. First watch is one hour, so that Will and Juanita get a fair chance to eat. Sacks and Don relieve them for two, and then Rob and I take over for two. This gives the two pilots a chance to oversee the refueling of the plane while on watch, and if they're not here, the flight engineer can take over for them."

Chapter 3

D on brought the C-130J down five miles from Nanoose Bay, on what looked like an empty meadow covered in clover. The landing strip was just outside the military port, with no markings except for a rough batch of daisies marking each end and a radio beacon that had been switched on when he was only ten kilometers away. Other than the beacon, he had been following the instructions from an unregistered, invisible tower. Like the beacon, the tower was operating on a highly unusual radio frequency, and Don's entire being had rebelled against obeying it's instructions. It wasn't until his wheels actually touched down on the grass and the plane rolled evenly to a stop that he really accepted it was there.

"Sir, I wouldn't believe it if I hadn't seen it," Don said. He looked down at his white knuckles, still wrapped about the stick and forced his hands to release their grip. The plane had come to a halt and had been directed by the tower to park near a cliff face on the western side of the field. Then a tanker truck had rolled out of a wide low tunnel in the side of a mountain to re-fuel them, and both Don and Juanita were staring around the field trying to spot the tower.

Hines unbuckled his seat belt and leaned over the back of the pilot's seats, pointed at a ranger station high on the mountain.

"Nanoose Bay tower is in the ranger station. In about fifteen minutes the ship and runway will be camouflaged to blend in with the surrounding countryside again, and when the next satellite flies by overhead five minutes after that, they'll see nothing."

"Who's got first watch?"

"I do," said Juanita, "Along with Lieutenant Post."

"Ok, let's get the rest of you inside the mountain and have some lunch."

A Canadian navy officer met them at the tunnel entrance, and after saluting Hines, he introduced himself as Captain Bali. The Canadian officer took them into a small guardroom and then along a concrete corridor to a small cafeteria. "I'm afraid it's only meatloaf and mashed," he said. "There aren't a lot of personnel stationed in the mountain, so there's no real cook. Usually they just run off to town and eat at the base, or order in pizza, but I've arranged for the regulars to all have a day's leave, though I've kept a few sailors to help with loading your plane. The problem of course, is we can only work when there's nothing overhead. Just about nobody knows about this place, and if I can help it, nobody's going to learn about it either."

"What sort of time frame are we looking at Captain?" Hines asked, picking up a tray and running it along the cafeteria counter, selecting a knife, fork and spoon from plastic bins. There was nobody else in the room except a burly non-com behind the counter, who carefully handed the General a plate of food, obviously intimidated by the stars on his collar. Hines grabbed coffee from an urn and a piece of rather sad looking pie from a display. Balancing it all on his tray, he carried his meal to a large table, motioning for the lieutenants to join him.

"I would say, six hours, sir," said Bali, bringing over his own coffee and sitting down across from Hines.

"You're not eating with us Captain?" asked Hines.

"I ate earlier, sir. As soon as I get you settled, the skies should be clear again and I can get my gang to work. This project is just too important to me to let anybody else supervise them.

"Lieutenant Fleet, you're load master?"

"Yes sir. Lieutenant Fields is the pilot, and I'm sure he'll want to help with balancing the load too."

Don nearly sighed, but recovered before he gave himself away. The flight had been more tiring than he had imagined, and he had expected an afternoon of luxury, waiting for his plane to be loaded, but that wasn't going to happen. He, and only he, had to fly the load they were going to put on his ship back to Nevada, so yeah; he wasn't going to get any rest. Not until he was sure that the plane was in perfect condition to fly back, with a balanced, well secured load. "If I might ask sir," he said, putting down his fork. "Could you give us an idea of the weight of the goods, and how they are packed?"

"The weight?" Bali looked as though his coffee was laced with garlic. "I never weighed it. No."

Don glanced at Hines, but the general was simply watching curiously, with no expression on his face. Don took a breath and continued. "Our hold is just over twelve meters long, by three meters wide by two point seven high, and our load limit is about nine and a half metric tons. If the goods are on pallets, a good forklift driver could have that filled up in about twenty to thirty minutes, including a coffee break and a washroom break, so, and I mean no disrespect sir, how are these goods packed if it's going to take us six hours to load the plane?"

Don glanced around, afraid that he was making a fool of himself and embarrassing the other officer, but both Hines and Anna were staring at Bali, waiting for an answer, Hines with his fork resting on his plate and Anna with her fork halfway to her mouth. After a moment the wait started to get uncomfortable and Don felt sorry for the man. "Sir," he said, addressing General Hines. "Perhaps I should just take a walk with Captain Bali and take a look at what he has for us to carry. I can eat later."

"No," said Hines. "You've been on duty all morning. Lieutenant Fleet deadheaded up here, and she's responsible for the loading. She'll check out the cargo, you eat your lunch. You can check her disposition later."

Pushing her seat back from the table, Anna gave Don a glare and stood to her feet. "Of course, sir," she said, her voice neutral. "I'll report back as soon as possible." Turning stiffly, she walked to the door.

Captain Bali stood as well. "General, I do apologize, I should have been thinking ahead. This base however is quite temporary, and we have neither a weigh scale, nor a forklift. The goods are sorted, but according to usage, not for transportation. They will have to be transferred manually into your plane."

Hines took a mouthful of the meatloaf, chewed it and swallowed before he answered. "Captain, you're a theoretical physicist, right?"

"Yes, sir."

"I don't think anybody, anywhere, expects a theoretical physicist to actually be a practical person, or at least I don't. Lieutenant Fields here is a physicist too, but he's also a pilot, and I'm glad he had the brains to ask the question. I didn't even think of it. If you and Lieutenant Fleet can come up with a load plan, I'll sign off on it and you can start loading.

"Are you flying back with us?"

"Yes, sir. I have a team of three, all vetted by CSIS."

"I'll need to see their paperwork before we go. That will be all." The captain turned and left, and Don picked up his fork, but put it down again when Hines turned to him, but first the general spoke to Rob and Sacks. "Doctor, Mr. White. Lieutenant Fields and I have something to discuss in private."

"Yes, sir." Both young men snatched up their trays and hurried away from the table, clearly pleased to be out from under the general's eye.

When they were gone, Hines turned a grim face to Don and said, deadpan, "It's lonely at the top." In spite of himself, Don laughed and a moment later so did Hines. Eventually, Hines said, "Mr. Fields, I want you to do me a favor. I want you to tell me about your relation ship with your team-mates."

Don felt a sinking feeling slowly flow through his gut that totally cut off the laughter. "In what way, sir?"

Hines looked thoughtful for a moment and then said, "Well, in every way. For instance, how do you feel about Mr. White for instance?"

"Rob? Well, I really like him, he's a heck of a nice guy, sir, much like Sacks, ah, Doctor Shackle. They're obviously very smart, but they're both introverts, very intense people. I couldn't think of a better pair of guys to have my back. Sir."

"And Lieutenant Post?"

"Well, I don't know him that well yet, sir. He was gone for a few weeks, what with the training at the university and the funeral for Lieutenant Franks. I would think he's the smartest of us all sir, and very dependable, an extrovert like Lieutenant Hernandez and I."

"And speaking of the very beautiful Lieutenants Hernandez and Fleet, what's your relationship to them?"

"Well," Don began, but Hines interrupted him.

"I want you to tell me the truth son. There's nothing going on between you three?"

"No, sir!"

"I like Hernandez a lot sir. I'll admit that right up front, but we've never done anything un-gentlemanly, if that's what you mean. Sure, we flirt a lot. We used to flirt even more. We started when we met on the train, before we knew we were going to the same base, let alone know we were going to be on the same team. Then one night Anna said we should drive to Vegas and get a room, and that poured cold water on us both. Then Lieutenant Shackle pulled me off to one side and told me that if I ever laid a hand on Juanita he would surgically amputate that hand for the sake of my, and his, careers. And then Rob said basically the same thing, only more graphically. I told Juanita, and we laughed about it and together we decided that we had plenty of time, and that loosing this chance over something like that would be stupid, so we agreed to distance ourselves from each other a bit."

"And lieutenant Fleet? Was she, or is she, jealous of your relationship?"

"Sir, no sir. There's been nothing between us sir. Actually, I'm pretty sure she thinks I'm an idiot, and that we're all in some sort of contest. Sir."

"What's your opinion of her as an officer, son? For instance, she's arrogant and she thinks she's better than you. She thinks she's the better officer, and she reported you to me, claiming you're sleeping with Hernandez. What do you have to say about that?"

Don reared back, his face red. "Sir, she shouldn't say those sorts of things about Hernandez.

"However, if she said it, then she must believe it. She's wrong, but I don't think she'd lie to you, sir. I don't know how to convince her otherwise, but I will try. If you believe her, I don't know how to change your mind either, but it's simply not true. As for her thinking she's the better officer, well, I'll admit she likes to take the initiative. She aspires to command, I don't.

"I'm sorry sir, that's bad phrasing. I do aspire to command, only she wants it now and I'm content to wait for my turn and hope that in the meantime I don't make myself look like an idiot. I do know somebody has to be in command though. A military unit isn't a democracy. Often it's better to do the wrong thing instantly than to stand around and do nothing while everybody debates what to do next, and the only way to do that is to have only one person making the decisions."

"And who commands your unit?" For a moment Don thought that Hines looked amused, but he wasn't sure.

"Well, right now we have you to command us, sir. Someday soon you're going to have to select a leader for us, either from inside, or outside the unit. We can't expect that you'll always be present and if we're going to operate as a unit, our unit needs a leader."

Hines sucked in his cheeks and then released them with a loud smack. "That's logical. And that need creates a contest, doesn't it? Any suggestions as to who should command your unit, lieutenant?"

"Sacks, sir," Don said without hesitation.

"Lieutenant Shackle?" The general didn't seem surprised, but his amusement was more obvious. "Why him?"

"He's the steadiest of the lot, sir. Call it maturity, or natural leadership. I respect the doctor, sir. I could follow him without question." The general was smiling now, and Don was getting nervous.

"But if you get into a shooting situation he'll be busy in his surgery, won't he? Pick somebody else."

Don took a deep breath. "If I use your reasoning, sir, then it would either be Juanita or me, sir."

"Not Mr. White?"

"I could follow Rob without question sir, but if this plane is as large as the personnel you have selected lead me to believe, he'll be in his engine room, sir, out of touch with the situation."

"Not Fleet?"

"She'll be shooting her guns, sir. Also, and I hesitate to say this, she may be a bit too aggressive to be in charge at this time."

"I agree. But that's also why she's an excellent gunner. So, why would choose yourself or Hernandez then? You'll be busy flying the plane."

"And in perfect position to see the developing situation and decide it's time to get out while we can, sir, or attack, if that's what we need to do."

"My thinking too." Hines reached into his pocket and drew out an envelope, which he then slid across the table to Don. "Congratulations son, you just made first lieutenant a year early."

Chapter 4

"First lieutenant?" Sacks demanded, staring at the silver bars on Don's shoulders. "When, and how did that happen?"

"I'm not sure, really," Don said. "One minute I'm telling Hines I'm content to wait for promotion, and the next he pushes over orders from the top Canadian brass that promote me. Then he hands me silver bars and tells me I'm out of uniform. And then he tells me to finish my lunch, grab you and get out here to relieve Will and Juanita, so I ate as fast as I could, and here we are." They were sitting on the ramp that led to the cargo bay of the C-130. When they had returned to the ship they had been early to start their shift, but Don had sent both Will and Juanita off to lunch anyway. After the others left, the first thing Sacks had done was to raise the main ramp a couple of feet off the ground to give them someplace to sit in the shade. In spite of the fact that Don felt that the silver bars on his shoulders stood out like billboards, neither Will, nor Juanita had even noticed them. Nor had Sacks until the other two had disappeared inside the mountain.

"Have you told Anna yet?" Sacks asked, a particular hesitation in his voice.

"No."

"Well, here she comes, and she don't look happy, mate."

Fields didn't notice, but walked up and slammed her fist down hard on the ramp. "These fools!" she snapped, talking to Sacks and not Don. It was something that she often did and Don wasn't surprised. She would simply pretend that he just wasn't there. "You should see the stuff they've got for us to load! I mean, there's only a couple of tons of stuff, some packed in crates, but enough loose crap that we'll be spending hours carrying it on and strapping it down!"

"It won't fit on skids?" Don asked.

"No, it's loose," She glared at him, as though offended that he would choose to interrupt her conversation. "Some of these frames are fifteen, twenty feet long, and they're all different shapes and sizes, and they've all got to be piled beside each other. You should have come to help me, instead of coming out here and slacking off!" she snapped.

"I'm on watch, Anna," Don said, reasonably. "You know that. You made the watch assignments."

"Not for another ten minutes you're not!" she replied. "Get your butt in there and see if you can sort it out. I can't."

"Are you relieving me?"

"Relieving you? No. Will and Juanita are still responsible for the watch. I'm going to go and try to get my lunch."

"If you're not relieving me, then I'm still on guard duty," said Don, his voice flat. "You know as well as I do that you never make a friend wait for his meal, so Sacks and I relieved the others early. General Hines ordered us to maintain two officers on watch at all times, and right now that's us. He also ordered you to sort out the load, and I strongly suggest you go back and take another look and see if you can figure it out. If not, ask Rob to give you a hand. He might be able to see it from a different perspective, or maybe he'll be willing to come and relieve me and I can swap watches with him. Either way, we're doing this operation according to orders."

Anna's face flamed, she turned and grabbed Don by the lapels of his jacket and she shoved her face to within inches of his. "And who died and made you god?"

Don stayed calm. "Nobody," he said. "But, as of a few minutes ago, I outrank you. Before you do, or say another thing, you look down at my shoulders. You see that I'm now a full lieutenant. Then you let go of me before I have you up on charges. And, you do what I've told you to do."

Startled, Anna looked down and saw the silver bar on Don's shoulder. Instantly her training kicked in and she let go. "How did you do that?" she shouted. "He put you in command of the unit? The fool!"

"Enough!" Don snapped. "I don't care if you used to snipe at me. I don't care that you ran to the General to tell lies about me. I don't know where you're coming from, but you will not speak about General Hines in this way! You will show him proper respect at all times, whether I'm in the room or not, whether he's in the room or not. This man has risked his career to give us the most incredible opportunity on this planet today, and you will not muck it up! Do you understand?"

For a moment Don thought he had gotten through to her, but then she said, "I want out. I want a transfer out of this unit."

"Denied. You may be selfish and opportunistic, you may be petty, you may be rude, you may be a liar, but you're still the best electronics engineer available, so, you are not getting out, we need you, and you're in for the duration. Dismissed."

"That went, according to plan?" Sacks asked when she was gone.

"What plan?" Don had almost forgotten Sacks was there. He was still staring at Anna's retreating back. "Do you remember what you told me about Juanita?"

"Uh huh." Don turned around and was surprised to see that Sacks was still sitting casually on the end of the ramp.

"I'll do worse to you if word of this little scene sneaks out."

"You could just order me not to talk."

"I don't think I'm ordering you to do anything. I'm just telling you, I'll use one of your scalpels to cut the tongue from your throat."

"Oh well, that's different. I thought you were threatening to cut off my hand or something."

"Not a chance. The unit needs your hands." They sat in affable silence for a while. "I wonder if the load is as much a mess as Anna made out," Don said finally. Then, "Heads up, we've got company."

Both young men stood to their feet as a rather homely blond dressed in a lab coat over a white blouse, short plaid skirt, dark blue tights and ballet flats stepped out of the tunnel and walked quickly to the plane. "Ah, hi," she said. "Who's in charge here?"

"I guess I am," said Don. "I'm Don, this is Sacks. Can we help you?"

"Name's Jill. I'm Dr. Bali's assistant, from Simon Fraser." Don detected a definite English, or Scottish accent hidden deep in her voice.

"Pleased to meet you," said Sacks. "And what can we do for you?"

"Well, Lieutenant Fleet has disappeared, and Dr. Bali has sent me out to take a look at the plane, to see if I can figure out..." she stopped in mid sentence. "You're wearing guns."

"Not a habit," said Don. "You were saying?"

"Well, the Doctor wants me to take a look at how much room you have, and see if we can fit the machinery in there," she waved vaguely at the hold. "I guess somebody's got to do it, and if this Lieutenant Fleet won't do it, and if this Lieutenant Fields she was talking about refuses to come and help, then I guess it's up to me." Her voice died on the last word as she read Don's name from the tape above his right pocket. "Lieutenant Fields, that's you. Why aren't you inside helping? This is important!" The tone of her voice was accusing and angry. Don started to reply, but Sacks interrupted him.

"Jill, I don't know what Lieutenant Fleet has said, but General Hines has ordered Lieutenant Fields to stay here until he's relieved. Don here is quite willing to help, but his boss has told him to stay here. You see how it is?"

"No. If he can help, he should. Besides, Anna told me you would say that, and that it was a lie."

"And now you've got two of us here saying she's wrong, and one of us is her commanding officer. Who're you going to believe?"

"If you're not going to help, then at least get out of my way so I can measure the inside of the plane."

"Ah, no," said Don, having caught his temper and knowing he was dealing with a civilian. "I told Captain Bali the dimensions of the hold, and you simply can't go on the plane. You're not allowed to."

"Listen you moron, I'm allowed on the plane! Captain Bali has sent me out here to measure it. I'm one of the scientists who're going to ride back with you to the states. You've heard about that, haven't you? I mean really, you are some looser! Americans!" She tried to push past, but Don moved directly in front of her.

"Until General Hines gives you clearance, you do not get on this plane," said Don. "I can give you the length and the breadth of the cargo bay again, but you will not go on board until I tell you that you can. Is that understood?"

She stepped back and stared at him, a look of perfect astonishment on her face. "I'm going to report this to your superior," she said. "I'm going to report this to Doctor Bali! You won't help, and you won't let me do my job! Military muscle heads!" Suddenly, she threw up her arms, turned and stomped off.

"Well now," said Sacks, watching her go. "You do seem to have a way with women."

"Don't I now? And there I was, actually being friendly with one and you had to go ruin it for me."

"Well, a man's got to do what a man's got to do. Hey, look, here comes Rob. And I thought being on watch over an empty plane was going to be slack. Yo, Rob, what's happening mate?"

"Well," Rob looked around with an exaggerated glance. Then he leaned close to draw the others in. "Did you ever hear the one about the two star and the second lieutenant who threw a hissy fit?"

"Oh, you've got to be kidding," breathed Don, closing his eyes tight against the real world. "Please tell me you're kidding!"

"Unfortunately, no, I'm not. It seems she knew, well I guess we all knew, that one of us had to outrank the others. Somebody has to be in charge when the boss isn't around, and basically, he's got a desk job, right?"

"I knew it," said Sacks, "Though I never said anything about it. Me, I'm a doctor and I can't be in charge of a flight crew. It just doesn't make sense."

"I knew it too, I guess," said Don, "though it shocked me when it happened. I thought maybe Juanita would get the tap. She's the better pilot."

"Yeah," said Rob, "but she's also a foreigner. Wait! Come to think of it, so are you! Isn't that interesting? Well, never mind that. It seems Anna thought it was a contest between her and me, because we're both Americans. She couldn't conceive of the idea that American officers might be subordinate to a foreigner while serving on American soil. And, well, you've probably guessed that she never liked you anyway, and then, blam, you're her boss. Disaster personified!"

"Yeah. Rob, can you do me a favor?"

"What, swap shifts with you so you can go solve the cargo thing?"

"Yeah."

"You got it dude, I sort of figured I should do that, which is why I'm out here, but remember, you owe me twice for today."

"Twice?"

"Well yeah! Once for covering for you, and once for not beating your time with Juanita."

It didn't take Don long to locate the cargo. All he had to do was follow the sound of Anna's cursing through a pair of large doors that led to a small gymnasium.

There was cargo all over the place, with the six sailors Bali had promised sitting and laughing silently while Bali, Jill and Anna stood in the middle of the room and argued. All six jumped to their feet as Don walked through the door. "You," he pointed at a sailor with the chevron of Able Seaman on his collar. "Get a hand cart and a skid."

"Right here, sir."

"Good. These two large machines, put them on the skid. Captain Bali I assume these two machines are necessary and can't be replaced?"

"Yes."

"You," Don pointed at another sailor. "Grab one of your buddies and start getting these small boxes loaded on another skid. You've got that first skid loaded? Use your hand truck and take it out to the plane, now. You," he pointed at another seaman. "Take these frames and haul them out to the plane. Strap them to the sides of the fuselage. Move." Instantly the last of the seamen were scurrying around grabbing the large sections of steel frames that were littered about the room. Don made his way to the doors and held them open while the two sailors carried the first frame through. "See that you don't bend that, but make sure is securely fastened," Don ordered.

"Yes sir," the man replied.

"Wait," shouted Jill, pointing to an electrical box a seaman was loading onto a skid. "That's delicate! You can't handle it like that!"

"Do you need it to set up your new lab?" Don snapped.

"Yes!" Jill replied, "but you can't just throw it on a skid! If it gets broken…"

"Grab something else seaman. The lady is going to either wrap it in bubble wrap for you, or she's going to hold it on her lap for the next several hours."

Ignoring the others, Don made a quick lap about the floor, selecting a few of the larger pieces of machinery for another skid and getting one of the seamen to help him load them. By the time the first men were back he had a couple of skinned knuckles and a second skid wrapped in plastic wrap and ready to go. When the team carrying the frames came back for a second load he noticed that one was wearing two stripes on his shirt collar, topped by a maple leaf. "Master Seaman, you're in charge of this group?"

"Aye, sir."

"Good. I want all of this stuff on that plane out there, got it?"

"Yes, sir. Will do."

"Thank you."

"Captain Bali, give me a hand here please." It was a risk, but Don knew he had to take it. If the sailors saw the officers standing around arguing it was bad for moral, if they placed orders, and then pitched in, then the seamen would work twice as hard and twice as fast just to show the officers up. Bali looked around, saw that all the sailors were busy and walked over to help Don lift a piece of equipment onto a skid.

"Should we be doing this, Lieutenant?" Bali asked under his breath. "The sailors are here for a reason."

"True," said Don. "But I want to get to bed tonight. Reveille is at 06:30 and I've got to get up an hour earlier so I can get in my morning run."

"You run every morning, Lieutenant?"

"Yes sir. Usually the whole team meets in front of our dormitory at 05:45 and we do a loop around the training field. It's about five

k. On three, sir." For a moment they concentrated on the lift, and then Bali pointed to another case of equipment.

"Perhaps we could run together sometimes," he said.

"I'd like that sir. Maybe we have more in common than I thought." They hoisted the case onto the skid and looked for another item to load.

"I think you both have more in common than you thought," Don recognized the voice and both he and Bali stood and saluted General Hines. "Stand easy," Hines said. "Lieutenant, you seem to be getting the plane loaded."

"Yes sir. It might be close, but we've got some great seamen here. All they needed was to be told where to put the equipment, sir."

"And the weight problem you brought up?"

"I knew it wasn't going to be a problem as soon as I saw the room, sir. I did have the seamen load the heaviest items first, a couple of what looked like welders. The only problem is that the rest of this stuff is fairly bulky, so I'm letting the ratings handle getting it all in. There's nobody like a sailor for squeezing a lot of bulky equipment into a tight hold, sir."

"And Captain Bali, you're all right with doing some of the work yourself? You don't have to, you know. As Lieutenant Fields has said, the sailors know what they're doing. All you have to do is get them to do it."

Bali shifted his feet and said, "You know I'm not regular navy, sir. I'm into physics, and when the navy offered me this job, well, I just jumped at it. I mean, this is my opportunity of a lifetime! I'd have done this sooner if I'd known how to handle the men, but I went from Kingston direct to Simon Fraser, and I've been working there ever since. I've never had to give a man an order in my entire career! Every once in a while I get a note from the military saying I'm getting a promotion, but nobody at Simon Fraser knows I work for the military, just that I have influential friends. Last year the board of governors even granted me tenure. Neither thrills me much. I live for my work and pretty much nothing else. This," he waved an arm at the rapidly emptying room, "is the culmination of my hopes and dreams. When we brought it here, it was on the lower deck of one of B.C.'s ferries, piled inside a couple of forty-five foot trailers. Then the navy tells me it's all got to go inside one airplane! Then you tell me I was supposed to organize that! How do you stuff your life's work into an airplane? Then one of your officers basically tells me I'm an idiot, and I thought my life was over!"

"Sir," Don said. "That was never my intention. I just needed the information, that's all. I apologize."

Bali shook his head. "Not you lieutenant. Notwithstanding what Jill told me, you've been very helpful. It was, what's her name, Fleet? She had me seriously angry for a while."

"Sir, Lieutenant Fleet is an officer under my command, and I apologize to you on her behalf. I know she was having a problem with the logistics, which is why I had one of my other officers cover for me so that I could come here and," he glanced at his watch. "Oops. Again I apologize for my officer, Captain." He turned to General Hines. "Sir, Lieutenant White is covering for my watch, and I'm late relieving him. If I may be excused, sir."

"Dismissed. Oh, and Lieutenant, if Bobwhite gives you any grief, tell him to come complain to me. I enjoy talking to lieutenants with complaints."

Chapter 5

R ob didn't have any complaints, and Anna stood at attention and saluted, her face as bland as an NCO's. Don saluted her back. "As you were, Lieutenant," he said, and she turned away, visibly scanning the runway for threats. "Rob," Don scowled at the officer and got a surreptitious crude gesture in response. "Any more room in there?" he asked.

"A little. It's going to be tight man. I'm pretty sure we can fit all this stuff in, though I'll admit it's danged awkward. I'm sure nothing is in order, and we had to re-pile several skids two high to make them fit, so we'll have to let Bali and his crew sort things out at the far end, but it's in, and it isn't broken, I don't think, so that's one for the good guys."

"You know Bali's got assistants coming with him."

"We left room for them," said Anna, from behind him, and Don turned to let her in on the conversation. He wasn't sure what to think about her. She had been rude, she had been antagonistic, she had tried to blindside him with the general and she had totally messed up on the job she had been given, and for some unknown reason he still wanted her to like him. But, whoa, she was gorgeous, and they needed her.

"Good. Did anybody think about where to put their luggage?"

"They have luggage?" Rob asked, and Anna simply stared at him.

Eventually she said, "There's the crew's rest bunk, in the main cabin."

"Good thinking," said Rob. "Though, I was sort of hoping to get in a snooze on the way back."

"Yeah. Rob, can you do me a favor? Find Bali and tell him they're allowed one bag each, plus a carry on if they can fit it under their seat, or hold it in their laps for the duration." He glanced at his watch. "Wheels up as soon as we have a satellite blackout. He should be able to tell you when that is. Bring me back word on that. Anna, did you ever finally have lunch?"

Anna straightened. "No, sir."

"Rob, find Will and have him go to the mess. He's to round up some sandwiches for Anna." He glanced over at her. "You may have missed the meatloaf, but unless you really, really like that stuff, you didn't miss anything good."

"Oh, and Rob, be sure to tell the general we're ready to go, and send out Juanita. I'm going to start the pre-flight walk around."

Stiffly, Rob came to attention and gave an exaggerated salute. "Suh, yas suh. And why do I gets to deliver the bad news, suh?"

"Cause you my whipping boy, Lieutenant," Don replied, deadpan. "And because I know you enjoy it."

"And who you callin, 'boy,' honkey?"

"Go!"

Predictably, Bali's assistant showed up first, followed only a few seconds later by Juanita. Surprisingly, when Jill started in on Don, Anna intercepted her and led her to one side. Juanita found Don doing his circle check of the exterior of the heavy cargo plane. "Silver bars, and I didn't even notice them," she said, giving a half salute mixed in with a modified bow. "Good work. Makes your shoulders look a good inch wider. By the time you're a captain you'll look like a bodybuilder."

"Right. Eyes on the plane Lieutenant, eyes on the plane."

"I hear you had a dust-up with my fearless compañero de habitación"

"Just a misunderstanding. Did Rob find out when the next satellite blackout was?"

"Uh-huh. 03:45. I'm jealous you know."

"Jealous?"

"Yeah, you've been checking her out. You're looking over there every couple of minutes."

"Well, there's nothing like a good argument with someone to make you notice them." They did a visual inspection of the starboard landing gear and walked over to the port gear, checking for low tires and hydraulic leaks in the mechanism.

"You want me to argue with you?" she said. "So you'll notice me?"

"Don't you get me started," said Don. "Besides, I've already checked you out. Every which way I can, short of getting a room that is."

They moved up to the front gear. "I knew it wasn't an accident when you walked in on me when I was in the showers that day."

Don colored. "That was an accident! The flag wasn't on the knob!"

"I still swear I put it there before I went in," Juanita said. "Though, if somebody did have to walk in on me, I'm glad it was you."

"Let's not go there. We're looking good out here. Let's check inside."

"You know," she said, as they climbed into the pilot's seats, "We've got un problema."

"I know."

"I meant every word I said. I'm all screwed up inside. I want you so bad it hurts. Almost as much as I want this assignment.

How am I supposed to live like this? I mean, we were just fooling around, flirting, and now I'm ready to throw my career out the window."

"I don't know," Don said. "My guts are totally racked up too, but I know we can't do anything about it. Seriously, we don't dare."

"Si." Juanita turned away and started checking out the controls in front of her, making sure everything was ready for takeoff. They could see the sailors outside clearing away the camouflage from around the plane and a moment later Rob came running up the stairs to the flight deck, carrying a bag in each hand. He quickly stowed them in the bunk at the rear of the cabin and then plopped himself down at the flight engineer's station, breaking the mood.

"Yo, is everybody ready to go home?" Rob demanded.

"Yo, just in case you missed the briefing," said Don, "I am home. My home and native land?"

"Right." Rob looked at his watch. "Just checking to see if you're awake. I hear the passengers climbing aboard downstairs, and I hear the rear doors closing. The time has come, the walrus said, to run through our pre-flight checklist." Will appeared and stacked another suitcase on the bunk and disappeared back down the steps. A moment later he re-appeared, followed by General Hines. By the time Hines had seated himself, Sacks had brought another case up and stowed it on the bunk. From the rear of the plane came the clunk of the rear hatch being locked into place, even as a light on the control panel flashed from amber to green. "Loading hatch secure," Rob announced, and a few minutes later there was another clunk from much closer and a second light flashed from amber to green. "Crew access door secure."

Don, sitting in the co-pilot's seat, got the nod from General Hines. "Lieutenant Hernandez, if you please." Juanita gave a nod and began the pre-flight checklist. When they were done with that, she turned the aircraft down the grassy runway and opened the throttles wide. They were over the Strait of Juan de Fuca when Don got to his feet. "Sir, permission to check on the passengers?"

Hines nodded. "Lieutenant Shackle," he said, "why don't you take this opportunity to sit in the control seat of a real airplane?"

Don slid down the stairs to the cargo deck. With full plastic wrapped skids filling most of the cargo bay in two solid rows, and both sides filled with masses of steel framework, there was barely room for the four people crowded together on jump seats. "How are we doing Anna?" he asked. "No sick civilians?"

Anna shook her head with a frown. "Ah, no sir. Nobody's sick, and there are no civilians."

"What?" Quickly Don looked past the Lieutenant. Everybody besides her was dressed in a Canadian military uniform, one male officer and two enlisted women. "Captain Bali," he said. "I didn't realize all your people were military."

"Oh, of course." Bali got to his feet, hanging on to the overhead for balance. "Let me introduce Warrant Officer Lucy Browning and Sergeant Daphne Hale. Unfortunately, Corporal Jillian Workman missed the plane."

"Corporal? Jill is a corporal in the Canadian Armed Forces? She was the first one out to the runway. She even had her bag with her." Something was nagging at Don's brain. "Anna," he said, "You were talking with her. Do you know why she missed the plane?"

"Possibly sir. We were talking and her cell phone rang. She answered it and after a moment she began to cry, dropped her bag and ran back into the tunnel. By then the other passengers were showing up and Rob grabbed her bag and carried it up to the flight deck. We had a narrow blackout window, so when she didn't show up again, I closed the door and we took off."

Suddenly Don understood, and it hit him hard. "So her bag is upstairs?"

"Yes sir. Did I do something wrong?"

Don ignored her question and grabbed the headset beside her seat. "Juanita!" he barked into the mouthpiece. "We have a possible emergency situation here. Maintain present altitude, notify air traffic control and go into a circling mode. Do not, I say again, do not change altitude, up or down, for any reason!"

There was silence on the line for a moment, and then the Mexican Lieutenant replied. "Yes sir, present altitude eighteen thousand, I repeat, eighteen thousand feet. Do not change altitude. Possible emergency situation."

Don threw the headset back in its cradle. "Anna, you're with me. Excuse us, Captain." Upstairs, everyone except the general was sitting stiffly in their seats. Hines looked like he was sitting calmly behind his desk. "Rob," Don snapped. "Which bag belongs to Jill? Bali's assistant? You brought it up to the flight deck."

Rob had to think for a moment and then pointed. "Green plaid. Stewart Hunting, Modern. I remember it because my grandmother was a Stewart and I resented that it had been used to cover someone's cheap plastic suitcase." Don did a double take and just shook his head. If Don's grandmother had been a Scot, then his own had been Inuit. He rushed to the cot and gently lifted the bag down, putting it on the table at the navigation station. "Out of my way Will, now."

"Sacks, I need a scalpel!"

"My bag is by your feet. There's a pocket on the side with a stethoscope and a half dozen scalpels."

"Got it." Don ripped open the doctor's bag and snatched out a scalpel, peeling off the sterilized cover. Deftly he slit through the middle of the plastic side of the suitcase, cutting the long way and stopping his cut at least two inches from each end of the bag. Then he used the scalpel as a probe, gently lifting the flap he had made to peer inside. "I see a uniform shirt, trousers, and bingo! It's either modeling clay or plastic explosive! I don't know which and I guess don't really care which.

"Ok, here's the plan. Anna and I are going to crawl over the cargo to the loading ramp. Then she's going to lower the ramp by about a foot and a half, and I'm going to slide the bag out through the opening. Any questions?"

"Do you have to destroy the evidence?" Will asked. "Couldn't you just disarm it?"

"I don't know enough about bombs to try, and there could be some type of booby trap in here, or an altimeter set to blow when the pressure goes up again. I say we've got to get rid of it. Anna, do you concur?"

"I should be able to disable it, but I don't want to take that chance with your lives, so yes, I concur."

"Then let's do it." Picking the suitcase up with both hands he followed Anna back to the cargo hold. "You," he pointed to the last technician, the one sitting beside the first skid. "What's your name?"

"Warrant officer Browning. I'm a physicist."

"That's good. I'm going to need to use your seat for a moment to climb up on top of that skid behind you, so I want you to please stand over there for a moment." Don handed the bomb to the warrant officer, turned his back to the skid and made a stirrup with his fingers, giving Anna a nod. Without speaking she stepped onto the seat with her left foot and into the pocket with her right, and for a moment he breathed in the scent of her, soap, shampoo and talcum powder, no perfume. Then there was a strain on his arms as she stepped up and thrust herself between the skid and the top of the plane. A moment later her head re-appeared above them, followed by her arms.

"I'm ready for the bomb," she said.

"Bomb?" asked Browning.

Don ignored her. "Coming up," he replied, taking the explosive from the startled warrant officer, stepping on the seat and passing it up to Anna. Bali quickly stepped forward and formed a stirrup with his own hands. Don gratefully stepped into it, and with Anna's help from above, was able to wiggle into the space between the top of the skid and the ribs of the plane. It was just high enough that he could wiggle forward, but not high enough for him to actually crawl. It was also dark.

"No light?" he asked.

"The fixture at this end of the fuselage is on the side wall, below the top of the skid," Anna explained, her voice making it sound like she blamed herself for this failure. She wiggled herself around to face the rear of the plane. "The next few lights are mostly blocked by higher skids."

"Ok," said Don. "Let's do this."

"Follow me," said Anna, pushing herself forward with her hands. Don, with the bomb clasped close to his chest, followed.

The first two skids were easy, relatively speaking. The area they had to crawl through was shallow and dark, but it was wide enough to move their arms and legs freely. Don knew they had done a day's work when they had covered it. Of the two skids in the next row, one rose completely to the ceiling and the other to within a few inches of it. "First obstacle," said Anna.

"But not insurmountable. You check that side, and I'll check this side and see if we can make it through over top of that steel framework, whatever it is." Don, who had crawled up on Anna's left, slid over to the side of the skid. Feeling with his hands he quickly decided that his side was impassable. Shaking his head at the ability of the Canadian sailors to pack the frames in, he rolled over to the other side. "Any luck?" he asked.

"I think so. It's really tight, but I think we can make it through. Ask me again on the other side."

"Well, I'm right behind you."

Suddenly, from behind them came the one shout neither of them expected to hear. "Missile!"

Forgetting everything else, Don hugged the bomb and tried to claw himself into the skid beneath him at the same time. With a jerk the plane jigged left, and then hard right. Then from about three feet away came the most blood-curdling scream he had ever heard, followed immediately by the double thump of flares and chaff being released.

"Anna! What happened?" Though his eyes were somewhat used to the dark, all Don could see was a black lump outlined against the dimly lit steel frames to the side. Letting go of the bomb, he rolled over to his right, finally coming to a stop beside the lieutenant, who was lying on her right side, her back to the steel framework, alternatively sobbing and groaning in pain. "What happened?"

"My back. Something… impaled me," Anna groaned in a soft voice.

"Where? You've got to tell me where! I can't see it."

"In my back, down at the bottom of my back."

"Ok, we've got to get it out of you, but in order to do that, I've got to find it. You understand?"

"Yeah." He could picture her biting her lip to fight the pain. "You do what you gotta do, just get me out of here." He wiggled closer, until they were almost touching. Sliding down so that he could put his right arm over her he started to feel down the length of her back. The spike was just above her left hip, digging directly into her back, but not near the spine. It was slick with blood and there was more blood coming.

"Good news, it's not in your spine. Look, tell me something about yourself. Talk to me. I know you speak Spanish, because I've heard you talking to Juanita. Do you speak any other languages?" Don slipped his left hand around her waist from below and took a firm grip on her hip with his right. They were laying no more than two or three inches apart and he hoped it was enough room.

"Greek," Anna said, sounding confused. "My mother was Greek

and taught me the language…" Don slid towards the front of the plane, until his shoulders were opposite Anna's hips, tensed both arms and pulled the girl to him. Feeling the spike give way, he clamped both hands over the hole in her flesh and applied pressure, hugging her close to him in the process. Anna screamed and then clenched her teeth and stopped. For a moment, Don was very conscious of the beautiful woman who he held against his chest.

"Anna? Don?" It was Sacks, calling over the top of the skids.

"Oh brother, am I glad to hear your voice! Anna's been hurt, impaled on a bolt. I pulled her off, and I'm applying pressure to the wound, but we've got to get her out of here."

"Hold her steady then, I'm coming up." Don could hear Sacks scrambling around to climb the skid, and all he could feel was relief at handing over Anna's life to someone else, but he also knew he couldn't.

"No, Sacks, hold on. There's just not enough room up here for three of us, nor is there any light. I'm going to try and move her towards the center of the plane, and then back towards you. Just hang tight for a couple of minutes."

From where he was laying, Anna's belly was about even with Don's head. "Anna, is your upper body free?" he asked. "There are no boxes or stuff directly in front of you?" He scrunched himself back a few inches and heard her whimper from the change in pressure on the wound, but she didn't scream.

"No," she said, "my head is to the right side of the next skid. You've got to try and lift my hips and pull me down before you try and slide me over." There was a pause. "Listen, this time, tell me before you move me, understand?"

"Yeah. Sorry about that." Don took a deep breath. "Are you ready?"

"Ready."

"Then now!" Don picked her up by the hips and with her help

managed to move her backwards by six inches before his strength gave out. "Are you clear?"

"Just about." Don could literally feel the pain in Anna's voice, but he steeled his mind against it.

"Anna, can you get your hand over the wound, to apply pressure while I get repositioned?"

"I'll try," she said, but almost as soon as she started to move, she stopped. "I can't. I could get my left hand there," she moved her hand till it rested on top of his, "but I can't apply any pressure. If I wedge my right arm under my body I have to move my hips up to do it. I tried and it's not working."

"Ok," said Don, "Don't worry about it." He bent his knees and succeeded in sliding his upper body down a few inches, all the while keeping his arms about Anna's waist, hugging her tight, his left arm under her side, his hand keeping pressure on the wound. "I need you to grit your teeth, because I'm going to move you again. Are you ready?"

Dimly he saw her nod in the dark. "Here we go," he said and slid her down a few more inches. "Is your head free now?" He pushed himself away from her towards the center of the plane where they would have more room to move.

"Yes. I hurt."

"I know. You were telling me about your father. He was Greek and taught you the language." He tensed his arms and drew her to him, immediately sliding back and doing it again.

"It was my mother, not my father. My father was Swiss."

"With a name like Fleet?" Slide and pull, slide and pull, they were getting into a rhythm.

"My maiden name was Schwartz. Fleet was my husband's name."

"What?" Don almost forgot to pull, and when he did it wasn't even. "You're married?"

"Widowed. We got married when I was seventeen, just a year

after I graduated from high school. The marriage was a mistake. Three weeks after we had our ceremony we had a fight. He went to a bar, got drunk, jumped into his Jag, fell asleep at the wheel. I joined the army as soon as the funeral was over."

Slide and pull, slide and pull. "Anna I'm sorry."

Slide and pull. "For what?"

"For what I said to you the night we met." Slide and pull. Don felt someone grab at his ankle.

"Don't be, it was only the truth." Slide and pull. Strong hands pulled him back a few inches and he pushed Anna down past him.

"Don, we've got her. Let go and we'll pull her out. You've got to get that bomb off this plane. Can you do it by yourself?"

Don let go and watched as Anna slid down past him to the edge of the skid.

"Anybody got a flashlight?"

There was silence for a moment. Then a voice said, "No."

Exhausted, Don turned to crawl back through the blood trail to the bomb.

Chapter 6

I t was easier, now that he knew where he was going.

He grabbed the bomb and pushed it over to the steel framework piled high on the left-hand side of the plane, and with Anna's body out of the way he could suddenly see much more clearly, noting that although the bolt that had skewered Anna still projected into the area he had to pass through, he should still be able to slip past it fairly easily. The only reason Anna had been caught had been the violent maneuvers Juanita had been forced to fly to evade the missile.

That stopped him for a moment. What had happened to the missile? Then he shrugged. Obviously, the missile had missed. Reaching forward, Don slid the bomb on top of a flat section of steel a couple of feet further towards the rear of the plane. Then he began the process of crawling through the jumble of metal. It wasn't as easy as he thought it would be. Almost immediately he got stuck, and it was only by forcing his leg into a position it wasn't supposed to fit in that he found the support he needed. Then, when he tried to move the suitcase it became stuck and only came loose with extreme difficulty after he moved past it. This time, however, he was able to shove it up on top of the next skid in line, and after disentangling his leg from the steel he was able to swing up beside it.

The next few skids were not easy, but they were nowhere as difficult as the climb through the piled steel had been. But the last skid was no more than ten centimeters from the rear ramp, and for several long moments Don had to fight down panic as he tried to figure out a way to access the rear door controls. No matter how flat he lay down, or how he stretched, they were still several centimeters below his reach. On the positive side, he had light, and he could see what he wanted to touch. And suddenly he knew what he had to look for.

When the Canadian sailors had been wrapping the skids in plastic, that plastic had come wrapped around a thick cardboard tube about fifty centimeters long, and like shippers everywhere, when they had finished a roll of plastic they had simply slipped the tube under the plastic skin to get rid of it, thus letting the receivers take care of the garbage. Situation normal. The tube was firmly attached to the outside of the last skid on the starboard side of the plane. Don ripped it out of the plastic and returned to where the controls were mounted against the fuselage wall. Being the pilot meant that he had never operated the door himself, but he had watched it done twice, the second time being just hours ago when Sacks had raised the ramp to make them a seat. If a medico could do it, he admonished himself, looking down at the switches, so could he. Now if he remembered correctly, there were three things he had to do. He had to unlock the door, he had to switch the hydraulic pumps to on, and he had to activate those pumps for only a couple of seconds.

Lying flat he extended the tube, holding it in his right hand and guiding it with his left. He thought that the lock switch was the toggle switch on the left, but he wasn't sure. There was writing on the panel, but he couldn't see it from where he was lying. Putting the end of the tube under the switch he applied pressure, forcing it into the up position and was rewarded with a metallic thump as the door unlocked. The next switch was the one for the hydraulic pumps, and he assumed that was the one in the middle, but when he flipped it over nothing happened, and the switch automatically returned to the off position. Don decided that was the power switch. He poked at the third and was rewarded with the whir of distant machinery. Hydraulic pumps on. Moving his tube back to the second switch, he again pushed up, and this time the door opened a few inches, letting in bright sunlight and freezing cold air.

Instantly the pressure dropped dramatically and the temperature plummeted by twenty degrees. The sudden roar of the wind and engines was both deafening and disorienting. Squinting in the sudden light he inspected the gap, but it wasn't wide enough to fit the suitcase through. Using his cardboard tube he hit the switch again and held it up longer. The temperature dropped sharply again, and now it was getting hard to breathe, there wasn't enough oxygen in the air to support his life. It was something he had expected and planned on, but the reality was still a shock. If he was going to do anything, he had to do it quickly, or he would suffocate, and they would all die.

Twisting, and shoving the cardboard tube into his pocket, he crawled over to where he had left the bomb, the noise and cold like a physical presence, battering him around until he felt he was ready to pass out. For a moment he just lay there with the bomb in his hands and wondered what he had planned to do with it. Then he looked up and saw the gap where the end of the ramp had separated from the top of the aircraft and he remembered. Somehow he had to get the suitcase through that gap, only, he couldn't remember why.

Sliding himself across the uneven cardboard boxes that made up the top layer of the skid, he pushed out with his arms and got the end of the suitcase through the slot, but his arms weren't long enough to push it far enough, and he lay there for a moment trying to think of what to do. Thinking was so hard. All he wanted to do was to go to sleep, with a nice warm blanket wrapped tight about him. Slumping down he felt something uncomfortable between him and his bed. Digging it out he realized it was some sort of cardboard tube. What did he have that for?

The door. He had the tube to close the door, but the suitcase was in the way. Tentatively, he poked at the suitcase with the tube, but it didn't move. Angrily, he poked at it again, and this time it moved just a little. He poked a third time and a piece of cloth popped out of the cut in the side. A cloth that the wind instantly grabbed and tore the suitcase free. Don smiled and sank into a deep sleep.

"Good morning sunshine."

Don thought maybe he recognized the voice, but he wasn't sure. Opening his eyes he looked around for the source. He was in a room, pale blue paint, lots of sunshine, no roar of turbocharged engines or hurricane force winds, and no freezing cold air. He decided that somehow he was off of the plane. He looked up and saw a dark, pudgy, middle-aged nurse standing over him. She held a memo paper in her hand and read, "Juanita says to say hi, she's gone home without you, but Anna's here to look after you. All the boys say hello."

"So, how are you this morning?"

"Fine, I think. Where am I?"

"Tacoma General."

"Tacoma, that's near Seattle, isn't it?"

"Pretty much. You'd think that pilots would know their geography a little better than that," the nurse said, with a twinkle in her eye. "You have heard of Seattle though?"

"Yes." Don laughed a little. "How long have I been here? And Anna, my friend, she's here too? Is she all right?"

"I'll be fine," said Anna from the doorway, but Don was prevented from seeing her by the nurse, who stuck a thermometer in his mouth.

"The back door," he mumbled. "I didn't close the back door."

"Will followed you," Anna moved past the nurse and carefully eased herself into the visitor's chair. Don noticed she was wearing a hospital gown and was dragging a rack with a saline drip attached to it. "He was going to help you, but when you opened the door he had to go back for an oxygen mask, and the line wasn't long enough for him to get to you. When you got rid of the package, he signaled Rob, who shut and locked the door."

"How?"

"There's an auxiliary panel at my station. Juanita says to tell you that we landed at Seattle Tacoma International, runway 16, at 18:52, at which time she took command of the aircraft."

The nurse took the thermometer from his mouth, checked the temperature and wrote something on a chart. She said, "Well, I think you're all ready to go." She tried a smile, but obviously wasn't in the mood for it. "Your buddies took your clothes for cleaning. They left you a parcel though. I'll bring it by."

"You're sure you're all right?" Don asked when she had left.

"Well, I can't do much. Sacks patched me up and shot me full of painkillers and he gave me a tetanus shot. He tells me I'll have a small scar, but it won't be bad. I'll need your help to change the dressing twice a day. Hines said we're just supposed to stay here until they let us go. Then we're supposed to rent a car and drive home. He left credit cards."

The nurse came back through the door and laid a couple of bags on the other visitor's chair. "Here are your clothes young man. I hope you like them more than she liked hers. Come along miss, he's got to get changed, and I've got to pop that tube out of your arm so you can go home."

"Nurse, a moment," Don asked. The woman stopped and looked back politely.

"Yes?"

"Who brought us in?"

"Ambulance," the nurse said. "There was some sort of accident on an airplane, and they brought the both of you in the same ambulance. I asked what had happened and they told me to forget my questions, like I was a curious twelve year old sticking her nose into somebody else's business. I'm a nurse, the health of my patients is my business!" With a final harrumph, she turned and herded Anna out the door in front of her, closing it behind her with a snap.

True to her word, when Don opened the bags he found everything he needed, socks, underwear, jeans, a tee shirt and runners, all brand new. Quickly he slipped them on and discovered a wallet and watch. He had never seen either of them before. His Visa card was there, but his driver's license and pilot's license were missing. There was also a new credit card in the wallet made out to Rapid International Flights Ltd. And a California state driver's license made out in his name, with a home address in San Francisco. There was also a letter from General Hines.

"We're ready to go?" Anna asked from behind him.

He turned and was stunned. His outfit was jeans and sneakers; hers was a short, strapless, bright yellow sundress with high-heeled sandals. "Wow."

"Yeah, right. Not my choice. I think Juanita picked it out. As a matter of fact, I know Juanita picked it out, just to spite me. I don't like dresses, I don't like high-heels, I don't wear sundresses, and I don't wear yellow. You can stop staring now, we have a car to rent."

It turned out that the closest car rental location was no more than a couple of blocks away, so they decided to walk.

"Are you sure you've got no problem with this?" Don asked as they stepped out onto the street. "We could call a cab."

"I've got problems with all of this, but I can still make the walk," Anna replied.

"I just wish I knew a lot more about what's going on than I do," Don said.

"Well, for once we're in agreement," said Anna. "I mean, you know I don't like you, never did, probably never will, even though you've saved my life at the risk of your own."

"I meant to ask you about that," Don said. "Can I ask why?"

Anna looked at him for a minute and then finally nodded. "I guess so," she said. "I at least owe you that. You talk too much, with too little substance. I call it verbal diarrhea."

"Oh." Don took the emotional blow hard. It was not what he had been expecting.

They walked on in silence, the words hanging between them like a slap in the face. After a while, Don took out the General's letter. The envelope only had his name on it, not his rank, and inside the message was printed in ink on plain white bond.

Dear Mr. Fields,

   I am sorry to hear of your accident.

   I know I was committed to get-together with you this afternoon, but pressing business, and your unexpected hospital stay has forced me to proceed home without us being able to meet again.

   Please forgive my absence.

   I hope to see you again soon at your office in San Francisco.

Hines.

Silently he handed the letter to Anna.

"What is this supposed to mean?" she asked.

"It means," Don said. "That we are going to San Francisco." He didn't speak again until they reached the rental lot, but he wasn't looking at the rental lot, he was looking at a car lot on the opposite side of the road. "Is that green car a '73 Capri?" he asked, and leaving her standing on the sidewalk, he jaywalked across the street.

A moment later Anna joined him. "Hey, we're supposed to

be renting a car, and I don't know why you're talking about San Francisco! Hines didn't say go there, he just talked about your office there, whatever that means."

Don was down on his knees looking underneath the battered sports car. He looked up and again noted how beautiful she was, and how short the dress was. He didn't get up but he did look away. "Look, you may have forgotten it, but I'm your superior officer. Speak when you're spoken to, and the usual sentence should be yes sir, or no sir. Now, there's a drug store just over there," he pointed down the street. "I assume Hines left you a credit card too?"

Anna stepped back like he had hit her. "Yes. Sir," she snapped.

"Fine. We need toothbrushes, that sort of stuff. You go get it. I'll take care of getting us transportation." He looked at his watch. "It's 10:00 hours. Meet me back here at 13:00, after lunch. We'll leave then."

He wanted to say how beautiful she looked in that yellow dress, but he didn't.

He wanted to say that if he bought the car he would buy it with his own money, but he didn't.

He wanted to say, hey, I don't know why Hines promoted me over you, but he didn't.

He wanted to say Anna, you have no ideal how much you've hurt me, but he didn't.

He said nothing, and knew he had said too much.

Chapter 7

"Weed?" Anna asked. "What kind of a name is that?"

"I don't know, but there's a restaurant open and I need breakfast." Don dropped the gearshift into third, and then down into second as they slowed and pulled into the parking lot that served both a small café and a self serve gas bar. Smoothly, he backed the car into a shady open slot on the west side of the building, and then used a couple of paper towels to wipe the sweat from his forehead. Climbing out, they both left their windows down a half-inch to let the hot air escape from the vehicle.

The day was getting hot, even though it was just past 06:00 hours, and the one thing the little car did not have was working air conditioning.

Most of the town was east of the highway, but from what they could see, Don decided that it wasn't very large, a few businesses, a few houses and a couple of church steeples. That was all. The highway ran west of the town, and the restaurant faced the highway, though it was set back a hundred feet behind the gas bar. To the north ran doubled railroad tracks paralleling the road that connected the town to the highway. The next business in line was a rundown motel with a broken sign and beyond that was a little mom and pop food store. The area was a desert, with low rolling hills, not really mountains, covered in sagebrush, tumbleweeds, and scrub. There were no buildings showing on the north side of the tracks, though a narrow paved road, guarded with wooden gates, lights and bells, crossed them just opposite the restaurant and wandered back into the hills.

The restaurant itself was mostly white stucco, with several large plate glass windows. To Don's eye it looked clean, if not affluent, and he guessed that was the best he could hope for. Inside, the floors were covered in worn linoleum, the walls painted a faded blue, the tables and chairs were made of wood, and the eight tables were all crowned with bottles of sugar and ketchup, salt and pepper.

Swinging saloon style doors and a food pass through window separated the back room kitchen from the eating area. In front of the pass through was a small alcove for the waitresses to keep their menus and just enough flat shelf to hold the cash register. Between the door and the window was a rack that held at least three-dozen large coffee mugs in as many different colors. Most of the tables were occupied, so Don and Anna took a table near the door on the north side of the dining room, Don with his back to the window, Anna sitting opposite him.

"Howdy," the waitress was a pretty redhead, in her forties, plump but not fat. Her makeup was thick, her blue cotton uniform was a little too small for her and her hair was pulled back into a ponytail. Her nametag said 'Lily,' and her smile was fake, but she was quick and pleasant.

"Good morning," said Anna, smiling back in what Don thought was a real expression, but he wasn't sure. "Coffee for me, and double that for him."

"That," Don pointed to a huge mug on the rack. "The red mug, that's for me."

Lily smiled. "You got it. What can I get you two to eat?"

Anna glanced at the menu and back to the waitress. "One egg, hard boiled, brown toast and marmalade."

Don chuckled and shook his head. "Four eggs, sunny side, four slices of toast, greased, a slab of ham, six rashers of bacon and a couple of sets of sausages."

"Done." Lily was back in a second with the coffee and then she passed their order through the window. Don tried to say something, but behind his back a trio of bright yellow Union Pacific power units began pulling a huge freight train through the level crossing. The rumble of the diesels and the clatter of steel wheels on iron rails, offset by the clamor of the crossing bells was deafening. A few minutes later the train was gone, and they looked at each other and laughed, the roar of the engines fading in the distance as the train picked up speed.

"So, verbal diarrhea eh? Pretty crude to say the least." Don said. It took him a lot of effort to say it without letting the hurt show on his face.

She flushed and looked down at her coffee cup, bit her lip and said, "Look, I'm sorry. I know words can't be unsaid, and the truth is, that's the way I felt. I should have been a lot more diplomatic about it though." She paused for a deep breath. "The very first thing you said to me was to contradict me, and worse than that, you were right. You couldn't get your baggage until it had been unloaded from the train. I did fall asleep at the wheel endangering all our lives. I had been awake for more than forty-eight hours before I even drove down to pick you up.

"The problem with being right most of the time is that the people who are wrong resent it. You know that. But the flip side is that we start to assume we're right all of the time, and I did that, and I'm sorry. I'm not used to being wrong. Ever.

"All six of us, you heard General Hines when he greeted us, we're all way past being very good at what we do, we're the top dogs. And it takes just one other alpha in the pack to upset the balance.

"I'm not outgoing like you are, I'm not the brave pilot, I don't have funny stories to tell and I'm not interesting because I'm from some exotic locale. I'm just me, very used to being the smartest person within a hundred thousand yards and suddenly I've been taken down about five notches.

"What do I have to offer this group? We've got incredible pilots, we've got a doctor, we've got an astronomer, and we've got a nuclear genius. Me, I just happen to know electronics and guns. You need a sniper on a plane crew? No. You need a loadmaster, and I haven't got a clue about spatial placement. I couldn't fill a coffee cup properly if I didn't use two hands!"

"But you can field strip an M-16 and reassemble it how fast?"

"In the light, or blindfolded?"

"How about a tank gun?"

"No fair. I spent last summer with the 3d Armored, H Company. You know I've worked tanks."

"And rail guns?"

"Need to know only."

"Bingo." He pointed a finger at her and waited while the waitress delivered their bacon and eggs. "What's the biggest difference between a tank cannon and a rail gun?"

She shrugged. "It's kind of obvious, isn't it? A cannon uses an explosive, a rail gun uses electricity."

"And which would work best in a vacuum?"

"You know the answer to that."

He smiled at her. "I also know the reasoning behind the yellow sundress."

Surprised, she looked him straight in the eye for the first time since they left Tacoma. "What?"

"Juanita and I, we had a bet."

She groaned. "You always have stupid bets!"

"Well this one was a bit more serious. We were trying to figure out who would get promoted first. I wanted to know what the terms were and she said, anything I wanted. I asked, anything? And she said yes. So I said, if I win, you've got to show me as much T & A as possible for a week."

Another groan. "You are rude, crude and socially unacceptable!"

"In your opinion. Juanita just laughed and just said 'you're on,' and we shook on it. What I didn't specify was who's T & A."

Anna didn't get to answer. For a second she froze, and then she shouted, "Down!" and dove for the floor.

Don didn't wait. Trusting her instincts, he dove for the floor, hitting the linoleum only inches from Anna as the front window of the coffee shop exploded in glass shrapnel. Almost instantly a large caliber bullet smashed right through the table where they had been sitting, embedding itself in the floor between them. Immediately, both young lieutenants sprang into action, racing around the waitresses' kiosk, through the swinging doors and into the kitchen proper. A moment later they were outside the back door, peering around the side of the restaurant. "I don't suppose you have a gun on you, do you Lieutenant?" Don asked.

"No sir," Anna replied. "One of the problems with seeing nearly everything, is that what you see is what you get." The distant shooter had fired only the one shot.

"You think maybe he's given up and gone away?"

"We could only wish." She paused and chewed her lip for a moment. "If he's a pro, then he's using a sniper rifle, one shot, manual re-loads. But if he's a pro I don't know how he missed. I wouldn't have."

"We were under the table by the time he fired." Off in the distance Don heard the wail of a siren. Closer still came the rumble of a second train approaching the crossing from the opposite direction. Inside the restaurant Lily was screaming, or at lease Don assumed it was the waitress. "How did you know?"

"A flash of sunlight off the scope. Amateur mistake, and there's got to be two of them, the sniper and a spotter."

"Yeah. If they stayed where they were, would they be able to see us while the train was running by?"

"Maybe. It would be a rough shot. If we ran straight from here to the car he wouldn't be able to see us for more than a second. If he's a pro, one of us is dead, if he's not, we might be able to make it." The lead power unit of the freight train began to pass over the level crossing and Anna sipped off her sandals, holding them in her left hand.

"On three. One, two, three." They both jumped from hiding and charged into the parking lot. They didn't hear the sound of the shot, but something crunched into the corner of the building as they raced by. Neither one of them gave it a glance. There was a brief moment of controlled panic while Don struggled to unlock the car, and then he dove in, snagging the lock button on Anna's side and starting the engine while she clambered in. Stepping hard on the gas, Don spun the wheels in the loose gravel, sliding the vehicle sideways before he was able to gain control, and then shooting out of the parking lot and down the street to the access ramp. By the time the little car had climbed back into the early morning traffic he was doing well over a hundred miles an hour, weaving desperately in and out of the slower commuters.

Twenty minutes later Anna laid her hand over his on the gearshift to get his attention. "Sir, I think we can slow down a bit now."

Don glanced at her, and eased off the accelerator, but still keeping the car well above the speed limit. "Somebody was trying to kill us back there," he said, feeling both stupid and obvious.

"Don't look now," she said, "but it's been going on for the last couple of days. A bomb on the plane, a missile, a sniper. This is getting really old, really fast."

"How did they make us? And for that matter, who are they?"

Don spotted what looked like a police car in the distance ahead of them and dropped to the speed limit. They were still gaining on it, but at a much slower rate. "I think it's about time Hines leveled with us. I mean, gimme a break here, people are trying to kill us, and we don't even know why, or how they're tracking us!"

"It's pretty obvious, I think, the tracking part anyway." Anna paused to sort out her thoughts. "Somebody was looking for us, and I think they've got a line on the credit card."

"Go on." Don noticed a sign indicating that a town called Redding somewhere ahead had a fair sized mall. He glanced at his watch. It was only getting on to 08:00. The mall wouldn't open for a good two hours yet, but if this Redding place was a good distance, he intended to drop in. Anna definitely needed to wear something that was a bit less obvious. He glanced down at her legs and then deliberately looked away, hoping she hadn't noticed. If she had something else to wear it would help his peace of mind anyway.

"Well, I'm pretty sure the guys used the card to buy our clothes." She put her hand on her back to hold her wound for a second and it came back red. "And by the way, that little bit of action back at the restaurant messed with my wound. I'm bleeding again.

"Anyhow, I don't know why they didn't pick up on the car yesterday, but I'm sure they picked up on the Hotel last night, and then followed us to the coffee shop this morning. And I'm thinking I'm a pretty obvious target in this dress, easy to spot and follow."

"I bought the car cash, with my own money."

She gave him a strange look. "Your own money?"

"Cash. It's a long story. Are you bleeding badly? Should we be finding a doctor?"

"A drug store, with clean gauze. I won't be able to go in, the back of my dress has a big bloody patch on it. Anyhow, I believe Hines thinks the R I F cover is still safe, but somebody's made us and wants us eliminated."

"Why?"

"Well, I'm pretty sure you've figured out some of it, haven't you?"

"Some sort of huge nuclear powered plane with, and I'm guessing, a rail gun or two, that requires an astronomer to navigate and pilots that need helicopter experience. Developed at Area 51, it's probably got some pretty kinky technologies behind it. The stuff we picked up in Nanaimo? I'm thinking nano fibers. The implications are a bit too fantastic for me."

"Speaking of which, tell me the long story, sir. Please."

Don glanced at her and then at the rear view mirror. The cop car they had passed earlier was pulling over a green jeep. "I think we just got a bit of luck," he said. "This morning, when we were pulling out of the hotel parking lot, do you remember that jeep that just about cut us off?"

"Uh-huh. You had to do some fancy driving to avoid hitting him."

"I think that's him, right behind us, getting pulled over by those cops we just passed."

She reached over and turned the mirror so she could look behind them. "Yeah, that looks just like them, doesn't it?" she turned the mirror back and Don re-adjusted it. "Now, tell me how you got the cash to buy this car."

Don flushed a little and then re-adjusted the mirror. He admired the mountains for a moment, but knew he had to answer the question, even though he didn't want to. "I have some funds, money I earned before I went to Kingston. There's not a lot, but every once in a while I phone my publisher and have him deposit some money in my bank account."

"Your publisher?" she leaned forward, interested.

"Yeah, well, as a teenager I wrote some kids books, and this guy in New York liked them. They don't bring in a lot of cash, but the agency collects the fees and hangs on to them till I need money. Mostly it's piped directly into an RSP every January, but if I need cash during the year they deposit it in this account I have at an American bank. Normally I'll just slip across the border and pick up some cash and I'm fine. There was a branch of my bank a block down the street from the car lot, so I waved twenty-five hundred in fifties in front of the salesman's nose and he just took it."

"A bundle of fifties."

"Yeah. It's more than the car is worth, but less than they were asking for it. I had to ask for the cash and specify I wanted it in a bundle. If there's one thing I've learned, salesmen like the look of a bundle of cash still in the bank wrapper. Then I needed another five hundred for insurance, and a hundred for plates." He opened the central console between the seats and she saw a pile of loose bills. "I've got about nineteen hundred in here. If the card's been made, then we'll have to work with cash for a while."

She sat back in the seat and winced in pain. The dress felt wet against her back. "And what's an RSP?"

"Retirement savings plan. Think 401k."

Chapter 8

D on found what he was looking for the moment he stepped into the mall, in the form of a highly decorated sergeant of marines, working in a small storefront recruiting office. The sergeant rose to his feet as Don walked through the door, noting both his haircut and bearing. "Good morning, sir," the marine said, his voice a pleasant baritone. "How can I help you?"

"Good morning, sergeant." Don glanced around at the recruiting posters on the wall. He took out his wallet and slid the R I F credit card out. "Sergeant, does this card mean anything to you?" He handed the card to the NCO and waited while the Sergeant read it carefully.

"Lieutenant Fields, sir. I was told you might show up." The marine handed back the card, came around his desk, closed and locked the front door. Then he hung up a neatly lettered cardboard sign that said, 'Back in 10 minutes.' "I suspect you need to contact your CO, sir?"

"Yes sergeant, I do. Do you have a secure phone?"

"Through that door there, sir." The sergeant pointed to the back of the office, where there was a single door. "There's a secure phone on the desk. Use line four, dial nine three nine, and then your number."

The general's phone rang only once before it was answered. "Hines."

"Lieutenant Fields sir. We have a situation here, sir." Don was surprised that the General had answered himself, and then realized he had been given the number for a direct line.

"Talk to me, lieutenant."

"Somebody's trailing us, sir. They took a shot at us this morning while we were having breakfast."

"Did you get away clean?"

"I don't think anybody was hurt sir, though the cafe was damaged. I'm at a marine recruiting office in Redding California sir. I've got to buy Lieutenant Fleet some new clothes…"

"Was she hurt in the shooting?"

"No sir, but her wound opened and she's got blood all over her dress, so she can't do much without drawing too much attention to herself."

"Does she need medical attention Lieutenant?"

"I don't think so sir. I'm going to change her dressing, and buy her a change of clothes."

"Do it, and I'll sign the expense forms. You didn't rent a car." It was a statement and a question rolled into one sentence.

"No sir, I had some money available to me so I bought one, sir. We think the R I F credit card has been compromised, and that gave away our location sir. Nobody came after us until after we used it to pay for the hotel last night."

"You have cash?"

"Yes sir."

"Good. Keep your receipts."

"I want you to pick up a disposable cell phone and drop your number at the recruiting station when you're ready to leave the mall. Then go home to San Francisco."

"Yes, sir," Don said, but the line went dead in his hand.

Forty-five minutes later Don was done his shopping and returned to the recruitment center. "Ah, sir, you're back." The Marine sergeant stood to his feet and brought out a slim aluminum suitcase from under his desk. "A gift from your friend Mr. Hines."

"Thank you sergeant." Don took the suitcase and hefted it. Its weight told him what was inside. He handed the NCO a slip of cardboard with his new cell phone number written on it. "Could you pass this information along to Mr. Hines for me please, sergeant?"

"Of course, sir. Good luck, sir," said the marine.

The motel where Don had left Anna was only a five-minute walk. The room was on the third floor, two down from the elevator, overlooking the highway. When he let himself in, Anna was standing at the window wearing a white terrycloth bathrobe and studying the traffic.

"Did you see anything?" Don asked. She had her hair down and he realized he had never seen her like that before. She looked good, really good, and she smelled deliciously clean.

"Well, two or three guys have taken a look at your car, but nothing suspicious has happened. There haven't been any green jeeps in the parking lot, but then again, I took a shower to get the blood off, so I haven't been standing here the whole time." She looked over her shoulder at him. "What's with the aluminum case?"

"Present from our friend Mr. Hines. I suspect it's mostly for you." Don laid the case on the bed and opened it, revealing the contents.

"Two Glock 18's, and a Colt M-4 Carbine. Nice. Look, he even sent us a couple of bayonets. I wish he had been able to include a grenade launcher, but you take what you can get." Anna had picked up the carbine and was busy field stripping it. Don reached over and took it from her hands.

"Speaking of taking what you can get, grab your new clothes and get changed. We've got a long way to go and you can play with your new toy in the car."

With one last look at the weapon in Don's hands, Anna snagged the bags he had been carrying and dumped them on the bed. Rummaging through the clothing for a moment she looked up and said, "You, are a philistine."

"What?" Don had gone to stand by the window, trying to get the smell of her out of his head, but her statement drew his attention back into the room.

She held up a thin red crop top and a short khaki skirt. "Obviously you like your women to be either naked, or at least halfway there!"

Don inhaled and held his breath for a moment before he allowed himself to answer. He wasn't sure if she was teasing him, or was angry. He decided to act on the first choice and hope he was right.

"True, but not deliberately," he said, even while he hoped she would wear the clothes she was holding. "I told the salesclerk that my girlfriend had lost her luggage, and I described you to her. I said you had hurt your back and you were lying down, but needed a few outfits. I gave her that list you wrote out of your sizes, she picked out some stuff she said was flirty and I paid her. Quite honestly I never even looked at the stuff!"

"Obviously, or if you did you were thinking about Juanita and not me." She grabbed a couple of items and started walking towards the bathroom. Then a look crossed her face, she dropped the clothes she was carrying and sank down to sit on the floor, weeping like a child.

"Anna?" Don was on his knees beside her in an instant, his arm about her shoulder. "What's wrong? Are you all right? Talk to me!"

"You wouldn't think about me. You don't know me at all! I've really blown it, haven't I?" she said, snuggling deeper into his arms. "The general is disgusted with me, you despise me, and the rest of the team must think I'm an absolute schmuck. And I wanted it to work." She looked up at him and there was hope in her eyes, but only faintly. "I don't make friends you know. Juan's as close as I've gotten for years. The other kids, they always called me names, they never understood. And now I'm working with people who just might understand and the old Schwartz with warts charm costs me this as well. I really wanted to make this work and what I did was stick my foot right in! I'm not getting any more chances, am I?"

"Anna, you're not down, you're not out," Don said. "You and me and the guys, we're a team. We're going to stick together; we're going to do this together as a team. I know how it feels to not have friends. No, look at me. The six of us, the whole team, we're all from the same basket of eggs, we've all had the same experiences, and we all know what it feels like to be the geek in the corner. But now we're going to have those friends, those guys you can talk math to, or electronics, or whatever you want, because we understand you, because you, me, Juan, Rob, Will, Sacks, we're all the same, we've all fought the same battles you're fighting. Nobody understands you like we do, and we need you, and we want you on our team."

"Yeah." Suddenly Anna pushed him away and dragged herself to her feet, running the sleeve from her robe across her eyes to dry them. "I'm sorry, I don't cry. And I'll start to believe you when I'm still with the team twenty four hours after we make it back to base." Abruptly, she disappeared into the washroom, popping out only a few minutes later with a clean face and wearing black slacks, a red v-neck tee and black flats. As soon as Don had fixed her dressing, she picked up the carbine, and slid it into the case along with the clothing from the rest of the bags. Then she took the cell phone and clipped it to her belt. Taking the small bag that the phone had come in, she checked the load on one of the Glocks, dropped it in and carried the bag in her left hand, like a purse. Don stuffed the other weapon in the back of his jeans and covered it with his shirt.

They made it to the car, and onto the highway before they saw the green jeep again, gaining on them from behind. Instantly, Anna flipped open the case in the back seat, snatched up the M-4 and rolled down her window. "You want I should kill em?" she asked.

"No," said Don, edging his speed up past the legal limit. "First of all, we don't know for sure it's the same jeep. And second, the person driving that thing is a real human being! This is not the movies! We don't want real people to die, no matter how bad they are, and especially at our hands. It'll be hard enough explaining to a cop why we've got loaded weapons in the car." The sound of a rifle firing came from behind them and a bullet pinged across the hood.

Don swung left and then slammed on the brakes, "Ok, now we know who they are. Three at the engine, but try not to kill anybody!" he shouted, the car swerving all over the road, the jeep shooting past to their right. Anna said nothing, but nodded, the weapon snuggled up to her left cheek, shooting left handed, pulling the trigger as the other car shot past. Two bullets smashed into the jeep's hood and a third bullet shattered the windshield. Don released the brakes and dropped the car into third, punching the accelerator for all it was worth. With a roar of power the little car leapt past the now spinning jeep. When Don looked in his rear view mirror a moment later the vehicle was gone from sight. "Good shooting," he said, his breathing ragged and tense.

Anna gave the carbine a little hug. "Great weapon. Did you know the M 4 was originally designed for shooting from a moving vehicle?"

She had such enthusiasm in her voice Don couldn't help but wonder at it. He shook his head, but said, "Yeah, I did. Do you think you hit him?"

"Nah, I hit what I aim at. There were two of them," Anna said. "I didn't recognize them, but I didn't have much time to look. Oh I hope I punctured the rad, or put one into the alternator. I doubt I could have blown through the block with this thing."

"Whatever you did, they're gone for now. Put your toys away and lets get out of here." He pointed at the trunk of a black Acura. "Hey, check out the grin. The car thinks we did the right thing."

It took Anna a moment before she saw that the lower edge of the trunk lid formed the shape of a huge grin, and then she giggled. "Don, who was your favorite TV personality when you were a kid?"

Don didn't have to think. "Tony the Tiger," he said immediately.

"He's not a personality, he's an ad campaign!" she protested.

"And a darned good one at that," Don retorted.

"Who was yours? TV personality that is?"

Anna grinned. "The Lone Ranger."

Don shook his head. "That's been off the air since way before we were born!"

"Yeah. Welcome to the world of DVDs! All I need to hear is the first few notes of the theme song, and wham, my heart races and my pulse shoots up and I'm ready to go!"

They rolled into Berkeley at 13:25, after stopping for a burger at a roadside restaurant. Interstate 505 had joined interstate 80 just out of town and now Anna consulted her map. "Take the bridge and stay on 80 till we get to the other side of the bay. Then we want to take the 280 south until we exit to the Cabrillo Highway. Take the Palmetto Avenue exit and Shoreview Avenue west and the address on your driver's license should be in the first ten or twelve houses."

The house was pink stucco, with a red clay tile roof. There was no evidence of habitation from the outside and all the curtains were drawn, but the garage door started to open as soon as they pulled into the driveway, and Don pulled the car right in to the garage. Will, standing inside, gave him a thumbs up and pushed the button to re-close the door. The lieutenant wasn't in uniform. "Nice car. Did you buy that in Seattle?"

"Yeah." Don swung out and flipped his seat forward, pulling out the bags from the back seat. "But some schmuck took a shot at us and look at the hole he put in the hood!"

Will grinned. "Don't worry, I'll help you fix it. I learned to do body work when I was in Venturers. Hi Anna," he said. "Everybody's inside."

Everybody included two new faces. "Don, Anna," Will did the introductions, "I'd like you to meet Jean-Paul Golden, a pilot and biologist from Israel, and Tessy Thewes, an electrical engineer and flight engineer from Luxembourg. Jean, Tessy, Don's a pilot, and recently appointed our CO. Anna's an electrical engineer."

"And a darn good shot too," Don shook hands with both officers.

Anna merely nodded at them. "A biologist," she said. "Now the plot thickens."

"I beg your pardon?" said Jean-Paul. "Does my assignment here pose some problem?" The Israeli was tall, dark and fit, with black eyes and a rough edge to him, Tessy was long, lean and graceful, almost liquid. Her golden hair was a lighter shade than Anna's and her smile was instantaneous. Don decided he liked them both.

"Not at all," said Don. "Anna and I, well all of us, are still trying to figure out just what this assignment is. I'm sure General Hines didn't give you any description when he welcomed you aboard."

"No, sir."

"Then you're as much in the dark as the rest of us." Don moved over to a couch and sat down. "When did you guys get in, and where's Juanita?"

Everybody else sat down except for Jean-Paul and Rob. Jean-Paul had taken up a position where he could keep an eye out the front window and Rob kept walking to the kitchen to look out the back door. "Juanita is shopping," said Sacks. "It's her turn to cook and she's planning on making real Zapotec food for supper. I think she muttered something about trying to find a store that sold fried grasshoppers. Jean and Rob are on watch. Now, before I pull Anna into the back and take a look at her butt, tell us what's been going on with you two."

"Nonsense. You know Juanita would want to fry the grasshoppers herself," said Don. "As for what happened to us, well, we got out of hospital the day after you left. We went to Tilden, but I saw a car I've been looking for in a lot across the street from the rental place, so I bought it and we drove it down. We were having breakfast in a town called Weed when somebody took a pot shot at us. We managed to escape and when we got to Redding, I called General Hines from a mall and he sent us some weapons. The bad guys took another shot at us and Lieutenant Fleet returned fire, disabling their vehicle. Then we came here."

"Right," said a voice from behind him. "First, we're not having grasshoppers for supper, and you couldn't tell a story if your life depended on it. Sir."

"Juanita," Don jumped to his feet and gave her a high five. "Buddy, old pal!"

"Who're you calling old?"

"You're a good two months older than me and you know it. It's your turn, tell me what happened with you guys!"

"Well," said Juanita, "Air traffic control was not thrilled with me calling an emergency. I mean, we had no flight plan filed, we weren't supposed to be where we were, and they didn't like our call sign. I had to get the boss on the phone to calm them down. Then somebody tried to shoot a missile up our butts. Well, I jigged and swerved and did everything I could to try and get the heck out of there. Finally I blew chaff and flares and it must have locked onto a flare, cause it didn't hit us, but we did see it explode.

"We heard Anna scream, and Sacks leaped out of the right hand seat and ran to the back. Hines slid in beside me and flew co-pilot. Imagine having a full two star as co-pilot. It gives me the creeps just to think about it.

"Well, a few minutes later I saw the door light go red and I heard it open. We all grabbed oxygen masks, but man was it cold!

Well, we had a few anxious minutes, but then the back door closed and General Kiwi got us a vector to Seattle Tacoma, asking for an ambulance to meet us there on the ground.

"Hines then sent me off with Sacks. We bought some civvies for you at a local mall and Sacks jumped into a taxi and took them to the hospital. As soon as he came back we piled back in to the plane and flew home. Bali unloaded his stuff and began setting up near the runway, but we didn't see much. Somebody had set up what looked like a circus tent, and he was working inside. Next morning Jean and Tessy showed up and as soon as they were kitted up we were thrown back into the plane with orders to come here, in civvies, and wait for you to show up."

"Anybody got anything else to add, broad strokes only? No? Ok, then this is what we've got.

"One, we have been called together to make a unit by several international authorities. Therefore, we can safely assume that what we're going to be working on is of tremendous importance.

"Two. Somebody wants to stop us, and they are willing to use deadly force to accomplish their mission.

"Three, with eight people we've got a good mix of abilities, but also a lot of overlap.

"Four, we've got several linguists in the group. Tessy is?"

"Poly-lingual."

"I'm bilingual, French and Algonquin Cree. Jean is…"

"Four languages, French, Hebrew, German and English. And I think you forgot that you speak English too."

"Fine, I'm trilingual. Juanita knows English, Spanish and Zapotec, Will what languages do you know?"

"Maori. Some Japanese."

"Sacks?"

"Mandarin Chinese, Vietnamese, some French."

"Rob?"

"Some Spanish, some Swahili."

"Swahili?"

"Don't ask, it was my dad's idea. Explore our African roots thing."

"Anna speaks Greek and Spanish."

"And Portuguese."

"And Portuguese. So we've got a multilingual group. Anybody think of number five?"

"We've got some very diverse training," said Anna. "Medicine, biology, electronics, nuclear physics, space sciences, astronomy, ordinance and pilots."

"Six," said Sacks. "That stuff we loaded in Nanaimo? It's got something to do with Nanotechnology."

"I agree," said Don, "But on a massive scale."

"Seven," said Juanita. "As we speak there's some sort of tank being loaded onto our plane."

"Tank as in, with a M256A1 cannon, or tank as in goldfish?" Anna asked.

"Tank as in great white," said Tessy, "but we think it's so we can transport some liquid, we don't know for sure what." She paused. "Is anybody a chemist? No? Well, we've got extremely critical power constraints connected to this tank, and it has it's own refrigeration unit attached, with standby power supply. We've also got four chemists from England traveling back with us." She licked her lower lip and said, "Has anybody else here besides me volunteered for space service?"

"Space service?" asked Will. "I didn't even know Luxembourg had an air force, let alone aspirations of going into space." Then he gave a theatrical sigh and raised his hand. "Yeah, me too."

Silently, Don raised his hand, and so did Anna, Sacks, Jean-Paul, and Juanita. All eyes turned to Rob, who was busy staring at his feet. Finally he sighed and raised his hand. "Though, what they might want with a traditional deep water sailor in space, I have no idea," he said.

"You are so full of it," said Anna. "Have you ever even been on a ship?"

"I did a couple of summer tours on the Harry S. Truman."

Anna nodded. "Ok, I'll concede that's a ship."

"It's a bloomin floating city it is," said Sacks, his accent exaggerated. "I've seen it. Did they let you in the reactor room?"

"No. They gave me a green jersey and I handled cargo all summer."

"And you're probably the smartest man they ever had on that boat," Sacks said.

"And that's why I applied for space, and that's why I'm here."

"For revenge against some moron who tried to mess with you big time?"

"No." Rob stared at them, passing his glance from one to the other. "I'm here because this crew is going into space, and I'm going to wear purple and supply the power. Don is going to wear gold and command it. Juanita and Juan Paul are going to wear yellow and fly it, Tessy, in purple like me, and Anna are going to help me and keep things in good repair, but Anna's going to wear red, because the guns are hers. Sacks is getting a white jersey, and Will is going to wear gold like Don, because he's going to be next in line for command."

Now every body was staring at Rob, mesmerized by his intensity.

Suddenly the cell phone clipped to Anna's belt began to blare the first few bars of the William Tell Overture, and the spell was broken. She answered the phone.

"Fleet here," she said. "Yes general. He can? We're on our way sir." There was an audible click and she deliberately turned off the phone. "I hate it when people hang up on me."

"He does that," Don said. "What's up, and just when did you get a chance to program my phone with your favorite ring tone?"

"That's for me to know, and you to find out," Anna answered with a smug smile, and re-clipped the phone to her belt.

Don sighed theatrically. "And the General said I was in charge. Right. I wonder if he's ever had to deal with women? Ok, everybody grab your bags. We're flying home." He exchanged glances with Rob and shook his head. "Or, to Nevada anyway."

Chapter 9

"He's going to let me what?"

"He's going to have you put your precious Capri in the trunk, his words not mine, and bring it with you," Anna said. "You and Rob drive it out to the airport, the rest of us are taking the van the guys rented when they got here."

"Hot dawg," barked Rob. "I needed a few minutes away from these jokers!"

Everybody scrambled out and into their respective vehicles, their luggage piled into the Capri's back seat. Anna took her precious Glock and her M-4. Most of the others only had toothpaste and razors, clean socks and underwear. Juanita was driving the van, with Anna riding shotgun and the rest of the crew in the back. Everybody had a weapon, mostly Glock 18s, but Jean-Paul had an Uzi. Juanita led the way and Don followed close behind.

"So, what was that place?" Don asked Rob when they were on the road.

"The safe house? The Marshal service lent it to the General."

"So is it true you had to change the dressing on Anna's butt?"

"Three times. Poor woman thought I was going to jump her," Don laughed out loud. "Like I would risk my life! I don't know what

Juanita was thinking when she bought that yellow dress. I think she was just being mean, but I'm not sure if she was being mean to Anna, or to me."

"Looked good did she?" Don noticed Rob was keeping an eye out for shooters, the window down and his weapon in his lap. He didn't protest. "Maybe, just maybe, she was being mean to both of you."

"Well, Anna is one good looking woman. Everywhere we went the men were staring. And I really do mean, staring, with good reason. So, there she was in this really short dress, with a strapless top and high heels, and looking more gorgeous than you can imagine. I'm as angry as I can be with her, I mean, you should have heard what she said to me, and no, I'm not going to repeat it, and I'm having to drive for hours and hours with this woman beside me, only inches away, and I'm going nuts.

"Then I've got to change her dressing. It wasn't as if she could slide the waist of her skirt down a bit and I could get at it. Nah, it's a dress. She had to lie down on a bed and undo the whole back of the dress so I could push the one part down enough for me to work on her, and of course, I was afraid to touch her, even when I had to, because I thought she might get offended and decide to shoot me!"

"I call that cruel and unusual punishment. What'd you do to Juan to get her so upset with you?"

"Nothing. Much. In Nanaimo she told me she had feelings for me, and I admitted I did too, feelings for her I mean. Then I told her we could do nothing about it, especially since I was now her CO. I tell you this bro, don't ever flirt with a girl you're not serious about." Juanita turned the van south on the Cabrillo Highway and Don followed suit.

"You're serious about her."

"And that's the problem. And on that note, I'll change the subject. I thought we were going to San Francisco airport? If so, it's in the other direction. I saw the map, and I memorized it. We, are going the wrong way."

"Did you ever hear of Half Moon Bay Airport? It's about ten miles south of here. Fewer prying eyes, and it was given to the local government by the Navy in 1947, so every once in a while they do a small favor for the government."

"Yeah, but how long is the main runway, and does it face into the prevailing winds?"

"Well, Juan is a little worried about that. It depends on the load we have to carry, and we'll have to do a full power up before we let the brakes go, and hope for a pretty strong headwind."

"And I just love a challenge." Don shook his head. "Well, we'll deal with that when we get there. What was all that stuff about wearing gold and red and purple?"

"It's flat top talk. The fuel guys on deck wear purple so you can identify them in a crowd. Yellow is for officers, green for operations, white for medics, red for ordnance handlers and brown for plane mechanics. I made up the stuff about gold, but I think it works, don't you?"

"Does the word incorrigible mean anything to you?"

"No, but my mama used to use it a lot. What do you think about that Thewes woman?"

"I don't know. I just barely met her!"

"Well, I think she's cute, and those legs, they go on forever!"

"You mess with her and I'll have you out of this unit so fast you won't know what hit you," Don said, but he was laughing as he said it. "Buddy, what you and I really need are a couple of chicks who don't carry weapons and don't wear uniforms."

"Tell me bout it, but where we gonna find em half this cute?"

Don was not enthusiastic with his first sight of Half Moon Field, though he wasn't as discouraged as he might have been. "Ok, it looks a little short, but, depending on the weight of the cargo, we just might be able to get out of here," he said, bringing his car to a stop beside the looming C-130J and behind Juanita's van. Climbing out of the car he showed his id to the six marines on guard duty, and noted that there was a stiff headwind coming directly down from the north, a good sign. Maybe this would work after all. He walked up the rear ramp and into the cargo space, followed by most of his crew. There seemed to be plenty of room, but he was curious about the weight of the cargo.

The front half of the cargo space had what looked like a steel re-enforced plastic bin that was securely fastened in place with cargo straps. It had a refrigeration unit fastened to one end that was running on airport electricity and a gas powered backup generator at the other. Don noted that provisions had been made to switch the refrigeration unit to ship power after the plane's engines had been started. The actual bin itself appeared to be about two meters high by three wide and four long, with the machines adding a meter of length to each end. Doing some quick math in his head Don estimated twenty-four thousand liters. At the specific weight of water that would be the same number of kilos. But the bin was only about four fifths full, so, maybe nineteen thousand kilos. Very close to maximum payload. A man came around the corner of the bin from the front of the plane. He looked like a civilian and wore a plastic military issue nametag. "Ello," said the man, his irritation showing in his voice despite his heavy English accent. "Who are you, and what are you doing here?"

"Good afternoon," Don said, reaching out his hand. "Lieutenant Don Fields. I'm one of the pilots. Are you responsible for this container?"

"You don't look like a pilot, and you're late," said the Englishman. "We should have been in the air hours ago."

Don nodded and withdrew his hand, not sure if he should be insulted or just amused. "Well, I have a few questions about the cargo and we're not going anywhere until somebody answers them, so I'm asking you again, are you responsible for this container?"

"What's in the container is none of your business," the man said, "You will either get this plane moving or I'll be calling your general and complaining. Now move!"

"Right. With all due respect sir, you go right ahead and you call. Juan, did any of you think to bring my flight suit?" Most of the crew had grabbed their flight suits from hangers strung along one side of the cargo hold and were piling back into the van.

"Over here," she said, shaking her head at the passenger's complaints.

"Thanks." Don found his uniform and boots and carried them back to his car, where he followed Juanita over to the terminal and they all separated into the washrooms to change into uniform. When they had changed, Juanita drove everybody else back to the plane and then came back to return the van to the rental agency. By then Don was ready to go and drove her over to the plane in the Capri, pulling directly into the cargo bay behind the tank. Getting out, he left Rob and Anna to tie it down while the three pilots began the pre-flight inspection.

"How much fuel have we got?" was Don's first question.

"About fifteen thousand kilos," Jean-Paul said. "With a six thousand kilo reserve, that gives us nine thousand to play with. Takeoff, depending on the load, and we still don't know what that is, will take us from seven to eight hundred. Call it eight thousand kilos at say, twenty two hundred an hour, cruising at 240 knots, that gives us three and a half hours. Call it eight, maybe nine hundred miles, or fourteen hundred kilometers. I'll get together with Will, but we're looking at about six hundred miles, or nine hundred and sixty kilometers from here to Las Vegas."

Don ginned. "You already had that worked out, didn't you?"

"Yeah."

"Good. This runway is a little short for us, but depending on the load, we should be able to get off the ground. Juanita, why don't you dismiss the guard? Jean, you've been cleared on this aircraft?"

"Yes sir."

"Fine. Juanita will fly left hand, you'll fly right hand. I'll be in command of the aircraft."

"Yes sir. We still need the weight of the cargo."

"I'm on it. You guys finish your checklists, but don't start engines until I give you the ok."

Not quite sure what to expect, Don went to the flight crew stairway and climbed aboard, going right up to the cockpit. Will was sitting at navigation doing some calculations and Tessy was sitting primly at the flight engineer's station, chatting with Rob about the instrumentation there. Sacks was sitting in a jump seat and gave him a thumbs up. "I see you met Doctor Smyth. I don't think he likes you very much."

"Our self important passenger downstairs?"

"That's the one. He's been complaining about you to everybody he could find, including the marine guards."

"I'm surprised they let me back onto the plane."

"Me too. What's the problem?"

"Well, we need to know the specific gravity of the liquid in that tank so we can compute the weight. We need that in order to know if we can take off or not, but he's not talking."

The doctor shook his head. "Good grief, the world is full of fools. Well, good luck."

"I'll need it." Don turned around and went back down to the crew door, but instead of going outside he turned and descended the steps into the cargo bay. Anna was just locking down the rear hatch. Besides her, there were four others in the passenger area, all of them sitting on jump seats. Don went down and introduced himself to the three he hadn't met, an older black man, named Lyondell, a pretty young woman who turned out to be his daughter, named Jezebel and a post grad university student from Cambridge named Dr. Neil Stills, Dr. Smyth's assistant.

"Well?" snapped Smyth. "Are we going to leave now?"

"Nope." Don sat down in one of the jump seats near Anna, and went through a mental relaxation routine he had learned from his karate instructor.

"Why not?" Smyth was getting angrier by the minute.

"Still one important piece of information missing."

"And what is that, if I may ask?" said Stills.

"Well, the runway here is just under a thousand meters and ends rather abruptly at the Pacific Ocean. Our takeoff distance, if your substance weighs close to water, is slightly longer than that. In other words, we have a fantastic plane here, but it can't swim. In order to calculate whether or not we are light enough to take off, and have enough fuel to reach our destination, I need to know the weight of our payload. I know it's about 19,000 liters, and if I knew the specific gravity of the liquid I could make my calculations. I tried to ask Doctor Smyth, but all he'll do is shout at me, so, we're going nowhere."

"I see." Stills glanced over at Doctor Lyondell, who nodded. "About point nine three, and it's closer to 18,500 litres."

"You fool," shouted Smyth, "That's highly sensitive information!"

"Nope," said Don. "Not on my plane. You do not berate anybody on my plane. I don't care how sensitive it is, nobody is childish enough to call anybody names. He picked up a spare headset. "Juanita? Go with a weight of just under eighteen thousand. You may proceed with your checklist."

"Stills," shouted Smyth. "You're fired, get off of this plane!"

"Doctor Stills," said Lyondell, "I've wanted you on my team for quite a while now. You're hired, sit tight."

"What?" boomed Smyth. "You can't do that!"

"I can do whatever I please, and hire whoever I please, and I just hired a heck of a good man," said Lyondell. "Doctor Stills has done most of your share of the work for the last five years anyway, and you signed the same papers I did. The goop belongs to the US government, and her Majesty's government has leased us to the American military. Did you read the fine print? We can either co-operate, or we can go home in disgrace, and nobody gets to publish. The boy doesn't belong to you any more. Besides, the pilot here is just doing his job, and he doesn't have a clue what the goop is. Maybe the information is worth something to us, but not to him."

Don looked from one of the arguing doctors to the other and wanted to laugh, but he didn't, though it looked like either Jezebel Lyondell or Sills might. The boy they were talking about was at least fifteen years older than he was. Smyth looked like he was ready to argue the point, but Anna interrupted him. "Gents," she said, sitting down in her jump seat. "I don't care about your arguments, or what your goop is. Lieutenant Fields and I have had a very bad day. We've been shot at twice and missed our breakfast. All we had for lunch were some greasy hamburgers a few hours ago that keep on repeating on me. On top of that, I've got a wound in my back that hurts a lot, so I didn't sleep much last night."

From outside the fuselage came the sound of engine number one turning over, and then firing. Immediately the three following engines started and both Anna and Don put on their headphones. A moment later the other four followed suit. "Put your seatbelts on," Anna said, "and keep quiet. This circuit is for crew use only. You may listen, but you may not talk. If you talk, I will unplug you." The plane started to rock from side to side as Juanita taxied to the down wind end of the runway. "As soon as the CO leaves the cargo hold and can't see me sleeping on the job, I'm going to catch a nap. You might want to do the same. Do not, under any circumstances, wake me up."

They reached their home base at 17:35, and it took nearly an hour to unload the one container from the aircraft, with the three Doctors all giving conflicting advice. As soon as it was unloaded and stored safely in a hanger with two airmen standing guard, Don dismissed his crew and asked Anna and Juanita to take Jezebel Lyondell over to the mess hall, but he stayed with the three Doctors while they ran some tests on the goop.

"It looks fine to me," said Stills after about half an hour of chemical analysis.

"Oh please," said Smyth. "You've barely scratched the surface."

"But that's all we need to do right now," said Lyondell. "Young man, Lieutenant Fields. I do appreciate you staying, but there really was nothing you could do."

"I appreciate that Doctor. I studied physics and math myself, so I knew I'd be useless around a bunch of chemists. However, I was concerned about your project surviving its flight."

"Not to be worried about Lieutenant. It's designed to survive much more rigorous conditions than you can ever throw at it."

"Like high radiation and extremes of hot and cold?"

Doctors Smyth and Lyondell exchanged worried glances, but Stills laughed. "Oh shoot, boss you should have seen the looks on your faces. Lieutenant Fields, you know we can't talk to you about this until you have clearance, but you know more than you're telling us, don't you?"

Don sheepishly ran his hand through his hair. "Can't tell you Doc. What I know, and how much, well, it's classified."

Chapter 10

A weary Don rolled out of bed at 05:30 in the morning and noticed that both Sacks and Jean-Paul were already dressing in shorts and tees. Putting on a burst of speed, he met with the other team members for their morning run in front of the cottage. He was pleased to note that his new people were taking their physical fitness seriously. Both Tessy and Jean-Paul were stretching with the rest, though Anna was taking a couple days off by doctor's orders. "Jean," he said, "Set the pace for us this morning."

The Israeli grinned evilly. "Sir, yes sir. Everybody ready? Then let's go!"

For the first couple of kilometers, running from the barracks to the base of hanger row, Jean-Paul set a fairly steady pace, not hard, but not difficult either. Then he turned and began to run the length of the runway, moving at a much more rapid pace. Fifty meters later he moved from a jog to a run, and after another fifty meters back to a jog for the third fifty, and then fast, and back to a jog, and Don began to regret he had ever suggested that Jean-Paul should set the pace. By the time they had circled the main runway twice and started back to their barracks, Don was regretting he had even gotten out of bed. Totally winded, except for the Israeli, the entire team collapsed on the front porch.

"You," Sacks protested, "Are an evil man."

"I try," said Jean-Paul with a grin. "You know doctor, exercise is good for your health. And your weight."

"I didn't expect that when I asked you to set the pace, Jean," Don wheezed.

"Ah, but it was my pleasure, Lieutenant."

"Fine. You're now responsible for unit fitness levels."

"Right, let's do half an hour's worth of calisthenics before we hit the showers then, shall we?"

Later, having sent the team off to their respective assignments for the day, Don took an hour to write up his mission report and stopped in to drop it off at General Hines's office, but the sergeant asked him to wait a second and picked up her phone. "General," she said, "you wanted to see Lieutenant Fields. He's in the office. Would you like to see him now?" She listened for a moment and nodded, pointing Don towards the inner office. "Yes sir, I'll send him right in."

Don stepped through the door, came to attention before the desk and saluted. "You wanted to see me, sir?"

"Stand easy. Is that your report Lieutenant?" The General held out his hand and Don passed the document over.

"Yes, sir."

"Lieutenant, I try to be blunt, and I don't mess around. Do you want Fleet replaced? I can do it you know," he snapped his fingers. "Just like that. I know you two aren't actually getting along too well."

"Sir, no sir." Don said. "Sir, if I may speak plainly, she was a pain in the butt about the loadmaster job, and for a while I really wanted her out, but when we were under fire she was a rock. She proved her worth, sir and whatever this assignment is, she's the kind of people I need."

"Meanwhile, I've kept her at loadmaster, but I've installed Lieutenant Thewes as Flight Engineer, with Lieutenant White as her backup. Rob is also working as Fleet's backup, and I think he's going to get her squared away. She's far too valuable to me for her talents to go to waste, and I think Lieutenant White can train her to do the job right."

Hines digested the news for a moment before he nodded and said, "Very good. Everybody is busy today?"

"Yes sir. Lieutenants Golden and Hernandez are scheduled for base CAP standby, Lieutenant Shackle is working a shift at the hospital. Lieutenant Fleet is on light duty, so she's giving a side arms refresher to Post and White. Lieutenant Thewes is getting her medical."

"And you?"

"I'm scheduled to report to Captain Bali, sir."

"Do you think you've guessed what's going on?"

"I think I have a pretty good idea, sir."

Again Hines was lost in thought for a moment before he said, "Then get going, and no, we will not call her Enterprise. Her name is the ES Intrepid."

For a moment all Don could do was stare, and then he found his voice. "ES, sir?"

"Earth Ship, Lieutenant. Earth Ship Intrepid."

All the way to the circus tent beside the main runway, Don was in a daze. He couldn't get the name out of his head. The Earth Ship Intrepid. It was like somebody knew for sure that there were others out there, people whose ships did not come from Earth. It was all right to see shows about space flight on television, or read about the idea in a book someone wrote, but to travel in a ship that had to be designated as coming from Earth. There was a sort of finality to that, because it meant that there were ships that didn't come from Earth. There really was something out there, and someone on Earth knew the truth, and he was going to experience it.

One of the airmen outside the tent blocked his way, feet apart, weapon at the ready, and his eyes flat and full of the knowledge that he could instantly kill. "Can I help you, sir?"

"My name is Fields, Don Fields, and I'm ordered to report to Captain Bali."

The airman had been briefed. Still looking as if he were ready to kill, he checked Don's id tag, stood to attention and saluted. "The Captain is waiting for you, sir. Please sign in, and turn to the right once you step into the tent. Sir."

Don saluted, signed in on the airman's clipboard with the time and date, and stepped through the canvas flap, only to discover that a solid steel door had been hung to the right, just inside the opening. Going through the door, he found he was in a short plastic containment tube that led to a steel and plastic trailer. Don guessed it was air tight, and wasn't surprised to see the seals around the second oval steel door. When he went up the stairs and let himself inside, Bali and one of the enlisted women from Nanaimo were seated at a Masonite table, both dressed in work clothes. They stood to their feet when Don came in. "Lieutenant Fields, good to see you. I understand you've had a bit of an adventure. You remember Warrant Officer Browning?"

Don shook hands with both. "Well, someone took a shot at us, that's about all."

Warrant Officer Browning was short and slightly plump, several years older than Don. "Well, from what I saw, sir, you were quite brave, getting that bomb out like that." She flushed slightly. "And you saved our lives. Thank you, sir."

"Warrant Officer, you're welcome," Don replied. "Of course, I was desperately trying to save my own butt as well."

Browning giggled a little. "Truth. Still, thank you."

"So Captain, I'm to work for you this morning?"

"Yes." Bali led them out through a third door, down three wooden steps and into the tent proper.

The lieutenants had been calling it the circus tent, but that wasn't what it looked like inside. Don guessed that it had to be over fifty meters across and over fifteen meters high. There was one tall pole in the center that looked like polished stainless steel. That pole was held up by guy wires that led to, Don guessed, at least thirty if not more, other poles along the outside perimeter of the tent, making a perfect circle. The inside of the canvas stretched over this frame had been covered with a thick black plastic, so that no outside light or air could enter, and lighting was provided by several extra bright lamps fastened to the poles just below the ceiling. The floor had been leveled and covered with what looked like a fine steel mesh. That floor looked so flat that Don suspected that if he putted a golf ball across it the ball would just keep on going until it hit the canvas on the other side. All along the sides, the walls of the tent had been weighed down with sandbags, and in front of the sandbags was piled the equipment he and his crew had picked up in Nanaimo, along with several ladders and tables of tools. "Welcome to the Bat Cave," said Bali. "A world of incredible scientific wonders hidden in the dark of day."

"There he goes with that Bat Cave line again," said a voice, and Don turned to see Sergeant Daphne Hale, Bali's other assistant. "Personally I hate that line, but I think it took him a day or so to write it and we hate to put him down, so we let him use it."

"Well, Lieutenant Fields, are you here to work?" Browning asked.

"Ready and raring to go," Don replied.

"Ok, let's grab a ladder and get started."

Real work, it turned out, was for the lieutenant and the sergeant to take the large parts of steel racking that had been piled along the outside of the cargo bay, and fasten them to the central pole in such a way that they eventually looked like a weird shaped wing, fastened vertically to the pole, and arranged to rotate around it in a perfect circle, its top and bottom just clearing the area between the guy wires and the floor, the outside edge forcing them to move several tables of equipment back as it rotated when they tested it for clearance. "Now this is more than strange," Don said when they were done. "What's this thing supposed to do?" He glanced at his watch and noticed it was well past midnight. It didn't feel that late, but he was exhausted and vaguely remembered eating at least twice during the day, both times in the steel trailer at the door.

"What, you don't know?" said Warrant Officer Browning. Don had decided that he liked both enlisted women. It hadn't taken them any time to get over the fact that they were in charge of an officer for the day and they had spent most of the time between jobs just kidding with him. "Ok, time to tear it down! We thought you were the one who knew what was going on here! If you don't know sir, then we're all lost!"

Don said nothing, but grabbed a wrench and walked over to a fitting that Hale had fussed with for over an hour. He was just adjusting the wrench to fit a rather large bolt when the Sergeant yelled, "No! All right, you win! It's an extruder, and now you have to go home and sleep on that tidbit of most useless information."

"An extruder. And what do you intend to extrude with it, if I may ask?"

"You may not. Do come back in the morning, but don't come inside. The next step is to sterilize the entire place, and to do that we're using ethylene oxide. Nasty, nasty stuff. Good night."

Juanita had fallen asleep on a couch in the sitting area, but sat up when he came in and turned on a lamp. "¿Ah, día largo, o acaban de decidir para salir para una cerveza con los chicos?"

Don flopped in a huge armchair, deliberately several feet away from her. She wore no makeup, her hair was tousled, she was dressed in bare feet and pajamas and she was yawning. She was looking great. "No beer, no boys, just work. Don't tell me you waited up for me?"

"Well, I bought you a present," she said, and handed over a neatly wrapped package.

"Uh-huh," he said as he tore the wrapping off. "An English to Spanish dictionary. How thoughtful of you."

She grinned. "Well, a man can't be considered educated unless he can speak Spanish, can he? You memorize the words and I'll teach you the inflections and grammar."

He noticed another book on the coffee table and recognized it instantly. "You're reading the Art of War again?"

"Si, though I prefer it in the original Spanish. El Arte de la Guerra, but the base library only has the English version. Sacks says I should read it in Mandarin, but the library doesn't have that either."

"Right. And you stayed up late to tell me that?"

Juanita yawned. "I've just missed chatting with you."

"I know what you mean. It's been a long few days. How was your day flying cap?"

"Bastante interesante. We had to scramble twice. One was a hot air balloon. The other was un hombre in a Cessna, said he just wanted a look. I told him we were armed and authorized to use deadly force. He turned around quick but I got his registration number and passed it on to the tower."

"I spent the day inside the tent with Doctor Bali and his circus."

"Oh boy, though those enlisted girls were kind of cute."

"They're both too old for me, and neither is as cute as you."

"You're just saying that because it's true." She sat back in the half-light. "What did you think of the dress I bought for Anna? I bought it with you in mind you know."

"I know. How could you be so cruel to me? I'd spend a couple of minutes checking out her legs, and realize it wasn't you, and then I'd be disappointed. Unfortunately, I think the dress is ruined."

"The blood, I know. Anna rinsed it out with cold water and we took it to the cleaner's here on base. They think they can get it back to looking like new, but no guarantees." She smiled elfishly. "They claim they have experience working with blood stains."

"Ouch. I hope so. I mean the getting the blood out part, not the experienced part. It looked really good on her, but I think it would look incredible on you."

"You better believe it would." Juanita pushed herself to her feet, picked up her blanket, stopped at his chair and put her hand on his shoulder for just a moment. "Good night," she said, and was gone, leaving him feeling lost and empty inside.

Chapter 11

For Don, morning came far too early, but he rolled out of bed with the rest, and when Jean-Paul suggested that they should run up and down the side of a mountain, he groaned like the rest, and then he dug his toes in and ran until his lungs felt like they were going to burst. This time when they got back to the barracks, they worked on self-defense techniques. "Will," he said when they were done, doing his best to control his gasping. "I want you to start teaching us basic astronomy tonight. Sacks, tomorrow night we'll start to review first aid. Both of you, one night a week for the next six weeks. And Doc, before you go, can I have a word?"

"Sure." Sacks sat back down where he had collapsed from the run, and stayed behind when everyone else tromped inside for showers.

"What's ethylene oxide? I know it's a gas used to sterilize, but I don't know much else about it," Don asked.

Sacks shrugged. "To be honest, I don't know a lot either. It's extremely hazardous, flammable and toxic, it's stored as a liquid and can freeze your hands if you touch the cylinder during discharge, its carcinogenic and can cause genetic disorders in your children. Oh, and it's heavier than air, so it could pool at your feet and you might not know it except for a bit of a sickly sweet smell or the fact that you might be standing in a pool of flame. I could download a copy of the MSDS if you want."

Don shook his head in self-disgust. "That's probably what I should have done myself. Thanks man. FYI, Captain Bali is using some at the circus tent, or, correction, he used some last night."

"Did I say it was extremely flammable? The tent is right near the runway! There are jets taking off and landing there at all hours. Which way do the prevailing winds blow? In other words, how much gas is he using, and how well contained is it?"

"He filled the tent with it."

"You gotta be kidding!" Sacks didn't wait for an answer. Turning, he ran into the building, shouting for a phone, Don at his heels. It took only a moment for the doctor to dial up the hospital and speak to his supervisor, explaining the situation. Finally he barked a rough, "I know!" slammed down the phone and raced into their room, stripping off his running gear. Throwing his shorts and Tee on his bed, Sacks jumped into his scrubs. "Don, I need the keys to your car, now!" Off in the distance Don heard a warning siren and he tossed over the keys even as the other officer raced back out the door. A moment later came the roar of the Capri's little engine and the side of the building was pelted with small rocks as the machine screamed out of the parking lot.

One thing Don knew was that when there was an emergency, you don't go to where the emergency is; you go to your emergency station. As of yet they had no such station, so he deliberately set his people back to their daily routines, showering, changing into uniform, having breakfast, and washing dishes. An hour later they were all sitting around the table in the kitchen when the phone rang and Tessy answered. It was General Hines. She grimaced as she handed the phone to Don.

"I understand it was Lieutenant Shackle we have to thank for our little brouhaha this morning," the officer said, with no preamble.

"I'm not sure what happened, sir, but I was asking him about ethylene oxide and he went out of here at a dead run. We haven't seen, or heard of him since."

"Doctor Lyondell, the chemist, he claims your doctor may have saved some lives this morning, but Doctor Bali claims he's nuts. What do you think? No political BS now!"

"Sir, Doctor Lyondell is a chemist, and I think he has a very level head. In matters of chemistry I would go with him every time. If I may ask, is everybody all right, sir?"

"As of now, everybody's alive, but Sergeant Hale got a good lung full, and Doctor Washington, he's our chief of emergency services, doesn't expect her to live."

Don wanted to curse and swear and smash something, but he knew it would do no good.

"There will be an inquiry," continued the General, "but there's nothing much we can do at this time. I think Bali was wrong to use a chemical he was unfamiliar with, but we can't change that. If Sergeant Hale dies, your crew will fly the body back to Canada for the funeral."

"Sir, shouldn't Captain Bali…"

"The Captain will continue his work until the inquiry. The enlisted personnel under his command are now assigned to your supervision for the balance of the project. All your personnel are to report to the ready room in Hanger 312 for a full briefing at 09:00."

"Yes, sir."

"And Lieutenant, that was your little car Shackle showed up in?"

"Yes sir." Don had thought he couldn't feel any worse, but the question was like rubbing salt into a wound.

"Is that a bullet hole in the hood?"

"Yes, sir. As soon as we get some time, Will and I…"

"I can't have you driving around in that. Every Tom, Dick and Harry will suspect what it is and demand an explanation, especially the cops or the MPs. Leave it at the motor pool, attention Sergeant Adams. I'll arrange for you to get the car back when the evidence is removed."

Nearly everybody was already there when Don and his crew walked through the door into the ready room in hanger 312. Captain Bali was pouring himself a cup of coffee, looking shattered, his hands visibly shaking. Warrant Officer Browning was standing at the back of the room, trying to hide from the officers, Doctor Stills was having an animated conversation with Jezebel Lyondell, Doctor Lyondell was sitting alone in the front row, studying some papers and Doctor Smyth was stamping around the room like a caged cat someone was prodding with a stick. There were several other officers present; making up a small clique to one side, but Don recognized none of them. There was no sign of General Hines, or Sacks. Don gave Juanita a, 'come with me,' nod and walked over to talk to Bali.

"Doctor? I'm so sorry to hear about Sergeant Hale."

"I too would like to express my condolences, Doctor," said Juanita. "It's very hard to loose a friend."

"She's not dead, she's only ill! Don't you go trying to put her in her grave!" Bali spoke loud enough for everyone in the room to hear and several faces were turned towards them, but quickly turned away again.

The two officers exchanged startled glances. "As you wish, sir," said Don stiffly. "We're sorry to have bothered you."

The door opened and Jean-Paul called out, "Attention." Immediately every military man stood to attention and saluted while Hines strode into the room, saluting them back.

"Everyone take a seat," the General snapped. "Fields, you're up here with me." Don moved up to the front, and while the General took a stand behind the podium, took a position of parade rest to his right.

"I assume everyone has heard the latest. Someone made a

mistake this morning and Sergeant Hale of the Canadian Armed Forces lost her life," he glanced at his watch, "Fifteen minutes ago, because of it.

"This was sloppy and careless work and will not be tolerated!

"As of now, I'm appointing Lieutenant Fields to be in charge of this project. It's his butt on the line and I don't give a hang if you out rank him, his word is final. When he's gone, and he is going to be gone quite often, Captain Hill," he indicated a short, hard looking man, "is now acting as safety officer for the project. If you want to do something, get his approval first, no ifs, or buts." He turned to look at Hill. "David, you're in charge as far as safety goes. If somebody, and I do mean anybody, doesn't clear an operation with you, then it doesn't happen. If it does happen, and anybody else dies, it's on you. Understood?"

"Understood, sir."

"Good. Fields, there will be a short runway service for Sergeant Hale at 08:00 tomorrow morning, and then you and your crew will fly her remains to CFB Halifax. You are expected to stay for two days and return on Sunday.

"I want you to be ready for anything, so I want your crew armed at all times, with live ammunition. Somebody out there is determined to stop us, and I think CSIS leaks like a sieve, so be extra careful in Halifax.

"Meanwhile, I believe it's time the lot of you were brought up to speed. Warrant officer Browning, I think it would be a good idea if you filled everybody in on your end of the project."

The NCO in question glanced at Bali and pushed herself to her feet. "Yes, sir."

She walked to the podium as the general relinquished the space. At the general's nod, Don sat down in the first row.

"As some of you know, and more of you have guessed, we are in the process of building a spaceship.

"I see that this information is a surprise to some of you, but not all of you.

"About five years ago, Doctor Bali and I were approached by the combined US and Canadian governments to do some research. What they needed was a hull, of a non-conventional design, size and strength. They needed it lightweight, and they needed it tough.

"I hope you understand, we were not consulted as to the means of propulsion, or controls, or sensors, like radar or anything like that, just the structure, and so this is what we came up with." She went to a large carton that had been lying against the wall and pulled out what looked like a hatch cover made from a black plastic like substance. "You probably think this prototype hatch is made of plastic, or steel, but you are wrong if you do. The hatch is made of sticky nanotubes. Doctor Bali and I have figured out a way to scale up the production of carbon nanotubes by a hundred thousand percent over the latest conventional technology. The best way to envision what we are going to do in that tent by the runway is to imagine a huge movable mold. Now that mold is going to rotate around the central pole holding up the middle of the tent, and extrude a spaceship. A flying saucer if you will, though as I told you, I have no idea how anybody is going to make it fly. I don't see any room in the design for engines, though there is a cramped space designated for a nuclear reactor, and cables that lead into empty floors and walls, but I have no idea what goes in those walls.

"But I digress. The saucer is fifty meters across by fifteen high, or just over a hundred and sixty feet by about forty-nine feet tall. By the time we finish building it, the walls, floors and ceiling of every room will be hollow, in two layers, ten to fifteen centimeters thick. There will be three floors, a control room, a climate control room, a reactor control room, three armories, bedrooms, a mess hall, a lounge, shafts for weapons of some kind, store rooms, labs and even a sewage recycling room. I can't comment on the design, although it's a fascinating subject in it's own right, but I can build the shell for you.

"Conventional nanotubes are incredibly short, but incredibly strong. The best quality ones are made with graphite, encapsulated in a helium atmosphere. Our ship will be built with the same quality of tubing, but much, much longer, and tangled together to produce a super hard, super strong skin with no natural weak points. And one of the most amazing things about this product is that we produce it out of an atmosphere of pure carbon dioxide flowing between our anodes and cathodes. The only impurity we can allow, indeed that we must inject in a constant stream, is a mixture of chromium, nickel and a third item that is super secret.

"It's so secret even we don't know what it is." There were a few scattered laughs at the old joke, but they were short and worried laughs. Browning quickly got on with her lecture.

"One of the problems with this method, ladies and gentlemen, is biological impurities. Germs, or other living tissue, like insects, would introduce hidden weaknesses into the matrix. Thus we chose to use ethylene oxide to sterilize the environment, but we were in a hurry, and we made a mistake. No, we made several mistakes. We did not study the properties of the sterilant we were using as closely as we should have. We ought not to have built our tent so close to an active runway. We should have done a pressure test on the tent before the gas was introduced, and we did not. We should have insisted that anyone near the tent wear a bio containment suit at all times, but we did not.

"And so, in spite of the fact that we have made incredible advances in science, we have done it at the cost of a human life. The life of one of my friends, and I would give it all up to have her back with us. It was a needless death, and I apologize to you all on behalf of doctor Bali and myself.

"General, you have a question, sir?"

"Warrant officer, how long do you think this process of extruding the shell will take?" Don assumed that the general had the estimate memorized to the minute, so he knew the question was to solicit information for him and his crew.

"All our calculations point to approximately three weeks. Sir."

"Does that have to be continuous process, or could it be done a section at a time?"

"No sir, we need to work in a continuous shaping."

"And how soon before you start?"

For the first time the woman seemed unsure of herself. She looked over at Bali, but the Captain was staring at the floor. Don thought he was crying, he couldn't see for sure. "We introduced the carbon-dioxide directly after the accident, as soon as we sealed the tear in the plastic liner. It would take us about fifteen minutes to do some final checks and then throw the switch."

Hines nodded. "Very good then. This next section of the briefing is on a need to know basis. If you and Doctor Bali could proceed with your preparations, Captain Hill will come over in a few minutes and check you out before you throw the switch."

The Bali stood and they saluted Hines before they left the room and Hines returned to the podium. "Doctor Smyth, perhaps you could proceed with the briefing."

Smyth stood and frowned at Don and his crew. "You won't be removing these junior officers from the briefing first, general?"

"No, I won't be. Proceed, and be complete."

Don was positive he saw a look of disgust flash across Smyth's face. "General I must protest. The information I have is of the utmost secrecy."

Hines was starting to get angry. "Doctor, do you remember who brought the original samples to you?"

"You did, General. Only you were a mere colonel at the time."

"And do you remember who delivered your research grant every year?"

"You did, General."

"And do you remember who I pointed out to you twenty minutes ago as being in charge of this project?"

"Yes, that rather rude young man standing beside you."

"Well that rather rude young man is far more important to this project than you are."

"Do you want to stay on the project, or would you rather I fire you and appoint Doctor Stills as your replacement?" For a moment the two men stared at each other. Then Smyth stepped up to the podium.

"Ladies and gentlemen," he began. "It is of dire importance that you remember that everything you hear in this room today is of maximum secrecy." He turned to stare at Don, and Don stared right back, simply tired of the man.

"As the general has reminded me, several years ago he came to me with a small portion of what looked like green Swiss cheese, made out of rubber. He told me at that time that he thought it might be part of a computer. An alien computer.

"It would be an understatement to say I was rather cynical, but together with Doctor Lyondell, I began to run certain tests on it. It took us more than two years to learn how to interface with the substance, but when we did we discovered that yes, it was part of some sort of memory bank, or at least that's what we thought it was.

"Working in complete secrecy was difficult, but recent developments in chemistry have enabled us to extract living DNA from the substance. Yes, it was, is, alive. Even more importantly, we have discovered a way to replicate that DNA by using stem cells from piglets.

"Elsewhere in this hanger is a large tank of liquid. If all goes well in the next several weeks, we will be pouring that liquid into the void between the control room floor of Doctor Bali's spaceship shell and the ceiling of the room below.

"We will then add a catalyst and a refined sample of the DNA. The alien DNA will then convert that liquid into a fully functioning computer, CPU and memory. We will then have to connect the interfaces, and do the programming. Yes?"

One of the unknown officers sitting in the second row had raised his hand. "I don't understand how that's going to work. Could you give us an example?"

Don didn't understand either, but he almost laughed when he saw how Smyth preened himself. "Of course. One of the great mysteries of all time is how a baby grows in its mother's womb. Why does a cow not give birth to an alligator? We know that the cow will give birth to another cow because the concept of cow is encoded into the fetus's DNA. What we have here are two liquids, each with the concept of computer written into its DNA. When we combine the two, in the presence of a catalyst, the two liquids produce a living offspring, a huge brain. In this instance, that brain will be encapsulated between the floor of the control room and the ceiling of the room beneath."

Don thought of questions he wanted to ask, but Jean-Paul spoke instead. "Sir, you've used the words living and alive, and that brings all sorts of moral questions to my mind. A living organism needs nourishment, and it excretes waste products. How is that handled? Also, is there any pre-programming in this alien brain? Or can we just download a copy of Linux and get on with our lives? If not, how do we program an alien brain? What is the capacity and speed of this computer, in terms that we can understand? And last, but not least, what about the moral issues? By growing and using a living brain are we indulging in some bizarre form of slavery?"

"And you are an expert in such things?" Smyth asked sarcastically.

"I'm a biologist, and yes, I did do several courses on computer programming in university, as well as religious ethics, but that doesn't matter. I don't care who you are doctor, but when there is a moral dilemma, even the lowest of the low have a right to ask such questions and to receive legitimate answers."

Oh, well said, thought Don. Smyth's face was turning purple and he was about ready to explode when Doctor Lyondell rose gracefully to his feet. "Doctor Smyth, perhaps I could answer these questions?" he didn't wait for an answer and Smyth stalked to his chair with a furious bad grace. Don kept a poker face, but inside he was disappointed. He wanted to see Smyth explode and be slapped down by General Hines. He wanted... to shut up, he told himself. This is too important. If it was more important than love, it was more important than petty revenge!

"From our research we have determined that the brain does need certain things to survive," said Lyondell. "First of all, we have to supply it with a sugar water drip and access to oxygen, though both are minimal. The only excretions we have found are carbon dioxide and hydrogen, again in very low concentrations. We have calculated that the amount of hydrogen released by the projected brain could be burnt off with a small flame every twenty or thirty minutes, and have devised an automatic valve that handles this for us, recycling every time the pressure builds up to a certain point.

"Imprinting computer programs onto the brain is tough, though I've never yet seen one of these bio brains crash, and yes, we have built three much smaller units already. Obviously, they have gone through extensive testing, using the most popular software available, and yes, strange as it may seem, we did settle on Linux as our operating system, mostly because it's open source and we could tinker directly with the program, though that's my daughter Jezebel's area of expertise, not mine.

"As for speed, well, there is no comparison."

"I'm sure that most of you are aware that when a large program is loaded into a conventional computer, only parts of it can exist in the internal caches at any one time. Now consider how much faster the computer would be if the CPU could access the entire program, all at the same time, as well as all of the memory simultaneously, and I don't mean 64k. This computer will be able to do that with more information than you or I could imagine.

"Now, for conventional computers there are only two states of being, on, and off. Jezebel has written the programs for the new computer as if there were ten different states of being, as if the transistor wasn't an on, off switch, but could be set for any one of ten different states. She's designated the first nine letters of the Greek alphabet, plus the last letter as her symbols for these ten states. I'm sure you're acquainted with them, Alpha, Beta, Gamma, Delta, Epsilon, Zeta, Eta, Theta, Iota and Omega. She will be available for the next few months if you want to talk to her about it. Actually I'm sure those of you who have studied programming will definitely want to talk to her about it.

"As for your last point, I've got to admit it's not crossed my mind. To me it would be like training a dog to do an elaborate trick. He could do the trick, and do it well, but in the end he's still just a dog. If there are moral applications I don't see them, and I'm afraid you'll have to figure them out on your own. It's just not part of our mandate. We were given an item and told to find out what it was, and how it was made. Then we were asked to replicate it. We have accomplished all that and more. Lieutenant Fields?"

"Yes sir," Don said. "Sir, have you tested your computer in several different environments? For instance, Captain Bali speaks of his shell as being a new substance. Is that substance compatible with your computer? And, if I may ask, where did this alien computer substance come from in the first place? What is the largest size it will work at, and you are talking about spreading it out in a fairly thin layer. Would it not be more practical to have it shaped like a cube, or even a globe to minimize the distance between components?"

Lyondell nodded. "Those are interesting points, son. I don't know where the substance came from, and I've long since run out of guesses. I know that when Colonel Hines brought it to us, Doctor Smyth and I were baffled. The DNA in this thing is incredibly complex, but we also know that complex DNA does not necessitate a complex structure. For instance, you may know the classic example of frog DNA being more complex than human DNA.

"We have done some calculations, and when we are finished creating the new computer, we will be able to determine weather or not it is living up to it's potential, but we can't determine that until after it's running. As for being compatible with Doctor Bali's shell, I think it important that we test that compatibility at the earliest possible convenience."

Chapter 12

"Auto pilot set and locked," Jean-Paul announced from the left hand seat. "Chicago, here we come!" there was a faint cheer from the back of the cockpit, but no real excitement.

"Big deal," said Will. "So we drops in, pulls up to the pumps, tell the laddie to fill er up with petrol, aviation regular please, clean the windshield and can he check the oil on engine number two, she's runnin a bit 'ot mate? Then we takes off and... Yes I got ya!"

"You got who?" demanded Juanita, who was sitting behind the other pilots and hadn't seen what the navigator had seen.

"Oh, I got Tessy good. One second she's listening to my marvelous New Zealand accent, and the next she's checking the oil pressure on engine number two! Ha."

"Hey, keep it down up here." Anna's head popped up from the cargo hold. She lowered her voice. "We've got a very upset non-com down here. She just lost a friend! A little respect maybe? Huh?"

"Sorry," said Will. "But I think we'd all better get comfortable. We're looking at two thousand, eight hundred kilometers, seven and a half, maybe eight hours of flight time here. And I'm sorry, but we can't remain somber for eight hours to Chicago, and then for another six up to Halifax, and then do a funeral and fly back for another fourteen hours without ever cracking a smile."

Don, who had been on the point of agreeing with Anna, had to change his mind. "Will, you and Juanita and Anna go downstairs and send her up. With all she's been through I can't imagine sitting with the coffin right there for fourteen hours. We'll all take one-hour shifts, in groups of three. Meanwhile, we keep the revelry down, but we don't have to be totally somber. Rob, you know where the coffee pot is, let's see if Sacks and I have taught you anything."

Rob sprang into action like he had been waiting for the order. "Shaft lube, one pot, coming up boss. Golly, how many year of college did ah go through to become a nu-cle-ar engineer, and how many bone did ah break on dat ol football field jas so's ah kin make ol whitey he weird coffee?"

Lucy Browning was just coming up through the hatch as Rob rolled into his tirade, and Don caught a glimmer of a smile on her face. "Hey, warrant officer Lucy," Don called, "Come on up and sit in the drivers seat for a while. Jean, give the lady a seat."

Lucy Browning, as it turned out, was thirty-five years old, and from the prairies. Born in Calgary she had been raised in Moose Jaw, joined the army as soon as she could and had never been back. She had loved school, and when she had been approached by the army to go undercover at Simon Fraser University, she had leapt at the chance, treating her cover as her life, getting incredible marks in subjects she loved, and she got a steady salary for doing it. "I've been living on campus, helping Doctor Bali on different projects for the last ten years! Can you imagine? I got a masters in chemistry for free, courtesy of the government of Canada, and currently I'm working on my Doctorate."

"Well," Don was shaken, and he didn't know how to ask the question. "If you know that much chemistry, why didn't..."

"You want to know why I didn't warn Doctor Bali about the

Ethylene Oxide and save Daphne's life? I tried you know. I really did try.

"I never knew Daph very well, she'd only been around for a couple of years, but she was studying physics, like Doctor Bali, and he decided he trusted her more than he trusted me.

"She was an under-grad in physics, and I know more chemistry than the pair of them put together, and they decided to use the stuff anyway!" Was there a bit of an, I told you so in there? Don wasn't sure.

"How well did you know Corporal Workman?"

"Jill? Nada. Frankly she'd only been with us for a few months, the spring semester. She was supposed to be a computer programmer, but there were times I'd stay behind and review her work, and she made some real amateur mistakes, dumb stuff."

"Did you tell Captain Bali about it?"

"Nah. He was a captain, we were stiffs, and he wasn't interested. I figured she'd settle down after a while and everything would be fine. No such luck. You know, these are the same questions the investigators were asking us."

Investigators? Of course there were investigators! He'd been debriefed himself for a good three hours. All of the new stuff that had been happening had driven that from his mind. "Was she friendly?" he asked.

"Jill? Lousy spy, trying to kill us! Yeah, she was friendly, in a strange sort of way. We all went out for a beer a couple of times a week. You know how you can sit around in the pub and brainstorm? Bali always encouraged it, and we came up with more than one or two good ideas that way.

"She always paid her way, chatted. All her stories sounded kind of thin though, but we laughed anyway. She said she was from Quebec, but she couldn't speak French. I tried, cuz I need to know more to advance in the army, you know?"

She shook her head. "Sorry. Of course, you wouldn't understand, you're an American. Do you speak any Spanish?"

Don shook his head. He had discussed this with Hines and here was the proof of his point. "Well," he said. "You know that official secrets act you signed a couple of days ago?"

"Yes, sir." There was hesitation in her voice, and behind her the noise of conversation faded.

Don raised his voice. "This conversation has just rolled under the banner of the act. The truth is, I'm a lieutenant in the same forces you're in. Will is from New Zealand, Sacks is from Australia, Juanita is from Mexico, Tessy is from Luxembourg, and Jean-Paul is from Israel. Anna is in the US Army, and Rob is in the US Navy, but we're all acting as American airmen under the auspices of the United States Air Force. Our ranks are real, but we're under cover, sort of. Somebody from the unit had to represent us at Sergeant Hale's funeral, and since Captain Bali is under site arrest, General Hines decided it was the crew. I couldn't go showing up in an American uniform, just in case I met someone I knew, so, in a few hours we're all going to change into our national dress uniforms and you were going to think we were nuts, but now you've been forewarned with the truth."

She stared at him for a while and said, "You know, I knew you guys weren't Americans, I think. None of you fit in down there, not really. And your secret identity is Captain Canada?"

"Sort of. More like Lieutenant Canada, but yeah, that's me. From Prince Albert, Saskatchewan."

"A flatlander, I should have known. From So-scratch-me-one, of all places! And the love of your life is from Mexico." She saw the look in his eye. "Sir."

Don lowered his voice. "Warrant officer, there are things you may say, and things that could get you tossed out the rear end of this airplane without a chute. Do you understand?"

"Sir! Yes, sir.

"Did you ever hear the one about the American couple who visited Saskatchewan and got lost in Saskatoon?"

Don shook his head. "Warrant officer, you have been warned!"

"Sir, yes sir.

"You know, I wish I could have stayed to watch the hull extruded." Browning looked down at her hands. "We've done some work on a smaller scale, like that hatch I showed you at the briefing, but building the hull, it's a huge difference, hundreds of times larger than anything else we've ever done before!"

"And you had a big part in that," suggested Rob.

For a moment Browning only stared at him. Then, "Yes, I had a big part in it," she said. "You'll never guess how big my part was. This extrusion has been the subject of my dreams for years, and now it'll be days before I get to see how it's working."

"Can I ask a question?" Sacks asked.

"Of course."

"Welders. You brought two with you, and when we got back to camp there were two more waiting for you. I may not know nanotubes, but I doubt you weld them together. Why four welders?"

Lucy smiled. "Actually, in a way, we are."

"You see, we form the tubes by using DC current through the mesh on the frame work and floor. "Lieutenant Fields, you remember the steel mesh?"

"The last thing we put on the frame, identical to the mesh on the floor of the tent."

"Right," Lucy said. "That mesh is connected to a very sophisticated computer program, and by swinging the frame very slowly, we form parts in selected parts of the mesh, which then grow away from it, or I like to say it extrudes the nanotubes. If there's power over here, then there is wall over there, if there isn't any power there, then there's no wall.

"The welders, well, the first one, and it's been totally redesigned and rewired, converts the incoming power to a very tightly controlled AC current. That current is then fed into the second rebuilt welder where it's converted to DC and a high frequency overlay is inserted. That's the power we use to grow the tubes between the squares in the mesh. The HF is actually what keeps the corners from being razor sharp."

"And the other two welders?" Rob asked.

Lucy shrugged. "Back up power, and a back up for the back up.

"I know the Doctor is going to do his best to control the reaction, but I sure wish I was there to keep an eye on it with him."

Thirty minutes out from Halifax they started to get changed, with first the men downstairs while Juanita flew the plane, and then the men at their stations while the ladies changed. Suddenly, all was somber; suddenly each man and woman was very conscious of the flag draped coffin sitting at the center of the cargo hold. Each knowing that it could be them, or, Don glanced at Juanita and met her eyes for a moment, someone they loved. Then the plane touched down in light rain and the pilots were far too busy slowing it down to taxi speed, and then taxiing across the runway to where a hearse waited for them near the main terminal.

Anna unlocked and lowered the rear door, and Jean-Paul and Juanita marched out, in full dress uniform, each armed with a P-90, and took station on either side of the ramp, their weapons at parade salute. Behind them followed the six remaining officers, carrying the flag draped casket, Don and Will in front, followed by Anna and Tessy, Rob and Sacks at the rear corners and with Browning following behind. On the tarmac, twelve enlisted members of the Canadian Armed Forces came to attention, and a Captain stepped forward and saluted. The Lieutenants carried the body to the hearse and slid it in. Then they stepped back as a group and saluted while the rear doors were closed and the hearse moved away. Don dropped the salute, turned stiffly and walked over to the Captain and saluted him.

"Sir. I'm Lieutenant Fields. I'm in charge of this unit. We have orders to accompany the body to Turo for the funeral, sir."

Two large black SUVs pulled up and the officer said, "Yes, I know. Grab your kits, and jump in. Two of your men are staying here?"

"They have the watch, sir."

"Let's go then."

Will, Sacks and Tessy joined Don in the first car with Captain Bowes, Anna, Rob, and Lucy jumped in the second car. "A most unusual unit you command, Lieutenant," Bowes said as they pulled away.

"You're Australian," he said to Sacks, "but you're not wearing regimental colors. And you young lady, I don't recognize the uniform at all."

"Luxembourg, sir," she said.

"I don't suppose you'd care to explain, Lieutenant?" said Bowes.

"I'm afraid that information is need to know only, sir," replied Don.

"I can live with that," Bowes said. "I've read the official cause of death, an inadvertent exposure to toxic chemicals?" his words made it a question.

Don nodded at Sacks. "I was the attending physician sir. Sergeant Hale was killed by an accidental ingestion of ethylene oxide, released in what I can only describe as an industrial accident."

"Can you give me any more details? I know Captain Bali only faintly, but he's not here with you, and I fully expected him. I knew that Sergeant Hale was working for him in British Columbia. Actually, I was their contact point for the last three years, though I only met him once and was not actually privy to what they were working on."

"Captain Bali has been charged with negligence causing death, sir," said Don. He slid an envelope from his jacket pocket and handed it over. "If you were his contact, then you will know who to give this to. The Captain has requested a Canadian officer as his defense counsel."

"Not you?"

"I suspect I'll be a witness for the prosecution, sir."

"So, a Canadian officer made a mistake on foreign soil, and a Canadian trooper was killed. Don't you think it would make sense to ask for a change of venue, have the trial here in Canada? I mean, well, the accident, it did happen in the US didn't it? I don't even know what state you were in."

"In the states, sir, but that's all I can tell you." Bowes pulled onto a highway and increased his speed to a hundred K, the second SUV close behind.

"Have you made reservations for us in Turo, sir?"

"There's a motel across the street from the funeral home. We'll be leaving the vans with you. Just drop them at the airport when you leave."

"Visitation will be from eleven to two, the service will be at the Salvation Army Citadel at 14:30 hours, internment will be at 15:00. I'll have an honor guard for all three. Will you want any of your people standing with them?"

"Yes sir. My officers and I will stand watch with your men."

"It's unusual having officers standing an honor guard for an enlisted trooper killed in an industrial accident," Bowes said, curiosity in his voice.

"Yes sir, but it's an unusual unit, sir. If I may sir, my men are all armed with live ammunition, and I suggest yours do the same."

Bowes stiffened, turned in his seat to look at him. "What? You're expecting trouble, at a funeral?"

"Sir, I can't go into detail, but we know that Canadian security,

CSIS, cleared a woman who was supposed to be part of Bali's command in B.C. A Corporal Jillian Workman."

"Corporal Workman, yes. Last year Captain Bali asked for a computer programmer and Corporal Workman was assigned to the post. Right now she's AWOL, and she's on a national wanted list on an unspecified warrant."

"Yes, sir. Corporal Workman smuggled a bomb on board my plane sir. Subsequently, we had a SAM fired at us, and then a sniper took a pot shot at two of us. With that kind of security taking care of us, we figure it might be better for us to maybe take care of our own."

"Then a Canadian officer shows up in an American C-130, with an international crew and a call sign normally reserved for American special forces black ops, and despite the fact that he only graduated from Kingston a couple of months ago, he's already earned himself a promotion. Then he suggests to me that the honor guard at a Sergeant's funeral should be armed with live ammunition. I see you're wearing a side arm as well.

"Mind if I suggest you're drawing more than a little attention to yourselves?

"The two guards left at your plane, are they using live rounds as well?"

"I'm very fortunate sir, in that there are several officers in this unit who qualify as expert with both long range and short range weapons. I even have one who has qualified as a sniper. Speaking of which, maybe you should notify your men in Halifax that under no circumstances should they approach the plane without making contact with it first by radio. One of the two guarding it is an Israeli, and you know how they teach their people to shoot before they're shot?" For a minute Don was worried that he had overdone it, but then Bowes fished a cell phone from his pocket and dialed a number.

"Todd? It's Captain Bowes here. Listen, that C-130 that landed today. Put a guard around it, about a hundred meters out, and do not approach it for any reason. They what? Yes, yes, let them have their pizza for crying out loud, just don't let anybody else near that plane, and yes, I know they're armed. No, they're not under arrest; we just want to protect them. I'll talk to you about it monday. Goodnight sergeant."

As promised, the motel was directly across the street from the funeral home, and Don paid for their rooms with the new card Hines had issued him just before take-off. Then, as soon as Bowes had left for the night, Don returned to the front desk and, requested that all their rooms be changed to the fourth floor instead of the second. Finally, he established a watch rotation; two officers awake at all times. Then he took a shower and went to bed.

Chapter 13

"Don, wake up."

"Anna? What time is it?"

"02:00. Get up, here's something going on."

Fumbling in the dark, Don slid out of bed and pulled on his flight suit and socks. Carrying his boots so that he didn't wake up Sacks, he grabbed his P-90 and slipped out into the hall. Earlier, Anna had switched off the hall lights to preserve their night vision. Now the only light came from the red exit lamps at the stairway and the elevator. Don slipped his feet into his boots and quickly laced them up. "Who's on watch, and what's happening?"

"Tessy is on the stairs, and she's heard voices, going down the hallway on the second floor. Somebody came up but she got behind him and put him to sleep with a strangle hold. Will was supposed to be in the lobby, but we haven't heard from him yet. Even as she said it, Don felt his cell phone vibrate in his pants pocket.

"Fields."

"Boss," it was Will, speaking in a whisper. Don had to hold the phone mashed tight against his ear to hear him at all. "Ten men, dressed in black, but they move like trained military. They're wearing night vision goggles."

"Arms?"

"Looks like AK47s. They went up the stairs, leaving two here in the lobby I had to put down before I called you." Ten men, with three down left seven, all well armed.

"Transport?"

"Two vans, idling at the curb, a driver in each."

"Anna, get everybody up, dressed and armed. Twelve guys, three are down. They're armed with AK47s. Will reports two in vans at the curb."

Don slipped back into his room and shook Sacks awake. Then he pulled a Kevlar vest out of his bag and slipped it on, along with a gas mask that he let hang from his neck. Anna was back in the hall and she too was wearing her body armor, with her gas mask handy. "You rigged the rooms downstairs?" he asked her.

"Oh, yeah," she said. "My guess is they'll try and hit all four rooms at the same time."

Like phantoms emerging from blackened caves, the rest of the team ghosted into the hallway. Don gave them a nod and led the way down the stairs to the second floor landing, passing Tessy's prisoner on the stairs. Don made note of the fact she had secured him with plastic zip ties and gave her a thumbs up. Stopping at the second floor landing he eased it open a crack to see what was happening in the hall.

He counted four men armed with door smashers, concrete filled lengths of steel pipe that had been equipped with steel handles, and three with their weapons trained on the doors. He was curious as to why they hadn't moved, and then he realized they were waiting for at least one more man to work with the fourth door smasher, probably the man Tessy had taken out. Trotting back up the stairs he pulled his leatherman from his belt and clipped the plastic ties holding the prisoner. Jerking off the man's night vision goggles and sweater, Don refastened the man's hands with plastic handcuffs and then pulled the sweater on over his flight suit and vest, shoved his gas mask in his hip pocket. Then he switched his P-90 for the AK47 and pulled on the night vision goggles. Instantly the darkness turned green and he could see. Pushing past the lined up officers of his unit, he stepped into the hallway on the second floor and walked boldly up to the intruders, taking his place as the eighth man of the team. Nobody spoke to him, so he said nothing. One of the men in the middle group held up a hand as soon as Don was ready, and almost instantly slashed it down, signaling the four door smashers to swing their concrete filled steel pipes into the locks on all four rooms, bursting out the locks. Quickly they dropped their heavy tools, swung up their weapons and seven men charged into the rooms. Don simply pulled off the goggles, closed his eyes and turned his back as four flash bang grenades and four tear gas bombs when off simultaneously.

Working swiftly, the multinational team moved in, securing each man with plastic handcuffs, gags over their mouths and doubled pillowslips over their heads. Leaving Tessy and Rob to guard them, Don led the rest of the team downstairs to the lobby where they hooked up with Will.

"Vans still at the curb?"

"Yeah, though I think they're starting to get antsy."

"Ok, Will, you grab a sweater and a pair of night vision goggles off one of these guys," Don indicated the men Will had put down earlier. "We burst out the front door; we each run to one of the vans, grab the side door, open it and jump in with our weapons out. Anna, you and Sacks give us five seconds, and then follow us. I want you to each take a van and drive it around back. On three, two, one!"

Throwing himself out the double glass doors, Don leapt down the concrete steps and raced for the first of two black vans that were parked at the curb, expecting at any moment to feel the shock and agony of a bullet smashing him down. Surprisingly, the bullet didn't come, and reaching the van he grabbed hold of the side door handle, threw it back, leapt inside and thrust the muzzle of his AK47 in the driver's face. "No heroics, no sudden moves," he demanded. "Turn off the van, but leave the keys in the ignition. That's right." Don took a quick look at the man's face, maybe thirty or so, tough looking, surprised.

"Move to the right seat and out the door, and don't make any sudden moves, because I will kill you. Do you understand?"

"Si."

Spanish? Was he speaking Spanish? It didn't matter. The man slid over and stepped out, just as Anna slid in on the driver's side and started the van up. "Hands behind your back," Don ordered, and with one hand slipped a pair of plastic cuffs over the man's hands and yanked them tight. There was a scuffle behind him and Don risked a glance, but Will had his prisoner in control, lying flat on his stomach on the sidewalk, Will's boot in the middle of his back. "You will walk, not run, to the main door. You will step inside and walk to the right, where you will find the elevator. You will wait until I open the door, then you will step inside and walk to the back of the elevator, facing the corner. No funny moves, no bravado."

To Don's surprise, the action went off without a hitch, and ten minutes later they had all twelve of the raiders searched and handcuffed in one of the bedrooms on the second floor. Don set himself up in another bedroom and ordered the prisoners brought in for interrogation, one by one.

"Name?" Don snapped at the first prisoner, when his gag and mask had been removed. Surprisingly, it was the driver that he himself had arrested.

The man said nothing.

"What were you doing here?" The man remained silent. All the men had been searched, but other than a couple of side arms, cigarettes and some cash, none of them had anything in their pockets.

"What was your goal, murder, or kidnapping?" Don asked. Again he was answered by silence. Unfortunately Don just didn't know the right questions to ask, or how to get the men to answer, so he spent a long and frustrating night with nothing to show for it. In four hours all he had achieved were twelve sets of digital photos and twelve sets of fingerprints. "Anna, Sacks? Load up our prisoners in their vans and drive them twenty klicks north of town, somewhere on a back road. Take their boots and socks. Then abandon the vans somewhere down the block here. Be sure to wear your gloves. Rob, you and Browning go with them to keep an eye on the prisoners while they drive. Everybody else back to your rooms to police them, no hairs, no nothing left behind. Wipe everything down for fingerprints with ammonia." He glanced at the dawn showing to the east. "Let's move people."

There were no significant surprises at the funeral, though Don was taken back for a moment when he found that the Canadian flag had been replaced with the flag of the Salvation Army. Checking with the Corps commander, a Captain Edwards, he discovered that Sergeant Hale had been an active solder in the Army, not just an adherent, and so the Flag switch had been done to honor her. After the funeral, they only spent a few moments back at the Corps meeting the sergeant's family and then the team ducked into the SUVs and shot back across the highway to Halifax.

"Sacks, did you take care of things like I asked you?" Don asked as they left Turo. It was their first chance to speak openly since the action the night before.

"Sure thing Don." Sacks shrugged. "I guess money really speaks. The desk clerk took a look at the doors, admitted we didn't stay in those rooms and pocketed his gratuity with a smile."

"Anna?"

"We left them on a gravel logging road at least ten K from any sort of civilization, in their bare feet, with their hands still in the plastic cuffs. We now have ten pair of night vision goggles and ten untraceable AK47s for future operations. We also have two side arms, Smith and Weston 1911 .45s, also untraceable to us, though one has some pretty fancy engraving."

"I don't care much if it's gold filled. Have you got a way to get them off the plane and to store them?"

"I do, and I will."

"I sure hope Juanita and Jean have that plane ready to go when we get there."

From twenty klicks out, Will, who was riding shotgun in Don's car, called Juanita's cell. "Hey babe, we just switched from highway one oh one to highway number two. We'll be pulling up to your doorstep in about twenty-five to thirty. Nah, we're in no danger, but you might want to be ready for a rush job on the take off. No, nobody's been hurt. We had a bit of a spat with some weirdo's, so we're coming in hot. Speaking of which, do you think you could order us a couple of pizzas before…Hey, she hung up on me!"

"How dare she?" said Don, deadpan. "And since when did, 'hey babe,' become the accepted way to address a fellow officer?"

"Well, she is a babe, isn't she?"

"You," said Anna, from the back seat, "Are so lucky I don't have a weapon in my hands. So very lucky."

"Luck," said Will, self righteously, "had nothing to do with it. I checked your hands before I called."

"You animal."

"What? I was hungry and I wanted her to order me a pizza…"

"It is going to be a long ride back to Chicago," said Don a few minutes later as they took the Bell Boulevard exit. Almost immediately he pulled into the airport Tim Horton's. "Bathroom break, everybody back in the car in five minutes."

Chapter 14

Almost as soon as they were airborne they received a radio call from Bangor looking for commander, SAM 1899. Don took the call on his headset, though he left the channel open so the others could hear. "Sierra Alpha Mike, eighteen ninety-nine."

"Sierra Alpha Mike eighteen ninety-nine, you are diverted to Hanscom Air Force Base, Bedford. Code seven, seven three. Report to Colonel Gene McDonald on arrival. Bangor tower out."

"Code seven, seven three? Are we playing spies now? What the heck is a code seven, seven three?" Will was rapidly flipping through his codebook while Don just sighed.

"It was my locker number in college," said Don.

"Your what? And how would he know that?"

"How does he know anything? Mr. Post, please plot a course for Hanscom Air Force Base, Bedford, and I wonder what they've got in store for us now?"

"A three day pass would be nice, " said Anna.

"But not probable," added Tessy.

"Pessimists," said Rob as he scooped up another slice of the pizza Juanita had ordered for them, and hooked a Tim Horton's donut with his other hand. "The world is full of pessimists. Personally,

I believe in a world of goodness, love and being able to avoid the SAMs."

"Everybody's on a three week training course to learn the ins and outs of your new electronics," said Colonel Cummins, when they reported to him. "You'll be staying at one of the residences at MIT and taught by three professors, who you will know as Professors A, B and C. Of course, you can't wear your flight suits, so you have the next couple of days to go shopping for suitable clothing." He made a performance of looking at his watch. "Well, it's getting fairly late, isn't it? Sergeant Tyne?"

A well-built man in his early thirties stepped into the office. "Sergeant, you've arranged transport for these officers and their crew?"

"Yes sir, there's a bus out back."

"Have somebody help them with their luggage. I understand they shouldn't have much. You've laid on pilots to take the C-130 home?"

"Yes sir, its being loaded as we speak and leaves in half an hour, sir."

Don exchanged glances with Anna. "Sir, we have been under attack several times, and are under orders to protect ourselves with deadly force if necessary. We request permission to carry arms."

For a moment Cummins said nothing, just stared at him. Finally he said, "Young man, this is American soil. Nobody is going to attack you here."

"Sir, so is California, and we were shot at there."

"No. Weapons. Period. Do you understand, Lieutenant?"

Don forced himself to simply bite his lip. "Sir, yes sir. We'll get our gear and report to the bus." Turning with the others he gathered his duffel and dress uniform from the plane. On the flight from Canada he had cleaned his carbine and sidearm and locked them into the rack. Now he quickly checked and made sure all ten AK47s were accounted for as well. Finally, he took his gear out and loaded it onto the bus with the others. The residence they were assigned to was on the north side of the Chessie System railway line running beside the campus, but it was very close to the building where they were to report. As soon as everyone had been checked into their rooms, Don walked down the hall to knock on Juanita's door.

"Don," she opened the door with a wide smile when she saw who it was. "Did you want to come in?" Don knew that Juanita was sharing a room with Tessy, but the other girl wasn't in sight and he didn't want to trust himself alone with her right now. He stayed in the hallway.

"Ah," he stammered. "Juanita," he could see the clouds forming and rushed to prevent them. "I, ah, was wondering if I could take you out to dinner."

"Dinner?"

"Yes."

"¿Sólo usted y mí?"

"Yeah. Just you and me. I checked the Internet with my laptop, and there's a seafood place, just a few blocks from here. That is, if you want to."

"Now?"

"I'd need about a half hour to shave, and to shower, but yes."

"Make it forty-five minutos. I'll meet you out front."

It was closer to an hour. Even as he rushed through shaving and showering and dressing in his American uniform, he felt like he had never felt before, scared, helpless and hungry, all at the same time. All his feelings seemed to dissolve into wonder when he saw Juanita coming down the steps to meet him in front of the dorm.

Somehow, Juanita had brought the yellow dress with her, and it did look even better on her than it had on Anna.

"You look beautiful," he said, simply taking her in.

"Gracias," she said, her nervousness disappearing from her face even as she smiled. "Dress uniform, wow."

"I tried," he said, offering her his arm. "Dress, shoes, black pearls even. How did you ever do this?"

"Well," she grinned shyly, wrapping her arm around his and taking his hand. "We all brought shoes. Significo, usted nunca sabe lo que sucederá. Anna brought the dress, and Tessy brought the pearls. I'd brought a skirt and blouse and some silver jewelry my mother gave me, and Tessy brought one of those denim skirts that looks like it's been torn off just below the hips, but we thought this looked the best. We tried all three outfits. Tessy did my hair, and Anna did my nails."

Don shook his head, grinning. "So everybody knows?"

"Por supuesto, todo el mundo sabe. What, you thought you could take me out to dinner and it could be kept a secret, eh?" She took his arm and steered him out the dorm door.

"I thought I was being cool."

"By keeping us apart? Are you telling some kind of joke? Tell me, why did you leave me back at the plane and take everybody else to Sergeant Hale's funeral?"

"Well, I wanted both of my pilots on the plane in case we needed a fast getaway, and I thought since you're Catholic, you might object to being in a protestant church."

"Half right, half wrong. Pilots on the plane, good reason. I'm Catholic, bad reason."

"How so?"

"Tessy is the Catholic. I'm actually Anglican. My mother was an orphan and the Anglican Church ran the orphanage."

"The crucifix you wear?"

"Was a gift from mi primo Reale. Half my family doesn't understand the difference between being Catholic and Anglican, so the Catholics treat me like a Catholic, and the Anglicans treat me like an Anglican. Anyway, Reale is my favorite cousin. He's handsome, and he's smart and he made sure I went to the best schools. He's why

I am who I am today, so when he gave me a Crucifix and asked me to wear it, I agreed."

"I'd like to meet your cousin Reale."

"I'd like you to meet all my family. As for Reale, you might meet him sooner than you think. As soon as I joined the army, Reale felt he had nothing to keep him in Mexico, so he went wetback to Los Angeles. He's living in country, though I have no idea where he is."

"Is that common?" Don asked. "I know a lot of Mexicans sneak into the states, but, well, aren't your people from the south part of Mexico?"

"I'm Zapotec, and the truth is, there are a lot of Zapotec in Los Angeles. A lot more than people realize.

"You know, it's not that we want to sneak into another country. I am a Mexican, and I am proud to be Mexican, but I have a job, I'm in the army. A lot of other people are not in the army. There are few well paying jobs in Mexico, and las personas necesitan dinero para comer."

"In Canada, we constantly worry about the manufacturing jobs that are leaking out of our country and going to the states, or to Mexico for that matter. Canada is one great big huge country, but we just don't have the population, or the infrastructure to support the size of the country. In reality we should be designing our own cars, clothing styles, building our own televisions and jet planes, but we're far too spread out, with most of us living within a couple of hundred miles of the American border, and way too dependent on them, even though some of our ideas are far better than theirs."

"Such as?"

Don thought for a moment. "The constitution. The Americans have this document that governs their very lives, and they think it gives them freedom, but what it does is ties them to the rule of law so tightly that in some instances they can't use common sense anymore.

They have the right to bear arms, guaranteed by their constitution. Great, if you're going to use that gun to shoot a deer so you can eat dinner. I can understand that, I was raised on venison, it was the only way my daddy could be sure there was always meat on the table, but that amendment was written before the invention of assault weapons, or sniper rifles. The American colonies needed to be able to defend themselves against the British domination. Fine at the time, but right now it's perfectly legal for an American to have a dozen AK47s or an M16 in his garage or even an automatic shotgun. Hello! Neither one is needed to shoot your dinner! It's insane, and they call it a right to bear arms. More like a right to shoot your neighbor."

"But Canada has a constitution too."

"True enough. A bunch of people just thought they would meddle with the social fabric of Canada because they were enamored with the American way of life. I call it constitution envy. They thought if the US has one, we should have one too, but we didn't need it, and in my opinion, we still don't. Now a lot of people realize just what a mistake that was, but it's too late. There's nothing we can do about it. Instead of the wisdom of common law, we have constitutional challenges where judges rule on the letter of the law, not on the spirit of the law, which is the same stupid mistake the Americans made. So, the law resulting from the constitution is being used to destroy the spirit of the constitution, not to protect the people, which is what it was about in the first place! When a law becomes more important than the people it was designed to protect, it's time to get rid of that law!"

"Did I ever tell you that you are cute when you start to rave about the things you believe in?"

"Did I ever tell you that I love you?"

"Not until just now."

"I do."

Chapter 15

"And, no, we never did have dinner." First thing in the morning, Rob had started in on Don and was letting him get away with nothing. "We wandered around a lot, under the streetlights. There was a bridge somewhere and we watched the water flow by for an hour or so. She got chilly and I gave her my coat, but I didn't feel cold. I felt for the first time in my life that I was really home, and I could tell her everything that ever went well with me, and everything that ever went wrong."

"When did you get back to the dorms?"

"I honestly don't know what time it was. It could have been one, or two, or even 03:00, I didn't check my watch. All I know is that after we got back, we sat on the porch and talked for a long time, about everything and nothing. I was just sitting there thinking how gorgeous she is. Then, when dawn came, we changed into our civvies and went for breakfast."

"So you've had no sleep at all for two days?"

"I got some shut eye on the plane, but last night, I didn't need it."

"You're going to have to admit this to Hines."

"I know."

"You could lose your promotion over this. He'll tell you that you can't have an affair with a subordinate."

"It's not an affair, but I know what you mean. He asked me specifically about Juanita, and I told him there was nothing between us, and I was telling the truth, or I thought I was. Then, yesterday, after the funeral, I was thinking about what's important to me. I was re-evaluating my life, and I realized that Juanita is more important to me than my life. Unless you've been there, you just can't understand. It's not lust, though she's a beautiful woman and I desire her, its more than that. I'm comfortable with her, I can talk about anything with her, and that's what we did this morning."

"You really mean that, don't you?" Now, instead of being accusatory, Rob's tone was full of wonder.

"Yes, I do."

For a second Don thought that Rob was going to actually take a swing at him, and then he stuck out a huge paw. "Congratulations man, you're in love. But you let me tell you something. If you ever hurt that girl, or take advantage of your position, man there won't be enough MPs anywhere that could drag me off you before I do you some serious bodily harm. You understand me? Serious, bodily, harm."

"And I," said Don, "would expect nothing less of you."

Professor A was a big man. Though he was not as tall as Don or Rob, he was still taller than Sacks or Will, and he could look Jean-Paul directly in the eye. Don could only politely describe his circumference as majestic. "My purpose in this accelerated course is to teach the functioning of semiconductors, not electronic engineering. We will discuss many different concepts, from electronic band structures and doping, transistors and solar photovoltaic panels. I can see that some of you understand what I am talking about, and some of you don't. Don't worry about it. Professor B," he indicated a shorter, much thinner man, "Will be taking those of you who need a refresher in the basics and bringing you up to speed. Professor C will be teaching you all about electronic engineering, with two classes, one in the morning for the advanced students, and one in the afternoon for professor B's students.

"I know that we, your instructors, have no knowledge of why you need this information, only that it's considered to be in the national interest. Rest assured however that our curriculum has been intensely scrutinized by those who do know your needs, and if we seem to be going off topic the reasons will eventually become obvious. Because of the relatively low ratio of teachers to students in these classes, you will be expected to excel, and there will be no excuses for failure. If you have questions, we will be available to answer them, twenty-four seven. Now, Fleet, White, Thewes, Fields, you come with me. You are about to undergo the most intense training in electronics this school has ever instigated. The rest of you, professor B is going to help you catch up."

For Don, the next three weeks of electronics school seemed to pass as fast as lightning and as slow as molasses. Time spent in the classroom seemed to drag, until there was no end to the day, and yet the hours spent with Juanita, whether studying or just chatting, seemed to fly away. It wasn't that he ignored his other work. He made sure that the team kept up their morning runs and calisthenics, and that every evening they spent time with Will studying astronomy, or with Sacks studying first aid. It was just that he had this one thing that seemed to fill him to completion, and that was Juanita.

And then the three weeks were over and they all hitched a ride back to Nevada aboard an army C-17 that was carrying several skids of cargo for Nellis base, their brains full of formula and schematics.

"No, I can't tell you what's on the skids," the Senior Master Sergeant said to Anna when she tried to chat with him about it. "Nor can I tell you about its weight. Mostly because I don't know. Well,

I know the weight," he corrected himself. "And it's fairly heavy for skids that size, but not too heavy for a Globemaster." He patted the fuselage of the heavy lifter with some affection.

"Then tell me about the Globemaster. Tell me about being a load master."

"Begging your pardon ma'am, what would a lieutenant want to know about being a load master for?"

"I have a job to do, and I need to know more about your profession. It's really important, though I can't discuss the details with you. I think the general has forgotten that I haven't had your training, so I need you to talk to me. Please."

Don heard most of the conversation, and he wanted to congratulate Anna on her initiative, but he knew that his promotion probably wasn't going to last much longer and he decided to hold off, and even as he did, his exhaustion finally caught up with him and he slipped off to sleep. Juanita, seeing him there, grinned and decided to sneak upstairs and see if she could get a chance to fly this bird.

They landed on runway 14 and had to taxi back the entire distance to the southeast end of the runway before parking the jet quite close to the circus tent. Surprisingly, General Hines was on hand to greet them. "Fields," he said as they trooped off the plane. "I'd like a word."

Here we go, thought Don. "You had an interesting time at the funeral?"

"We were attacked by several men, sir."

"Yet you managed to capture them without any shooting, and without compromising the mission. I find it interesting that you didn't hand them over to Canadian authorities."

"No, sir, we didn't. Sir, I didn't know who those men were. They could have been terrorists, or enemy agents trying to capture or kill us, or they could have been innocent men and officers sent to capture what Canadian Forces considered enemy elements on Canadian soil. All Canadian intelligence knows is that you're running a secret operation down here. They don't know if it's right or wrong. I know the people on the west coast, and possibly Captain Bowes are bad guys, because Bowes was Jillian Workman's control, but were they thinking for themselves, or was Workman simply operating in good faith when Bowes sent her instructions to plant a bomb on our plane? We'll never know unless we capture her, and I suspect she may be dead by now.

"And if we go further back, did Bowes order the attack, and if he did, does he know the reasons? Or is he simply a good soldier just obeying orders from his superiors, or from someone he just thinks is his superior? For all I know the orders for our elimination could have come from CSIS, or the CIA, or MI5, or some crazed commander of the defunct KGB. We don't know, and we didn't want to kill anybody who might be innocent.

"Now, understand, my men were armed with live ammunition, and all it would have taken was one thing to go wrong and we would have opened fire, but nothing did go wrong, thank God.

"The only Canadian authority we knew was Captain Bowes, and I didn't, don't, trust him, so we neutralized the attackers and isolated them."

"The photos and fingerprints you sent over came back empty from the national databases, but we'll keep looking." Put in Hines. "And how did things go in Boston?"

Don's heart sank. "Our studies went well sir, though it's imperative for me to report to you that Lieutenant Hernandez and I, we..."

Hines's voice was neutral. "Professor A gave me the rundown on that. The jury is still out on my response. Tell me your side of it."

"Sir. Since I last spoke to you about this, my life has been threatened three, no four times. Juanita's has been threatened twice. Our earlier decision to wait was based on the idea that we had plenty of time, but with people shooting at us, bombs and SAMs to worry about, we may not have that time. There is a distinct possibility that one of us will be dead tomorrow."

"So you decided to just go ahead and have a sexual fling. Is that what the trust I put in you is worth?"

"No sir. We have not had a sexual fling. We have however, fallen in love."

Hines grim face did not change. "Fascinating."

"Before you went to Halifax I ordered you to be armed at all times. Yet when the C-130 came back, all of the weapons we had assigned you were on it."

"Yes sir. The commander in Boston refused to let us go armed, and so we had to improvise." Don drew back his jacket and let the officer see the butt of the Smith and Weston 1911 strapped to his belt. "Those attaché cases my people are carrying sir? AK47s. Sir."

A hint of a smile touched the officer's face, but abruptly the General turned toward the circus tent. "Get your people together, Lieutenant."

Don raised his arm. "Team, here!" he shouted, and the crew came running.

They caught up with the General just outside the tent, or actually, just outside the smaller tent that had been set up beside the larger tent to obscure the opening. There were ten tough looking airmen guarding the passage into the smaller tent, and many more spread across the field around the larger tent. After they had all signed in at the security desk, the general ushered them inside.

"I see you have added Warrant Officer Browning to your team, Lieutenant," Hines said, flatly.

"She has become part of the team, sir. I know she actually reports to Captain Bali, but she fought with us in Turo, and trained with us in Boston. I feel I can depend on her. Sir."

After a moment Hines nodded, his eyes hard. "I'll make the arrangements."

"Just after you left for Halifax, Captain Hill inspected Captain Bali's work and gave him the green light to turn on the extruder. Two days ago, the hull form was complete and the process was turned off. Subsequently, Captain Bali committed suicide."

Don cast a glance at the flap that covered the door to the circus tent, desperately wanting to see what was inside, but holding himself in check by sheer power of his will. "Suicide sir? May I ask how?"

"He hung himself. In his room. With a wire from one of his pieces of equipment."

"You have an investigator on it, sir?"

"Should I?"

"Sir, yes sir! I know the Captain was upset about what happened to Sergeant Hale, and I'll admit I know nothing about psychiatry, but suicide is a huge step. A suicide by someone working on something this secret and delicate needs investigation."

The general's face was grim. "You're right, and we do have a team working on it Lieutenant. If you will follow me," Hines said, and pushing aside the flap, he walked into the larger tent.

Don had imagined his first sight of the Intrepid's shell would be overpowering. What he had forgotten was that it would pretty much fill the interior of the tent. When he walked through the flap the steel doors had been removed and all he saw was a flat black wall less than an arm's length in front of him, a black wall that soared several meters up, and curved out of sight to both left and right. A black wall that was covered with mounting points and recesses for equipment, a black wall that curved back under itself, starting about waist high, so that the wall actually touched the ground in a smooth curve about a meter under the shell of the ship. Reaching out his hand he touched it and it felt smooth and glassy to his touch. "Ladies and Gentlemen, I give you the ES Intrepid," said General Hines. "Your home for the next several years, and if you don't screw up," he glanced meaningfully at Don, standing next to Juanita, "your job for the rest of your lives."

Hines had moved to the right when he came through the flap and now he began to walk purposefully that direction. "Follow me."

After they had walked about ten meters, there was a hatchway molded into the side of the ship, with no hatch mounted. Someone had set up a pair of wooden steps and Hines stomped up the steps and inside. Here there was a string of bare hundred watt bulbs that had been fastened to the ceiling with duct tape, and Hines flipped a switch to turn them on. Don noted that the exterior wall was about twenty centimeters thick, and that those same walls seemed to simply absorb the light from the bulbs instead of reflecting it. There was a large number 'one' written on the wall in white chalk.

"This is airlock one," the General said. "The corridor you see before you leads to the reactor room. Mr. White, I fully expect you to spend the next several weeks in that room preparing your reactor for its initial cold start up. There isn't a lot of room in there, but everybody will co-operate with Mr. White until we are generating electricity. You will of course clear everything with Lieutenant Fields or Captain Hill before you begin your start up sequence.

"Mr. Fields, the control room is to the left down this corridor, one floor up. You will make it your priority to assist Doctors Lyondell, Smyth and Stills to get your computer installed under the floor there and running. You will then assist Doctor Jezebel Lyondell to get it programmed, and then get that room set up to work.

"Lieutenant Fleet, Lieutenant Thewes, electronics. There are more readouts, electric displays and sensors to be installed on this vessel than there are on a trio of C17s.

"Lieutenant Hernandez, mechanicals. Doors, servomotors, that sort of stuff. Some of your priorities should be the hatches, the kitchens, refrigeration and heating. When you have time, assist in the control room.

"Shackle, there's an infirmary to the right, or there will be when you finish it.

"Post, there is a complete suite of controls and displays you have to install, including radars, distance measuring lasers, optical sighting, the lot. Fields, Fleet and Shackle will assist you when they have time.

"Golden, you help Fields and you set up the environmentals. Hernandez will help you with the heating and cooling, that sort of stuff.

"Browning, after you do your inspections of the ship I need you to prepare a complete report for me, any problems with the process, any mistakes you want to correct.

"Since Captain Bali is not able to impart his knowledge, I have a team of physicists that need to be trained in setting up and running his machine. And when you're not doing that, you help Golden, make yourself useful.

"There are full plans in the small tent outside. I'll be rounding up a few more people to help you, since there are literally miles of cable to be run in this thing, but, take a few minutes now to wander around and sort yourselves out, then go have supper and get an early night. You start after chow in the morning."

"And Mr. Fields?"

"Yes, Sir?"

"My office, 08:00. Bring Hernandez with you."

Chapter 16

D on didn't sleep at all, and he suspected that Juanita didn't sleep either. First thing in the morning they did their run with the team, showered and changed into clean uniforms. By 07:45 they were in Hines' waiting room, where they sat, not speaking, but surreptitiously holding hands until 08:00 on the dot. Then the phone rang and Sergeant McCowan listened for a few moments. When she put the phone down she said, "Go in, but be careful."

Don led the way in and snapped a ridged salute. "Sir, reporting as ordered, sir."

Hines finished reading the report in front of him and initialed it twice before putting it down and returning their salute. "Mr. Fields," he said. "I have given you the biggest opportunity I've ever known to be given to any serving officer, anywhere, at anytime, and you have come dangerously close to just blowing it out the window. I could have you; both of you, out of here so fast you wouldn't even get the chance to pack your bags. Do you understand me?"

"Sir, yes, sir."

"Instead, I spoke to the President of Mexico, to the Prime Minister of Canada, and to the President of the United States on a conference call last night. We had some other matters to discuss, but I had to admit to them all that you blind-sided me. Do you have any idea what it's like to admit to the three leaders of the western hemisphere that you've been blind-sided by some collage age wiz kids?

"Then the Prime Minister laughed at me. Nobody laughs at me, but those three thought it was a hoot. Well, that's the only hoot you get! Now, get your butts out of here and get to work before I decide to simply throw you out anyway!

"Go!"

They got, almost running, almost forgetting to salute, but they got themselves gone. Or at least they tried to. In the antechamber, McCowan held up her hand to stop them, pointed at Don to go, and Juanita to stay. Doctors Smyth, Lyondell and Stills were waiting for Don when he reached the circus tent. "Got a lay in, did you boy?" snapped Smyth. "I thought you were supposed to be one of these gung ho types, out to save the world. The least you could do is be on time."

"Sorry sir," said Don. "I had to speak with the General before reporting to work."

Stills, who at least had a vague idea what was going on, laughed. "Lieutenant, I understand you can fly just about everything that has wings?"

"And some that don't have wings as well, sir."

"But can you drive a lorry?"

"A truck? If it's not too big, yes."

"Do you remember that tank of liquid that you picked up in San Francisco?"

"Yes, sir."

"Well, it's over there, in that hanger, and we need it over here, and we've been waiting for you to show up to get it for us."

"Yes sir, I'll see what I can do. Was there anything else to come with it?"

"No, it's all ready to go."

Quickly, Don walked over to the hanger, to where he found the required tank of liquid, sitting on the back of a large flatbed truck, along with a hose and several other pieces of equipment. The tank was covered with a large gray tarpaulin. There were three airmen guarding the truck. "Morning," Don said, saluting the three airmen. "We need this piece of equipment over at the circus tent. Do any of you know how to drive it?"

One of the guards raised his hand, "I've driven commercially, before I joined up, sir."

"Great. You drive then, and the rest of us will just come along for the ride."

"Yes, sir. Are those crazy Englishmen over at the circus tent, sir?" The driver swung himself into the truck and started the engine, which turned over with a raw rumble. Don climbed in the passenger side and the other two guards jumped up on the flatbed, where the tank was held on with heavy canvas ratcheted belts.

"I gather you've had some dealings with them?"

"Well, the girl's all right sir, kind of cute actually, and she treats us like real people, but the other three, well, the old white guy, he's bonkers, and the other two just seem to ride herd on him. Sir." They pulled out of the hanger and the driver used the radio to get permission from the tower to cross the runway. "I don't suppose you can tell us what this sludge is, sir? They've spent hours in the hanger every day, running tests, adding a pinch of this or that and arguing. And arguing! Personally I keep expecting one of them to punch one of the others, or make a human sacrifice of the or old guy, or maybe just wave his arms over top of the vat and mutter something like, well, 'fillet of a fenny snake, in the caldron boil and bake,' you know?"

"And the rest to join in with, double, double, toil and trouble. Well, don't worry, we should be rid of them soon, airman," said Don. The driver pulled around the side of the tent, put the truck into reverse and backed up to where Stills was standing and waiving beside the tent entrance.

"As you know," said Dr, Lyondell, "Our objective is to get the base liquid from this tank here," he pointed to the back of the truck, "to the computer bay tank, just below the floor in the control room, with minimum damage to the liquid. In other words, we don't want to use a pump, because that harsh on and off again throb of pressure could harm the liquid."

"I've not been to the control room yet," said Don. "Only just inside airlock number one and a quick glance at the reactor room and some corridors."

"Then if you will come with me," Dr. Stills said. "I'll show you what we have to do and hope that a bright young man like yourself can figure out how to get this," he patted the tank affectionately, "from here to there."

They signed in at the security desk and went back through the flap and almost ran into Warrant Officer Browning. They exchanged greetings with the unhappy soldier and were just about to go their separate ways when Don thought of something. "Browning," he said. "I've not had much of a chance to explore the ship, but I know there's an access hatch just down this way. Is there anything like it, or even a smaller port of some kind on the second level?"

She rubbed her eyes for a moment, her exhaustion written large on her countenance. "What size access do you need?"

"Eight, maybe ten centimeters, for a temporary plastic pipe."

"Eight, maybe ten centimeters. No, no hatches, but there are missile tubes. Each one is about three meters long, and forty-five centimeters across, built like a torpedo tube; only the inner and outer doors haven't been installed yet. There are six installations on the flight deck level, with a cluster of seven tubes in each installation. Would that do the job?"

Forty-two missiles? Don thought. What are they expecting me

to do, fight a war? "I'm positive it will, Warrant Officer, thank you."

"Well," said Stills, "You can get a hose in, but somehow we've still got to get the base liquid up there without bruising it."

"That would be the least of our worries," said Don. He swung himself in through the hatchway into the airlock and out the door on the far side. Quickly stepping along the passage in the dark he almost missed the ladder leading to the second floor, but eventually found it and scrambled up one level, where he found another string of the ubiquitous construction lights fastened to the ceiling. Beside the access ladder, there was a chalked note with an arrow pointing toward the open doorway to the control room.

Carefully they made their way along the passage, finding first a long narrow room with several missile tubes, and then, several feet further down the corridor, the control room.

The control room was octangular. Don guessed it at about seven meters across, with no furniture or molded in features like he had seen in several other rooms, black walled and with an arched ceiling no more than two and a half meters high. Near the center of the room he found four circular holes in the floor, each fifteen centimeters across and covered by a removable flat plate. "Is this it?" he asked. "Four holes, being equal to four computers, each one checking on the other three?"

"You've got it," said Sills. "The question being, how do we get the base liquid up here, and like I said before, without bruising it?"

"You have a flashlight in your pocket, don't you?" asked Don, who had already seen the light.

"I do."

"May I borrow it?"

Taking the flashlight back to the missile room, Don selected one of the tubes at random and turning the flashlight on, he placed it in the tube. Then, followed by an amused Sills, he went back down the ladder and outside the ship, walking along beside the ship until he saw the light from the flashlight shining on the outside wall of the tent. Taking a discarded stub of chalk from the ground he drew a large arrow on the side of the ship, pointing up, and wrote 'missile tubes,' beside it. Outside the tent, he grabbed the airman he had dubbed Hamlet and sent him for a cargo loading truck and went himself in search of a stepladder, which he found almost immediately in the small tent. Carrying the ladder back to the mark he'd made, with a simple flip he set the wooden ladder up in the corridor between the tent wall and the ship. Then he climbed up the ladder and cut a slit though the tent canvas with his pocketknife. Climbing down, he went back outside and supervised while the three airmen from the hanger used a winch and transferred the tank of liquid to the back of a luggage loading truck.

"I think I've got you figured out," said Sills, and he climbed up on the truck with the tank and a long section of hose. Don gave Hamlet some directions and had him back the truck up beside the tent. Using the truck's built in hydraulic scissor lift, they raised the level of the truck so that the outlet from the tank was level with the hole Don had cut, and Sills started feeding the hose through it. Dr. Lyondell laughed and followed Don back inside the tent. While Don raced up the ladder to grab the hose and feed it into the missile tube, Lyondell climbed up inside the ship and took the end of the hose to the control room. Doctor Smyth simply stood and cursed the whole time.

"Are you ready?" asked Stills from outside.

"Wait a second," said Don, and he passed the question on to Lyondell by shouting into a missile tube.

"Turn it on," shouted the senior doctor, and Don passed the order outside. A moment later a heavy, green, viscous liquid started to flow through the tube, and it was all Don could do to hold the weight of the tube up.

"What'ya doin up there big boy?" Juanita called from below. "¿Tener un abrazo con una serpiente verde grande?"

"Haven't you got a door, or a CO2 scrubber you're supposed to be installing someplace?" Don replied.

"Aren't you going to ask me what Sergeant McCowan wanted to talk to me about?"

"Maybe later, someplace more private," said Don.

"Eh, what was that?" Shouted Lyondell from inside the craft.

"Nothing," called Don. "I was speaking to someone else."

"I am not nothing," said Juanita, "And we were talking about birth control. How would you like it if I started tickling you?"

"What?" Don nearly dropped the hose.

She started tickling him and he jerked back. "Juanita Concepcion Hernandez y Romero, if I drop this thing on your head Dr. Lyondell will be so upset, and Doctor Smyth will be upset, and General Hines will throw us both out on our butts, and I will be upset, and you will be the most upset of all, so go away, we are not alone here!"

"Eh, what was that?" shouted Stills. "Should I be turning it off?"

"No, let it flow!" Don yelled.

"What's going on out there?" yelled Lyondell, and Juanita blew Don a kiss, ducked under the ladder and through the hatch into the ship.

"Nothing!"

Eventually, the flow of liquid stopped, the last few liters flowing cleanly away, leaving a sticky green scum inside the clear tube, and Don was able to feed it back outside to Dr. Sills. Even as Don was folding his ladder and taking it back to where he found it, Dr. Sills and Jezebel Lyondell met him in the smaller tent. "Put that against the wall and come with me," said the Doctor. "You've got to see this, it's the most interesting thing." Don put the ladder against the wall and Sills handed him a small case, saying, "Bring this," then he hurried off back inside the ship. With a bit of a shrug, Don followed, down the side of the tent, through the airlock, past Rob, who was busy working with a couple of airmen trying to manhandle some heavy equipment down the corridor, up the ladder and into the control room, where Sills and Jezebel were already on their knees beside the four holes in the floor. Squeezing to one side they made room for Don. "Open the case," Sills instructed and Don did, finding four identical rods.

"What are these?" Don asked.

"The catalyst," Jezebel explained. "Here," she handed him a pair of thin plastic gloves. "Put these on. Now, gently, slide one rod into each pool."

Don did as he was ordered, sliding the heavy rods into the gooey liquid and finding that the liquid seemed to almost solidify around them, holding them in place and not letting the rods sink to the bottom of the pans. "Now, quickly," said Smyth, and Don looked up, surprised that the man was even there, "Pour in formula B, quickly, quickly!"

Almost as excited as the elder doctor, Lyondell took four small bottles from his pocket and handed three of them to the others. "One in each compartment, gently now."

Don quickly unscrewed the lid of his bottle, lowered the lip and poured the liquid into the pan below the floor. Instantly the goop began to rubberize and turn color, first a dark green, and then to lighten till it reached it's final shade, a lively green that was as far distant from the first sample Don had seen as red was from blue. Lyondell snapped four covers over the four holes, looked up and grinned at his daughter. "Now we wait," he said.

"In a week," she replied, "If the keyboards and monitors have been installed, I'll start my work. Then it won't take long before we know."

But before the week was out, Don got orders to report to General

Hines's office. "I'm busy and I just got a hornet's nest dumped in my lap, so I've no time for questions. Here's a mission for you, take care of it," Hines said, totally ignoring his rage from their last conversation. "I've got a Lear Jet 85 in civilian colors out on runway 14-35. I've got a geologist down in Brazil that I need picked up, pronto, and I've got two hot pilots, yourself, and Mr. Jean-Paul Golden who need some seat time. Mr. Golden is qualified to drive that plane, and you're not doing a lot over at the circus tent."

"Sir, I'm working hard, sir," Don protested, knowing his protest was useless. "We're all putting in fourteen, fifteen hour days, sir."

"As I was saying, fly to Caracas for fuel, to Rio for the pickup, and you're back here in a week or so, tops. There are some civilian style pilot's uniforms that have been delivered to your barracks. You've got about an hour before I expect you to be in the air. Lieutenant Fleet is going with you and she'll finish the briefing on the way."

Don left the general's office bewildered, but the feeling was becoming second nature. Running to the circus tent he found Juanita helping to install some cabling, screwing it securely to brackets that had been attached to the ceiling and walls with fast acting epoxy. "Babe, I've gotta go," he pushed her into a dark alcove and kissed her quickly. "I'll be back, I don't know when." Then he turned and ran for their billet.

Chapter 17

J ust over an hour later Don and Jean-Paul were wheels up and heading just south of due east. The leer jet fuselage, they had discovered, was split into three main compartments, the flight deck, where they were sitting, a main lounge with eight large executive chairs, and behind the lounge a small bedroom, dominated by a queen size bed. Between the bedroom and the lounge was a narrow hallway, or more accurately, two doors with a kitchenette on one side and a small washroom on the other. "We'll turn a few more degrees south after we pass over Dallas," said Jean-Paul as he tucked the landing gear up and received permission from Las Vegas tower to head up to thirty five thousand feet. "With full tanks we'll have maybe a five hundred mile cushion, call it two and a half hours. It'll be close heading down to Rio though." He clicked on the autopilot.

"Actually, we have clearance to land in Caracas to refuel," Anna stuck her head through the door to the flight deck. Don noticed that she was not dressed in one of the civilian semi uniforms he and Jean had been issued. Instead, Anna was wearing what looked like an expensive blouse and slacks, open toed heels. "I've copies of the written orders here. Basically, our job is to pick up a civilian scientist down in Rio and bring her back to base."

"She couldn't jump on a plane and maybe fly someplace closer?" Jean-Paul asked. "Not that I mind a few days of sun and relaxation, but this job seems to be getting weirder and weirder. I don't know about you two, but I'm really into the ship. I want to be in Nevada, piecing the thing together, not out here playing nursemaid to a scientist. Really, a geologist on a spaceship?"

Anna laughed, but Don could empathize with the Israeli. "You're right man. I'm getting involved, digging right into the guts of the Intrepid, learning things that will be invaluable to us later on. I think I know how Lucy must have felt going to Daphne's funeral. I want to be here, because it's my job, and I should be there, because it's where I've invested my life! Right now I have my next six weeks worth of work laid out clearly, and then, bang, it's just the three of us alone on this plane flying to South America.

"And speaking of us being alone, no offense people, but the last couple of times I've left home I've had people coming at me with guns, and I know you two are pretty good shots, but there aren't any weapons on this plane, and we're going unarmed into a foreign country! That doesn't make me comfortable."

"Well, I wouldn't say we were totally unarmed," said Anna. She walked over to a bulkhead and switching off the overhead light, gave a pull on an ornamental piece of woodwork. A panel in the wall slid open to reveal three Glock 18s and three P-90s. She turned the light back on and the compartment closed with a snap.

"And that's not all," said Jean-Paul. He pointed to a group of switches at the bottom of the control panel.

"I was going to ask you about those," Don said. "As far as I can see there's no use for them in this plane."

"Ah," said Jean-Paul. "This one," he pointed to the first switch, "turns on the fire control HUD. You control it with this little joystick. The second switch can arm either one, or two air-to-air missiles, and when you get a solution, the third and fourth switches fire them."

"And I thought this was a civilian ship."

"It was," said Anna. "It once belonged to a very rich, very civilian smuggler. There are a few more toys, like extended fuel tanks, and two concealed cannons, one in the front, and one at the rear."

"Yeah," said Don. "And why wasn't I told about all this?"

"Need to know, baby," said Jean-Paul. "Speaking of which?" he cast a meaningful glance at Anna.

"Right. I've met the geologist, Doctor D. Pamela Wright. She's one way cool black chick from South Africa. She's about thirty-two, gorgeous figure, skin black as ebony, and the last time I saw her she had just shaved her head so she wouldn't have to worry about hair. As they like to say in books, she does not suffer fools gladly, in any way, shape or form. Trouble is, the CIA considers her persona non grata, so we've gotta sneak her into the states."

"Right," said Don. "Now we'll have the CIA on our tails too. Too cool. Where are we supposed to meet her?"

Anna glanced from one to the other and snorted. "You're going to love this," she said.

"From the way you're laughing, I doubt it," said Jean-Paul.

"So, I'm a rich heiress, and I'm vacationing in Rio. You two are my pilots and boy toys. We park the plane, lock it, check into a certain hotel and spend the next week on the beach. She's supposed to contact us."

"Hold it," said Jean-Paul. "You and me on a beach, in Rio, for a week, waiting for some gorgeous black chick? Did you bring your string bikini and suntan oil?"

"Yes, but it's you, and me, and him," she jerked a thumb at Don, but she didn't sound resentful that he would be there.

"Well, you could get lost for a while, couldn't you Don?" Jean-Paul asked.

"Hum? Get lost?" Don was staring at nothing, imagining Juanita on a beach in Rio in a chain mail bikini. Ah, never mind the chain mail. Just a string bikini. "No. I don't get lost. Once I go somewhere I've got it memorized. My parents took me to Rio when I was a kid, oh, ten, twelve years ago. It was an award for skipping from grade four directly into grade six. It made me so excited I skipped a lot more, but they couldn't afford a second trip like that, so they took me to the West Edmonton Mall. It was a bit of a comedown from Rio, you-know?"

"Come on," said Jean-Paul. " You know what I was talking about! Get lost, as in give us some space, like you and Juanita need space occasionally?"

"I know exactly what you mean," said Don, still staring off into space. "And if Anna ever gave me the nod, I'd get lost and give her some space," he looked over at his fellow pilot and dropped the dreaminess from his voice, "Because we've been under fire together. She can rely on me, and I can rely on her. That's good enough for me. I've dressed her wound, and she's quite possibly saved my life. That sort of thing builds a bond, you know?

"But, we're on a mission. If that means she gets to lie on a beach while you rub suntan oil on her back, that's fine as long as you both stay diligent. Up to a point, what you do on your own time is no concern of mine. However, I'll tell you what both Will and Sacks said to me. If she complains, I'll cut off your right hand with a machete, for the sake of your career and mine. What Juanita and I have, that's a mutual understanding, and doesn't intrude during working hours. Usually." His voice softened. "Though, I wouldn't mind getting paid to rub suntan oil on her back for a week in Rio."

"So, you've really been to Rio before?" Anna asked, ignoring Jean Paul.

"Yeah. We didn't have a school for advanced students in Prince Albert, so what the school board did was have different teachers spend time each week tutoring me. Every couple of years they would claim I had just skipped a grade, but I think I spent maybe a month in grade one, and a couple in grade two, and then they started bringing in the tutors. When I graduated grade twelve I'd only spent eight years in school and had what the local university considered a masters in math. I spent the next three years at the University of Saskatchewan, and was a couple of courses from getting my PhD when I chose to go into the military. Of course, that meant I had to go back to first year studies in a different field, so I chose physics and space sciences, which gave me the time to pick up the other math courses. My instructors in Kingston, they used me to instruct other classes, that sort of thing." He grinned.

"I even had a couple of my instructors in one of my classes. That was a joke, grading my instructors calculus exams.

"Anyhow, yes, my folks took me to Rio to celebrate my skipping a grade or two."

"And your math degree?"

"I finished it. I just have to defend my doctoral thesis, and to do that I need the time to physically go to the university and meet with the instructors."

"I guess that explains why you're not intimidated by all the guys walking around the base with PhD after their names," said Anna.

"Way I hear it," said Jean-Paul, "You've got your own alphabet you haul around."

"Of course," she said with a grin. "Doesn't everybody?"

"No," said Jean-Paul. "Well, I've got two or three degrees, but…"

"But you went into the air force. Been there, done that," said Anna. She took a couple of wallets out of her bundle of papers and handed them over to the pilots. "These are your identities for the next couple of days. Memorize them." She held out her hand. "I need your wallets and anything else that could identify you."

Rio was hot, but dry, the beach was long and overflowing with the whitest of white sand. And though it wasn't high season as far as the Brazilians were concerned, there were still enough foreigners on the beach for all three team members to be able to vanish into the crowd. Don found he loved the sea, often starting his day by swimming straight out from shore for twenty or thirty minutes, and then just lying on the waves, soaking in the sun before sliding into a relaxed Australian crawl back to shore. The third morning he was emerging from the surf and walking past a trim black woman wearing a black one piece, sitting on a hotel towel under a huge beach umbrella, when she looked up and winked at him. "Good morning, Mr. Fields," she said.

"Doctor Wright?" he guessed.

"True enough." She patted the towel beside her. "Sit down."

Don lowered himself to the towel, shifting his eyes around, trying to spot his friends. "I thought you were supposed to make contact with Miss. Fleet," he said.

"Well now, I thought I was, but a couple of friends of theirs showed up and all four of them went away somewhere."

"They did?" Don was doing some rapid thinking and didn't like where the thoughts were taking him. "I don't suppose you got a good look at them?"

"Well, your team seems to have a habit of being tall, well built and beautiful, though I doubt that Anna's string bikini was Government Issue. Maybe that scar on her butt is. Government issue that is."

"She bought the bikini at the hotel. I told her it was scandalous and she said well, that made it perfect, but it wasn't my friends I was talking about, it was the other couple. Anna was under strict orders to stay here on the beach, waiting for you to show up. Jean was to stay with her until I came back from my swim."

"Oh, he's been staying with her all right. Almost like he was hoping she would fall in the water so he could give her mouth to mouth."

"Yeah, I saw that too, but I'm pretty sure Anna doesn't return his feelings. Look, I hate to be rude, but if my friends are missing then I've got to get out there and look for them. How long ago did they leave?"

She glanced at a large gold watch on her wrist. "Half an hour. So, your friends weren't supposed to meet someone else?"

"No. And the password is?"

"Alabaster."

"Venice is my favorite city too. Look, my friends wouldn't leave without me. Excuse me for a moment." He pushed himself to his feet and walked over to where Anna had sprawled beneath another large beach umbrella. It was similar to Doctor Wright's, though Anna's was red, and the geologist's was yellow. He settled to his knees and ran his fingers through the sand, hoping that one of the two had left a note, but there was nothing. Getting back to his feet, he made his way back to where the geologist was getting to her own feet. "Well, I guess the next step is to inquire at the front desk, and check our rooms," he said to her. "You're staying here?"

"Under the name Greta Muller. No note?"

"Nothing." They walked across the beach and into the main lobby of the hotel, but didn't speak again until the door of the elevator closed behind them.

"What floor?" Don asked, punching in his own floor fourteen.

"Fifteen. Let's go to your suite first and you can change and check to see if your friends are there. If not, we'll go up to my suite so I can change as well. Then we'll check out the desk."

Neither Anna, nor Jean-Paul was in the room. Don took a quick shower and then dressed in his pseudo flight officer's uniform, white shirt with blank blue epaulettes and button down pocket flaps, black slacks and shoes. He left the shirt un-tucked and slipped his Glock through his waistband. Upstairs, he waited while the Doctor changed to low shoes, a knee length jean skirt and a Hawaiian shirt. She took the proffered Glock without comment and slipped it into her bag. Then they made their way downstairs to the front desk.

"No, there are no messages for you, sir," said the young woman at the concierge's desk. "Perhaps your friends have just gone for a walk."

"Um, perhaps," said Don, and made his way out onto the street, not sure where to start. Pulling his cell phone from his pocket he stepped into he shadow of an alleyway.

"Hines," said a familiar voice at the far end.

"It's Fields. I've contacted Wright, but Fleet and Golden have disappeared. Wright saw them taken away by two men, average height, pale complexioned."

There was silence for a moment. Finally, Hines said, "I have contacts in the government there, from a G-eight security meeting with the plus five. I'll make a couple of phone calls." The phone went dead and Don slipped it into his pocket.

"Any news?"

"They haven't contacted him. Maybe some of the locals saw something."

Don looked around and felt an instant wave of despair. There were millions of people in the city who might have seen something, and he didn't even speak Portuguese. A moment later an older Asian woman in a beautiful green and gold sari rounded the corner, bowed slightly and smiled at them.

"Doctor Pam," the woman said with a trace of accent. "Are you perhaps looking for a white minivan, with diplomatic plates and two young people inside?"

"Ruby Khan," said Wright in surprise. "I never thought I would run into you in South America, though it is a pleasant surprise. I'd like you to meet Mr. Fields, my new boss."

"Ruby Khan?" asked Don. "The anthropologist? I've read your books." Don shook hands. Her grip was firm and dry.

"Well, Ruby isn't my real name, but you couldn't pronounce my name without offending me, so you can call me Ruby. You're looking for your two friends who were forced from the beach an hour ago at gunpoint?"

Don shook his head in wonder. "Yes."

"White van, diplomatic plates. One of my sons followed it to the Swedish Embassy. I stayed to see what happened to Pamela."

"One of your sons?"

"Of course. They refuse to let this old woman out of their sight."

"And where is the Swedish Embassy?"

"Well, not really the Swedish Embassy. The Consulado Geral da Suécia. The consulate in Rio, it's on the Praia do Flamengo, not too far from here." She led the way out of the alley and climbed into a large sedan parked at the curb. Don and Wright slipped in beside her. There were two large men sitting in the front seat. Ruby didn't introduce them, but Don assumed they were her sons. Ruby said something in Hindi and the car pulled away from the curb. No more than five minutes later they were parked down the street from the Swedish consulate. "So how do we play this?" Ruby asked Don.

"We play it square. We've got to find out if our team members are in there. If they are, I've got to get them out. Somebody pulls a gun on us and starts firing, I'll shoot to kill. Having said that, does anybody have a scrap of paper?"

Ruby spoke sharply to the men in the front street and one handed back a steno pad. Don took it, tore out a page and wrote quickly. Then he took a fifty Reais note from his pocket and stepped out of the car, approaching a young man on the street. Using Don's French and the youth's halting Spanish, Don asked him to take the note to the guard at the Swedish consulate. Then, accidentally, he let the young man spot the grip of the automatic tucked into his trousers, just to remind him to do what he had been paid to do. While the youth trotted over and thrust the note into the hand of one of the guards at the gate, Don stood on the opposite side of the street, counting the cameras and guessing at their angles. The guard with the note disappeared inside and a couple of minutes later the air was filled with alarm bells and there came the distant sound of sirens. The front door of the consulate flew open and people started to walk from the building, quickly, but in good order, crossing the street to assemble in groups down the block. Don quickly noted two things. One, they had apparently been drilled in this sort of thing before, and two, the place they were assembling was upwind from the Consulate building. The security man in charge had obviously done his homework.

Then the side door of the consulate opened and two men hustled out Anna and Jean-Paul, forcing them into he back of a white van. Don noted they were both wearing handcuffs and had on raincoats over their swimsuits. Quickly closing and locking the van's back doors, the pair of guards climbed into the front seat, and one of them must have punched a control, because the steel gate that blocked the driveway began to swing ponderously open. Don didn't let it open all the way before he slipped through and stepped up to the driver's door. He instantly shoved his Glock through the open window into the driver's face. Behind him he heard a noise as Ruby's sons took out the remaining consulate guards. He hadn't asked of they were armed, but he suspected they were very good at what they did. He didn't look to see who won the fight. "Turn off the van, or I will kill you," he said, surprised that his voice wasn't shaking. Grabbing the van door he wrenched it open and pulled the driver out, fishing the man's weapon from a fancy shoulder holster under his jacket and throwing him to the ground. Don knocked him out with a kick of his uniform boot to the jaw.

"Good. You," he pointed to the other guard with the muzzle of his weapon. "Take out your weapon, using only your fingers of your left hand, and slide it into the back of the van." The man did as he was told, reaching for the door handle after dropping the gun.

"No, you're not going anywhere yet. Do you have the keys to the cuffs? Good, take them out and toss them to the lady in the back. Now, sit on your hands. That's right, sit on them! I'm going to drive out of here with this van, and that means I've got to put my gun away." He took a glance back and noticed that Anna had acquired the guard's gun. He tossed the Beretta he had taken from the driver to Jean-Paul. "What you've got to understand is that the lady in the back is one heck of a marksman, and I'll bet she's mad. I hope for your sake you didn't hurt her in any way, because she just might kill you for fun." Don climbed into the driver's seat and pulled the van into the street, racing off towards the hotel. Less than an hour later Jean-Paul had them airborne.

Chapter 18

"Mountain Bluebird eighteen ninety-nine, this is Brazilia Flight Control. You are requested to change your heading to three, three, zero true and descend to sixteen thousand feet."

"Affirmative Brasilia Flight Control." Jean-Paul took off his headphones and looked over at Don. "Looks like our goose is cooked," he said. "The Brazilian authorities want us to land at the capital."

"It's not happening," said Don. "This could be a legitimate inquiry, or it could be whoever it is trying to stop us using a new tactic. We can't risk it." He switched on the intercom. "Everybody please find a seat and strap in, we're going to have to do some fancy flying here." He waited for a five count, letting Anna and Pam get settled, and then gave Jean-Paul the nod. Instantly the pilot rolled the plane to the right and dove for the treetops.

"What's that river there?" Jean-Paul asked, and Don quickly checked a map.

"The Rio Jequitinhonha. Nothing here about it except that it goes east northeast to the South Atlantic. Get down there and hug the water." He reached over and deliberately turned off their transponder. "There are a few towns but I'll bet they're not terribly well connected. If you see one, fly as far away from it as you can. Slow down and let's hope the Brazilian air force doesn't find us for a while. We should hit the coast in sixty minutes, give or take a few."

It was almost an hour later that they heard the radio squawk, almost simultaneous with two blips appearing directly behind them on the radar screen. "Mountain Bluebird eighteen ninety-nine, this is Captain Roberto Silva of the Brazilian Air Force. I am armed and authorized to use deadly force. I order you to climb to sixteen thousand feet and turn to heading two seven five. I repeat, heading two seven five." Suddenly they flashed across the streets of a small city. Don got a glimpse of sandy beaches; a few empty wharves and they were at sea.

"Punch it," said Don. "All we've got to do is hold on for ten minutes and we'll be in international waters." He keyed the mike. "Captain Silva, this is Captain Fields of Mountain Bluebird eighteen ninety-nine. We are peace-loving tourists, and while we were enjoying the beaches in Rio, my employer and one of our crew were kidnapped, and your government did nothing about it. We had to search for and rescue our people by ourselves, no thanks to you. I see no reason for us to return to your country, or to trust your government. Our rights were violated, our people were kidnapped and assaulted, and you are again violating our rights by threatening us with violence. We will not be detained simply because we wish to leave."

"Mountain Bluebird eighteen ninety-nine, I am not here to argue with you, I am here to arrest you. Once again, turn on your transponder, change course to heading two seven five and climb to sixteen thousand feet, or I will fire."

"You would fire on an unarmed civilian ship?"

"I will fire on suspected smugglers if they do not turn around immediately. This is your last warning."

"Target acquisition signal," said Jean-Paul.

"Be ready with chaff," said Don. "He's probably getting so many trash returns from the waves that his missile won't be able to hold that lock for long. I hope."

"Pursuer has fired. We have a missile in pursuit."

"Wait for it, now, deploy chaff, deploy flares. Yes! The missile went for one of the flares. Captain Silva, we are now in international waters." Don reached over and turned on the transponder, but on a different frequency. "This plane is now reverting to being an asset of the United States Air Force. If you fire at us again, it will be considered an act of war, and we will respond in kind, only my missiles are a heck of a lot smarter than yours. Do you understand?"

"You have missiles on a Leer jet?"

"Do you really want to find out?"

"I can't let you go."

"And I don't want to kill you. You've done your job. You're now in international waters. I am sending this conversation to my home base by satellite uplink. Like I said before, if you fire again, it will be considered an act of war by my government."

"An act of war?" Jean-Paul asked, when Don clicked the microphone off. "What kind of drugs are you on?"

"I had to say something," Don replied.

"About what?" Anna asked, slipping through the door into the control cabin.

Don noticed she was still wearing the bikini and raincoat. Of course, she hadn't had time to change. He forced himself to refocus. "Brazilian Air Force, they seem to want to kill us."

"Let me talk to them," she said, grabbing the mike. "Brazilian Air Force, this is Sierra Alpha Mike eighteen ninety-nine," she said in Portuguese, "Hold your fire. Repeat, hold your fire. We are Sierra Alpha Mike eighteen ninety-nine. You have orders about us directly from Seniore Barra, don't you?"

"I have orders about Sierra Alpha Mike eighteen ninety-nine. I don't have any orders about Mountain Bluebird eighteen ninety-nine. Which are you?"

"Look at this face," Anna said. "Would it lie to you?"

"Unfortunately, yes, it would. It already did, didn't it?"

"Yes, we did. That's why we have these cloak and dagger call signs, isn't it? The president of Brazil gave you an order, expecting us to lie to you, didn't he? So, what are you going to do?"

Silva said something in muttered Portuguese and looking at the radar, Don saw both pursuing pips break off. "They've gone home. Anna, you're a darlin, though you could have told me about the call sign thing! Jean-Paul, turn left to course oh three oh, and what's our fuel supply like?"

"I know we can't reach Miami," Jean-Paul said.

"Well, let's try for Saint Kitts. I always wanted to go there."

"How about Port of Spain, in Trinidad and Tobago?" Anna asked. "I knew somebody from there once, he said it was absolutely gorgeous."

"Port of Spain it is," Don said, feeling as though the weight of the world had been lifted from his chest. He reached over and picked up the satellite phone from its cradle. "I guess I better call the boss and tell him the good news. Maybe he can get somebody from the American Consulate in Rio to sanitize our rooms."

"And Anna? Thank you. Now please, go get dressed!"

Ten minutes later he hung up the phone. "Would you believe the rest of the crew is going to meet us in Port of Spain?"

"Oh boy," Jean-Paul said. "Who's going to shoot at us now? And, how's the ship? Are they getting anywhere?"

"Well, let's go back and talk to Pam, so everybody hears at the same time."

"Autopilot it is."

"We're going to Spain!" Juanita did a little dance around the restaurant lobby as they waited for their table, and then ran over and gave Don another kiss. "I've always wanted to go to Spain. Madrid, here we come!" Like the rest of the crew they had opted for civilian clothing for the evening dinner, and Juanita's idea of dressing for dinner in Trinidad was a short tan skirt and a green tank top over heels, and Don had to admit it worked. It worked well. As far as he was concerned, anything she wore worked well.

Just an hour before, Juanita had flown the C-130 in from Nevada with the help of a two man crew that was even now flying back to the states in the Leer.

The whole crew was there. Don, in a conservative blue shirt and Khakis, Juanita in her skirt, Anna in tan Capri's and a white blouse, Rob in a multi colored Hawaiian shirt and khaki shorts, Doctor Wright in a simple knee length black dress. Sacks was wearing a button down white shirt and jeans, Will a green tee, Jean-Paul an olive green button down with dress slacks and a Yarmulke, and Tessy was wearing a short orange dress with spaghetti straps and high heeled sandals. Jean-Paul, Don noticed, was starting to grow a beard. Off to one side Lucy Browning was wearing shorts and a tee. The one person he was surprised to see was Jezebel Lyondell. When the maitre'd called their table, he arranged to sit half way down the table, and for the young black woman to be across the table from him.

"Hello Jez," he said as they sat down. "To be honest, I'm rather surprised to see you here. I thought you'd be safely ensconced in the control cabin teaching junior how to talk."

"Well, so did I." Don noticed the lines of tiredness in her face, and felt sympathy for her. There had been a few hours of excitement before leaving Rio, but before that he had spent three days just lying in the sun, doing nothing. "But, it seems I've been assigned to your crew. Surprise, surprise. Daddy knew it was going to happen, but I didn't. Well, I suspected it might. I hoped it might, but I refused to get my hopes up."

"I see," Don said, and he did. "But how did they tear you away at this stage in the programming?"

"Well, I was getting tired. Junior's doing great by the way. It took us a little while to get the inputs and outputs organized, but then I downloaded the central program, and he understood right away."

"He?" Juanita asked.

"He," Jezebel said. "It's part of the programming. Junior thinks he's alive. Well, actually, he is, and he loves it. I've never ever seen a computer, ah, entity that could absorb so much information so fast. Sister is just the same. So are Grandma and Pa, but Junior is the fastest and the brightest."

"What?" asked Jean-Paul, who was sitting on Jezebel's right. "I thought we had one computer on board, and his name was Junior."

"One. Well, we actually have one interconnected computer, but it has four lobes, and each lobe has a distinct personality. Grandma was the first lobe activated. She could handle all of the calculations herself, but we've basically assigned her to navigation and communications. Then comes Pa. Pa is assigned to weapons systems." Don noticed Anna's face light up down the table when Jezebel mentioned weapons systems. "We won't have a lot of them for a while, but he knows how to speak to several types of guided missiles, torpedoes, machine guns and such. Junior's brain is actually about five to ten percent bigger than any of the other three, and we've assigned him to flight control. Sister of course, is assigned power conversion and life support. Other specialties will be assigned as different systems are integrated into the unit."

A waiter appeared and they all ordered supper. After the waiter left, Jezebel continued. "Anyhow, things are going great, and then all of a sudden I'm called into Hines' office, he puts a piece of paper in front of me and gives me a choice. Sign up for the ES Services, or be locked up for life under the official secrets act. Lemme see," she held up both hands as though they were scales weighing her life. "Sign the paper and go into space, and get paid for it, which has been my secret dream for about a gazillion years, or not sign the paper and go to prison in Area 51 and not get paid. So I signed up, and I'm locked in at the rank of ensign for one year, at which time my performance will be evaluated."

"Just like us," said Rob, "Only we get evaluated in six months."

"You've been counting?" Will asked.

"Duh!" said Rob. "And you haven't?"

"Speaking of," said Don. "How's the power room coming?"

"Well, it's a little weird," said Rob.

"How so?" Don asked.

"Well, we've got the equipment set up for the rods, and those are wired into sister, and she can raise them and lower them perfectly, but we've got no hot stuff, and once my baby starts giving off the rads, we've got no way to protect ourselves, and no way to convert it to some useful type of energy."

"Mind you, I've been told the second part will be solved when this trip is over, so I'm guessing we're picking up some sort of shielding, and or maybe some kind of strange power conversion technology on this trip. Or maybe I'm just blowing hot air."

"That makes sense to me," said Sacks. "The engines will be the last component we'll need. It just makes sense to get the reactors operational first."

"How about the mechanicals?" he asked Juanita. "How are they progressing?"

"Actually, we're way ahead of schedule," she said. She was sitting on his right and sitting close. "I've got all the exterior hatches hung, and wired for power. We've spent literally days outside, hanging off ladders, wiring for video cameras, heat sensors, laser distance finders, proximity sensors, gas sensors, radiation sensors, and other sensors that go into bands I've never heard of. Inside there are CO_2 sensors, heat, humidity, air pressure, and a dozen other things that need to be physically installed and calibrated, intercoms and computer feeds, with redundant backups, and after the wiring is installed we've got to actually install the cameras and sensors themselves. It's a huge job. I guess that's why Hines decided to give us this break. I hope."

"That may be true." Don slid an envelope from his shirt pocket and stood to his feet. "My friends, we have something to celebrate tonight. I have an envelope here, signed by the Canadian Chief of the Defense Staff.

"I don't know what it is about this project that hates non commissioned officers, but, Warrant Officer Lucy Browning, please stand up." He waited while the soldier stood to her feet. "By order of the Government of Canada, you are hereby raised to the rank of probationary Second Lieutenant, in the Canadian Armed Forces, which of course, will translate to ensign in this service. Congratulations. You've got work to do to catch up, and courses to take, but it should be no problem. I hear you're only working sixteen to twenty hours a day now, so you should have plenty of time."

Chapter 19

Dawn found them staggering out to the C-130, each one dragging their gear and exhaustion along with them. They had talked, and celebrated long into the night, and though the pilots were forbidden to indulge themselves in drink in the hours before a flight, none of the others had felt themselves thus restrained. It was finally Don, Juanita and Jean-Paul, assisted by Pam, who had shepherded the rest of the crew back to the hotel, set their alarm clocks for 05:00 and were then free to indulge themselves in no more than four hours of precious sleep. Almost, Don decided to forgo the external inspection of the plane, and it was with bleary eyes he finally noticed the crude bomb fastened into the starboard side wheel well. It took no expertise to figure out that the trigger was set to go off when the flap covering the well closed. Anna, headache in hand, inspected the bomb with a critical eye and then took several photos before she lightly peeled it off. Disarming it with a yawn, she carried the parts on board. Following her in, Don called the entire crew to gather in the main hold.

"Listen up people," he announced. "We found a bomb, a crude device designed to be discovered. Now I'm assuming that whoever it is that we're up against isn't stupid, so I think that where there's an obvious bomb meant to be discovered, there's another bomb very well hidden, that's not. So now we've got to tear this ship apart until we find the one that's not obvious. Will, you take command of the starboard side, Juanita; you take command of the port side. Pam go over to the tower, demand to see the airport's director, and make as much noise about this bomb as you can. I need you to see any surveillance videos or photos they may have, any log books for entering this part of the airport. After you've looked at it, fax anything they might have that will help us figure out who is responsible to base." He handed her a paper with a number written on it. "This will print out in the boss's office. Move it."

It took two hours, but when Pam returned she told Don that the intruders didn't seem to be able to open the locked doors, but had done something with the engines. Will climbed up through the top hatch and leaning down over the number one engine casing found a small package of C-4 just behind the propeller reversing mechanism. There was another bomb behind the mechanism on engine number two. "I guess the idea being that when we landed in Spain, you would reverse the propellers, and both engines on the Starboard side would blow off, causing an uncontrolled crash thousands of miles away from where we fuelled."

Don watched from below while Anna climbed up through the hatch and out on the wing. Then she quickly took digital photos, disarmed the bombs, and stowed the explosives on board the plane for Hanes' investigators to break down later. This time there was no yawning. Thoughtful, he gathered the crew back together in the cargo compartment. "Anything else before we take off? Nope? Ok, Juanita, you and Jean get set to fly us out. I'll relieve Jean in one hour, he comes back to relieve Juanita in one more.

"We've filed a flight plan for Miami, but we'll make our apologies as soon as we lift off, though we don't tell anybody where we're really going. We've got maybe thirteen hours worth of fuel. Ten hours of flying time gets us about four thousand four hundred kilometers, so I'm planning on dropping into Amilcar Cabral International Airport in Cape Verde for fuel, maybe make it an over nighter. They've got a runway we can use, and I've contacted base to set it up."

As soon as the plane was wheels up, Don stood up, stretched and was about to go down to the cargo hold when Will said, "Boss, can I have a word?"

"Sure. Why don't we go out to the back hatch where we can be sure of some privacy, if that's what you need."

Will glanced around the cabin. Juanita and Jean-Paul were at the controls, and Rob was at Tessy's engineering desk, though the function was almost obsolete on the 130J. "Well, not really a word, more a package." He took a sealed bag from his luggage and handed it over. "General Hines asked me to give this to you as soon as we were in the air, not before. I know nothing else about it. I haven't seen what's inside."

Curious, the Lieutenant moved back to his seat and opened the seal. He had been about to go below and suggest that the crew find places to stretch out and catch up, but decided that this could be more important.

Opening the bag he pulled out a black loose-leaf binder, stamped top secret. Opening it, he noted that the first page was a letter to him from General Hines.

> *Lieutenant Fields,*
>
> *I want you to read the enclosed document very carefully. We found it in Bali's things when we cleaned out his safe. If it is real, and I have no reason to believe it isn't, then it may change our concept of things radically. I'm not going to bore you with my ideas; I don't understand the math well enough to be sure I understand the mechanics, though I do understand the personalities and egos involved.*

Make your own conclusions and report back to me. I must stress that secrecy is of utmost importance.
Hines.

Turning the page, Don saw what he did not want to see. The title, and the author's name spelled out in a sixteen-point font. 'Building from the Room at the Bottom, or the Problem of creating Macro Structures from Nano Technology, Solved,' by Lucy Browning, University of British Columbia. It was Browning's doctoral thesis. The question was, did she write it before, or after Bali came forward with the same ideas? He glanced at the date and noted that it claimed to have been written five years previously, which would have been before Bali had become involved in the construction of the space ship.

So, did Bali steal Browning's ideas, or did Browning steal Bali's?

If Browning had stolen Bali's ideas, then there would be no way for her to sneak it past him. He would probably be one of the peers who would review her work before she was awarded her doctorate. But if Bali had stolen Browning's work, then why hadn't she been screaming blue murder? Don knew he would have been if anybody had done that to him. The big question of course would be was she angry enough to endanger the project, and to murder doctor Bali?

No, that was nonsense. She had been with him in Boston when Bali had died. But she could have paid someone else to kill him. Sitting back down in his jump seat, Don turned to page one and began to read.

"I think the only solution to our problem would be for us to get married."

"Huh?" Don looked up from the thesis and stared across the console to Juanita. "What did you say?"

"I said I want to marry you, but you weren't paying any attention." It was ten minutes after Don had relieved Jean-Paul. Everyone else had left the flight deck and were all trying to find someplace comfortable to grab some shuteye. The plane was on autopilot and Don was still concentrating on the thesis in his lap. He glanced at his watch and discovered he had been sitting there reading for over two hours.

"Married? We haven't even discussed that at all."

"I thought maybe this might be a good time, though I see you're kind of busy."

Don glanced down at the binder in his lap. He hadn't made much sense out of it yet, but it certainly looked authentic. Maybe it was time to take a break. He closed the book, slid it into the bag and locked it. "Are you serious? About getting married and all that?" he asked. Flirting and sexual innuendo had been fun, falling in love had been confusing, and now marriage? It seemed the obvious next step, but he found he was shocked when she suggested it.

"Never more serious. We're not going to move in together, we both disagree with extramarital sex, I've decided that I love you, you've told me that you love me. Were you telling me the truth?"

Don didn't hesitate. "Yes."

"Do you plan on marrying me?"

"I guess I was, though in an abstract way. I never really thought the word. You know we're living in an artificial environment, forced together like this. Marriage is a huge step. You also know it could get us thrown out of this program."

"There are advantages as well as disadvantages."

"Name one."

She reached over and grabbed his ear, pulled him close and then whispered for a moment. "You shameless hussy," he said when she was done. "I'm blushing, aren't I?"

"Yes."

"So how do we go about getting married?"

"As soon as we're back in Nevada we drive up to Reno for the weekend."

"No big church wedding, no cake, no reception, no nothing? I thought that it was this huge thing for women."

"Well," she said, "My family can't be there, unless you want to fly down to Mexico, but that's not going to happen, and from the way you talk, your folks won't be there either, and if we called our friends together, most of them would wonder what was going on with us on assignment in Nevada. To tell you the truth, I think the best plan is just you, me, and two witnesses."

"Rob."

"And Anna."

"You drive a hard bargain, but it's a deal."

"Only, you've got to ask me right."

Fortunately, there was no problem in Cape Verde, and after the crew had a quick break for a hot meal, half standing watch while the other half ate, they all piled back aboard the plane. It was just dawn in Madrid when Don and Jean-Paul brought the ship in for a landing at the Aeropuerto de Madrid-Barajas, where the airport authorities assured them that they had been expected, and then shuttled them off to the end of a long runway, where a huge old hanger gave the C-130J cover from the air.

"Your machine will be safe here with us," said the Brigada in charge of the Guardia Civil force sent to guard the craft. He was a very fussy, precise man that Don instinctively trusted. "We have been given very specific instructions from our government to ensure that nothing happens to it during your visit here."

"I hope so," said Juanita in Spanish. "If anything happens to my plane I'll be very disappointed."

"Señorita, I would never disappoint one so beautiful as yourself." He paused and made a show of looking disappointed. "Except in that the parties who are to meet you here, they have been delayed." He pulled a notebook from his pocket. "We expect them to arrive, ah, the day after tomorrow."

"Do you know what time?"

"No Señorita, I don't. If you could leave me the number of the hotel where you will be staying, perhaps I could arrange to call you when they arrive."

"No, that's unnecessary. It's not that we don't trust you, but we have been ordered to maintain our own personal guard at all times. With at least two of our people on the plane, and your people outside it, we will surely be safe. Good day, sir."

"Wanna bet he had another reason to ask for your phone number?" Don asked as they piled onto the bus that was to take them to their hotel.

"Wouldn't do him any good. Anna, Tessy and I have the next two days totally scheduled."

"I don't get to take you out to dinner tonight for a romantic candle lit dinner, to make up for our missed dinner in Boston?"

"Of course," she said, with an impish grin. "That's in the schedule. I'll meet you in the lobby at eight. I don't suppose you have a suit you could wear, do you?"

"I'll try."

The charcoal gray suit cost him three hundred and fifty Euros, the shirt and tie seventy-five, and the shoes nearly a hundred, but when he met her in the lobby, he was wearing a suit, and had a diamond ring in his pocket. She had gotten her hair done, had on three inch heels and was wearing a gold lame mini dress that clung to her every curve. "Wow," he said. "You look gorgeous."

"Anna picked out the dress." She made an attempt to tug the hem down and failed. "I thought it was too risqué, but she said risqué is good. She also said something about revenge for the sundress, which I don't understand at all."

"You should thank her for me. Nah, never mind, I'll do it myself." He kissed her and led her out to the curb where the doorman had a taxi waiting. He handed her into the car and then slipped in beside her. "Now, I don't know this restaurant myself," he said, after he had given the driver the address, "But the hotel manager swears it's the place. He even claims to have proposed to his wife there."

"You have reservations?"

"The manager arranged for everything. He says our table is to be right beside the band."

"And can you dance?"

"Sort of. It's not really on my list of accomplishments. You know until I met you I've never been a ladies man. It doesn't make for much dancing."

"I'll teach you. My Uncle Phillipe taught me, and he was amazing."

The restaurant was in a cellar, with brick walls, an old fashioned wooden bar, and a three-piece flamingo band, a singer, a guitar and a dancer, a woman whose heels seemed to move with the precision of a university drum line. Their table was right beside the dance floor. "You're not seriously going to try and dance like that are you?" Don asked after the band's first number.

"Not on your life. Maybe with a longer dress and thicker heels. I've tried it when I was a child of course. No, I didn't realize it was a flamenco place you were taking me to. I was thinking there might be a band that could play a waltz, or maybe," Don could tell by the glint in her eye that something was up, "A tango."

"A waltz maybe you could talk me into, but not a tango. Well," he grinned, feeling like a schoolboy on his first date. He pulled the little black velvet covered box from his pocket, opened it, sank to one knee, and offered it to her. "Will you marry me?"

There had been a pause in the music while they had talked and the flamenco dancer walked over and leaning down whispered something in Juanita's ear that Don couldn't hear. Juanita answered in a whisper and a giggle, and the dancer threw Don a sly glance and whispered back.

"And what was that about?" Don asked when the dancer had retreated to the bandstand.

"Girl talk," Juanita answered with a smile. "Of course I'll marry you! I've known it since we met on the train!"

"Did I ever tell you…" Don began, but the male singer making an announcement over the PA interrupted him. He couldn't understand all the Spanish of course, but he understood enough to know that their engagement was being announced to the entire restaurant. "Am I blushing?" he asked.

"Of course you are," Juanita replied. "Oh, look, the singer plays guitar too. And they are asking us to dance!"

"Us the restaurant, or us the couple?" He knew the answer before he finished the question, because the music was definitely slower, and in three quarter time. Sighing, he stood to his feet and held out his hand, helping Juanita to hers.

They danced several times that night, but Don knew that nothing in his life would ever equal that first dance, where he held his fiancé in his arms and they shared their love so uninhibited, and so completely.

Chapter 20

The sound of the shot drifted in from far away in the dark, from somewhere where it didn't seem to have the power to harm anyone, and from one moment to the next Don's world was destroyed. One moment he was walking back into the hotel with his beautiful, vivacious fiancé, and the next he was crumbled to the sidewalk, holding her lifeless corpse in his arms, her beautiful golden dress drenched in her blood, her eyes slack and motionless, her heart shattered by a single bullet.

"Don, come on, it's Sacks, man! Please, please, let go! Let me try and help her!"

"You can't." Unwilling, but unable to stop them, Don let them slide his beautiful Juanita from his arms. He looked up at his friend, his face lacking any understanding. "She's dead, Sacks. I was going to marry her. This week, in Vegas. We were going to get married." Sacks had taken one look, as soon as he had eased Juanita's body from Don's arms, and knew there was nothing he could do. He tried, but there was nothing he could do, and when the police arrived, and the ambulance, there was nothing they could do either. And then Anna and Tessy were there, and all they could do was get down on their knees beside Don on the sidewalk and weep with their arms about him, while the ambulance drove away without a siren. Without hurry.

"Come on man," said Rob, lifting him to his feet, and half carrying him into the hotel, where they all sat in the lobby until long past dawn, until long past the point when the police had gone. Latter, Rob led him up to his room and put him into his bed, and he fell into an exhausted sleep. When he woke at three thirty in the afternoon, Doctor Wright was sitting in the corner, reading a dog-eared copy of Guns and Ammo. For a moment he couldn't remember who she was, or why she was there, and then he remembered and the pain hit him anew.

"I see you're awake."

"Yeah," he muttered, "I am. I wish I wasn't. How long have you been sitting there?"

"Oh, we've been taking one hour shifts." She paused and studied his face carefully.

"I'm so sorry Don," he could see tears at the corner of her eyes and knew she was telling the truth. "I don't know what to say."

She took a deep breath. "Sacks has taken over while you were asleep," she said, finally. "He's quite a competent young man. He says you're in shock; so don't trust yourself to make logical decisions.

"Our cargo hasn't arrived yet, but he's taken most of the crew out to the airport to wait for it. I think it was just to give them something to do.

"Anna has been acting as our liaison with the local authorities, since she speaks some Spanish.

"Rob, of course, has been hovering over you like a mother hen. He's the one who's been speaking to Hines and the American State Department. Speaking of which, there are three men downstairs, waiting to speak to you. A Mr. Gregory Huff, from the American embassy, a Mr. Carlos Costilla, from the Mexican government, and a Mr. Joshua Ross from the Canadian Consulate. They all wanted to speak to you earlier, but we put them off until three thirty." She pushed herself up from the chair. "I'll go tell them you're awake and order you some breakfast in the dinning room. Take a shower, shave and get dressed."

There were actually four men waiting to see Don when he finally got downstairs. He had thought about putting on his uniform, but had opted for slacks and a short sleeve shirt instead. "Good afternoon, Lieutenant Fields," a middle aged, dark haired Spaniard in a neat uniform met him in the lobby. "I am Comandante Roberto Lorca Guerrero of the Benemérita. I have been sent by my government to assure you that we are doing everything in our power to investigate this incident."

"Comandante," Don repeated, shaking hands and searching his memory for some of the things Juanita had chatted about so freely the day before. "I would think of you as a Major. Sir, I seem to have three important visitors waiting for me in the restaurant. Would you join us for coffee?"

The three men in the restaurant were sitting and sipping their own coffees with Anna and Rob, and they all stood for handshakes. The waitress came and brought Don a generous helping of bacon and eggs, scrambled, and they all sat down. Huff, who looked like a former military man, got right to the point. "Lieutenant Fields, as I hope you can understand, there is a considerable international concern over the loss of your officer."

"My fiancé," Don said flatly, and took a bite of toast. The food seemed to have no taste in his mouth, and he ate mechanically.

The man from the State Department was surprised, but he covered it well. "I'm sorry, I didn't know."

"My condolences, Lieutenant," said Ross. He was the youngest of the three, still in his thirties, heavy, but not fat, balding, but not gray.

"And mine," said Costilla.

"We seem to have a jurisdiction problem," said Ross. "I'm here because you're a Canadian citizen. Mr. Costilla is here because Subteniente Hernandez was a Mexican national. Mr. Huff is here because in order for you all to work inside the American Air Force, the President of the United States granted you all American citizenship. It seems when certain other countries heard that, most of them, including Spain, granted each of you citizenship as well. It's a complicated mess, but that's how governments work things out, by making them complicated beyond belief."

"Wait," Don held up a hand. "How many governments?"

"Twenty-six," said Huff.

"And again, why? And why is it so important?"

"Because," said Huff, "Every nation that has been participating in this endeavor, and you should know at this point that none of us is privy to the details, so we don't really know what that endeavor is, wants to claim you, all of you, as it's own. If something happens to one of you, then there are twenty-six governments asking for answers. I'd like to find those answers myself.

"Obviously this is an unsecured room, though I've had my people sweep it for bugs before we agreed to meet you here. As I said, I for one wanted to find out what was so important about you, so I sent an inquiry back to the US. This morning I got a phone call from the Secretary of State, who tells me she got one from the President. I have been ordered to use every facility at my command to find out who did this, and bring them to justice. But I haven't been told who you really are. I don't mind telling you I don't like working in the dark, but with that kind of authority behind the order, I have no choice."

"Have you been told that this is the fifth attack we've been through?" said Anna.

"No," said Ross, "We haven't."

Don looked over at Comandante Lorca. "Comandante, I

apologize to you. I wonder if you have the security clearance for any of this? As you probably know, some things it's better not to know."

Lorca gave a grim smile. "I work in the international brigade, Lieutenant. I was made aware of much of this when I was given this assignment this morning, including the fact that you have been given citizenship by twenty-seven different nations."

"Twenty-seven?"

"Two days ago, Japan granted you all citizenship."

"Japan?"

"Si."

"That's ridiculous! I've never even been to Japan!"

"Which is beside the point, when you think of it."

"Yes. Mr. Costilla, I assume you will want to repatriate Juanita to Oaxaca?" Don asked.

"Si. The consulate is arranging for Señorita Hernandez y Romero to be shipped to Mexico, and then to be buried with all honors. If you would like, we will arrange for you and a few of your crew to accompany her."

"We have a job to do here," Don said, but his heart was elsewhere.

"I have an order here from a General Hines," said Huff, "Detaching you, Ensign Fleet, and Lieutenant White." He pulled a paper from his briefcase and handed it over to Don. "He's commandeering a pair of pilots from an air base down in Morón de la Frontera, near Seville. They should be here today. They're going to fly your plane home."

"Mr. Costilla is arranging for the funeral, of course, and provided the medical examiner is finished with Subteniente Hernandez, you're going to fly directly from here to Mexico city on an Aeromexico flight at eighteen thirty tonight.

"General Hines will meet you in Mexico City and you will then catch a flight to Oaxaca, for the funeral mass, and then she will be buried in the military cemetery there."

"Juanita was Anglican, not Catholic." Don turned to Costilla.

"Her family is Zapotec. You will have to arrange for an Anglican Priest who speaks the language. It shouldn't be too difficult, there was an Anglican orphanage in her village." He looked over at Huff. "The other person you should be looking for is Reale Castro y Hernandez, her cousin. Evidently he went wetback to the US a year ago, probably in the Zapotec community in Los Angeles."

"And what about you?" asked Ross. "Do you have family that should be there?"

Don thought about it for a moment, and then shook his head. "My folks never met her, and I never even wrote them about our relationship, for reasons of security. I think this would be a lousy time to tell them, there would be too many questions I'd have to answer."

"You said there were other attacks on your unit," said Huff. "Can you tell us about them?"

"It's hard to explain without violating security, but there's a Canadian Army Corporal, Jillian Workman. She snuck a bomb on board our plane in the province of British Columbia, Canada, in June, and the next day Anna, that is, Lieutenant Fleet and I, we had a running gunfight down the West Coast of the US from Seattle to San Francisco.

"Then Sergeant Hale died in August, and we were attacked by a military assault style force in Turo, Nova Scotia. A couple of our team members were kidnapped in Rio last week, and now this."

"You seem to get around a lot," said Huff.

"I'll say," agreed Ross. "And in spite of all this, you still thought you could just go out on a date? In the open?"

"Well, were we supposed to hide in a hole for the rest of our lives?" Don shouted back, shooting to his feet. "Is that it? We have a job to do, and somebody doesn't like that, fine, but it doesn't stop us from having private lives! Besides, we were both armed! Who was expecting an assassin's bullet in the middle of the night? In Madrid of all places?"

Chapter 21

"Don, come on, sit back down." It was Rob, his arm about his friend, easing him back into his seat. Don did not want to sit. He wanted to weep, but he could not. He wanted to smash something, he wanted to kill someone, but he could not. Instead, he allowed himself to fold back into his chair.

"I apologize," he said, looking down at his half eaten breakfast. He picked up his fork, and then put it down again. "I'm afraid I'm not acting very professional at the moment." He looked straight at Ross.

"To answer your question, yes, we thought we could just take an evening off and go out to celebrate our engagement. We were in a different country, a different continent entirely, registered under different names and nobody knew where we were going except the hotel manager."

Lorca leaned forward. "The manager has been interviewed, and I believe him, though he is going to have to be questioned at length. He told no one where you were going. It could have simply been a random shooting, but I doubt it. I believe the gunman may have been waiting for any member of the team he could spot, and when you came home late, he simply took a shot. The preliminary estimate is that the shooter was just over six hundred meters away, in the bell tower of a church."

"At that distance he must have been a very good shot, probably sniper trained. I think therefore we are looking for someone with military training."

"The men who assaulted us in Turo were definitely military," Rob said. "We thought they could have been Canadian Military, so we deliberately didn't harm them."

"You thought they were Canadian Military?" Ross demanded.

"Yes, sir. We thought, or Don did, that the local provost marshal or, military police, or whatever you call them, thought there was something fishy about our unit, and decided to arrest us without making the right phone calls first."

"And?" asked Lorca.

"And we left them twenty miles up a gravel road with no socks or shoes. Then we went to a Tim Horton's for coffee and went home."

"I see," said Huff, with just a trace of a smile. "And the other incidents?"

"Could be American military, and the one in Rio could have been Swedish military, or consular personnel," Don said, his voice nearly calm. "What we're dealing with here could be just a few fanatics who've found out what we're doing, or planning to do, or the more likely scenario is that they could be a broadly based paramilitary organization, against what we're doing, but we don't know why." He held up a hand to stop their questions. "Look, what we're doing is legal, it's popular with at least twenty-seven governments all over the world. It's big, bigger than you could imagine, and it could be dangerous, or construed as dangerous, by those governments who do not have participants. Nor can we overlook dissident members of the governments that hold us in favor, but that's about all I can tell you. Your governments, all four of them, have signed on as participants."

"I think," said Huff, after a few moments, "That Lieutenant Fields should be left alone for a while."

"Thank you," Don said. "Rob, would you and Anna drive me out to the plane? I'd like the pair of you to be witnesses at an interrogation."

"Lucy, could I have a word?" Don asked, indicating a small empty office in the hanger. He had kept his voice low because he didn't want to interrupt Sacks, who had been giving a lecture on first aid.

"Sure Lieutenant," She replied, and preceded him into the office. Inside, she noted Rob and Anna and looked a little surprised. "What is this?"

"Could be anything," said Don. He looked into the black top-secret binder he had recovered from the safe in the plane. "What can you tell me about the differences of nanotube construction with hot gas, spark or laser blast technology?"

"Quite frankly, I don't think much of any of them," she replied. "They don't compare to the crystalline, CO_2 combination we used to build the Bluebird." She used the code name for the ship. "Sure, they were fine in their day, but most of the nanotubes produced were either twisted, or defective or of uncontrolled diameter. We have complete control of all three parameters. Did you know that some of the nanotube fibers we used to create the shell were almost eight or nine centimeters long? Did you know that I had to deliberately radius the corners of every right angle on the ship or they would have been sharp enough to cut you?"

"No, but I do know that you were the one who came up with the theory, not Doctor Bali." said Don, "and I know that he was claiming your work as his own. Work that could have led to a Nobel Prize. And you kept your mouth shut, and let him do it. So I need an explanation. Now."

Browning looked down and mouthed a curse.

"What did you say?" snapped Don.

"I said, yes, he stole my doctoral thesis, and claimed the work as his own. Well, he didn't steal it, sort of. He forced me to sell it to him." She sat down on the edge of the desk and slumped into a shapeless blob.

"And you let him get away with it."

"Yes."

"Can you tell us why?"

"No."

"Ensign, I'm making this a direct order, witnessed by two other officers. Tell me why you let Bali steal your work. Understand, if you do not answer this question, you will be in disobedience to a direct order, subject to a courts marshal and you will give us sufficient reason to suspect you of compliance in Bali's death, plus, you could be implicated in the subsequent attacks on us and Juanita's death. Now tell me why you let Bali steal your work."

"No."

Don stared at her for a long moment. Then he said, "Ensign Fleet, please take Ensign Browning into custody for refusing to obey a lawful order from a superior officer."

Later that night, as they sat aboard the Aero-Mexico Flight from Madrid to Mexico City, Anna came over and sat down beside Don. They were all in business class, and since there were very few passengers they had spread out to try and catch some sleep. "Don, are you still awake?" she whispered.

"Yeah."

"So, you were going to get married?"

"Yes." He paused. "She was going to ask you to be her maid of honor."

"She asked me a while ago, after your moonlight walk in Boston. She just didn't know when the wedding would be."

"We weren't going to wait very long. The plan was to get a weekend pass and drive down to Vegas."

"No white dress, no church, no family?"

"She said she didn't need them."

"She probably didn't. I've never met anyone who knew what she wanted like Juanita did." Anna paused, and Don didn't interrupt. He knew she had something else on her mind. "Do you think maybe you were a little hard on Lucy?"

"She disobeyed a direct order, Anna."

"You were under a lot of stress, and your order may not have been appropriate. You disobeyed a direct order from Captain Golden, remember?"

"The marine?"

"Yeah, the marine. I've got a gut feeling, and that is that she's innocent of whatever it is you think she's done."

"You think so?"

"Yes I do. She's got a brilliant mind, and yet Bali took her work, and she supported him. Now I think she must have a good reason for disobeying you, just as you had a reason for disobeying Captain Golden."

"Did you know Captain Golden was Jean-Paul's uncle?"

"You've gotta be kidding me."

"Nope. I saw them run into each other on the base. Captain Golden started to raise a fuss when he saw his nephew the Israeli pilot in an American uniform, and Jean-Paul told him he was on a joint mission for the Mossad and the CIA, which shut the captain right up. It was a lie, but it did the job."

"And Lucy?"

"I thought about it, and told Sacks to hold her in minimum security, room arrest and or working on the plane."

"Thank you. Did our cargo ever arrive?"

"Just before we took off. Sacks sent me a text on my phone. Two large liquid containers just like the thinking liquid. He thinks it could be the result of the same technology."

"Yeah, but who's technology? They never did explain that properly."

"Little green aliens in space suits."

"And on that note, I'm going to sleep," Anna said, but Don heard her weeping in the dark, and he had no comfort he could offer her.

Hines met them at the airport in Mexico City and they all stood at attention and saluted while Juanita's coffin, draped with the national flag of Mexico was carried from the plane and transferred to the flight to Oaxaca by six enlisted men of the Mexican Air Force. The sight of the flag, and the strange uniforms of the enlisted men, and the officers who accompanied them suddenly brought home to Don how little he knew about his fiancé, how little he knew about her country, and because of that, how little he knew of her. He wanted to weep, but he couldn't, he was an officer, he was on duty, he would not.

Juanita's mother was a miniature, older version of her, and when he introduced himself he was pleased to discover that she spoke English with only a trace of an accent. "So you are Juanita's man?" she stood back and eyed him from head to toe, and Don felt weighed in the balance. "Yes, I see why she liked you. She wrote me about you, you know."

"No," Don said, a little embarrassed, "I didn't know."

"Two months ago, she wrote that she had met the man she intended to marry, and that he would make me proud, just as she has made me proud. Tell me, did you ask her, before she died? Did you ask her to marry you?" Don was acutely conscious of all of the rest of Juanita's family, all lined up, sitting across the front of the church, aware that all conversation had stopped and her mother and father, her brothers and sisters were all waiting to hear the answer to her question. He was also aware that General Hines was beside him, and that he too was waiting for his answer.

"Truthfully? First she told me we should get married, and then I asked her, and she said yes."

There was a sigh down the line. "That sounds like my daughter. Then you are family." She drew him down and kissed him on both cheeks. "Come, I have someone I want you to meet."

Leaving the reception line, Señora Romero took Don by the arm and led him across to some chairs on the far side of the room, where she introduced him to her three brothers. Then there was a small, dark man, of no more than thirty, sitting in a chair by himself, everyone else keeping a respectful distance. "This is Juanita's second cousin, Reale. Reale lives in Los Angeles, in America."

"Señor, es mi placer de encontrarle. Juanita sólo habló de usted una vez, pero ella me dijo que sin su ayuda ella nunca habría tenido éxito," Don said as they shook hands.

"She succeeded because she was an intelligent woman who worked hard," said Reale, speaking in heavily accented English. "I understand you were to be married."

"That was our plan."

"Then you are family. You will sit with us during the service, and at the graveside. Tell me, who did this to my cousin, and why? How did it happen?"

Don took a deep breath. It was not a question he wanted to answer, but he knew this man had to have the truth. "Juanita and I were working together on a top secret project, and somebody, I don't know who, is trying to stop us. We were in Spain, in Madrid, on a mission to pick up some highly secret cargo, when we decided to go out to dinner to celebrate our engagement."

"Juanita wore this gold lame dress, and she looked so beautiful that words could not describe her. I took her to dinner, and I gave her the ring I had bought." He gestured towards the open coffin, where Juanita lay in full dress uniform. The ring that was on her left hand was clearly visible. "Then we went dancing. It was late, after midnight when we were walking back to the hotel, and some coward shot her in the back from several hundred meters away. She died right there, in my arms, and there was nothing I could do about it. We have police from America, Spain and Mexico looking into it, but to be honest with you, I doubt they'll ever find out who did it, though if I could, I'd want to kill him myself."

Reale studied Don's eyes for a moment, and then glanced down at the crossed rifles and pistols on his sleeve. "I think I believe you. These patches on your sleeve, they mean you are trained in the use of these weapons?"

"They mean I am an expert in the use of these weapons."

"I see that you are carrying a pistol in a shoulder holster."

Don grimaced. "The cut of the uniform is supposed to hide that, but yes. I am armed. As was Juanita when she was shot, not that a pistol can protect you from a sniper's bullet."

"I will look into this," said Reale, looking grim. "Perhaps one of my friends may be able to tell me who has done this thing. If so, I too would like my revenge on this sniper who shoots in the dark."

Chapter 22

The Intrepid had not changed much in his absence. It had only been a couple of weeks, but Don felt as though he had been away for a lifetime. He was surprised that the video monitors he had been installing in the circular control room were still sitting in boxes just inside the door, right where he had left them. The two large pilot's control panels still sat in a crate to the left as he entered the room, and the navigator's station was still pushed up against the right hand wall. None of the radios had been installed, nor had the command seat been taken from it's packing and bolted to the floor. The only thing that had changed was that someone had replaced one of the three burnt out lights that hung from the strand across the ceiling. Even the fact that Jezebel Lyondell sat on the floor, typing on her laptop, with it's array of eight wires dangling seemingly unheeded through the four computer access holes in the floor seemed unchanged. The whole scene seemed to re-enforce the disconnected feeling that Don had, that the last few days had been a dream, except for the pain.

"Good morning, Jez," he said, and she looked up, startled.

"Morning? Already?"

"It's 07:30. Don't tell me you've pulled another all-nighter?"

"I, ah," she looked confused. "I guess I must have. Ah," her expression turned to sheepish. "I don't suppose you could tell me what day it is?"

"Tuesday, the second of November," he replied, totally not surprised at her disorientation.

"Yes, you went to Mexico. How was your flight?" he could see that she was eyeing her computer, wanting to get back to whatever it was she was doing. Then, unintentionally, she yawned.

"Jez," he said, "you've been in here too long. Go get something to eat, and go to bed. That's an order."

"But I'm right in the middle of..."

"And you haven't been out of here for more than washroom breaks for at least three days, right?" He could see on her face that he had missed at least a day. "Four days? Five? Get out of here, right now, and don't come back for at least two days."

She left, and he was alone in the room, and he didn't want to be. He wanted to call her back, just for the company. But he shook the feeling off and started to unpack the video equipment he had to install. First he unpacked the cameras, each about the size of a half grapefruit and installed them in the molded in brackets about the room, firmly twisting down the connection screws, and then securing them with the provided clips. When he was finished he had nine cameras, all mounted just over two meters high. Then he began installing the video screens just below the level of the cameras. At a meter and a half tall, and two point six long, they were quite the largest he had ever handled, but he found them quite light and easy to connect. First he placed them leaning against the wall upside down and backward, sitting on the top of a large cardboard box. This brought the bottom of the screen up to where he could engage the clamping mechanism in the provided bracket. Then he attached the power, video and sound feeds to each one before swinging it up and locking it in place.

Distantly he heard Rob giving instructions to the guard detail on how to pour the radioactive shielding into the void surrounding the reactor, and wondered how they would ever get the rest of the equipment needed to generate electricity into the reactor room after the jell had hardened. The room was small, and the shielded airlock that led to it was also small, with smaller doors than the rest of the ship. As captain, it was his business, but he also know that Rob had assured him the job was taken care of, so he had chosen not to question his officer more deeply, only to trust what Rob had told him.

Suddenly there was a flicker of light overhead, and the entire ceiling began to glow with a soft, warm light. He walked to the door and looked down the hall in both directions and noted with satisfaction that the nanotube light panels were living up to their advertising. He knew that certain nanotubes, excited with a low current, could create a light, and that was one of the innovations Lucy had used in her design for the Intrepid. Field emitters they were called. But they were supposed to be in a vacuum. He reached up and stood on his toes, just barely able to slide his fingers across the ultra smooth surface of the ceiling and once again shook his head at Lucy Browning's ingenuity.

He had been to see her since they had arrived back from Mexico, but though she had admitted that most of the design and construction ideas for the Intrepid had been her work, she had been adamant that she would not explain her silence, and that troubled him. If she had done something, something to compromise this marvelous craft he had to find out now, before the work of transforming the shell into a spacecraft was finished. Before it was tested. If she had directly, or indirectly been the cause of Juanita's death, or Bali's... He pushed the thought from his mind. Hines had her confined and he had his best people on it, relentlessly questioning her and her motives, searching deeper and deeper into her background, but they were getting nowhere. They surely didn't need him to interfere.

Leaving his own work for a minute, he stepped down the corridor until he came to the access hatch for the power room. Most of the crew were there already when he stuck in his head. "Hey, Rob, you've got the lights on! Congratulations!"

"Not intentionally!" Rob replied, standing over his console, while the professor that had come from Spain with the goop stood in the background and grinned. He spoke some English, not much, so Anna had been assigned to translate for him, and she stood at the console, behind Rob, fairly closely he noted. "They didn't tell me. They deliberately didn't tell me! They just said let's test the insulator, please expose a small portion of one rod. One rod mind you! Well the insulator takes the free radioactivity released by the plutonium, and converts that directly into electricity. They don't need me here at all, just some idiot sailor to watch the dials. Look at the power this thing puts out! It's so simple and so incredibly complex, both at the same time! Just look at those conversion rates. We're talking nearly one to one."

"Yeah, right, keep it up man."

"No, don't go!" Rob grabbed the sleeve of Don's new blue-gray coveralls, a uniform variant that Hines had pointed out when they had come back from Mexico, a new uniform for a new service. Don wasn't sure if he liked the idea or not, but he had let the point slide. "Do you know what this means?" Rob asked, and then answered his own question while Anna grinned. Obviously she had already heard a variation, or provided some of the points. "A normal reactor works by heating water to steam, and then using that steam to turn a turbine, which in turn powers a generator and produces electricity.

"Bang, all of that technology is obsolete, it's gone. We get radiation in on one side, and somehow it's shoved into line and eaten, with the by-product being free moving electrons, or electricity on the other side! Nothing gets through, not light, or x-rays, or heat, or gamma radiation, no Alpha, no Beta plus or minus! Did I say no ionizing radiation gets though? I've got readings here, on dials that aren't even moving! If you sprayed this stuff on an antenna then it wouldn't be an antenna anymore, just a highly charged lightning rod!

"The question here is how long it will last? If it gives out continuous performance at nearly one hundred percent efficiency for a long time, then, well, say there was a landslide and a town's power plant was destroyed. The power company could pull up a brand new nuclear reactor mounted on a short tractor-trailer unit and just plug it in. I don't care what the goo costs, and Philippe here tells me it's actually quite economical, electrical power will become as cheap as though you were burning air to produce it. Electric cars, no problem, electric planes, no problem, electric trains, no problem, no pollution, no lingering toxic waste, no nothing! And the best thing yet is that it could run on all that nuclear waste stockpile we've already got!"

Don almost caught his friend's enthusiasm, but the incredible pain in his heart held him fast. "I'm thinking we're probably looking at a long development period while this transition takes place, right? Just play it cool, ok? You have our reactor working. Yes! You've got to keep your nose pinned to those digital dials that read nothing other than output, ok?

"Now, do you think you'll have to turn off the power again for testing, or can we leave it on, and if we're leaving it on you should be sure everybody knows not to touch any live leads, hum?"

Back in the control room, Don was startled to find that the monitor units he had already installed were lit up with a picture of the control room itself. Even as he walked in each of the monitors changed, every pair showing the image picked up by the cameras he had mounted above them. "Well, at least I know the equipment was installed right," he said, though here was no one there. "You would have loved this, seeing the ship come to life, piece by piece."

"Hi," said Will, poking his head in the door.

"Yo. So, what are you doing here?"

"I thought I'd drop by and see if you needed any help with those monitors, though it seems you're doing a fine job all by yourself. Even if it's been four hours with no breaks."

"Yeah, I am," Don replied, "but four hours? Maybe I could use some help."

They worked in silence for a while before Don asked, "Does it ever get any easier?" He didn't have to explain what he meant, because Will understood. Will had been there before him.

"Um? No, not yet, not for me, but then, I never wanted it to get any easier." Don could feel the pain in Will's voice; he didn't have to look at his face.

"Because if it gets easier, then it means you're being disloyal, you're forgetting."

"Something like that. I don't think it can be put into words."

"No, it can't."

"Did you hear they think they've got a lead on our buddy Jill?"

"Jill? Jill who?" For a moment Don wasn't able to place the name.

"Corporal Jillian Workman."

"What? When? Where? How?"

Will put down the screwdriver he was using to attach leads to one of the final monitors. "Atlantic city, at the Showboat Casino. You know how they have face recognition software these days? Well, the yanks do love their technology, and that whole hotel is wired for video," he glanced around, "Just like this room I guess.

"Anyhow, it seems the feds have made a file available to the Casinos for download, you know, like, download photos of your favorite international terrorist here, because he may be planning to blow up your hotel! If he is, you want to be the first to know, because having a murdering terrorist as a guest can be so bad for business, you know?

"Somebody, we don't know who, added Jill's official i.d. photo to that list. Could have been the FBI, or the CIA or the ABCDEFG, we don't know, we don't care. Casino security got on her trail and they've a couple of strong leads.

"I see that look in your eyes boss, and it ain't good, and killing her would do nothing to bring anybody back to life, though, believe me, I thought about it myself."

"Your fiancé died in a plane crash."

"And the plane had a SAM up its butt, and I'd like to kill the guy, or guys who fired it, but I can't, and even if I find the guys who did it, I won't. I, will, not, reduce myself to their level."

"Are you serious?" Don had suspected something like this, but since he had no evidence, he had kept his speculation to himself.

"The FAA investigator showed me the proof, in twisted and burnt metal. While I was on the astronomy course, right there at the end, they threw me on a plane and flew me east. They had a huge hanger in New York, and all the bits and pieces of the aircraft laid out like a picture puzzle, an engine here, a child's running shoe there. And over here a spot where all the metal bits around this hole bend in, in a perfect circle, and then they twist and bend out again, as though a missile went through the skin of the craft and then exploded." He shook his head.

"Sorry, I'm getting carried away. No, I will not let you shoot her, we need to know who sent her, and why." Will said it in such a calm everyday tone that Don felt his rage slide away. There were others who had a right to the truth, and to justice, the same as he did.

"Don?"

"No, I'm not going to kill her. I want to, but I'm not. Do you know what happens now?"

"No."

"The General will see you now," it was the same sergeant outside Hines' office, yet she seemed more kindly than she had before. "Lieutenant, I'm sorry for your loss. She was a beautiful girl."

Don smiled at her, possibly the first time he had smiled in weeks. "Thank you sergeant. It's been a tough road."

Don came to a stiff attention before Hines' desk and saluted. "Sir!"

"You wanted to see me, Lieutenant?"

"Yes sir. I understand Jill Workman has been arrested. I was hoping you could tell me if anything more has been learned about her actions."

Hines looked like he might bark, but visibly forced himself to relax. "No, Lieutenant. We know she was a member of a couple of subversive organizations, but that's all."

"I see sir. What about Lucy Browning?"

"Lucy Browning. Quite honestly, we don't know if she really committed a crime."

"She's refusing to respond to a direct order, Sir."

"She's refusing to answer on the grounds that she may incriminate herself. That is not proof that she's committed a crime. The operative word is may, which means she's possibly not sure if her actions were criminal or not. It's in our American constitution son, and I for one am glad we have that document, even if it makes things awkward occasionally.

"Now, what about our friend Doctor Wright? Is she settling in well?"

"Yes sir. She's a remarkable woman, sir, though I'm surprised. She's much older than the rest of the team sir, and she's non-military."

"The younger women are looking to her for leadership?"

"Well, we all are, sort of. It's still my team, sir, but Pam, I mean Doctor Wright, is helping us be centered as a team, if I can put it that way."

"Have you decided on your executive officer?"

Don hadn't given it much thought, but he didn't have to. "Ensign

White, sir. The others look up to him as well, and he's got a real eye for detail. I've seen him settle several disputes, and he's got a keen eye for finding humor in a situation and helping us settle down when we're all on the edge," he paused. "And even though I outrank him, there have been several times he's just grabbed me and taken me aside and put me down a notch. I respect the way he's done it, and I respect the man for doing it."

"Understood," the general nodded as though he understood every word, and the reasoning behind them.

"Speaking of team members, sir," Don swallowed the lump in his throat. "We will be needing a replacement pilot. Sir."

"True enough." Hines opened a drawer in his desk and pulled out an envelope, handed it over. "This is Lieutenant White's promotion. Why don't you give it to him? See the sergeant on the way out; she'll have a two-day pass for the pair of you. Today's Monday, get a Hummer from the motor pool, take Tuesday and Wednesday off, and Wednesday night drive down to Kingman and pick up your new pilot. There's also a chap coming from China who will be a real help to you." He handed over another envelope. "The details are in there."

Suddenly Don thought of something he had wondered about, but never asked. "Yes, sir. May I ask a question, sir? Why the train? We're pilots sir, and we love to fly, it's our natural element, yet you've brought several of us in on the train, sir."

"Did you enjoy your train ride, son?"

"Yes, sir."

"Well, I like trains. Sometimes it's important to just sit back and let someone else drive, to let the train carry you along, and not fly. It gives you time to think."

"Dismissed."

Chapter 23

They spent their two days just lying beside a pool in Las Vegas working on their tans, Rob ogling the girls in their bikinis, Don trying not to notice them, and being angry with himself and feeling unfaithful when he did. At mealtimes they sat and chatted about life in general. Although it wasn't long, the break was something Don had seriously needed. "You know, I still haven't told my folks about Juanita," he blurted at the end of supper on the second day. They had eaten early, cognizant of the fact that they had a long drive ahead of them that night.

"For real?"

"For real."

"How's your relationship with them? And I don't mean to pry, but, being your exec, you know it's my job to look out for the things you don't." Rob had been more than pleased when Don had gathered the entire team together outside the circus tent that had become their second home and ordered them to form ranks, two files. Then he had stood in front of them and ordered Ensign White, "Front and Center!"

Bewildered, Rob had obeyed, even going so far as to actually saluting Don when he stood before him. "Ensign White, on the recommendation of your commanding officer, you have been appointed executive officer of the Intrepid Team. As such, it is my pleasure to promote you to the rank of second lieutenant." He had then handed Rob the orders and a small box containing his silver bars of rank. "Congratulations man!"

"My relationship with my parents? Good, I guess."

"Do they know where you are?"

"Detached duty at a secret destination is all they know. They send my mail to a postal box in Chicago, same as yours. They don't know anything else about where I am, or what I'm doing. I haven't even told them I've made lieutenant yet."

"Then, my suggestion, for what it's worth, is don't tell them till you see them. Protect them from knowing what we're doing, and what's happening to us. I mean, how would it sound? Hi mom, I've got to tell you something. I met a girl, and fell in love, and we got engaged, but she died, so now I'm devastated. I'm sorry mom, that's all I can tell you. Don't worry about me, I'm doing fine, I've survived all of the attempts on my life."

"You have a rather blunt way of putting things," Don said.

"In perspective," Rob replied. He glanced up as a very pretty waitress swung by their table with a coffee pot. "Ah, here comes some perspective now."

Later, as the big Hummer rumbled along the road to Kingman, Rob, his hands wrapped around the wheel and driving solidly at the speed limit, asked him about his car. "So what ever happened to that '73 Capri you picked up in Seattle? I haven't seen it around."

Don grinned. This was a subject he could get into and enjoy. "Have you ever heard of a Sergeant Longford in the motor pool?"

"Yeah," Rob stretched the word out as long as he could, as though giving himself time to think. "Big redhead? He's the guy who races on weekends isn't he?"

"He's the guy you bet on two weeks ago and won the forty bucks, remember?"

"Yeah, I remember him. What about him?"

"He's helping me hot rod it."

"Like Sergeant Adams helped you repair the hole in the hood by making you a new hood from carbon fiber?"

"Well, Bill, Sergeant Longford and I, went to a local scrap yard about three weeks ago. I had a one-day pass and Juan was scheduled to take a course in something, I don't remember what. Anyhow, we had been talking about fixing the car up, and were searching for a new motor, cus the one it's got is a little tired. Anyway, we found the remains of an almost new Lotus Esprit. It had a three point five liter v-eight. You know, about three hundred and fifty horses at sixty five hundred RPM. We're putting in dual turbochargers under the rear seat. Couple that with a six speed standard, huge disk brakes on all four wheels, and he's got a buddy who can redo the interior, and I can do the suspension work myself. And Sergeant Adams is helping me with the bodywork in my spare time. We're shaving the door handles and putting in door poppers."

"A turbocharger under the car?"

"Two. We don't have room under the hood, so the sergeant suggested we route the intake from under the car, with the turbos piped in just behind the crossover in the exhaust. It's a little extra work, like when we put the battery in the trunk, but we took out the rear seat and put in a bench, twenty centimeters up and actually have the turbos where the back seat was, with custom intakes through grills on the sides of the car. Then we put a hinged shelf on top of it another ten centimeters up, but this one's accessible from inside the car. Anna's helped me put a small armory in there, a couple of the AK-47s from Nova Scotia, and the two handguns. We covered it in black carpet and it looks like the trunk in a hatchback. You can't even tell it can be opened unless you know how. And as a bonus, the shelves stiffen up the car a lot!"

"As if either you or she had the spare time. What color are you painting it?"

"Well, if I ever get it finished, Plymouth has this shade they called Radiant Red. I figure some of that, some gold sparkle, and six or seven layers of clear coat, and the inside in black leather and carpet, it might look pretty good."

"And who died and left you all this money?"

"Well, I told you I wrote some children's books."

"Yeah."

"Did I tell you they actually sell fairly well?"

"How well?"

Don was looking industriously at the scenery. "I'm, ah, comfortable.

"But you don't seem so bad off yourself."

Rob grinned. "Yeah, well it's what got me into the navy in the first place. You remember my dad was in the marines?"

"Yeah."

"Well he died in the middle east. It was some classified mission and we never were told exactly where, or how. That was when I was about twelve. When I was fourteen, my mom and I went to a remembrance gathering. You know, it was one of those things where a bunch of widows and children get together for mutual comfort, and some big shot politician comes in to drop some hot air on you in order to further his career?"

"That wasn't bitter, was it? Much. But go ahead, I'm tracking you."

"Well, like yourself, I had a lot of accelerated schooling, and I had already graduated high school and I was playing around with physics and stuff. Anyhow, I got to chatting with this admiral, Vice Admiral Shane. I told you about him before. He's the guy that signed the orders sending me here. Well, we started talking about the sighting mechanism on an anti-aircraft gun, and I made a suggestion.

"Would you believe, Shane had my suggestion drawn up into a patent application, and then he forwarded it to the Pentagon, with a suggestion that they buy the idea from me?

"Hence, neither I, nor my mother, have wanted for money ever since."

"And?"

"And, at this point I've got about seven patents in my name, all of which are making reasonably good money. Also, Admiral Shane sponsored me to the naval academy. And yes, I've talked to Anna, and yes, she's pointed out a couple of improvements, and yes, we've submitted a joint patent application on them. I'll bet you every one of our people have the same sort of story."

"True enough." They sat in silence for a while, and switched drivers after an hour, stopping for gas at a small station beside the highway. "But doesn't the government own any ideas you come up with while you're a serving officer?" Don asked, eventually.

"Normally. However, the admiral had a special clause written into my contract when I signed up. You see, I was a formal naval consultant before I was a navy officer. You wanna hear a good one?"

"Sure."

"Remember when I told you I had served on a flattop?"

"Yeah."

"Well, the last week before I went back to the academy, I went down to look at one of my modified sighting mechanisms, and I told the gunner that his sights weren't set up right. I mean, I should know, I designed them! However, the NCO in charge of the gun tub complained to the lieutenant in charge, who complained to guns, who complained to the exec, who called me on the carpet for touching one of their precious guns. He was about five minutes into tearing the hide off of me when the captain walked in.

"Well, Captain David, he was a friend of Admiral Shane's and he knew about me. He also knew about my patents. He took the exec into a back room for a couple of minutes and explained, loudly, and when they came back out the exec explained to guns, and then guns explained to the lieutenant, who explained to the NCO.

"Now, I may be a beautiful shade of black, but that NCO, he was red!

"So, there I was, chatting with the Captain, who I'd never actually seen before, and he asked me about my courses, and did I enjoy being in the reactor room all summer, and I said, well, sir, I've never actually been in the reactor room. I've been schlepping stuff on the deck all summer, and he hit the roof. Again he went into the back room with his exec, and then the exec called the ship's personnel officer. Did you know carriers have personnel officers? I didn't.

"Anyhow, the personnel officer found my file, and somebody had blackballed me because I was a friend of Shane's. It was written right there on a paper clipped to the front of the file! Ooh-wee, I got shipped off that ship so fast I barely had time to pack my diapers, and this clerk from the personnel office, he got shipped off too, and it wasn't pretty at all. Hey, coffee shop, on the right. This time you're buying."

When they were on the road again, Don said, "Did I ever tell you I was going to ask you to be my best man, and Juanita was going to ask Anna to stand with her?"

"Not in so many words. I knew about Anna of course. Juan asked her before she spoke to you about it."

"Sounds like Juan." Don was silent for a long time, and Rob let him hold his peace. After a while Don said, "It was strange, at the funeral, the Anglican Priest talking about eternal life. I did the church thing you know, went to Sunday School, and learned all the choruses, all the stories they told us. I memorized them all. But I never thought it meant much, because I was young, and I was going to live forever. And now Juanita's dead, and I thought she was going to live forever too."

"Sometimes it takes a personal knowledge of something to begin to understand it. Like church, like getting saved. A child might ask saved from what, but only if you know death, then you can be saved from it," Rob said.

"Baptist?" Don guessed. "I know you don't drink, but you're usually fun to be around."

"Assemblies of God," Rob said. "Baptists have got the right idea, but, going to church down home is like, 'shouting in the aisles' and 'Amen pastor, you preach it now,' every few words."

"Humph. I always wanted to go to a church like that."

"I'll take you, next time we get leave on a Sunday."

"Deal man," Don held out his hand. "You got a deal."

The train station in Kingman was the same as they remembered it, and since they were an hour early, they dropped into a nearby coffee shop for another brew. "So, are you and Anna trying to reach an understanding?" Don asked as they sipped their coffee, and Rob gagged.

"Who told you?" he sputtered, wiping his face with his napkin. "That's supposed to be the deepest, darkest secret in the world! I haven't even told me, or Anna!"

Don laughed, loud and long. "You've got to be kidding," he said when he could finally talk. "Secret? Have you seen the way you two moon at each other? The way she stands close to you? Anybody else would be violating your personal space, but you look like you just want to reach out and put your arm about her. So, level with me. Are you keeping protocol? Remember, I have the right to cut your hands off at the elbow if you mess up this job over a girl, or mess up the girl. Remember, she's crew too, so if you hurt her, I get to shoot you."

"Speaking of which," Don glanced at the locked aluminum

suitcase in the back seat. "We're back on duty, and we're in uniform, even if the uniforms are these gray things."

"I'll have you know that these uniforms are sort of identical to a US Naval officer's, and except for the gray cloth, and black braid instead of gold, you're a Lieutenant, Junior Grade."

"And so are you, Mr. Executive officer."

"Why thank you, Captain. I never really wanted to be an Ensign."

"Captain." Don shook his head in wonder. He was going to be Captain of the Intrepid. How cool was that?

"Captain Hitomi Tanaka, pilot, of the Nihon-koku, and Lieutenant Xiang Wu from Taiwan, military construction specialist." Don recoiled like he had been bitten by a blacksnake, even as the short Japanese woman gave a small formal bow. "Are here to join the Mountain Bluebird Project."

"Lieutenants Don Fields and Rob White," Rob said, filling in the gap, while Don tried to organize his thoughts. He felt he couldn't breathe. She was a Captain, and outranked him.

"Captain," Don snapped a shaky salute. "Our orders told us to expect a Lieutenant Tanaka, not a Captain."

"Have long desired promotion and have powerful sponsor in parliament who pushed for advancement." She smiled, but it was not a friendly smile. "You question rank, Lieutenant?"

"I'm the commanding officer of Project Mountain Bluebird," Don admitted, "and Rob here is my executive officer."

She bowed again, but not quite as low. "Will select own executive officer."

Chapter 24

"Have arranged car?" Tanaka snapped, even while Don shook hands with Lieutenant Wu.

"Yes, we have. There is a Hummer in the parking lot."

"Correct answer would be, yes, sir." Tanaka held out two yellow baggage stubs. "Meet there." Stunned, Don took the stubs and exchanged a horrified look with Rob while Tanaka walked away.

"Guys," said Wu, his voice lowered, his accent pronounced, his face serious. "Be very careful. I've only known her for a couple of hours, but Tanaka told me she received her promotion at the airport in Tokyo, just before takeoff, and she's very protective of her new rank. She's very gifted, and feels she should have received the promotion a long time ago. You don't want to get her angry."

"That may be so," Don said, and his snarl surprised him, "But I'm Captain of the Intrepid, not her."

Rob slid the baggage slips from Don's fingers. "Come on bro, it's just about midnight, and we've got a long drive ahead of us. Let's get the baggage, get her put to bed and let Hines straighten it out in the morning."

Don turned and followed his friend to the baggage area, watching as the self-assured Tanaka strolled across the platform, exchanged a few brief words with a loitering policeman and disappeared into the ladies washroom.

Tanaka didn't like the idea of sitting in the back seat, so she told Rob to sit in the back with Wu, and Tanaka didn't like the sound of their voices talking, so she told them to be silent, and as soon as they were on the road, she ordered Don to tell her everything about Project Mountain Bluebird.

"I'm sorry, sir," Don said, "But until you've been vetted by General Hines, the Lieutenant simply can not speak to you about the project. I'm sure you understand."

"Do not understand," Tanaka snapped, "and unless learn to co-operate, will regret ever volunteering for project."

"With all due respect, sir, we are under orders, from our commanding general," said Don. "We're operating under orders, and will co-operate with you to the limit of those orders, but we will not discuss the project."

"Realize disobeying lawful order from superior officer?"

"No sir, I'm not. I'm obeying a strict order from a much higher officer. With all due respect, you will have to ask your questions of him."

"Then will. Drive faster?"

"No sir, I can't. This is the speed limit."

"Now doing?"

"I'm stopping for gas, sir."

"Should have done that before picked up. You stupid?"

"No sir. I am not stupid. I am an officer who just noticed that his fuel is low and needs to pull into a gas station. Sir. We have a two hour drive before we reach Vegas, and then another three hours after that before we reach base."

He made to get out, but Tanaka said, "White handle gas. Driving through Las Vegas?"

"Yes sir, it is the quickest route."

"Planning to do what in Las Vegas?"

"To drive through, sir. We will also be changing drivers and getting more fuel."

"Don't think like you, Lieutenant Fields. Too flippant and rude, too quick to talk back."

"Yes, sir," Don said, hoping she would shut up, but he had no such luck.

"What qualifications, Fields?" she demanded. "When graduate air-force academy?"

Don could see no reason to not answer the first question. She could be trying to be friendly. "I'm a post-grad mathematician waiting for a chance to defend my doctorial thesis. I also have advanced degrees in physics and aerospace engineering. I've studied electronics. I'm qualified as command pilot on several different aircraft. I rate expert in rifle, small arms, and hand to hand combat. I have also attended a three week course on paratrooper training."

"And you liar."

Stunned, all Don could say was, "No sir, I am not."

"Twenty, or maybe twenty-one, and have all this education? You liar, can't stand liars. Repeat question, what qualifications?"

Don thought a moment before answering. "Captain, unfortunately, you do not accept what I say to you to be the truth. However it is, and since I can not convince you of it, and I can't tell you anything else but the truth, I will refer you to General Hines, who will answer all your questions."

The rest of the trip passed in silence, with Don and Rob changing places in Las Vegas, and Tanaka grilling Rob the same way she had grilled him, until they finally rolled up to the base gates and the officer of the guard stepped up to his window. "Would you please step out of the vehicle and present your identification, sirs."

Don, who was driving again, recognized the sergeant who had worked with him to unload the thinking liquid, guarding the gates.

"Yes, Sergeant." Don got out of the Hummer and handed over his identification, and while Rob and Wu did the same, Tanaka stayed in the truck. "I think she wants you to go to her, and not lower herself by having to come to you." Don said.

The sergeant picked up something from Don's tone, though he said nothing. "Yes, Sir. Ma'am, I'm going to have to ask you to step out of the vehicle."

"Lieutenant Fields," Tanaka snapped, "Tell soldier who am."

"I'm afraid I can't do that, Sir," Don said. "I haven't actually seen your documentation, and unfortunately, the sergeant must see it himself, and search our vehicle."

"You embarrass deliberately?" Tanaka demanded. "Because outrank you?"

No, thought Don, I'm embarrassing you deliberately because you so abundantly deserve it.

"Ma'am, I have asked you to step out of the vehicle," the sergeant said, walking around and opening her door. "You will comply with my instructions immediately, or I will physically take you out of the vehicle and place you under arrest until you can be cleared by the base commander." The other two visible airmen raised their weapons and pointed them at the hummer. Don and Rob, who had returned their side arms to the locked case in the back before driving up to the gates, stepped away from the truck and out of the line of fire as they heard the click of safeties being disengaged. Wu quickly followed them.

"Captain Tanaka, get out of the vehicle," Don said. "Now!"

"Will not…" the Japanese officer didn't get to finish her sentence, because in a move too quick to be seen, the sergeant had her out of the passenger seat and flat on her face on the ground, her hands locked in nylon handcuffs.

"Malone," the sergeant beckoned to a corporal who Don hadn't seen until then. "Take this officer and put her in a cell. Hobden, search the truck. Lieutenant Fields, I need your keys please. Please lead your group over there towards the road and wait until I'm finished."

Don was at breakfast two hours later when his cell phone rang. "Fields," he said, fishing it out of his pocket, switching it on and raising it to his ear.

"Hines," the general barked. "My office, now. Bring White and Wu."

Don stood up and pointed to the two indicated officers. "You two, you're with me," he snapped, turned and ran out the door.

"Sounds like he killed and ate a bear for breakfast," said Sergeant McCowan at Hines' office. "Knock and go right in, and please, no jokes about Davy Crockett."

Don did as instructed, followed by Rob and Wu, stepping up to the desk and snapping a salute, his eyes straight ahead. Tanaka also stood before the desk, as well as the sergeant of the guard. Sitting in the background were a couple of senior officers. "Sir, reporting as ordered, sir."

"Stand easy," Hines snapped. "Did you witness Sergeant Fuller arrest Captain Tanaka last night Lieutenant?"

Don had moved to an at ease position, but he was not relaxed. "Yes, sir, I did."

"Describe it."

"Yes sir. The sergeant stopped us a 04:58. He asked us to step out of the vehicle to have our papers examined. Lieutenants White, Wu and I complied. Captain Tanaka did not comply and the sergeant told her a second time, telling her she would be physically removed if she did not step out. Captain Tanaka did not move, and so the sergeant arrested her."

"Was he physically or verbally abusive?"

"No sir. His actions were strictly professional."

"And then?"

"Then the sergeant examined her papers, but he could not read her orders because they were in Japanese. His list told him to expect a Lieutenant Tanaka, not a Captain Tanaka. He sent for the officer of the guard, and told the rest of us to proceed, so we did."

"And you didn't think to vouch for your fellow officer?" The general in the background asked, his voice deep and gruff.

"Sir, I had only known the officer in question for a few hours, I have not seen her papers, and I did not know for sure that she was who she said she was. Her rank was wrong and she had not talked to us during the drive from Kingman."

"She says she asked you to describe your qualifications and project to her, and you refused to answer on both counts."

"Sir, I described my qualifications, and she called me a liar. I refused to describe the project because she has not yet been vetted by my commanding officer, who is very strict about security." Don wondered who the officer was, but he kept his eyes straight ahead. "Then she ordered us not to speak until we reached base. Sir."

"Must have been a long five hour drive," the officer said. "Lieutenant White, do you have anything to add?"

"Sir, no sir. Lieutenant Fields has described the situation accurately, sir."

"Well, I think I've heard enough," the officer said, and got up from where he had been sitting on the credenza. "Sergeant Fuller, you are of course, exonerated from all charges. You and your men did exactly what you were supposed to do in an unpleasant situation. Good work. That will be all."

"Sir," Fuller came to a rigid attention, saluted and left. When the general turned, Don was finally able to see that he wore three stars on his shoulders. One more than General Hines. This then, was Hines' superior.

"As for you, young lady," the officer turned to Tanaka, "I'm going to leave disciplining you to General Hines, but don't you ever dare to bring a charge against one of my men again. The enlisted man is the backbone of any military force, and Fuller is an exemplary example of the kind of man I need. He's honest, he's forthright and he's tough enough to do whatever he has to when he's following my orders. My orders. Do you understand?"

"Hai, sir."

"I'll take that as a yes. All yours general." He turned to go, but before he reached the door he turned back.

"Lieutenant Fields?"

Don had to turn around to face him. He came to attention. "Sir?"

The general held out his hand. "On behalf of the President of the United States, and on behalf of the Prime Minister of Canada, my condolences on the loss of your fiancé."

Don took the proffered hand and shook it. "Thank you sir, it means a lot to me."

"Alright," said Hines when he had gone. "Somebody has thrown a monkey wrench into the works. Captain Tanaka, your promotion was not anticipated when we requested you. Lieutenant Fields is, and will be, the captain of the Intrepid. Lieutenant White is his executive officer."

"We are not playing games here Captain. Out of about twenty military personnel on this base who have known the details of Project Mountain Bluebird, I've had to send three home in body bags. That's fifteen percent if you want the statistics. However, Sergeant Daphne Hale, Captain Michael Bali, and Lieutenant Juanita Hernandez are not, and never will be statistics. They were living breathing people somebody loved, not cold numbers in a ledger."

"Two more personnel died before they even reached this office. Lieutenant Fleet has a scar on her back because of a missile fired at the plane she was in. Every man jack in this crew has been fired upon by a person, or persons unknown. Some have been kidnapped, some in danger from a bomb. When someone around here tells you that security is tight, and information is restricted to those I myself have vetted, he means exactly that. When someone tells you that you do not enter the base unless your paperwork is perfect, and you have to present it politely to any guard who asks you, you will."

"Now, according to your file you were not due to be promoted until next spring, when both Fields and White would be promoted at the same time. But we cannot have a lieutenant giving orders to a captain, and we cannot promote him again until spring. Therefore, if you want to stay here, you will voluntarily restrict yourself to the rank of lieutenant and be subject to their orders. Both Mr. White and Mr. Fields."

"Meanwhile, you have stomped all over their rights and generally made yourself repugnant to every officer on this base. It would probably be in the best interests of this command if I were to turn around and send you back to Japan in disgrace, but I have old friends in the Defense Force, whom I will not dishonor."

"So what do I do with you? Lieutenant Fields, do you have any suggestions?"

"No problem, sir, if you'll let me take care of it." Don said. At Hines' nod he continued. "Captain Tanaka, Lieutenant White, Ensign Wu and I are about to leave, so that you may have privacy to communicate your decision to General Hines. You may stay, or you may leave, it's your decision. If you do decide to stay, report to me at my office in hut fifty-two. For the next two weeks you're the clean-up crew in the kitchen, and I happen to know a construction site where there is a lot, and I do mean a lot, of cable to be pulled." He turned to Hines and saluted. "Will that be all sir?"

Hines saluted back, a thin smile on his face. "Dismissed."

Chapter 25

By the end of December the fitting out of the Intrepid was nearly complete. The video feeds, both inside and out had been installed. A dozen radios and their back-ups, and the back-ups to the back-ups had been installed in the command center, where the flight console, the command chair, with it's own control console, and the navigation center were up and running. Two-dozen different aerials had been installed on the roof, on the circular outside rim, and on the bottom of the ship, along with hundreds of sensors.

Jean-Paul Golden, with the help of Lieutenant Tanaka, had the organic earth beds in the biology lab up and running, constantly recycling the atmosphere, and Sacks, along with Lieutenant 'Lucky' Wu, had the surgery all prepared for it's first patient. Rob had the power room ready to go, and Anna finally had missiles for her tubes, and three highly modified Mark sixteen Phalanx Close-In weapons systems installed at strategic points along the outside of the rim. On December 31, six days after Christmas, Lucy Browning decided to talk.

"Hello Lucy," Don said, lowering himself into a steel chair. Both the chairs in the room and the table were bolted to the floor. There was a large armed airman guarding the exit and a thick one-way mirrored window across the wall. "General Hines says you asked to speak to me."

"I did," she mumbled, and stared down quietly at the table for so long that Don thought that perhaps she had changed her mind. "I don't quite know where to start," she said finally. "You know that Doctor Bali had a hold over me. Did you know that he was my distant cousin?"

"No." Don had insisted on reading her file before talking to her, and that fact had not been recorded.

"When we were young, my mother used to take my brother Will and I to visit the Bali home every few months. I was actually named for my great aunt Lucy, Doctor Bali's mother."

"He was your cousin, yet you call him Doctor, and not by his name?" Don asked.

"He insisted. You see, my mother was an illegal immigrant from India. She had no papers and status in Canada. In India she was very poor, and the Balis wanted to move some of their money out of the country. At that time it was highly illegal for people to take large sums of money with them when they immigrated, so people like the Balis would sponsor a family, such as ours, to come to Canada, where a person like my mother would work for several years to pay back the sponsorship. In our case, she was ordered to marry a Mr. Browning, my father, who paid several thousand dollars in dowry."

"I've heard of it," said Don. "The custom is a virtual slave trade. The person is brought into the country illegally and then forced to work, turning over their earnings to their sponsor. Because the immigrant is not knowledgeable about our laws, they think they will be sent to prison and then expelled from the country when they finish their sentence. Thus they voluntarily live as slaves in order to protect the inheritance of their children."

"And it's still better conditions than they lived under in India. My mother came here and was forced to marry Carl Browning. It was a forced marriage, but it was pretty well what she had bargained on when she took the original money from Doctor Bali's father. Many Indian women are raised with the idea of an arranged marriage. Marriage for love is a foreign concept to them, so she adapted easily enough."

"Yet you were born here, and your mother had papers that were good enough to convince CSIS when they did your background check," Don said.

"My older brother wasn't."

Don checked his memory. "Yes he was. Grace Hospital in Vancouver."

"Doctor Bali said those records are false. When he found out about my research project he forced me to give him my research, claiming Will would be deported to India if I ever spoke up. Lieutenant, Will doesn't even know the language. He has no idea that he was born outside of Canada, and he certainly doesn't have the money for the lawyers he would need to stay in Canada."

"Yet, you were born in Canada."

"Yes."

"And Will is your older brother?"

"Half brother actually. I don't know what his father's name was; only that he was white. Dutch I think. And I don't know what Will's real name is. I started calling him Will when I was one or two, because I couldn't pronounce his name and maa just copied me."

"Maa?"

"Mom."

"So your mother came to Canada as a single mother, and this other family had her totally under their control for years, including forcing her to marry." Don idly drummed his fingers on the tabletop for a moment, and then asked. "So why are you speaking up now? What's changed? Where's your father? Your mother? Why don't we have a full record of your brother?"

"Will had Aids. He died two days ago. As soon as that happened, Maa insisted that she was ready to take the risk for me, that I had to speak up now that he was gone."

"And you kept silent this long just to protect your brother." It wasn't a question; it was simply a statement of fact. "Lucy," he said after a moment, "You know that there are many charges that can still be used against you. You may still end up facing a courtroom, either here, or in Canada."

"Yes, I know."

"Will you tell me something else then?"

"What?"

"How did your mother know how to keep in touch with you? You've been locked in a maximum-security cell for over a month now. How are you communicating with the outside? Somehow your mother knew what was going on, and where you were, somehow she was able to tell you about your brother's death. That information didn't come through a phone call."

"Well," and for the first time since he had known her, Lucy Browning became visibly frightened. "I used to tell her everything. I'd phone her and tell her where we were going, what we were doing. Later, when they locked me in here, a guard came to see me. I don't know his name, but the Balis helped his family immigrate too. He said he could contact Maa for me, and we've been exchanging information."

"And all this time your mother has been under the thumb of a known criminal, and you've been feeding her information." Don felt the rage building inside of him and it took a serious effort to hold it back. "The people that died, the danger that we've been in, the threat to our lives, it's meant nothing to you."

"No." She cringed and said, "They meant a lot to me. It's just that my Maa and Will meant more. Could you imagine what would have happened if they had been deported back to India? An abandoned woman whose son was dying of Aids? In India?"

Don pushed himself to his feet. This woman and her selfishness were directly responsible for the death of Juanita. He could take no more. Turning, he staggered from the room, wanting more than the world just to reach out and smash her, anything.

Rob was in the hall waiting for him. "You all right, big fellah?"

"No. But we found the leak."

"We found a leak. That contact Lucy spoke about, he's still out there. You know he's been feeding information to somebody."

"Bali's family."

"My money's on someone else controlling the Bali family. They may have started this on their own, the human trafficking, but the assaults on us, there's got to be a reason behind it, and we still don't know who or what's behind them. Focus old man, we've still got a long road to travel here.

"Meanwhile Lucy…"

"Can rot in there for the rest of her life!"

"Meanwhile Lucy deserves some compassion. She just lost everything she ever had, and it's your job to plead for clemency."

For a long moment Don just stared at his friend, and then he began to shout. "What? Are you out of your mind? This woman compromised our entire project! Would you feel the same way if Anna had been killed instead of Juanita?"

Rob remained calm. "No, I'm not out of my mind, and I probably wouldn't, but you need to listen to me for a moment."

"No!" Don stalked from the building and slammed the door behind him.

"Don't tell me you said something to upset him?" a voice behind Rob asked.

"General?" Rob turned. "You were in the room behind the mirror with we, you heard what Warrant Officer Browning said, and you saw his reaction. I'm afraid I suggested he speak up on Lucy's behalf, and he wasn't ready for the suggestion yet. Sir."

"Nor am I." The senior officer looked at his watch. "You've got five minutes. Talk to me."

Rob took a deep breath. "Sir, there is a possibility that Lucy Browning is the bad guy here. It's possible that she sold us out in order to save her mother and her brother. Actually, that's what it looks like she did."

"I agree." The general started walking towards the exit. "Walk with me Lieutenant, I want to hear what you have to say."

"Well, sir, everything Browning said in the interrogation room indicates that Bali was simply a small time creep. What's been mounted against us is an organized international offensive. Bali may be a cog in the wheel, and Browning may be too, but I don't think either has the resources, or the reason to mount this kind of an offensive.

"Between you and me sir, and anybody else that's qualified to listen, I think it's one of the contributing countries, wanting to take all of the glory for themselves, or worse, a loose agency in one of those countries that heard about what's happening and wants in. For pity's sake sir, it could even be the CIA, or FBI for that matter, playing a game of, 'if I can't have it neither can you.' Like two year olds!

"Frankly, sir, and I think you agree with me, or you wouldn't be listening to me now, this thing is so big, and so many people have been briefed, that it's pretty ridiculous to call it a secret project anymore. There's how many countries involved, twenty-seven? And if only the leaders knew what was going on, then it wouldn't be a secret any longer, and well, here in the US, who knows? The President, the Vice President I'm sure, two or three of their top aides, the Secretary of State, the Secretary of Defense, their aides, the Chief of the Defense staff, his top two or three aides, and probably their wives too."

"You forgot the speaker of the house, the governor of Nevada, their aides, twenty or thirty men on this base, everybody that works for one of the secret labs that helped develop the technology, the men who found the spacecraft we salvaged the original DNA samples from," the General said.

Rob was so surprised he stopped walking. "I don't think you were supposed to tell me that last part, sir."

"Well, where did you think we got the technology from, son? Did you think we made this kind of scientific leap overnight without outside help? Yes, we found a crashed spacecraft in Roswell. There were a lot of different kinds of goop leaking from it and one of our guys was smart enough to grab as many pure samples as he could."

"Who was that general? Was it you?"

"I wish it was. It was a good friend of my father's named Ross Denyer. He was one of three men who got up close and personal with the craft. The reactor room must have been leaking because he died of radiation poisoning within the year. With his death the project was passed to my father and then to me, and I distributed the samples to eight different labs around the world, and most of them have been able to replicate the original product."

"Most, not all?"

"Two of the samples withered and died, and we have no idea what functions they were supposed to perform. However, that brings us back to Lucy Browning. If she's not to be the scapegoat, what function is she to perform?"

"So you agree sir, that if we prosecute her now, all she'll be is a scapegoat?"

"You should be a lawyer son. Actually, you did study law, didn't you?"

"For a few years sir. I picked up a couple of degrees, and eventually got called to the bar, but I was more interested in nuclear physics.

"Sir, I respectfully suggest that Lucy Browning be given a neutral discharge from the Canadian Army, and that we buy her technology from her, at a reasonably low price, grant her and her mother American citizenship and ship them off to a lab someplace where she will never be heard of again. After all, she's a victim, and that victim single-handedly developed a technology that built us a radically advanced spaceship shell in less than a month and a half. If this ever gets out, and eventually it will, public sympathy will be on her side. Even Don admits what she developed should earn her a Nobel Prize. Can you keep her in prison forever? I don't think so. If she ever steps into court and sues, and the public finds out that the military is using stolen technology, especially technology this unique, well, it'll cost us a whole lot more than just paying her off, believe me. Sir."

For a moment Hines just stared at the Lieutenant. Then he said, "You're going to have to sell this to Lieutenant Fields, and that won't be easy."

"Yes sir. But you're going to have to sell this to the President. Sir."

Chapter 26

"How in the world," Don shouted, throwing the papers he was working on across the room, "Am I supposed to do a performance review on Jezebel and Pam? I've only seen them a half dozen times since we got back from Spain, and that was in the mess hall!"

"Come on Don, show some respect for the organization," Rob's smile wasn't quite a grin, but it was close. "The world, especially the military world, runs on red tape, you know that."

"And that's why I want to leave it as soon as possible!"

"You schmuck, you've been itching to get that line in all day, haven't you?"

"Are we interrupting something?"

"Huh?" Don had grabbed Rob and was trying to wrestle him to the floor when the ladies in question walked into the unit office.

"No," grunted Rob, twisting out of Don's hold like a varsity wrestler and pinning him down over the desk. "Look, I'm having some trouble communicating to the commander here. Do you think that if I hold him tight you might hit him a few times for me?"

"I don't think so," said Jezebel, but in a tone of voice that suggested she had thought about it before replying. "You had best let him go, we're here on business."

"Aw, no sense of adventure." Rob let Don go and began gathering up the files from the floor.

"If I may ask," said Pam, "Just, what was the cause of this little exercise in machismo?"

"Ah," Don actually blushed. "I was doing your performance reviews, and I got rather fed up. Really fed up. I mean, how am I supposed to do a review on you, when I don't know you? I haven't a clue what you've been doing for the last month, and, well, whatever!"

"I, see," said Pam. "Well, I may have solved your little problem for you. It seems the FBI and the CIA have been chatting, and they've discovered that I'm here."

"Oops," said Rob. "Then we've gotta get you gone!"

"Exactly what we thought. Perhaps a trip to Canada might be in order."

"Where in Canada?" asked Don.

"We thought, oh how about, So scratch me one?" suggested Jezebel with a straight face.

"The Toon, or Regina?"

"Perhaps, Prince Albert?"

"Nobody in their right mind goes to Prince Albert in January." Don said, with a bit of a twinkle in his eye. "Well, nobody in their right mind even goes anywhere near Saskatchewan in January. Or February, or March or April for that matter. You are in your right minds, right?"

"I'll tell you what," said Jezebel. "You fly Pam and I to Prince Albert, in the Leer, and I'll do her performance appraisal, and she'll do mine. Deal?"

Don looked at Rob and then back at the two women. "You know something I don't."

"You've probably forgotten that it's your parent's twenty fifth wedding anniversary this weekend," said Pam. "General Hines has authorized us to get out of here for a week, anywhere we want to go, as long as it's out of the country, and he's authorized us to take a pilot or two along to fly the plane. What do you say?"

"Hi, Dad?" The payphone at the airport was old and beat up, but Don knew he couldn't use his cell for fear that it might be traced.

"Don? Is that you? Where are you, what are you doing? How are you doing? Julia! It's Don on the phone! Son, you know we haven't heard from you in months! It's so good to hear your voice!"

"Dad, I'm at the airport. I just flew in with some friends, and I was hoping we could stay at the house for a week." He didn't know how much he could say, how much he should say.

"Of course! Some of your army buddies I suppose? We can throw a couple of your friends in the guest room, son, you know there's no problem. My goodness, it's so good to hear from you. Do you need me to come and get you, or did you plan on grabbing a cab?"

"Ah, we're going to rent a couple of cars."

"A couple?"

"Yeah. Ah, Dad, there's six of us. I think we'll have to go to convention mode, if that's all right?"

"Six."

"Yeah. The ladies can share my bedroom and the guest room, and Rob and I can sleep in the rumpus room."

"So, it's like a guys and girls week in the country?"

"Not exactly. You'll see when we get there, OK?"

"Sure, Don. Only, no fooling around in my house! You make sure your friends know that, alright?"

Thirty minutes later, when the two rental cars pulled up in front of his father's house, Don jumped out and literally ran up the steps, grabbing his mother around the waist and whirling her around in a big circle on the front porch. While he had been away he hadn't realized how much he had missed the farm, and now that he was home he didn't ever want to leave. Eventually he put his mother down and threw his arms around his father, and then went through the same little whirling dance with his little sister Michelle. At twelve she seemed to have grown a good foot since the last time he had seen her. Then he introduced his friends.

"Mom, Dad, the beautiful woman in the red is Doctor Jezebel Lyondell. This beautiful woman is Doctor Pamela Wright, she's a geologist. This is Captain Hitomi Tanaka, a pilot of the Nihon-koku. The tall black dude is first lieutenant Rob White, and this is second lieutenant Anna Fleet."

"Welcome to our home," said his mother. "I'm Julia Fields, and this is my husband, Greg, and our daughter Michelle. Now, I see that five of you, including my son, are armed. I would appreciate it if you didn't go armed inside the house." She looked at Anna and did a double take. "My, you are beautiful! And you carry two pistols and a rifle?"

"Mom, as far as Anna is concerned, that is unarmed. And I wouldn't be surprised if she had an ankle back up, just in case."

"Two," said Anna with a grin. She stood on her toes and did a quick spin. "Not bad. There are good sight lines. We'll be able to see if anybody's coming."

"Now, is that an M16 you're carrying?" Greg Fields asked, eyeing Anna's weapon which she had ready in her hands, not slung on its strap.

"No sir, it's a M110 SASS. I requisitioned it from the Marines. This one has a M8541 day scope on it, but at sundown I'll be changing that out for an AN/PVS-10 night scope..."

"Anna," said Rob and Anna flushed.

"Ah, Mrs. Fields," she said. "I apologize, but in light of the, ah, adventures we've had, I like to be careful. If you don't mind," she indicated the other officers. "We'll just run through the house and check the barn before we put down our weapons."

"Don?" his father asked, "what's going on here?"

Don shook his head. "Dad, I can explain some, but first, as our tactical expert has suggested, we're going to do a quick sweep of the grounds. You'll understand when I explain."

His father used his fingertips to rub his forehead, and said, "I think we have a bit of an idea. You go ahead, do what you have to do, and then you and I can sit on the porch with a coffee and talk."

Five minutes later, they were doing exactly that, dressed in their shirtsleeves and enjoying the Chinook blowing down from the west.

"So, we saw you at graduation, and you said you were off to a special assignment in the states. Eight months later you show up at the house wearing first lieutenant's bars on a strange uniform, and there's this Japanese Captain that salutes you and calls you sir. Then you have your own armed guard, an American Naval officer and an American Army lieutenant, who walks around with several handguns, and just took a sniper rifle upstairs to her room. You look about as down in the mouth as you possibly could be and still be alive. Plus you have two lovely and well-educated black ladies with you, and they all look to you for leadership, and, well, we saw you on TV. Spanish TV, and Mexican TV."

"How did that happen?" Don asked.

"You don't deny it was you?"

"No. I never have, and I never will lie to you. There are just some things I can't tell you."

Greg Fields nodded at his son. "I appreciate that. And I'm very glad you came. We'd hoped to see you at Christmas, but your mother is elated you remembered our anniversary."

Don gave an embarrassed grin. "Quite frankly, I'd forgotten, and it was Doctor Jezebel who reminded me that it was this week."

"But at least you came."

"I did. Now, how did you ever see the Spanish news?"

Don's father took a sip of his coffee and settled back in his chair. "Are you all right son? Maybe I can't know the details, but I saw you standing as part of the family, in an American uniform, at a Mexican Funeral, shaking hands with the president of Mexico."

"Yeah." Don had thought long and hard about this moment and he still wasn't sure how to say it. "Maybe you should call mom. What I have to tell you, I have to tell you both."

His dad put down his coffee and stepped over to the door. "Julia, could you come out here please? Don wants to tell us together."

There were worry lines on his mother's face that Don didn't recognize, but he was pretty sure what had put them there. "Maybe you should tell me how you saw me on TV before I go on," he said, when she had joined them on the porch.

"Michelle is taking Spanish in school this year," his dad said. "Her teacher taped the news off that Latino channel for an example in class. Michelle recognized you right away of course, borrowed the tape and brought it home. So why were you there?"

Don swallowed, and felt his eyes fill with tears. "The funeral was being held for Lieutenant Juanita Concepcion Hernandez y Romero. She was a member of our unit. A sniper shot her while we were on a mission in Spain. We had been out for dinner and dancing in Madrid, celebrating the fact that we had just gotten engaged. It was the happiest day of my life, and it ended with her dying in my arms."

"Engaged?" his mother looked bewildered, "To a Mexican Army Lieutenant, who got shot? In Spain?"

"In Madrid. Juanita was a Zapotec, from Oaxaca, that's southern Mexico. A native."

The word native got through to his mother like no other. Her father had been a Scottish immigrant, her mother a Metis, descended from men who had fought in the war of independence in 1885. As a young woman she had given tours of the Batoche church site in period costume and had learned the Cree language from her Grandmother. Don could see the reasoning file through her mind. His fiancé had been a native, a young woman much like her. Throwing her arms about her only son, Julia Fields let her tears mingle with his as she wept for his broken heart.

Chapter 27

"You mean you were going to get married to some girl I didn't even know, and I wasn't even going to be at your wedding?" Michelle protested as they all sat about the table that night. The farmhouse didn't have a separate dinning room, just a big kitchen with neat homemade cupboards, a simple plank table and hand carved chairs. There were cotton curtains on the windows that matched the white stove and refrigerator and a checkerboard floor of blue and white tile, but everything else was pine with a beautiful patina of age.

"It wasn't that simple," said Anna, as she helped to clear the dishes from the dinner table. "They were very much in love; we could all see it, but because of our assignment and the people that want to hurt us, well, we can't just call home and say, 'Mom, I've just met a guy.'"

"Somebody might just trace that call and find out who we are and go after our families."

"Do you mean we're in that much danger?" Julia Fields asked. "I'll be frank, you people and all the guns make me nervous."

"You people," she said. "I'm sorry, that just doesn't sound nice at all." She shook her head. "That's not what I meant. The guns, they make me nervous, but you, you are my son's friends; I think the best he's ever had. You are welcome here, even if you do carry guns."

"We don't think you're in danger," Don said. "We think our opponents are aware of the unit, but not of who's specifically in it, not our real names. Also, we're traveling under false documents, and the transponder codes and registration on our jet have been changed. We wouldn't have come here if I thought we were putting you were in danger."

"So, Lieutenant Anna," Michelle said, "tell me more about Juanita."

"Don't you think your brother might do a better job than that?" Anna asked, sitting down and pouring herself a cup of tea. Like all of them she had settled into civvies, jeans and a sweatshirt, and a thin gold chain about her neck that Don had never seen before. Rob caught him looking and grinned at him in an embarrassed kind of way, and Don grinned back.

"No. I want to hear what you thought of her, as a person."

"As a person," Anna paused, reached into her shirt pocket and brought out a snapshot she had taken with her phone. She handed it to Michelle. "You can keep this copy," she said. "I took this photo just before they went out for dinner in Spain. Weeks before Don proposed, Juanita asked me to be her maid of honor. And as soon as I said yes, she told me I had to wear the yellow dress."

"Hold on, you don't have to tell her about the yellow dress," protested Don.

"Oh yeah," said Rob, "tell her about the yellow dress."

"One at a time please," said Don's father. "I think we're going hear a story about a yellow dress." He glanced at his son. "Unless there is another reason why we shouldn't hear it?"

"No, dad." Don shook his head and sighed. "Go ahead, Anna."

"Well, it was just after Don had saved all of our lives by throwing a bomb off the plane."

"A bomb?" Mrs. Fields asked.

"The story started before that, when you got wounded and he dragged you to help, and got all his clothes soaked in your blood," Rob threw in.

"I'm telling the story, you butt out."

"So, I was wounded," she twisted a hand to her lower back. "Down here, and Don was in the hospital too. No, it wasn't anything serious, though yes, Don did save our lives at the risk of his own, by opening the ramp at the back of the plane and shoving out this bomb he had discovered."

"Hey, what she's leaving out was that it was the two of us that set out to dispose of the bomb, and the reason she was wounded was because she exposed herself to that risk in order to save our lives," Don threw in.

"Obviously, he succeeded, as evidenced by the fact that we're sitting here in front of you right now. The general even gave him a metal for bravery."

"A medal?" Julia demanded, but Greg hushed her.

"Anyhow, he got rid of the bomb, and in doing so oxygen deprivation compounded by extreme cold knocked him out, so we both needed hospitalization. The general had to get the cargo on the plane back to base, so he had dropped us off at a hospital in Tacoma, with instructions to rent a car and travel down to San Francisco to meet the rest of the team. Well, we were supposed to travel incognito, so the unit doctor went and bought Don some trousers and a shirt, and Juanita went shopping for me. When it was time to leave the hospital I found out that the minx had bought me this incredibly sexy little yellow sundress. Understand, I hate wearing dresses, I hate the color yellow, I hate, hate, hate, short dresses, and I really like crew neck tees, or sweatshirts and jeans."

"Wait a minute," protested Don. "What about the bikini in Rio?"

"That wasn't a dress, nor was it yellow." Anna replied smugly.

"And the little yellow dress was?" Julia asked, making a face at her son, as if to say, 'I love you,' and 'shut up,' both at the same time.

"The shortest dress I've ever worn, very bright yellow and strapless. Worse, I had just been stabbed in the back and needed Don to change the dressings twice a day. I could have, well, anything." She stopped, looked at Don and shook her head. "Sorry. It was a poor choice of words. The point is, she had a very twisted sense of humor."

"Outrageous is the term I would use," said Rob.

"I like twisted," said Michelle, and grinned at her brother.

"It gets worse," Anna said, glancing at Michelle, "but maybe I shouldn't..."

Julia put a hand on her arm. "My husband and I want to know more about this minx that could have been our daughter, and Michelle wants to find out about her almost sister. Tell us what you know, and don't pull any punches. Please."

"Well, it's a little embarrassing for me." She glanced over at Rob, who gave a little shrug. It was obvious to everybody there that he knew what was coming next.

"Back then, I had, well a bit of a crush on our fearless leader." Don looked up, startled. This was the first time he had heard this. "And, well, Juan and I had a bit of a bet going. That's what we called her sometimes, Juan. On the flight up, she told me she had him wrapped around her little finger, and I laughed at her. I told her that all I had to do was flash him a little leg and wiggle my butt at him and I'd have him under complete control. Twenty-four hours latter, thanks to her, I was showing him a whole lot more flesh than I had bargained on, and he was still her rock. Worse, I had a meltdown. There was a point that I would have done anything he said, just so he wouldn't be mad at me anymore, but he never made a pass at me, I never even caught him looking, and I do have some assets to look at, if I have to say so myself..."

"You don't have to say so yourself," said Rob. "I'll say it for you. She does have some assets!"

"And that was why Juan insisted that I wear the yellow dress. Speaking of which, I still owe her the twenty bucks."

"What twenty bucks?" Rob asked.

"The bet."

"Wait a minute," said Michelle, "She bet you twenty bucks you couldn't snag my big brother, and then she set you up to succeed, and you still lost?"

"Ah, but you should have seen how Juan looked in the dress herself!" said Don, and everybody laughed. "Mind you, she didn't earn that twenty honestly."

"What do you mean?" asked Greg Fields.

"Well, dad, come on! There I was, racing down the west coast of the United States in my favorite car in the world, a seventy-three Capri, with one of the most beautiful women in the world sitting beside me, danger all around, and you think I never looked? I may have been in love, but I'm still human!"

"Oh, compliment taken!" shouted Anna, a fist in the air. "And your cell phone is ringing."

Don snapped the instrument open. "Fields."

He listened for a few moments, said "Yes sir," a couple of times and hung up.

"Important call?" asked his father after a few moments of silence.

"It's a great call, Dad. Guys, they've arrested Lucy's contact."

"Who is it?" asked Rob.

"Well, he's basically a nobody, a marine guard named Phillips. But he has a strong connection with Marine Captain Golden."

"The dork, I mean, the Captain who went after you and Juanita about the helicopter training?"

"That's the one. It doesn't mean he's involved, but it's a lead and the feds are following up on it as we speak."

"You're flying helicopters too?" asked Michelle.

"Your big brother can fly just about anything that flies," said Jezebel, "And he does it well."

"Which brings me to a question," said Don's father. "Why does a unit like yours need a computer programmer?"

Jezebel grinned. "I'm also a sociologist, and I've studied psychiatry."

"I believe she's keeping notes on our unit," said Rob deadpan. "Something about how not to put together a team of child geniuses."

"Child geniuses," said Julia. "Are you all like Don? Is that why you're all such good friends?"

"And they were hand picked," said Pam. "There's not a person in the crew who's not certifiable. They're either geniuses, or they're mad, one or the other. Well, some are arguably both."

"And you, Captain Tanaka, how do you fit into this crew?" Julia asked. The captain hadn't said anything all night, except to assist with cooking the meal and clearing the dishes, as had all of the crew.

"Am very new," she said, in a very stiff, polite voice. "Do not know if fit into crew yet. Am pilot, linguist, and trained nurse. Also have degree in biology."

"You're a linguist?" asked Michelle. "How many languages do you speak?"

Tanaka gave a small bow. "Several. Have not counted in years, but learn maybe three new language a year. Am afraid English not the best. Have only been speaking for three months."

"You do have beautiful eyes," said Michelle.

"You speak Japanese?" Tanaka asked.

"No, but I looked you up on the Internet, or at least your name. Are you from Fukui Prefecture?"

"Hai. You very smart girl."

"Smarter than Don. I'll bet he doesn't even know what your name means."

"It's a name," said Don, not quite sure what he had missed.

Tanaka gave a polite smile. "Lieutenant, would like to speak with you."

Don stood up. "Of course. Shall we take a walk?"

Outside, they crossed the small grassy yard to the main driveway, a quarter mile of straight gravel road, lined on both sides with fifty-year-old willow trees that were feeling the touch of January. Don said nothing, letting his newest officer lead the conversation as she wanted. Eventually she said, "Have been very good, to me. After way I treated you, thought would be nasty, but have not been. Have been better officer, better leader of men."

Don smiled. "I was tempted, but you're a good officer. You work well with Jean-Paul, and I'm responsible for your well-being. I couldn't punish you for your assumption of authority. After all, as the general said, we didn't expect a captain, we expected a lieutenant."

"Did not expect to be captain. Orders came only hours before flight, along with uniform markings."

"Insignia."

"Hai. Lieutenant, think superiors pulled deliberate joke that not funny."

"You think they knew exactly what they were doing, trying to mess us up?"

"Hai. Think should be very careful. Government of Nippon involved, could be very dangerous."

"Have been given very strange order. Do not like, but must obey, for family sake. Not by government, but by friend of family."

Don stiffened. These were not the words he expected or wanted to hear. "And what was this order?"

"To seduce unit commander. Earlier, did know, but did not want to know you unit commander. Did deliberate try to alienate, but have been kind when did not have to. Took into own house, ate with father, mother, sister, rest of crew. Very strange. Make like friend. Am very sorry for order. Not tell General, please. Already angry, me."

Don glanced at her, not sure how to take her words. To seduce unit commander? Not in this lifetime. He looked at her again, wondering what the truth really was. She wasn't pretty, but rather handsome, not tall, but maybe one point seven meters, or possibly one point seven two, her most striking feature was her hair, which for the first time she wore loose. It was glossy and thick, hanging down over her shoulders like a black cape that reached to the middle of her back. "And what should I tell him? Any attempt to subvert the leadership of this team has to be reported back. People have died, and we need to trace the problem to its source and cut it off."

"Problem happened before came." She looked at him with a frown, concentrating before she said, "Use please, not report, me."

Chapter 28

"Use her? What does she mean by that?" Rob asked. It was well past midnight and neither Don nor Rob could sleep. Instead they were sitting on mattresses on the floor in the basement rec-room, which had become their impromptu bedroom. "And who the heck gave her an order like that, and why?"

"I'm going to assume that it means she wants me to feed her false information. But, like you said with Lucy, we don't know if this is the leak that's against us, or if it's just another country's government trying to get a hold over the project." It had taken Rob a lot of talking to get that point across to Don, but eventually he had conceded that it was not only possible, but also probable. "As for who gave her the order, well she admits it was a friend of the family, someone who loaned her father money, but he died before he could repay it.

"As for why, well, I don't think it's because some benefactor wants me to be a happy camper, and neither does Hitomi. I think it's a ploy to get control over me, to re-enforce their control over her and to ultimately gain control over the project."

"So what are you going to do?"

"I don't know, but for the next while I'm going to stick close to her in public, to the point that anyone watching, like corporal Phillips, thinks I'm possibly under her control. The way I see it is to handle everything like this trip. Keep everybody in the dark, leave false clues and be ultra careful."

"The General said go away, so we did, and we didn't even tell him where we were going. Thus, the only people who know where the six of us are are your parents, plus your little sister and us.

"By the by, that little sister is smart as a whip, and cute too."

"A little young for you I think."

"Only by about eight years. I can wait." Rob picked up Don's old guitar from where it had been leaning in a corner and quickly tuned it. "Anybody for some Jim Croce?" He strummed a minor chord and started singing 'Time in a Bottle.'

"I prefer 'I Gotta Name,'" Don said. "I always thought it was his best song, but, you know he wrote 'Time in a Bottle' for his son, not a girl?"

"Like 'Hey Jude' was written for Julian Lennon. Yeah, I know."

"And what song should have been written for Captain Hitomi Tanaka?"

"'For Your Eyes Only?' No, I know, 'The Mission Impossible theme!'"

"Nice." Don shook his head. "How do I get myself into these things?" he asked.

"I think," said Rob, "That you just happen to be Captain of the biggest, baddest, well, the only real, though it's still got some building to do, spaceship Earth's got." He grinned. "And, it's black!"

"And that's an advantage?"

"You better believe it, Honkey!"

"Yeah. The question is, will it fly, and how? The thing's got no motor, no engine, and no zip. How's it going to fly, mister engineer?"

"Danged if I know Cap'n, but I'm given 'er all I got. And speaking of not knowing, what I want to know is why we've never been given any spacesuit training, or weightlessness training, you know, like they have for all those astronauts on TV, and in the movies. You know, the barf bag scenes."

Don stared down at his hands. Finally he said, "There are several possibilities, and I'm sure you could list them better than I could.

"First, it's possible that this whole thing has been a farce, something designed to mess up some government agency, or even a foreign government. What bothers me about that scenario is the products that have been installed already. The computer, the radioactive shielding, the shell of the ship! That much is real, and every last one of them has been a marvel of technical innovation. All of those are far and beyond what anybody could imagine.

"Second, and this is what I think is possibly the truth, and though it's an amazing possibility, it's still lousy, because it's way less than we imagined. They have some liquid that fills the remaining voids around the ship. That liquid will do it's metamorphosis into a jell, just like the other liquids, and through some weird grasp on reality, it will cause the ship to fly, but only on Earth, and we just won't need spacesuits, or zero gravity training.

"Third, everything is going to operate as planned, but they don't expect us to leave the atmosphere for the first while, so there will be plenty of time for us to take those courses."

Rob put the guitar back. "You know, we've been operating under some pretty tight resource restrictions," he said, lying back on his mattress, fingers interlaced under his head.

"What you mean, tight restrictions?" Don demanded. "Flights to Brazil and Spain, secret labs, ultra advanced technology, and we've got military personnel from all over the world!"

"Pocket change," said Rob. "Remember that saying, a million here, a million there, pretty soon you're talking serious money?"

"Yeah."

"Well, what's Israel invested? A junior pilot. What's Canada invested? Another junior pilot, an eccentric scientist of a Captain, a couple of NCOs, some advanced nano-technology they didn't even know existed, a lab at a university. What's the US invested? A suave navy ensign, a gorgeous Army lieutenant, some empty space at area fifty-one, a couple of planes and a lot of lip service. Where's NASA in all this? They're the experts. I think we're just Hines' part time hobby, trying a long shot to get a ship into space before the big boys do. There's no real money here. You and I are the cheap alternative."

Don sighed. "You're right, I know it. So why don't we turn out the light so you can get your beauty sleep. After all, you just ruined my dreams, you don't want to ruin Anna's as well."

Don's cell phone rang at 16:00 on Monday. "Fields."

"Sergeant McCowan."

"Yes Sergeant?"

"The crisis has been resolved with a presidential pardon Lieutenant. General Hines says it's time to bring everybody back home. And Lieutenant?"

"Yes, Sergeant?"

"Saturday is General Argue's birthday, sir. There is to be a formal ball at the officers club Saturday night. Attendance is mandatory, unless you're dead or on duty, no exceptions. Dress uniform for men; ladies may wear uniforms or conservative gowns. Your crew will be there. Sir."

Chapter 29

One thing Don could say about the party was that the food was good. Soup, salad, pasta, baked trout, prime rib with roasted potatoes, gravy and green beans in oil, vinegar and garlic, chocolate cake and thick, thick coffee. He and his crew were seated around a single large table, and after dinner Don held up his single glass of red in a toast. "Gentlemen, I give you the ladies of our crew, who have one and all done us proud. I have never seen a more beautiful and stylish group of ladies anywhere."

"To the ladies," Rob replied, and they all sipped their wine. "And speaking of the ladies, I hear a waltz. A waltz is the one formal dance I know! Anna, if you would be so kind." They both stood and Anna took Rob's arm. "We might be back," she said. "We might not."

"I don't suppose you would like to dance, Don?" Hitomi asked, with just a touch of longing in her voice.

Hitomi had let her hair down, and was wearing a calf length, blue silk wrap-a-round, closed with half a dozen fancy broaches, and it made her look positively elegant. Don wished he could be better company for her, but he knew he could not. Even the thought of trying to be gallant to the ladies simply disgusted him. The death of Juanita was just too fresh in his mind. "I'm sorry," he said. "I can't."

"I understand," she said, in a voice that suggested that maybe she really did understand. "By the way, who's that?" the Japanese girl asked, looking over his shoulder. Don had to turn to look and was surprised to find a tall, older woman in a light green gown, trailing a young Air Force Captain behind her, and heading for their table.

"Lieutenant Fields?" the woman asked, and Don rose to his feet.

"Yes, ma'am?" she looked familiar, but he couldn't quite place her face. "I'm Lieutenant Fields." He wanted to salute the captain, but the woman was busy shaking his hand while assessing Hitomi with her eyes. For a moment Don almost felt left out.

"My, young lady," the woman said. "Is that dress an original Tanaka?"

Don looked from one to the other and was surprised to see Hitomi blush. "Hai. Mother designed it for me."

"I'm sorry," said the woman with a touch of condescension. "You must have misunderstood. The house of Tanaka is a Japanese design center. Very high end."

"Hai. Mother is my very best designer."

Suddenly Don started to understand what was going on, and he wanted to laugh but restrained himself. The older woman expected the two young people to recognize her, and though she looked familiar, Don couldn't place her. The problem was, the older woman should have recognized the younger as well, but she hadn't realized it.

"Excuse me," Don said, "may I present my date for this evening? Miss Hitomi Tanaka."

"*The* Hitomi Tanaka, of Tanaka House?"

"Hai."

"My apologies Miss Tanaka. Of course, I saw you at the spring collection in Tokyo."

"Hai, Tanaka House was honored that you could attend." Again Hitomi surprised him by using a pronoun in her sentence, something she rarely did.

"Andre," the woman addressed the Captain. "Take Miss Tanaka and show her that you know how to dance, and be very nice to her, she's an important designer," she said, and turned back to Don. "Now, Lieutenant Fields, ask me to dance."

"I'm not much of a dancer, ma'am."

"You will do well enough, I'm sure." A moment later Don was gliding across the floor. The woman was an excellent dancer and consistently covered his mistakes. "You should take lessons young man. It's essential for an officer to know the social graces," the woman said.

"I haven't had much time for waltzing, ma'am."

"Oh, I know, but you will have to learn. Now, in a few moments this dance will be over and a young woman will come and chat with you. The young woman has had more than a passing acquaintance with a plastic surgeon. As a matter of fact, she's purchased enough silicone to get a frequent flyer discount."

"Not a look I admire, ma'am."

"Good, though most men do a double take when they first see her. Whatever you do, don't react to her chemical enhancements. She's going to take you to see her friend, whom I'm sure you will recognize. Do not mention their relationship to him; do not be anything but absolutely courteous to both of them. Smile, nod, and shake the man's hand if he offers, you do not offer if he doesn't. He'll say some nice things, but if it's not in writing, there's plausible deniability. Do you understand?"

Don took another look at the woman he was dancing with and suddenly he recognized who she was. The music stopped and he gave her a little bow. "Thank you for the dance, madam secretary. I hope that if I'm ever lucky enough to have the opportunity to dance with you again, my technique will have improved considerably."

"Heads up lieutenant. Here she comes."

Don did a double take, just as the secretary of state had predicted.

The woman certainly had more than a passing acquaintance with plastic surgery, with an emphasis on the word plastic. And, she definitely was not hiding it. "Lieutenant Fields?"

"Miss. Georgia?"

Perfect botoxed lips hinted at a sultry smile. "You've seen my movies?"

"No," the lips pouted, "but one of my friends mentioned them with enthusiasm."

She smiled again and wrapped a hand around his arm. "Somebody would like to meet you," she murmured in a voice that could make most men do anything, but Don still hurt too much to care, and he certainly wasn't going to flirt with the president's mistress.

"Lieutenant Fields, how good to meet you at last." The president of the United States reached out to shake his hand and Don responded in kind.

"I'm honored, sir." The president was a tall, good-looking man in his fifties. He had always been athletic, but now had a bit of a belly and his short hair was thin and graying. Don wasn't sure if he liked him or not. The man's mistress had let go of Don's arm when they shook hands and moved quietly away, a few of the secret service men following her. Don didn't know the details of the relationship, didn't want to.

"I'm sure General Argue extended my condolences on the passing of your fiancé son, but I would like to extend them personally to you." He didn't pause for Don to answer.

"Tell me, how is the project going? Do you honestly think you have a chance to have it up and running in the next few months?"

"There always seems to me that there's more to do, sir." Now that he had an idea what to look for, he spotted two more men dressed as waiters, and a couple dancing on the floor who were definitely out of place. "I know I don't have general Hines' overview. Since the project is so secretive we're mostly working on a need to know basis, and though I'm overseeing day-to-day operations, there are still huge gaps in my knowledge, things that I can only guess at."

"I'd love to come over and see it," the President said, and Don instinctively cringed. The man was carrying at least a dozen security men, plus two aides and an Air Force Colonel with a briefcase handcuffed to his wrist.

"Well, sir, we'd love to have you come and see it, but your escort would have to check it out first." He had tried to be as subtle as he could, but felt like a skier racing down a slope in front of an avalanche.

"And while I trust them with my life, some secrets are just too sensitive," the president mused. "Or at least this one is. Young man, I'll let you get away this time, but when it's revealed to the world, you've gotta bring it over to my place and let me have a look." He took a card out of his pocket and handed it to Don. "This is my personal number son. There are maybe two-dozen people in the world who have access to that line. If you ever need to call it, you'll know."

"He what?" Rob demanded as they walked home from the party.

"The president of the United States gave me his card."

"For real?"

"Hey, I checked, it's even got a phone number on it."

"Speaking of which, your cell is ringing."

Don fished his cell out of his jacket pocket. "Fields."

"Lieutenant, it's Sergeant Fuller, at gate three."

"Yes, Sergeant. How can I help you?"

"Sir, there's a couple of tanker trucks here. They have a purchase order signed by General Hines and your name as contact. The bill of lading says it's for Project Bluebird, sir. They've got a gent with them that speaks no English, but he sure speaks a lot of excited Spanish. The trucks have Mexican plates, sir."

"Hang on to them Sergeant, we're on our way." Don closed

his phone with a snap. "Anna, you and Rob are with me. I need a translator."

"Ah, boss," said Anna. "Party dress, remember?"

Don hadn't remembered. He actually looked over to see what she was wearing, and was surprised Anna was still dressed in a beautiful crimson gown that he suspected was also House of Tanaka. "Ok, to the barracks and change, on the double. It looks like the engine gel has arrived."

Chapter 30

Two large blue semis with stainless steel trailers were idling just outside the main gate when they got there, the heavy diesels rumbling loudly in the night. Five spotlights seemed to pick out every feature in garish detail, and Don could easily see the chromed bulldogs that sat proudly atop both radiators. He looked down and spotted the license plates, humbly bearing the name of Oaxaca, before Sergeant Fuller stepped up and saluted. "Sir. Their paperwork seems to be in order, but arriving in the middle of the night like this, I thought you might want to check them out first before I let them in."

"Thank you for calling me, Sergeant. Do you have the Spanish gent handy?"

"They're all Spanish, Sir, but the leader is over here in the guardhouse, sir."

The man's name was Professor Julio Romero y Lopez. "Señor Fields," he said, shaking Don's hand. "Reale sends his greetings," Anna translated.

Don quickly stepped back. "You know Señor Castro y Hernandez?"

"Of course, I am his godfather," Anna said, "At least, I think it was godfather."

"Then you knew my Juanita?" Don asked.

"Si, I heard of her passing on the news. So sad. She was so young and alive, and should have taken my advice. She should have been married years ago and be sitting in a warm kitchen with a baby at her breast. Did she tell you that she flew my first prototype?"

"Prototype?" Don demanded when Anna was finished. "She flew a prototype of this engine?" *Until I flew something faster*, she had said, and been awarded the Mérito Técnico Militar.

"Si. Mach three in a highly modified F-5 airframe."

"So, the government of Mexico is using this substance in its planes?"

"No. They have one jet fighter that almost shook itself to pieces, totally un-airworthy by now."

"You said it was highly modified?"

"No engines, except for this gel in the converted fuel tanks and an electrical generator in the back. It was an amazing test flight, but we had to bring her down before the plane destroyed itself, and that was a near thing."

"And the tanker trucks?"

"Hold the two components that mix together to produce the sludge. Lieutenant, the components have a limited life span apart. We have been on the road for three days. If we don't mix them and install them in your planes within the next few hours they will die. If we are to do this, we must do it now."

Don looked at the man and decided that he seriously liked him, and that he trusted him. "Sergeant Fuller?"

"Sir?"

"My recommendation is that you let the trucks through."

"Sir, yes sir. You will be responsible for the professor and his men while they are on the base, sir." He handed over a clipboard. "Please sign here, sir."

Don signed the form and ushered Anna, Rob and Romero y

Lopez to the hummer they had commandeered from the motor pool. With the two huge Mack trucks following close behind, they drove across the base to the circus tent. "Señor Romero, how do you plan on getting the liquid out of the tankers, and mixing it?" he asked, pulling up close to the canvas side.

"This is no problem," the Mexican replied. "Have the trucks park side by side, close to wherever you want to pump it to. I'm assuming that the target vehicles are inside that tent, for security reasons?"

"Yes," Rob said. "Just how delicate is this operation Professor? Do we have to figure out some way to lift those huge tanks up for the liquids to flow out?"

"Ridiculous!" replied the Mexican, looking as though Rob had just put on a monkey costume. "You have heard of pumps, haven't you child?" Anna was translating with a straight face, but Don could see that she wanted to laugh. "Max's truck has a massive pump attached to the underside of the trailer. In words simple enough for you to understand, we pump the contents of Adolfo's truck into Max's truck. Then we run the pump in a loop for about five minutes, taking what's in the bottom of the tank and shooting it into the top of the tank. That mixes the two liquids together. Then we have about half an hour to pump the resulting liquid into your selection of aircraft, and I'm assuming you have a lot of aircraft to pump it into."

"And how big is your hose?" Rob asked.

"Ten centimeters. I sent General Hines a connection sample to be fastened to your equipment. Young man, really, these ridiculous questions..."

"Señor," said Don, "unfortunately there will be a lot of questions, and none of them are ridiculous. We had a soldier die a few months ago because we didn't know enough to ask the right questions."

Romero y Lopez looked from one to the other and shrugged. "Someone died?"

"Si," said Rob, "somebody died. Next question, is this product flammable?"

"Until it cures." Anna shook her head. "I think that's the word, cures. Ages, matures, ripens?"

"And how long does that take?"

"A few days, perhaps a week, depending on how large a mass you put in any one place. A larger concentration takes longer to cure."

"If it was all in one place? Hypothetically?"

"Hypothetically?" said Anna. "I speak the language, not teach it!"

"So find some other way to say it!"

"Hipotéticamente?" the professor looked amused.

"Si, todos en un solo lugar."

"Dos semanas. Tal vez tres semanas."

Don pulled the hummer up beside the tent and everybody piled out to be cleared by security. Then Rob and Anna directed the two trucks to park parallel to the tent, with the output of the pump next to the entrance. The two drivers, Adolfo and Max quickly rigged up a pipe between the two trucks and using a pump powered by a power take off, added the contents of the second truck to the tank of the first. Disconnecting the pipe from the second truck, they climbed up and fitted it to a connection near the top of the tank. At the professor's nod, the swarthy Mexican named Adolfo climbed down and re-engaged the pump. All this was done with a constant loud Spanish commentary, verbalized by both drivers and the professor.

Meanwhile, leaving Anna to guard the entrance to the circus tent with her M16, Don climbed to the top deck of the Intrepid, where he lowered a rope for Rob to lash to the end of a couple of sections of flexible pipe they had unloaded from the truck. Then Rob climbed to the upper deck and helped him clamp the pipe to the filling connection on the very top of the ship. Five minutes later, when the Professor was satisfied with his mix, they coupled the end of their pipe to a hose that connected to the part the drivers had been using to mix the two substances. Then Rob climbed back up to the top of the Intrepid and opened a gas release valve to allow the air to escape while the liquid engine was pumped in.

The filling seemed to take forever, though Don timed it on his watch and decided that it only took twenty-two minutes before a trickle of green goop started to drain from the relief valve. Rob called down for them to stop pumping and then he shut the valve, closed the secondary valve on the end of the pipe and reversed the procedure to disconnect it from the ship, still filled with liquid.

"So, what are we going to do with the excess?" Rob asked. "We never planed on it."

Hines, who had joined them during the pumping started to say something, and then paused, thinking. "We still have the tank the computer came in, sitting in hanger number three, don't we?"

"Yes sir," said Don.

"White, you run over there and get that tank, bring it back over here." He said something to the professor in Spanish and the older man nodded in agreement. "Professor Romero y Lopez says we can store the solidified gel for several months without using it, though it does need a little electrical power and a sugar drip to keep it alive."

"Does he have any suggestions as to power requirements, or how to use it, limitations, that sort of stuff, sir?"

Anna passed on the question and the Mexican chemist trotted over to the cab of Adolfo's truck and returned with a thick blue binder, which he handed over to General Hines. By then, Rob was back with the tank previously used for the computer liquid and the remaining goop was transferred to that. Finally, near 03:30 in the morning, Don ushered the professor and both tankers out of gate three.

Chapter 31

And then, suddenly, everything was done. Don found himself wandering through the ship, his clipboard in hand, with his thick dog-eared to do list, not sure if he could believe everything was checked off. He came upon Rob and Anna in the library, a small closet sized room on the third level, where Rob was sitting on the floor, studying a maintenance manual, and Anna was sitting opposite him with her laptop.

"Yo, boss man," Rob said, "grab a chunk of floor."

Don did just that, since there was no room for chairs. "You're finished too?"

"We done mon. Gonna ask de cruel ovaseer for dat tree day pass mon. Mebee he be good ta me an let his people go mon."

Don threw a punch at him, but missed. Anna laughed and put down her computer. "Everything's been installed and tested three times, including the coffee maker. The only thing we haven't tried yet is the drive gel. Jean-Paul doesn't want us to mess with that for another week. I'm thinking you've finally got some time to work on that old car of yours. How's it going anyway?"

"Well, I've actually found a good bit of spare time in the last couple of weeks. You know Rob helped me rebuild the suspension and put on new brakes. Will and Sergeant Adams have helped with a lot of the bodywork, and I've got to thank you again for all the help with the electronics. Sergeant Longford has finished rebuilding that new motor and we popped it in on Saturday. It took us a little time to set up the timing, but I took it for a test run and that thing can move!"

"And the extras?"

"Ceramic armor around the gas tank and the back of the trunk. Thick Kevlar blankets inside the body panels, hood and headliner, stuffed inside custom leather seats. Four point seat belts, re-enforced glass, and an arsenal in the back seat. Just your everyday custom car."

"For Bond, James Bond."

"No radar, no machine guns."

"Large screen GPS."

"Well, yeah. It's pretty much ready for the paint shop. Sergeant Adams has this buddy down in Kingman who has got an amazing reputation for custom paint." Don's eyes went vacant for a moment as he thought of Juanita, and what she might have thought about his car. Then he snorted a laugh, thinking she would have insisted on driving. And he would have let her.

"Yo, Earth to Don! Wake it up!"

"Yeah. Best way to wake up is with coffee, right?"

"There are other ways, but a good pot of shaft lube helps."

"I'm off to the office. If you see Hitomi, ask her to drop by, will you?"

The Japanese pilot stuck her head inside the office less than an hour later. "Wanted to see?" Like the rest of the crew, Hitomi wore the blue-gray Earth Service overalls, though her zipper was lower than it should have been. He suspected she had adjusted it just before coming in. It was one of the things she insisted on doing, in spite of being ordered to stop. When he had directly confronted her with it she had shrugged. "So send home. Have been ordered by friend of family to seduce. Please to let try."

"Why?" Don had demanded. "What's this friend got over you that gives him a right to ask such a thing? It's disgusting!"

"Find disgusting?" she had protested.

"No, not you, the order. Nobody should have the authority to give a young woman an order like that!"

"Innocent, innocent lieutenant. So naive. Father gambler. Owe much money. Father die in car crash, friend pay debt, finance House of Tanaka. It's very important that I pay back that debt. If I do this for him our debt is paid. Do you understand?"

"And again, suddenly with the personal pronouns?"

"Want lieutenant understand, hai? Besides, lieutenant kind of cute when angry."

Frustrated, Don had given in, and, he mused as she came to sit in a chair before the desk, it was definitely flattering. "Hitomi, I've been thinking about the attacks on the unit. They all happened before you joined us, but they have left a wound on the rest of us that needs to be tended."

"Have decided to use?"

He grinned. "Hai. Have decided to use you."

She grinned. "Use in what way?"

"I'll tell you later." She frowned, but said nothing. Don took a paper from his pocket and slid it across the desk. "This is a three day pass, starting the day after tomorrow. I'd like you to come to Vegas with me for a couple of days. I've booked a room for us at the MGM. Actually it's a suite, called a Glamour Suite. I want you to call your friend and tell him. We'll be registering as Mr. and Ms Joyceman."

She looked at him hard for a few moments. "Anything special should bring, or wear?"

"Sharp, I want you to look sharp and sexy. We will probably go out for dinner both nights, so if you have a couple of dresses, bring them. We'll leave right after breakfast, day after tomorrow."

"Hai. Sir."

Hitomi was ready on time, as efficient as ever, dressed in skin tight black leggings and a form fitted white shirt that hung over them down to her hips and was gathered at the waist with a wide gold lame belt. She wore knee high, high-heeled black boots, a dark blue blazer and a half dozen loose loops of red stones over her shirt that was unbuttoned half way down. Her hair was worn loose and her manicure and her light makeup were perfect. She looked amazing, and Don told her so as he handed her into the car. Then he loaded her three large suitcases into the trunk and laid her garment bag atop his on the shelf behind the front seat.

"How did your conversation go with your friend?" Don asked, after they had cleared the front gate.

She gave him a strange look and said guardedly, "Not friend me, friend family. Personal friend would not give order."

"Distinction noted. How did the phone call go?"

"Friend most interested. Wanted more information, but did not have. Told him share room."

"And what did he say about that?" he glanced over and saw she was blushing.

"Told me make very happy."

"I'll bet. Listen, you don't have to worry, I'm going to sleep on the couch. I meant it when I said I don't believe in using people like that, though I would like it if you could act a little more than friendly when we're in public."

"Play dangerous game," she said, though she looked relieved. "Friend much money, much influence. If cause of attacks on unit, could attack today, tomorrow."

"Well, I guess that leads us to the big question, doesn't it? Hitomi Tanaka, where does your loyalty lie? With the Unit, or with the people who sent you to subvert it?"

He could see her squirm for a moment, and then it was obvious she had made up her mind. "Came this far," she said, gesturing at her clothes and the car. "Am willing to go much further. No line between obeying friend and obeying lieutenant. Now ask risk not virtue, but life, will make love, but ask risk bullet." She was quiet for a moment, and Don understood. For him, his principles were his life; to risk the first was to risk both. He knew a lot of people thought that way but stopped at the actual reality of risking their lives for their principles. He waited for her to continue.

"You draw a hard line across the rock," she said eventually, her accent all gone. "However, I have done everything I could do to fulfill my obligation to the family friend. I respect your principles that make you say no, and because I respect you I will say yes. I will do whatever you ask of me, no questions."

"Thank you."

They drove for an hour in comradely silence before Don said. "So, tell me about this company, the House of Tanaka."

Hitomi smiled. "House of Tanaka," she said, "Ten year, owned by mother, sister Katsu and Hitomi. Mother, Katsu and Hitomi designers, Hitomi general manager."

"And what kind of clothes do you design?"

"Gown, formal dress, expensive clothing."

"The secretary seemed impressed."

"Secretary rude. Persona non grata all store."

"Ouch. How many stores do you have?"

"Tokyo, London, Sidney, San Francisco, Paris and Rome. New store in New York next year, maybe."

"That was a beautiful dress you wore for the party. I actually suspect you had something to do with all the ladies gowns, didn't you?"

Hitomi chewed her lip for a moment before saying, "Had heard of party before trip to Lieutenant's home. Gathered sizes, E-mailed San Francisco. Parcel waiting when come back."

"But doesn't that give away our location?"

Hitomi laughed out loud. "Location not secret. Friend knew location before order. Knew more than Hitomi."

"Probably more than me too. Well, we've silenced Phillips, and Workman has been captured. Maybe that's cut some of their pipeline."

"Why no interview Workman?"

"Pam is going to interview her when we get back. She had a chat with Workman a couple of days ago, and the conniving little weasel refused to talk, saying she wanted to talk to her lawyer. Pam told her the truth. Told her that she was on the staff list. We'll see if that loosens her tongue up after a few days in solitary."

"Staff list? Not heard of staff list."

"We made it up, Rob and I. It's supposed to be a joke, but we played it like it was an unfortunate anagram selected by Homeland Security. Staff stands for suspected terrorist, arrest and forget forever."

"No trial?"

"Nope."

"Glad only simple dress designer from Tokyo, not on staff list."

"Yes, the designer. I assume you brought a special dress for dinner tonight. Is it from the House of Tanaka?"

Hitomi grinned. "Brought two dress, designed by Hitomi Tanaka, sewn by house seamstress, but not House of Tanaka."

"Well, if you designed them, and your house made them, why aren't they House of Tanaka?"

"Eight year when study design. Decided four philosophies of design."

"First, utilitarian, clothes keep body from being naked. Not really need designer."

"Second, body as platform for clothes. Look stupid, make laugh, but sell for lots of money. House not make clothing like this."

"Third, risqué. House not make clothing like this. Clothes as platform for body."

"How risqué?"

"Showed to Anna when told to look sexy. Called first seduction dress, second plumber dress."

"Plumber dress?"

"Very low back. Hitomi have good low back. Strong. Well muscled, you see."

Don wanted to ask how low, but resisted the temptation. "And the fourth philosophy? I assume it's the way the House of Tanaka operates."

"Hai. Clothing as a platform for personality. The person who wears the clothes must be more important than the clothes themselves. Therefore the clothing must enhance and support the person who wears them. To my mind, all things in life should be designed this way."

"But you designed two dresses to be risqué? Doesn't that upset your philosophy? And by the way, you're forgetting your accent again."

"So sorry. Have read about Carl Jung's idea of opposites in personality?"

"Yes."

"Then understand, sometimes want to be appreciated for intellect, sometimes want to be appreciated for nice body. All woman like told look hot." Don sighed and just let it go.

The suite was gorgeous, and Don tipped the bellhop generously. Then he glanced at his watch. It was noon. "Shall we go for lunch?" he asked.

"Hai. Wash, change." She walked into the bathroom, and a moment later he heard the bathtub filling. She didn't re-appear until 13:00 hours. She was wearing a dress, but not one of the ones she had described in the car. It was knee length, blue, with a relatively low neckline, but certainly not scandalous, at least by Las Vegas standards. In the afternoon they moved about the hotel and up and down the strip, being careful not to stick out, nor to fade into the woodwork. Don did a little shopping, but not much, Hitomi mostly just hung onto his arm like a blushing bride and was seen but not heard. At 19:00 hours, after Hitomi had changed again, they moved into the casino, played a little baccarat and mostly broke even, though Don knew with a little effort he could win more. He hadn't really studied them, but he had read methods of counting cards, and once read they were his for life. Unexpectedly, Hitomi chose to sit in on a poker game and he was shocked when she won three high stakes pots in a row.

"Father taught," was all she would say, and Don left it at that. He wasn't sure he wanted to know more.

At 21:30 he mentioned that his dinner reservations were for 22:00 and they had to hurry upstairs so that she could change again and do her face for dinner. "Want seduction dress, or plumber?" she asked on the elevator, and Don blushed. An older man standing at the front of the elevator started to turn and say something, but changed his mind.

"Subtle you're not! What you're wearing is sexy enough," he whispered. "You really don't have to go this far. We're just setting ourselves up as bait to see if your friend is out to kill us."

"Settled. Wearing plumber dress," she said, and it took her half an hour to put it on. When she did he realized it had no back, and was aptly named. After they were seated she leaned forward and whispered. "Designed dress, never thought would actually wear, so designed too far. Feel like naked in public, but like reaction from man."

"Yeah, well any man who doesn't react to that thing is hardly a man. Designed too far? You could go no further. How do you keep it on?"

She leaned forward again, lowered her voice and whispered, "Double stick tape," and Don started to laugh, the first real laugh he had had since Spain.

Chapter 32

"How would you like to see the Hover Dam?" Don asked in the morning, between combing his hair and brushing his teeth.

"That better place to take Xiang Wu than pilot?" Hitomi teased him, rinsing toothpaste from her mouth. This morning she had on yet another outfit, and Don was beginning to understand why she had brought as many bags as she had. He was wearing his shirt and trousers from the day before, his suit back in the garment bag waiting for supper. Hitomi had retreated to the bedroom after supper, though she never actually closed and latched the door. He had slept on the couch and had actually slept well for the first time in weeks. It had been a good night, and Hitomi had been a good companion, but nothing more.

"Maybe, if he were here," Don said. "But he's not. I've driven, or been driven past it three times since I came to Nevada, but I've never had a chance to stop and look at it."

"Have breakfast first?" she asked. "Then change."

"We can have breakfast. When we get back to the room we'll take ten minutes for you to do whatever you have to do. If you're not ready, I'll either leave without you, or just pick you up bodily and drag you out to the car in whatever you have on at the time." He realized he was flirting, and decided against hating himself for it. Juanita was gone, and she had been for months. There was nothing he could do about it except go on living.

Breakfast was in a large dining room, with snow-white linens, gleaming silver and thick, thick coffee served in ridiculously small teacups. "Bacon, home-fries, four eggs scrambled, a slab of ham, real ham mind you, not some paper thin slices, some sausages, white toast, four pieces." Don said to the waiter, whom he recognized from lunch the day before. He had left a good tip and the man had spotted him when he came in the door and quickly seated them both in his section.

"Very good sir." The waiter had just turned to go when the grenade rolled through the door. Without thinking, Don shoved him violently behind a planter, grabbed Hitomi by the arm and threw her to the floor, landing on top of her. A moment later the grenade exploded with a bang. Almost simultaneously there was the sound of a shot, the two sounds overlapping each other so fast that Don was never sure which came first.

Instantly the room descended into chaos, a dozen people injured, a hundred others screaming. Anna burst through the door from the hallway, her gun held high, pointing at the ceiling. "Boss, you all right?" she snapped, dropping to her knees beside Don. "I shot the schmuck and he's down, but I don't think I killed him. Rob's putting him in handcuffs."

Don tried to lift himself up, but found he couldn't. His right leg wouldn't hold his weight. With an effort he rolled off of Hitomi and then pushed himself to a sitting position. "Youch," he said, examining the chunk of shrapnel in his thigh. "Best get Sacks in here and working on those civilians. Hitomi, you and Anna are going to have to do some first aid."

"What about you?" Anna asked, while Hitomi just stared at her, stunned. Nobody had told her the rest of the team was coming.

"Serious enough, but I won't bleed out." He waived them away. "The two of you, go help those people."

Hotel security started to burst through the doors even as Anna and Hitomi started sorting the wounded, pointing out the most seriously hurt to Sacks. A few minutes later a house doctor came around to see to Don's wound, accompanied by hotel security. "Mr. Joyceman, we do apologize, but it seems your bodyguards have the situation under control. I have no idea how that man smuggled an explosive device into this hotel. We take very extensive precautions, you understand."

"Well, it seems you were out maneuvered this time." The doctor slit open Don's pant leg and using forceps, grabbed the chunk of steel, pulling it out of his leg. Don wanted to scream, but instead kept his mouth clamped tight. "But then again, so were my people. Has anybody recognized him?"

"He's a cop," Rob said, stepping forward and handing Don a wallet, complete with a badge from the Arizona Department of Public Safety, Arizona Criminal Investigations Division. "Name's officer Bernie Chisholm."

Hitomi looked at the photo on the man's id and said, "Recognize from somewhere, don't know where."

"I know where," said Anna. "The Kingman train station."

Suddenly, Don remembered. "The first time I saw you, at the train station, you gave him something, and he gave you something back."

"I gave him my phone number, he gave me a watch for my birthday. I didn't tell you because I didn't know you then, it was my business, not yours. He's my uncle, but I hadn't seen him for several years. Told me he was keeping an eye on the station, that there was some drug traffic coming through the station and headed to Las Vegas, using military personnel as couriers. Said he had been carrying the watch in his patrol car for three months, trying to decide if he should send it to me or not." She looked up, tears in her eyes. "Uncle Bernie and mom have been estranged for a few years, I don't know why. I didn't see why I shouldn't tell my uncle the cop where I was based. We hadn't been told anything then, not even that what we were doing was top secret. I always thought it was just a lucky fluke that we ran into each other like that.

"He's been calling me every month or so, just for a chat. But, well, he's my uncle, my mother's brother! I used to sit on his knees and read him my storybooks when I was only four years old!"

"Did you ever tell him where we were going?" Don asked. Sacks had come over and helped Rob lift him into a chair. Then he opened his bag, put on a fresh pair of vinyl gloves and swabbed the wound with a disinfectant. Again, Don wanted to scream, but didn't. Sacks started to sew him up.

"No." She thought for a moment and shook her head. "Not a chance. We talked about this and that to do with family and friends, but I'd been told not to discuss our work, so I didn't."

"Do you have the watch with you?" Don asked.

"No, Rob," she looked down at the watch on her wrist. "Uncle Bernie's watch stopped working a few days ago, so Rob bought me a new one." She stared at her wrist for a moment. "You think I was wired?"

"I think there was a bug in the watch he gave you, and anything you heard us say, or discuss was transmitted to a repeater on base. Phillips probably knows where that is. Come to think of it, there's probably one each on the two planes we've been using. I wouldn't be surprised if there's a hidden squawker on the C130 as well.

"Anyway, I'll bet that the watch died because the bug was using the battery. And I'll bet that whatever your uncle heard, he knew it was going to be the last bit of information he was going to get, so he needed to finish what he started. That's why he attacked us here. He knew we were going to be at this hotel, and he knew you were going to be here as well."

Don stared at the wall for a moment and then asked, "I wonder if he was counting on you to stop him? So that he could go through the motions but not really hurt anybody, because you stopped him."

Anna stared at him for a moment. "You think he expected me to shoot him?"

Don shrugged. "We won't know until we ask him. Do you think we can get him in here?" There were Las Vegas Police all over the place, as well as several ambulance crews, and as Anna rushed off to check on her uncle Don asked, "Sacks, these people, the ones that got hurt in the blast…"

"The injuries range from mild concussion to fairly serious boss." Suddenly the enormity of what he had done hit Don like a sledgehammer. Not only had he risked the lives of his crew, but the lives of many innocent people as well. "It's my fault they got hurt," he said. "I underestimated the opposition. I never thought they would ever attack us here. There was a chance, but only a chance that someone would take a pot shot at us, but there would be too much risk of being identified in a crowded place. That's why we were going to the Dam this morning, to give them space to instigate their attack."

"Mr. Joyceman?" a tall, strongly built man with a crew cut, a faded blue suit and a badge joined them.

"An alias," Don said. "First Lieutenant Donald Fields, US air force." Don pulled out his fake air force identification and handed it over to be copied.

"Right. I'm detective sergeant Charles Dupree, Las Vegas PD. I'd like to ask you a few questions if I may."

"We'll co-operate with you sergeant, up to a point. Unfortunately, we may not be able to answer all of your questions at this time."

"I'll need some answers at least, and I'll need them quick." Don glanced at Rob and gave him a nod.

"Well detective," Rob said, "It's pretty simple." He took a

business card from his pocket and handed it over. "Lieutenant Robert White, attorney at Law. We are conducting an investigation into some fairly serious breaches of the Official Secrets Act, and subject to the provisions of that act, we will co-operate to the best of our abilities.

"I will admit that we were conducting a sting, exposing two of our own with the expectation that someone from a certain subversive organization would come after them. We had, however, no way of knowing, or even suspecting, that the perp would throw in a grenade; experience led us to believe that the expected assault would be in a much more private location. We know that the hotel has some very sophisticated surveillance, and we registered our presence and our firearms with hotel management, with the full expectation that if we were assaulted it would be in a far more secluded location, with limited to zero danger to the public at large.

"As we see it, somebody committed an act of terrorism, and an armed air force officer shot him," He looked over at Anna. "Lieutenant Fleet, please surrender your side arm to the detective."

Anna did as instructed, first popping out the magazine and clearing the breach. "One shot has been fired. There should be seventeen shots left. My brass will be in the hallway to the left. I was about five meters away, walking towards the subject, because I recognized him. He didn't see me. I was about to call out to him when he took a grenade from his pocket, snapped out the pin and threw it through the door. As soon as I saw the weapon I called his name and he jerked, possibly spoiling his aim. By then I had cleared my weapon and shot him. If you don't know already, he's a cop, though we have enough information on him at this time to have him charged with espionage."

Sacks finished his tailoring on Don's leg and began to bandage the wound. "You do have the right to continue your investigation." Rob continued. "I would if I were you."

"However, if you attempt to investigate us further, well a word of caution. If you think we're stepping on your toes, wait until you see what those schmucks from the FBI and Homeland Security do to you."

"And detective? These people who have been hurt, I don't know what you're going to tell them, but to us they aren't collateral damage, they're people. If you could please arrange for someone to give me a call with an update on their condition, I would appreciate it."

"Detective?" Two ambulance attendants stood at the door to the dining room. "We'd like to shoot this one over to Valley. Looks like he got shot in the stomach."

"I assume you're going to send a uniform with him?" Rob asked.

"What do you think?" said Dupree. "You think I'm stupid?"

"No. I think you're trying to do your job, and I'm sorry to stymie you like this. I'd like to go with him, ask a few questions on the way."

The officer stared at him for a moment, openly assessing him, and then he said, "Fine. Rogers!"

A shorter man in a Las Vegas police uniform came running over. "That's the perp," he pointed at the gurney, "this is a lawyer," he pointed at Rob, making it sound like both were equally guilty. "Go with the two of them to the hospital and keep your ears and eyes open."

Chapter 33

"She said what?"

"She said uncle Bernie had died five years ago," Anna reported. "She said that the man I met may look like him, may sound like him, may even have the same smell of him, but he wasn't my uncle."

"And then?" Don asked. They were all sitting around the table in Don's suite having a meal, though Don didn't know if he should call it breakfast, lunch or supper. The only one actually sitting close to the table was Don, though the rest of the crew were close enough to grab more sandwiches from the platter the kitchens had sent up.

"Then I got on the phone," said Rob. "I told her who I was, and that we were conducting an investigation into Mr. Chisholm's activities and she just broke." He glanced at Anna and sighed. "It seems there were some serious questions about some sexual misconduct a few years ago. An underage prostitute. And then the charges just disappeared into thin air. Which means to me that somebody got to the judge, or the prosecutor, or possibly both. Somebody very powerful."

"Any guesses as to who that might be?"

"No, but it does tell us he's right under someone's thumb."

"Did you get a chance to question him directly?"

"He looked me right in the eye and dared me to shoot him again. Then he asked for a lawyer."

Don sighed. He wanted to sleep, he wanted to go home to the base, find his bunk and crawl in. "Right. The rest of you back to the base, Rob, you're with me. It's 15:00 hours, let's see if we can make Kingman by 18:00."

In the car, Rob pulled a couple of papers from his pocket and passed them over to Don. "I printed this E-mail for you just before we left, after everybody else was dismissed and Sacks was changing your band-aide."

From: General G. Hines
To: Lieutenant Donald Fields
Re: Trial of Corporal David Phillips.

It has come to my attention that you should be advised of the following circumstances.

A general courts marshal has been convened by the Judge Advocate General, charging Corporal David Phillips with one count of espionage against the Government of the United States, one count of violation of the Official Secrecy Act.

Prosecution is proceeding in a military court, but under the scrutiny of the White House, the FBI and the administration of this base.

Corporal Phillips has reached a tentative plea bargain with the government, allowing him to plead guilty, but with the administration of a lighter sentence, probably five to ten years in prison, as opposed to twenty. He admits to selling the information Browning and other sources provided him to one Shridher Deolalikar, who is an associate of Doctor Bali's father, Serinder Bali. Deolalikar is known as a member of an organized crime ring in Delhi. They deal in theft, prostitution, and drugs, not information, so it seems he may have been branching out into new territory.

Deolalikar has also been known to associate with one Valhad Tusk, a polish immigrant to Vancouver, who is also known to be involved in slavery and prostitution, transporting girls from the far east, Poland and Ukraine to Canada, getting them hooked on heroin, or crack and then selling to the highest bidder. Currently, Tusk is out of the country, supposedly on a recruitment drive for his nightclubs, of which he has seven in the lower mainland. (List attached.) Canada Customs is watching for his return and claims he will be arrested as soon as he sets foot on Canadian soil. CSIS has agents at all boarder points, but I have no faith in the system. We have sent requests through Interpol for his arrest in Poland, or any location where they have authority, but again, that would require faith in the system, and I just don't have what that requires.

Don snorted his agreement. He had no faith in the system either. He assumed that if Canada Customs arrested the man, within the half hour there would be a lawyer, or a judge, who would claim his rights had been violated under the charter. Good-bye suspect.

We don't have any ideas as to where Tusk might be passing his information on.

In connection to this, we have also arrested three other corporals on the base who have confessed to related charges, including passing Phillips the visa numbers related to every credit card I've issued you, and your whereabouts each time you were off the base, or out of the country.

Captain Greg Bowes, Canadian Army, has been investigated by CSIS and exonerated. This time I believe them, mostly because I know the chief investigator as a personal friend and I know that he is the ultimate professional.

I'll end on a rather curious note. I have received a message from a Comandante Roberto Lorca Guerrero of the Spanish Benemérita. The letter is in Spanish, but he claims to have hunted down and slaughtered, that's the word he used according to my translation, a certain Paulo Lopez y Garda. He says you will understand why. I assume he was the investigating officer into Lieutenant Hernandez' death. He also mentioned a couple of hints from a Mr. Castro y Hernandez led him to Mr. Garda. Hines, Major General, USAF

They discussed the message for a while, but eventually Rob asked about his day with Hitomi.

"Weird. She would change into a new ensemble every half hour, and take an hour plus makeup to do it. Outside the room she was acting like the blushing bride, and inside like an old married couple. Did you see that dress she wore for supper last night?"

"Uh-huh."

"Wow factor, Mr. White?"

"Wow factor nine, Captain."

"Not a ten, Mr. White?"

"Well, Hitomi's a lovely girl, but imagine if Anna or Tessy had worn that? No, cancel that, I don't want you imagining anything like that about Anna!"

"I'll try and restrain myself, though it's a temptation. Except for those people that were hurt, and I pray none of them dies; I'm glad Chisholm decided to attack us today. She's got an even worse dress she was going to wear tonight, and what was that you said about Tessy?"

"Well, I'll admit Hitomi knows how to dress to her attributes. And I know Tess is the quiet one, but if Hitomi's a nine, Tess is a definite ten and a half. And you didn't notice?

"Fascinating." At it's best, Rob's Spock imitation was lousy, and they both laughed. "So, what are we doing in Kingman, and should you be traveling with thirteen fresh stitches in your leg, and do you think you'll get a purple heart?"

"Don't care about purple hearts. I'm a Canadian, not a Yankee. We are off to see the police chief, the wonderful chief of Oz."

Captain Kevin S Jacobi chose to receive them in his office, "Second floor, corridor to the left, at the end of the hall. Go right in." The sergeant on the front desk pointed to metal stairs that climbed the wall on the far side of the lobby.

Don thanked him and they took the stairs, Don taking more than twice as long as usual. "I should have asked if they have an elevator."

"You shoulda let me bring your wheelchair."

Jacobi stood when they came in, a serious frown occupying his face. "You two here about the allegations against my officer?" he demanded, before they even sat down.

"I," said Rob, handing the policeman his card, "was there, and I saw what he did, and my partner gut shot him as he was throwing the grenade. I would have shot him myself, but she's a better shot than I am. Lieutenant Fields here had a golf ball sized chunk of steel pulled from his thigh about four hours ago, so there's no allegation about it. I've still got blood under my fingernails from trying to help his innocent victims, so knock off the outrage, it's not going to help your cause." Don helped himself to a chair, and Rob took the second. They didn't offer to shake hands, and neither did Jacobi, who slowly lowered himself back into his seat. They had both decided that this interview would go better if they were in uniform, so both young men wore air force dress blues.

"According to our information, about six years ago this officer was charged with a felony, but the charges were dismissed. Why?"

Jacobi threw Rob's card on his desk and purpled with rage.

"Just who do you think you are, barging into my office like this, demanding confidential information about one of my officers?"

Don took a more consolatory tone. "Captain, for now, we are just two officers investigating a case of espionage. We want to co-operate with you, but you can either talk to us, or the FBI. Those are your choices."

"Espionage?"

"We have proof that officer Bernie Chisholm planted an electronic transmitter inside a federal military compound and was responsible for passing the information obtained to a subversive organization. We believe that his earlier misconduct was used as blackmail against him to force his hand today."

Jacobi swore softly, picked up the phone from his desk and punched in a four-digit number. "Jill, I need the Chang file, hot. Thanks."

"Your records aren't computerized?" Don indicated the monitor on Jacobi's desk.

"We came in one morning and this one was purged from the system." It was obvious that the policeman didn't want to admit this, and obvious that he was telling the truth. "We don't know who did it either. I'd had a bad feeling about it beforehand and personally filed a hardcopy in archives under the name Chang. All the evidence disappeared at the same time." He clapped his hands together to emphasize the point. "Bang, everything was gone! I know Bernie couldn't have had anything to do with it, because I had locked him up myself and he hadn't yet made bail. Most of the guys don't even know anything about it, except me and a couple of my senior staff."

An extremely fat, middle-aged woman walked in and passed Jacobi a red file folder, tied shut with a gray ribbon. She didn't say a word and Jacobi barely glanced up at her. When she had left, he untied the ribbon and pulled five sheets of paper out of the folder.

Leaning across his desk he handed the top one to Don, the second to Rob. Don saw that his paper was the arrest report, and Rob's the victim statement. Both were stamped 'charges withdrawn.' It only took him seconds to speed-read the report and then swap papers with Rob. Silently they handed both back to Jacobi, taking a two page investigator's report and prisoner's property report in exchange. Again both officers read through them quickly and handed them back to Jacobi.

"My original question remains captain. Why were the charges dismissed? Statutory rape should have gotten him fired, and at least five years in prison."

"In Arizona, if the offender is over eighteen, and the victim is under fifteen, 13-1405 says the presumptive sentence is twenty years," Jacobi said. "The girl was a good girl, and the perp was a cop, who used his influence and position of power over her. I think judges in Oklahoma have the right to assign the death penalty. Indiana would have given him a minimum of thirty years with twenty more added for aggravated assault. I would have been happy if he only got five years, in open population. Cops aren't too welcome in prison. His odds of survival would have been about nil."

"And why was he released?" Rob asked.

"Because the evidence disappeared, same way it appeared, the victim moved out of state and the district attorney ordered us to forget the charges and put him back to work, under strict supervision of course. He didn't want to get sued for false arrest."

"And you did it."

"Lieutenant White, when you've been in this job as long as I have, you learn to keep your mouth shut and your eyes open. Yes, I saw the proof. I assessed the case and was convinced he committed the crime, at least the sexual interaction with a minor. There was a positive match with the DNA in the sperm. However, there was something fishy about the whole thing, but I didn't know what. It's possible he was deliberately tempted and gave in. He was a weak man, but there are a lot of men who are weak in one way but can do heroic things in another. The beating could have been done by someone else, after he left."

"Quite frankly, sir," Rob said, quite calmly, "I don't mean to sound callous, but I don't care if he is guilty of anything else other than what I saw today. That was enough. What I care about is that he was put in a position where he could be blackmailed. I want to find the person who corrupted him and nail his butt to the wall. I want the blackmailer, which should put you and me on the same team."

"Lieutenant, I don't know if we're on the same team or not, but the district attorney let him go because he was told to so by his boss. John Beale, the attorney general is headquartered in Phoenix. I did some digging into his past and found that he had done four years in the marines before law school. It was fairly hard to get at his records, but I found out that he had been stationed in Japan, actually learned the language and married a Japanese girl about five years younger than himself. I've seen her at a political rally, and she's gorgeous. When he finished law school he moved to Arizona as a public defender, and moved up the ladder from there in leaps and bounds, finely moving to attorney general eight years ago. There has never even been a hint of corruption in his record. I could go no further than that.

"The rumor is he's going for Governor, and he's jumping on a Republican nomination with a law and order mandate.

"That last part isn't public knowledge yet. There's quite a bit of time before he's got to declare.

"Anyway, I don't see how any of this could be relevant to your investigation."

Rob and Don exchanged glances. Finally, Don said, "Captain Jacobi, you've been fair with us, we want to be fair to you.

"Without going into detail, our investigation already shows

us a significant link to Japan and other countries in the far east, specifically India. Part of the pattern we have seen is where women are blackmailed into compromising otherwise decent and upright men. I don't know exactly what you can do from here, but I will be arranging for an investigation into Mrs. Beale's life."

"I know this is awkward, because the victim was a minor at the time, but it would help us to know her name, and present whereabouts, if possible."

Jacobi sighed. "Awkward isn't the word I would use, Lieutenant. It's not legal for me to give you those details, because she was a minor at the time, but I will give you her name, only because of what you just told me. Brahmacharini Chautala. The last I heard of her, she was living with her mother in San Antonio, Texas."

Chapter 34

It wasn't hard to find her. He just looked her up in the phone book at Lackland Air Force Base. "Did you find what you needed, Sir?" the flight sergeant asked when Don returned the book to him.

"Yes, thank you." He glanced over at Hitomi who was chatting with the mechanic checking over their F-22s. General Hines had been most co-operative when Don explained what they had found out. "We'll need quarters for the night, probably fly back to base early tomorrow, if we can get our business finished tonight." He glanced at his watch. 12:00 hours, time for lunch. "Where's the officer's mess?"

"One second sir, and I'll have someone drive you over."

Lunch was slim by Don's standards, but fairly good. Later, picking up a car at the motor pool, they drove to the address he had found in the phone book.

"She's at work."

Don looked down at the diminutive woman and tried a smile. Mrs. Chautala was not making things easy.

"And where does she work, ma'am?"

"What do you want with my daughter?" the woman asked. She wore a rumbled sari and her breath smelled like alcohol.

"I want to talk with her," Don said. "We think she may be able to help us in an investigation. Can you tell us where she works?"

The woman stared off into the distance. "She dances, at a bar." She had to think before she remembered the name. "I think it's called the Gazelle. Stupid name for a bar."

It took them a while, but they found the right bar, only it was called the Pink Gazelle. The hostess however was no Gazelle. "Hey," she snapped as soon as she spotted them, lumbering over to the door. "We don't allow lookie loos! Get otta my bar!" She looked Hitomi over and shrugged. "She can stay, you can't. Freaking voyeurs!"

Hines had arranged for both officers to be given credentials identifying them as special investigators for AFISRA and Don flashed his now. "Not voyeurs. Investigators who want to speak to one of your staff. We can do it quietly in a corner with no fuss. I would prefer that, and I think you would too. I'd like to keep this as low profile as possible." He glanced over the crowd and saw maybe three dozen women, all shapes, all ages and all colors. "Your call."

"Cops?"

"We would prefer to leave the cops out of this," said Hitomi. "They messed it up the first time, and we're trying to fix what they screwed up. We want to chat with Barhmacharini Chautala. Probably just five minutes of her time, that's all. Then we leave and you go back to business as usual."

The woman thought for a moment and then pointed to a booth near the kitchens. "You both buy drinks, you buy Barbie a drink. You get ten minutes." Then she lumbered off to the bar, where she spoke to a pretty, skinny waitress dressed in short shorts and a flimsy halter-top, with lots of long black hair, worn straight. The waitress spoke to the barkeeper and then brought three whiskeys to the table.

"I'm Barbie," she said, sitting down opposite them. "What do you want?"

Don introduced himself and showed her his credentials. "A few days ago one of the women in my team shot Officer Bernie Chisholm in the stomach," Don said. "At the time we expected him to live, but he didn't survive for more than twenty-four hours."

Her face twisted at the news, but ended up in a smile. "Good. I hope he was in horrible pain when he died?"

"He was," said Hitomi.

"Though I doubt it means as much to you as you thought it might."

"I don't think you have a clue about how I feel. My mother was born in a brothel in Calcutta, and I was born in the same room fifteen years later. One of her customers took pity on her and brought her to America to be his live-in concubine, and she did it, for me. As long as she slept with him he kept me in school, food and clothing, but he wouldn't marry her. He wouldn't give her an ounce of self-respect. When I was fourteen, he decided to put me on the street to earn some cash, but I went to the police, and I met officer Bernie Chisholm. Funny the way things go, huh?

"Officer Bernie did things to me, things I'll never forget, or forgive. He's dead? Good! Are we through? I want to go celebrate with some of my friends."

"No, I want to know who rescued you from Chisholm. I want to know who gave you the money to move away from there," Hitomi said, "And as long as we're feeling sorry for ourselves, I too was blackmailed to seduce someone, but when I went to the authorities, they helped me, Lieutenant Fields helped me.

"We know for a fact that the people who helped you escape also set you up to run into Chisholm in the first place. They didn't care about you, or anything else, they cared about getting their hooks into him, so they could force him to betray his country. Now, will you help us catch the guys who did this to you, and to me?"

Chautala looked from one of them to the other for a long moment. "Not a word of this leaks out," she said at last.

"Agreed," said Don, and Hitomi nodded.

"There was this lady, I don't know her name, but she was Japanese, like you. She was married to some attorney. She gave me fifty grand and told me to get lost. We came here and put a down payment on a condo, and I've been working here at the bar ever since. We didn't have enough money, and I was tempted to start turning tricks on the side, cus I was only a freshman in high school, but Lulu told me if I'd dance nights as well as tend tables, she'd take care of us. I finished an accounting course in college last spring, but I owe Lou so much I just can't leave."

Don glanced around and for the first time spotted a couple of glass cages, designed to look like whiskey tumblers sitting on a platform on the far side of the room. "Is that where you dance?"

"Yeah. The back of the glasses are hinged, and there are about eight of us waitresses who dance for the crowd every night, taking turns. Sometimes a richie girl will give us a tip to start dancing early, but the show don't start till about eight."

Hitomi took a business card out of her pocket and wrote on the back of it in careful Japanese. "If you ever want to get out of this business," she said, handing over the card. "Drop into this address. The manager is a friend of mine."

Chapter 35

A week later the Leer dropped from overcast skies to land at Vancouver International. Anna, Pam, Tessy, Will, Don and Hitomi climbed down from the plane, stretched and piled into the two waiting cars, Anna, Pam and Will in one car, Tessy, Don and Hitomi in the other. Jezebel had downloaded maps to their portable GPS units and they had no problems locating the first stop on the tour, a condo apartment owned by Valhad Tusk, located near UBC. It was locked of course, but Tessy punched the lock, and Anna disabled the alarm. Still, they moved quickly, searching the suite, donning hair nets, cloth booties and latex gloves in the hallway first.

None of the crew wanted to be here, each of them knew that what they were doing was illegal, and every crewmember in the unit had volunteered. They should have been back at the Intrepid, testing her engines. Don glanced at his watch, it was 13:30 and they should be just finishing lunch and starting their normal after lunch bull session. Instead, a call had come to General Hines, saying that Tusk had been arrested by CSIS. His lawyer had taken less than the predicted thirty minutes to get him free and no more than a day to have the charges dropped. Don hadn't been able to sit back and accept that. He just wasn't, so he had picked five members of the crew and flown to Vancouver.

Each crewmember had a specific room to search, and had been given very precise instructions on how to search, and what to search for. Soon they found a safety deposit key and a thumb drive, both secured inside an electrical outlet. Tessy had made the discovery and brought it into the office, where Don and Will were carefully separating Tusk's computer from it's peripherals, loading it and every paper file they could find into boxes they had brought with them. "Looks like we've got what we want boss," she said.

"It does," he agreed. "But let's keep working."

A few minutes later they heard a vacuum start up in the hallway, and knew they had to get moving. When Tessy had punched the lock it had left a hole in the door, and if the maid noticed and called the police they were done for. Don took a quick look around the living room and knew it would never pass even a casual glance by the maid, so opening the door was out of the question, and there was no way they could hurt the woman. She was innocent of any crime. He was about to ask for suggestions when Hitomi stepped up to the door, glanced through the peephole, opened the door a crack and slipped out. Instantly Anna took her place at the door.

"Everybody grab your boxes," she snapped, and the crew obeyed. "We go down the stairs on the count of three, two, one." She opened the door wide and scrambled down the hallway to the stairs, the crew following her, Don trailing the rest, carrying Hitomi's box as well as his own. Hitomi met them on the street, jumping into the back of Don's car.

"You got rid of the maid?" Tessy asked.

"Told, horrible mess, third floor, come quick, clean," Hitomi said. "Stayed on elevator, walk out." She smiled at him. "Use Italian accent. She no remember Hitomi,"

Yeah, thought Don, she no remember Japanese girl who speak with bad Italian accent. Right. Who was trying to kid who?

Halfway to their next stop Don spotted a motel that offered Internet connections and quickly rented a room. Then he installed Pam and Tessy in the room with two laptops and all six boxes of data taken from Tusk's condo. "Search for what you can find, and contact us if you find anything. The name of his bank would be great."

They were heading down South West Marine Dr. toward the Knight Street Bridge when Don made his big mistake. Looking ahead, he noticed a car racing towards them, followed closely by two police cars, their sirens howling. Without thinking he fishtailed his rental car sideways to the road, and Anna, following behind, copied him. Moments later the car screeched to a stop, the driver's door flew open and a man scrambled out, trying to run, but two men had already jumped from the first police car and tackled him.

"Name?"

"Fields, Donald, Lieutenant, United States Air Force, in Canada on vacation."

"Yeah. Why'd you stop the perp, Fields, Donald, United States Air Force, in Canada on vacation?"

Don fished his id from his wallet and handed it over.

The cop made a face, "Special investigator for AFISRA? Whatever that is. Cute, but you're in Canada. Now, why'd you stop the perp?"

"Air Force Intelligence, Surveillance and Reconnaissance Agency," Don said, trying to keep the anger out of his voice. "It says so, right there on that paper. It means I'm a cop, much like you, only on a different scale. I saw a police pursuit and my training sprang into operation." As soon as he said it he knew he shouldn't have said anything about scale. The cop's frown deepened.

"When did you get to town, Mister, on a different scale?"

"Officer," said Anna. "Did we do something wrong by helping you out, or is there some other point to this? We're here on vacation, checking out your beautiful city, and you're going to roust us just because you can?"

The officer looked at her and a faint smile touched his lips. "Lady, there's something about you four that seems wrong. I'm not sure what. You all claim to be Air Force officers, but his accent," he gestured at Will, "and her accent," he gestured at Hitomi, "They don't fit. In Canada, sure, you bring an accent to Canada and you keep it to the end of your life. In the US, you loose that accent tout-sweety, especially if you're in the armed forces. The only accent that sounds real American is yours. Where you from, Idaho?"

"North Dakota."

"Bingo. If the three of them spent four years in an American military academy then I'm deaf, blind and mute."

"Nonsense," said Hitomi, and her accent was Parisian French. "You may have a good ear for voices, but you were not listening to what Lieutenant Fields said." Suddenly her accent was English. "We're intelligence agents. We can sound like anybody we want to sound like! If you want, I can do Liverpool instead of London, or how's this for Glasgow? Not bad would you say?"

"Pretty good, actually," the officer admitted.

"The other point," said Anna, speaking with a definite Spanish accent, "About our being intelligence agents, is that our backgrounds are secret. You could arrest us, and take us in for questioning, but soon enough CSIS is going to come knocking on your door and explain to you that you just embarrassed them. Now, we were honest enough to explain to you who we are, and why we're here and what we're doing here. Everything up front and legal. If you want to waste your time, and ours, you know what to do. If not, we're going to get back in our cars, drive back to the airport and fly to some country where the police respect foreigners who are willing to help." Turning her back she walked over to her car and got in the driver's seat, Will only a step or two behind her.

Hitomi grabbed Don's arm. "Come on lover, we are so outta here."

"I blew it, totally. That cop was good, with good instincts. He didn't know what we were up to, but he knew we were up to something," Don admitted to the general when they landed back at base.

"Well, I knew it was a risk when I let you go. You probably want to know that Jezebel went over the contents of that thumb drive, and we found he's paying rent on two properties the cops weren't aware of. One was a unit at a self-storage facility where the RCMP found a large stash of addictive drugs. Evidently he's trafficking, as well as using them on his own girls. The other was a farm down in Langley. It was a brothel, with seventeen women, addicted to cocaine, held in sexual slavery. Unfortunately Tusk escaped, but when Jezebel searched his hard drive she found some archived copies of his E-mails. He was passing information to a man named Grzegorz Chmielewski, don't ask me what it means, or if my pronunciation is anywhere near correct.

"We've traced this Chmielewski to Poland, and the Policja are raiding his apartment in Łódź any minute now. It seems they were very anxious to co-operate with Interpol when they knew Tusk was luring young women out of the country to be used as prostitutes.

"Obviously, working with Interpol leaves us wide open. Anything can leak, and probably will, so it's time for you to get back to work. The rest of your crew have been doing some clean up, but I think it's time we actually tested the engines on the ship, don't you?"

Chapter 36

They had, of course, driven past the circus tent on their way to the barracks the night before, but it had been dark and they hadn't actually stopped to look at it. The first thing that Don noticed now was that it was no longer a tent. While they had been gone in Canada, the poles and guy wires supporting the canvas cover had been removed, as well as the walls, though the canvas roof itself was still in place, lying loose on top of the ship itself.

The second thing he noticed was that the ring of guards around the site had been doubled, and when he looked up he saw two fighters circling the field as cap, with two more on standby on the runway. "Are they expecting an attack?" He asked Rob as they pulled their hummer up close to the Intrepid.

"Nothing specific," his exec replied, parking the truck and climbing out. "But I guess it's important to always be careful."

"I suppose," Don said. "All this extra security makes me nervous, like telling an actor good luck before opening night. It's bad luck, because the general is assuming everything is going to work. What if we give it a little juice and nothing happens?"

"Then we trouble shoot until something does happen."

"Yeah," Don said, and picking up his briefcase and laptop,

he made his way to the access hatch, followed by the rest of the Intrepid's crew. Inside, each person found his or her place quickly, Rob disappearing down the corridor on the first level, to take his position in the reactor room, followed by Xiang Wu, who was acting as his assistant. Next Sacks broke off to his emergency station in the infirmary. The third to split off from the main group was Anna. Her launch station was at fire control in the armory, but before she left she grabbed Don's arm and kissed him on the cheek. "For luck, Captain," she said, and disappeared inside.

In the main control room, Jean-Paul took his place at co-pilot, and Hitomi sat in the left seat as pilot, but not before she had herself kissed the Captain for luck. Don, blushing now, took his seat in the command chair and got blindsided by Tessy, who also kissed him before taking her place at the reactor controls, Don looked over at Will, who had taken his place at navigation and was answered with a quick shrug of the shoulders. Pam was next, taking her place at communications and then Jezebel, who quickly took her place at computer control.

"Everything ready to proceed?" demanded the general over the two-way radio, and Don was glad that Pam hadn't yet turned on the video feed.

"Everything here is just fine, sir." The video screens around the room flickered to life, showing a three hundred and sixty degree view of the desert, interrupted only by the hangers and a few distant buildings on the base proper. "We were just wishing each other good luck."

"There's no such thing as luck, Lieutenant," Hines said, but that wasn't what Don was thinking about at all.

"Stations check," Don ordered.

"Reactor on line," Rob said over the headphones. "Rod one unlocked and ready to be pulled, electrical output is minimal. Radiation in the reactor room is negligible."

"Infirmary ready," said Sacks.

"Armory ready," said Anna. "Pa is on line, all missile tubes are secure."

"Navigation ready," said Will.

"Power control ready," said Tessy, and Don noticed she was blushing too, which made him feel good.

"Computer on line," said Jezebel. "Junior has control and is conversing with Sister, Pa, and Grandma. Diagnostics show all four lobes are operating within guidelines."

"Communications on line," said Pam. "Transponders activated. Video and audio feeds five by five. All ground personnel have been cleared from the field."

"Co-pilot ready," said Jean-Paul. "All outer doors have been closed and sealed. I am green across the board. Initiating pressure test." For a moment all was silent as the pressure inside the ship built above normal. "Pressure holding. Hydraulics up and running." Jean-Paul flipped a switch and the pressure returned to normal. "Ship is ready to launch."

"Pilot ready for countdown," Hitomi said. "On mark."

"General," Don said into the microphone attached to his headset, "We are ready for launch. Request removal of the canvas cover, sir."

A moment later four trucks, attached by ropes to the canvas cover, pulled away in four different directions and the Intrepid stood totally exposed to the sunlight for the very first time. "Cover removed," came the response from the headset. "Chase planes launched."

"Acknowledged," said Don. "Guys, this is for Juanita, and for Daphne Hale, for Sarah Franks and for Andre Dupuis, who all died to make this ship a reality. Pilot, prepare for launch. Power, on my mark, pull your first rod to twenty percent power."

"One rod to twenty percent power, sir, on your mark," Rob replied, and Tessy made ready to duplicate Rob's action from bridge control.

Don eyed the clock on the display before him and counted off, "In three, two, one, mark, power to twenty percent."

For a long moment nothing happened, and then like a smoothly operating elevator, the Intrepid shot up from her resting place. "One thousand, five thousand, twenty thousand, fifty thousand meters and climbing," reported Hitomi.

"Power to minimal," snapped Don, calmly. "Reverse power, slowly! Bring her to a stop if you can."

"I make us to be about fifteen hundred kilometers out," said Will, a few moments later, "and we have come to a halt." He glanced at the chronometer and announced, "That took us about ten minutes."

"Nice. Ninety thousand kilometers an hour?" Don asked.

"Well, a bit more sir, we've been braking for seven minutes. I calculate we were probably going about a hundred and fifty thousand when we started braking." He glanced around. "You know, at that speed, we could make it to the moon in four and a half hours. Just in case anybody's interested."

"But we'd be awful hungry by the time we came back," said Don. "The only food on board is coffee, and that's only one of the three main food groups."

"Three main food group?" asked Hitomi, her eyes never leaving her console.

"Coffee, ice cream, beer and pizza," said Anna, appearing in the doorway. "Usually we leave out the coffee, but the Captain doesn't drink and neither does Rob, so they sub coffee for the beer."

"Ah, make joke. Understand. Three main food group, like sake, rice and squid."

"Yeah, well my main worry right now is breakfast. Ham, bacon, eggs, sausage, toast and coffee," said Don. "I know I should have eaten this morning, but I couldn't, so now I'm starving."

"You and me two," threw in Anna. "Breakfast that is."

"You and me three," said Rob over the headset.

"Mountain Bluebird, 1899?" came a thin voice over the headsets. "What's your twenty? Repeat, where are you?"

"Base, this is Mountain Bluebird, 1899."

"ES Intrepid has exceeded expectations by an incredible margin, sir. Request permission to re-calibrate controls and practice maneuvering before returning to base. I'll have navigation give you our co-ordinates so you can redirect your radars.

"Hitomi, work with Rob, Will, and Tessy to try and put us into a synchronous orbit with base. Jean-Paul, I need an environmental assessment, including air pressure. And, can anybody guess why we still have gravity in here?"

"Can I ask one question?" Jezebel asked.

"Which is?"

"Do you always bring this much luck when you get kissed by five beautiful women, or was it just a fluke?"

"Well, we'll just have to try it again some time and see," Don said. It just slipped out, his words totally out of control, and for a moment he felt a deep sense of shame. And then Jezebel smiled gently and gave his shoulders a little hug, patted him on the head and murmured, "In your dreams big boy, in your dreams!"

Chapter 37

L anding the Intrepid was far easier than takeoff. With the controls recalibrated for actual power as opposed to estimated power, Hitomi brought the ship into her new landing area behind the hangers with just a kiss of the now extended landing skids to the ground.

"Ground floor," Jean-Paul intoned as they settled. "Coffee shop, ladies and men's clothing, curious onlookers and senior officers. Exit to your left, mind the doors, mind the step, mind the armed guards."

"What was that, Mister Golden?" Hines said over the intercom.

"Ah, nothing sir, I had thought that the intercom was closed. Sir."

"Very good. Attention all crew members, meet me for lunch at the officer's mess. My treat. Oh, and Don, don't forget to lock the doors behind you."

"Sir, yes sir." Don felt a wave of tension just flowing out of his body, glad to be back on solid earth, yet at the same time already missing the glorious freedom of space.

"No, sir, it didn't hit me until I looked up from my instruments and saw that every screen was filled with the blackest of nights and thousands upon thousands of stars. Stars without number, Sir.

"Once we had the ship under control and on cruise, the entire crew went upstairs to the lounge. Then we opened the shutters over the skylight and just stared out through the glass at the stars. Sir, you have never seen anything like it. You've just got to come up and see what we have seen. It's like staring at the naked elements of creation."

"And you say you still felt gravity, the full time you were up there?" Captain Hale asked.

"Everywhere inside the ship, sir. I'd say it was way less than half that of Earth. We didn't have the precise instruments to measure gravity inside. We measured it outside, and there was a weak pull from Earth, but almost negligible. It was an incredible ride sir."

"And nobody had difficulties with motion sickness, anything like that?"

"No sir," Don had convinced the cooks to whip him up the breakfast of his dreams, scrambled eggs, a slab of real honeyed ham, eight rashers of bacon, several sausages, a huge mound of home fries, toast and coffee that tasted almost as good as home. He paused to take several bites and drink his coffee. All down the table his crew seemed to all be eating the same thing.

"No breakfast lieutenant?" Hines asked, eyeing Don's heaping plate somewhat skeptically.

"How could I eat this morning, sir? My stomach felt so tight it thought I was going to be sick, until I sat in the chair, and then everything became clear, and we launched."

Hines nodded. "I've been there, except when it was me, I was jumping out of an airplane into an active combat zone. Speaking of which, I need your crew to prepare themselves for a mission."

Don put down his fork. "A combat mission, sir?"

"Quite frankly, I don't know. After lunch I want you to all report to hanger C for final fitting of your space armor."

"Space armor, sir?"

"Yes. Then I want you to stow the suits on board your ship and set about provisioning your vessel for a three month tour."

"Sir?"

Hines lowered his voice. "A certain astronomer has brought a piece of information to my attention. Now, this astronomer and I have a history, which reflects on your vessel's history." His explanation was cut short by the sudden roar of a phalanx, followed moments later by a second. Don jumped to his feet.

"Action stations, move it!" he shouted, and almost immediately there was a loud explosion from outside, followed by sudden silence.

Racing through the door of the mess hall he almost collided with Anna. Moments later they were able to see a cloud of black smoke, not more than a thousand meters from where a crew were busy trying to camouflage the Intrepid. "Boss, Pa must have shot down a missile," Anna yelled at him. "Here comes another! Incoming!"

Without hesitation, Don followed Anna's lead and dove for the dirt, even as the two phalanx gun platforms on the starboard side of the Intrepid opened up again, the brass shell casings spraying away from the guns in a huge arc. A moment later there was another explosion, and Don, with the rest of the crew, hauled themselves up from the dirt and sprinted towards their charge. Inside, they each raced to their action stations, leaping to their consoles and powering up for instant take off. As soon as Tessy, the last crewmember to arrive, dove through the hatch, Sacks slammed it shut behind her and Jean-Paul reported a green board. "Launch," Don snapped from his chair, and Hitomi did, slapping the controls into a fast accent, even while Rob pulled two rods to maximum. Almost instantly they were in space.

"Engineering, pull the power," Don ordered, and saw the indicator on his screen drop to less than a quarter rod. "Hitomi, bring us back to low orbit." He donned his headset. "Guns?"

"Guns," said Anna. "I have laser tracking online. Unauthorized aircraft forty miles south of our last position. Turning away, transponder non operative."

"Put it on screen. Hitomi, I want that plane to have a big black flying saucer right up his butt, now!"

"Aye sir. Mister White, I need two full rods for a five second burst, then reduce to one rod at twenty percent, on my mark. Mark." Instantly the Intrepid began to curve back towards Earth, at a lightning speed, and then began to slow and swing down through the atmosphere, finally coming up behind a US Air Force F-22. "Captain, that's one of the planes we flew to Texas! It's based at Nellis!"

"Understood. Pam, get that pilot on the radio!"

"Captain, he's punched out," Hitomi announced.

"Follow him down. Anna, grab me two vests and P-90's, we'll pick them up as we go by. Rob, leave the reactor room to Lucky Wu and get up here, you're in command of the ship. Tess and I are taking a walk. Tess, you're with me, let's go!"

They jumped from a dozen feet up, hit the ground and rolled, bouncing to their feet and raced towards the collapsing chute, where the pilot of the F-22 was struggling to free himself.

"Move again," said Don, placing the muzzle of his P-90 against the pilot's knee, "and you're a cripple." The pilot froze, and Tessy reached over to remove the gun from his shoulder holster. Then she pulled a double pair of plastic handcuffs from her vest, connecting the man's wrists together with one pair, and his wrists to the pilot's seat with the other. Finally she unhooked his flight helmet and pulled it off.

"Captain Golden?" Don demanded when the man's face was revealed. "What are you doing? You just fired on an American base!"

"What do you think I was doing?" the marine snarled. "I was trying to destroy that ship!"

"But why?" Don demanded. "Have you no idea how this will

benefit mankind? Have you no idea what a great achievement this is?"

"Achievement? It's nothing, just a copy of a copy!"

"What do mean by that?" Tessy demanded.

"Don't you know?" Golden asked, his eyes laughing at them. "Oh, this is precious! Nobody…" His words cut off as a machine gun started to rattle. Don and Tessy hit the dirt. Overhead there was the swoosh of a small missile and then an explosion to the east. The sound of the machine gun was abruptly cut off.

"I think I got em, boss," came Anna's voice in his ear.

"Ten-four, keep your eyes open and your finger on the trigger." Don rolled to his feet. Golden was a mess, one round had destroyed his side and another had blown both his hands off, the left at the wrist, the right at the elbow. Tessy instantly began applying tourniquets to both stumps while Don began stuffing padding from his first aid kit into the wound on the major's side. "Sacks, we need you down here. Tessy and I are all right, but there's a man down!"

"Bringing the ship down," Hitomi announced, and the Intrepid seemed to drop from the sky, it's main hatch sliding open only feet away.

"On three," Don said, "One, two, three." Tessy grabbed Golden's flight suit on one side while he grabbed it on the other, lifted him and shoved him through the hatch. Then they scrambled up and into the ship, slamming the hatch behind them.

Chapter 38

"Sir," Sacks and Don both came to attention and saluted General Hines.

"Stand easy," the general said. "What happened?"

"Sir, Marine Captain Golden died on the operating table. His time of death was approximately 01:38 this morning, sir."

"I understand. I will arrange for notification to his next of kin. Did he say anything before he died Lieutenant?"

Don opened his mouth to tell about when Golden had said the Intrepid was a copy of a copy, but before he could speak up Sacks said, "He did mutter something, Sir. He cursed the men who shot him, claiming they had no loyalty. Then he said something about being in their pay for five years, and what had it got him?"

"Five years?" said Hines. "Most of this technology hasn't even existed for five years!"

"Sir," Don interjected, "Major Golden also said that the Intrepid was merely a copy of a copy. I get the part about being a copy. You told us that most of the products we used were copied from alien DNA. But what about the double up, a copy of a copy? Does that ring a bell with you?"

"No, unless, you've probably figured out that Lieutenant

Hernandez was the original test pilot, flying a jet fighter where the wing tanks had been filled with the engine liquid. I wonder if," he snatched his phone from his desk and hit a speed dial button.

"McCowan, I need the number to contact Professor Romero y Lopez." He paused for a moment, waiting for a phone number. When the number came he scribbled it down on the back of a business card. Abruptly, he hung up and dialed the international code and then the phone number. What followed was fifteen minutes of loud Spanish, sometimes calm, sometimes excited, and once, very angry.

"The absolute moron!" was the first thing Hines said after smashing the handset back down onto the cradle. "Why, why, why, was I so stupid as to trust that idiot? Do you know what he did? Do you have a clue as to what he did?"

"I think he didn't follow protocol for disposing of samples, sir," Don ventured. "I could understand some of what you said, but not all of it."

"He took a small piece of goop, and built a radio controlled airplane around it, as a gift for one of his grandchildren," said Hines, enunciating each word with painful accuracy. "Not only did he let a piece of incredibly secret information out of his grasp, he gave it away. He put it in a model airplane and gave it to a twelve year old child!"

"Ah, sir, does the child still have the airplane?"

"He's checking." The phone rang and Hines snatched it up. "Hines. What? No puedo creer esto! Sabes que vas a ser educado en el cargo! Que nunca trabajar para los militares de EE.UU. de nuevo, y si puedo, me veras en la cárcel!" Hines was literally shaking with rage when he hung up the phone. "The grandchild entered the airplane in a contest. The authorities claimed he was cheating and confiscated the plane."

"What happened to it, sir?" Don asked.

"He thinks it was sent to Spain for analysis." Hines sank slowly into his seat. "Mr. Shackle, you're dismissed. Thank you for your assistance in this matter. Fields, you stay, we've got some things to discuss."

"I know this could be problematic for you lieutenant, but I would like you to go back to Spain. Take Fleet, Thewes and White with you. Tanaka will drop you in a field and we'll arrange for a local contact to pick you up."

"I suggest Comandante Roberto Lorca Guerrero of the Spanish Benemérita, sir. He's already somewhat aware of the project."

"Very good. You've all moved your kit aboard and the ship is provisioned?"

"Yes sir."

"All right. I want you to take a couple of days to see if you can figure out what happened to that sample. If a dangerous biological product were imported into Spain without a permit it would be against the law. If there was a permit issued then it should be easy to trace. See what you can find out. Then I want you to take a quick trip to the moon and see if there's something fishy going on there. I have it from a reliable source that something, and I don't know what, has been seen moving around the edge, from the light side to the dark and vice versa. Dismissed."

Outside the administration building, turning his back to the cold February wind, Don called Rob on his cell phone and asked him to organize the trip. Then he made his way across the square to the offices of the Air Force Security Forces. Returning the crisp salute of the blue beret at reception without stopping, he made his way down the hall to the offices of the Ravens. Opening the unmarked door beside interrogation room three, he politely greeted Captain Hall. "How's she doing, sir?"

Hall turned down the volume on the speaker mounted below the window that looked into the next room. Pam, dressed in a dark blue power suit, complete with white shirt and tie, sat across the table from Corporal Workman, who was wearing an orange jumpsuit.

"Nothing yet Lieutenant. They've just gone over her background. I think Workman's lying, but Ms. Wright seems to know what she's doing. Did your crew get all the stuff I sent over stowed away?"

"Yes, sir. We're primed to lift at a moment's notice. I've read about how the submarines went out during the Second World War, but I never thought I'd find cases of canned fruit beneath my bunk, sir."

"It happens to the best of us son, and canned fruit is at least good for you and not tempting." He reached over and turned up the speaker.

"Now, Jill, I need you to tell me who you were working for when you were at CFB Nanaimo," Pam asked.

"Shouldn't I be telling the Canadian authorities this?" Workman asked. "What authority do you have? You don't even sound American."

"I'm not. Please answer the question." Pam was keeping her voice calm and light, as though she was laughing at a joke inside that she could not share.

"I want a lawyer."

"And I want to win the lottery. Tough. Life goes on. Please answer the question."

"I said I want a lawyer!" Workman was no longer quite so sure of herself, but not panicking yet.

"And I don't care what you want. Please answer the question." There was a touch of steel in Pam's voice now, though it was still light and non-threatening.

"Hey, this isn't legal! I'm not answering any of your questions until I have a lawyer!"

Pam made a notation on her pad. "What you don't understand is that you're not getting a lawyer. You're not getting the due process of the law. What you're getting is life in prison, in solitary confinement, until death, with no parole, or death by injection. Or, you can talk to me. Personally I don't much care which."

"You cops can't do this to me! I know my rights!"

"Ah, well, you're wrong on two counts. The first one is, I'm not a cop. There are no policemen watching this interrogation, and it's not being recorded. Nor is there an officer of the court watching this interrogation. Ergo sum, until we release you back to the police, you have no rights, and when we do release you, you won't be able to prove that this interrogation ever happened.

"Speaking of rights, you have rights under whose laws? The US? You didn't commit a crime in the US. If they had you, which they might not, all they could do under law is hold you for extradition. Do you have rights under Canadian law? Well yes, but you and I both know that both Canada and the US will deny that the flight you tried to bomb ever happened. The FBI agents who picked you up have been told you're being held for extradition, the Air Force crew that blindfolded you and flew you here have returned to the States. Nobody knows who you are, or where you're being held."

"Oh, I understand there's a Captain Bowes in the Canadian armed forces who wanted you for desertion, but he's not looking too seriously, since he recently resigned his commission and took a job in the private sector. Nope, sorry. Nobody outside this base knows you exist." Pam smiled pleasantly and Don was glad it wasn't him facing her across the table.

"You're lying to me!" Workman said, but Don could hear uncertainty in her voice.

"Of course," admitted Pam. "The problem is, you don't know which points I'm lying about. Do you want to take the chance? Now, I'm going to make you an offer, and it's a one-time offer; you don't get a second chance at it. Are you interested?"

"What's the offer?" Workman asked, regaining some of her former self-confidence.

"I asked, are you interested?" said Pam, quite calmly. "I did not invite questions."

"Of course I'm interested, you moron!" snapped Workman, and Pam calmly leaned across the table and slapped her hard across the mouth.

"Insults will get you hurt," Pam said. "I hold your life in my hand. If I grow tired of you, the offer is withdrawn. You will tell me everything you know about this conspiracy. Everything. Names, dates, places, goals, accomplishments, everything. In return, I will see what I can do to help you. I'll make no promises however."

"That's it?" Workman asked, bewildered.

"Yes. Awful, isn't it? Now, who are you?"

"My name is Regina Douglas. I'm from Toronto. I was a first year programming student at Seneca collage when they approached me. I was broke and I couldn't finish paying off my tuition."

"Who approached you?" Pam asked, making a note of the name.

"They never told me their names. It seemed they had been trying to recruit an army corporal named Jillian Workman, but she had died. I looked quite a bit like her, and I was the same age. I also had some training in computers, so they thought I could maybe pass for her. They offered to pay my bills and send me to UBC to get my degree, so I agreed."

"Did you know they were planning an act of espionage?"

Douglass closed her eyes. "Yes."

"Did they tell you how Jillian died?"

"Somebody pushed her in front of a subway car. I don't know if it was in Toronto or Montreal. They said if I didn't co-operate with them it would happen to me. I gather the body was a mess, and had my identification on it. They took me to the cemetery and made me watch my funeral from a hundred yards away. There weren't very many people there."

"Then they flew me to Vancouver and set me up with Captain Bali. I don't know how they got onto him, but Lucy Browning was the brains of that outfit, not Bali. He had something over her, but she was the smart one. But there was something strange about her. She couldn't talk it, but she could understand Hindi. I know cus every once in a while Bali would say something in Hindi and she would answer him in English, as though nothing had happened."

"Did you ever find out what they were working on?"

"No. I had a guess, but I never knew for sure. By then I just wanted out, but there didn't seem to be any way out."

"Who was your contact in Vancouver?" Pam asked.

"Valhad Tusk. I never knew what he did, but a couple of times he brought some sleazy looking women with him when he met with me. One of them called him Valhad, and one of the goons he had with him called him Mr. Tusk. I don't think he noticed, because he never let on, and I just filed the names away for later."

"Did Tusk ever let on who he was working for?"

"No."

"How many times did you meet with him?"

"Six, or seven, I'm not sure. I wasn't in the inner circle, and didn't know much about the details of the project, but I passed on what I knew. When I told Tusk we were going to the States he gave me the suitcase, with the bomb, and told me to plant it on the plane. He had a car waiting down the road, and by the time that plane took off one of his goons was driving me down to Sidney for the ferry ride back. I didn't trust them, and managed to get away from him on the ferry, just before it departed and grabbed a bus over to Victoria. Then I snuck on board the ferry to Port Angeles. I just about got caught getting off, but I made it. I've been living in the states under the name Susan Clifford ever since."

"And there's nothing else you can tell me?" Pam sounded very disappointed.

"No. Wait, there was something. When I told him we were going somewhere in the States, he made a call, overseas I think. I think the woman who answered spoke in Italian, or Spanish, one of those languages." Having broken her barrier, Douglas now seemed to do everything she could to please.

"No names?"

"Ah, yes. The woman must have passed the phone to someone else, because Tusk called him Señor Calderón, and was yelled at in Spanish. Then Tusk said 'Yes, yes, Señor De Borbon. Let's just get on with it! What do you want me to do?' I thought it was funny because Tusk had forgotten the man's name."

De Borbon Calderón. They had a name. A Spanish name. "Captain Hill?" Don said, knowing in his heart that what he wanted to do, and what he was about to recommend were two separate things. "My suggestion is that you blindfold this young woman, put her in a car and drive her into California someplace. Pull over to the side of the road and tell her to get out. Then drive away."

Chapter 39

Jean-Paul brought the Intrepid down in the middle of an empty field eighty kilometers north of Madrid. Rob disembarked first, followed closely by Anna, Tessy and Don. All wore jeans, hiking boots, warm sweaters, caps and jackets. They also carried their Glock 18s in shoulder holsters and AK-47s in steel attaché cases. Rob glanced at the GPS unit he carried. "The road is about a hundred meters that way," he pointed east. "It's nearly 01:00 hours, and we should expect Comandante Lorca to meet us about two kilometers down the road at 01:30, so we should get a move on."

"Agreed," said Don. "Everybody watch your footing in the dark, and for pity's sake, anybody spots a bull in this pasture, speak up, got it?" A dozen times since they had left Nevada behind them, Hitomi had teased him that she was going to find a pasture full of fighting bulls to drop them off in, until he had gotten nervous, with the possibility that she just might do that. She made no excuses about the fact she wanted to go with them, to take Tessy's position, but Don was having none of it. General Hines had told him whom to take, and so that was who he was taking.

He was getting tired of Hitomi's constant attempts to compromise him. She said she was acting under orders from the mysterious friend of her family, but Don doubted that she had heard from him since Las Vegas. He had never been happy with the idea anyhow, nor had he really forgiven her for her abrupt assumption of his authority in Kingman, though he tried to hide his true feelings from her. If the choice had been his, Tessy would have been top of the list to come along. Anna was with Rob, and she didn't have to act a part at all. Pam and Jezebel, though both remarkable women, would have stood out for being too much older than him, and he had wanted to get to know the quiet girl from Luxembourg better.

Not that he had any sort of personal interest in her, but he had discovered when doing her six month evaluations that he barely knew her at all, and he didn't think that was fair to her, or to the unit. So, when Hines had told him whom to take into town with him he had simply said, "Yes sir." And now he was watching out for bulls.

"Sir?" Tessy had grabbed his arm in the dark. "Watch where you're going to step." He looked down and noticed a darker spot in the grass. "I think that's a cow patty."

"Yeah. Hitomi might not have found a bull, but she found the next best thing. Thanks Tess." They continued in silence for a while and quickly found the fence, which thankfully, wasn't difficult to climb over. The road, a rather narrow, obscure back way, was hard pressed gravel, running for miles through open fields and scattered patches of forest, scattered oak and beech, interspersed with pines. It was bordered on both sides by grass filled ditches and pole fences, which were sometimes covered in bush, sometimes not. Occasionally they would pass a driveway with a cattle gate and occasionally a log and wire fence gate. The air was redolent with the smell of cattle and their byproducts. The temperature was fairly cold, and Don was glad for his duffle jacket and cotton gloves.

"I thought," said Tessy, "That Spain was supposed to be hot." She blew a cloud of frosty breath. "That is not hot."

"I'd guess it's at least three or four below," Don said.

"It's not that cold," said Rob from in front of them. "I'd say it's only about twenty nine, or thirty."

"Right. Fahrenheit. Good for Americans only. Us cultured folk back here are talking in Celsius."

"Metric shmetric," said Rob, and pulled up short at a crossroads. "This is where the Comandante is supposed to meet us," he said. He looked at his watch. "Anytime in the next five minutes."

"I'll bet that's him," said Anna, pointing at a pair of headlights coming from the south. Easing her Glock from its holster she slipped off to the side of the road. Tessy, without instructions, drew her AK-47 from its case and moved off to the other side. Then Rob stepped behind a tree and disappeared in the night, leaving Don alone on the road to meet their contact. When the older Mercedes pulled up, the driver turned off the engine, rolled down the window and turned on the interior light.

"Señor Lorca?"

"Si. Are you alone? I thought there would be others."

Don raised his arm in the all-clear signal and the others all hid their weapons and joined him in piling into the car. Lorca started the car and did a u-turn, driving back towards Madrid. "So tell me," said Lorca. "What are your plans? What do you hope to accomplish here in Spain? What is your goal? How can I help you?"

Don had thought about this moment for two days, and still hadn't decided how much he could tell the policeman. "About three years ago, just outside Mexico city, a child by the name of Amando Perez Lopez was flying a model airplane in a contest sponsored by El club Teledirigido del Vuelo de Madrid," he said. "One of the judges confiscated his plane, saying he was cheating, and brought it back to Spain. We need to find out what happened to that model. The man who made it had access to some very sensitive products, and he foolishly incorporated one of those products into it, and the people I work for want it back.

"As you know, the people I'm working for include the governments of the US, Canada, and Spain.

"The date of the contest was July twenty seven, the judge's name was Señor Aquilino Carrión de la Peña.

"Also, we are looking for a man named De Borbon Calderón. I don't know his first name, but he is working in association with two men, named Valhad Tusk and Shridher Deolalikar. They're into drug smuggling and human trafficking."

"El club Teledirigido del Vuelo de Madrid?" asked Lorca. "I've never heard of it, but then I'm not into model airplanes. De Borbon Calderón I may have heard of. There is a Roberto De Borbon Calderón who works for El Ministro de Asuntos Exteriores. He's known in police circles as a pretty bad man, but slippery, like he's coated in fish oil. Do you understand what I mean?"

"Yes. Do you have any idea how we should proceed?"

"Si, I do. First we will get you to Madrid. I've made reservations for you in the name of Jack Macy at a small inn in Alcobendas. It's right near the metro station Marqués de la Valdavia."

"We'll book you into the hotel, and then I'll go back to headquarters to begin searching for connections between Roberto De Borbon Calderón and a man named Tusk. When you've rested, check the phone book for hobby shops. I doubt El club Teledirigido del Vuelo de Madrid is listed, though you can look it up if it is. What I think you should do is ask at the hobby shops if they know anybody associated with the club. You brought laptops? Good. Check to see if the club has a website, or a link on a website associated with one of those stores."

When they had rested for a few hours, Anna and Tessy booted up their computers, since they were the two who had the most Spanish. Though both Don and Rob had been doing their best to absorb the language as quickly as possible they still felt they would be prone to miss something that might be important. Twenty minutes later they had a list of thirty-two shops in different parts of the city. Some of them had web sites, some did not, and none had a link to El club Teledirigido del Vuelo de Madrid.

"So tell me why we're not just phoning the hobby stores?" Anna asked.

"Ever been in one?" Rob asked in reply. "I don't think I've ever seen a hobby store that didn't have some sort of bulletin board where hobby clubs come in and post their meeting times and dates. If we phone, then you might get the model railroad guy, who doesn't care a whit about your airplane. On the other hand, we drop in and Tessy smiles at the guys behind the counter and asks them what they know, and you my dear, find the bulletin board and check to see what's listed. And Tess, don't forget to ask about Señor Aquilino Carrión de la Peña. And can somebody tell me why all these dudes have got fourteen names? How'm I supposta remember alla dese names masta? It weird mon!"

Anna grabbed him by the ear and marched him towards the door. "It's simple," she said. "Carrión was his father's last name, and de la Peña was his maternal Grandfather's last name. Get it? You would normally call him Señor Carrión. The rest is …" He cut her off by picking her up and kissing her. Don exchanged glances and shrugs with Tessy and they marched off to check out the stores.

The first six stores were a dead loss. One had been closed for over a month, two had only a few cheap plastic models in stock, one was for model railroads, and two were only toy stores. Store number seven had a sign advertising the bi-monthly meetings of the club, but no phone numbers. Store number eight was a dead loss, but store number nine, at the extreme south end of Madrid, just east of a metro station called Buenos Aires, was where they hit pay dirt.

It was a small shop, overstuffed with merchandise, but clean and neat, wedged in between two large buildings that nearly made it disappear from view. The floor was worn white linoleum, the shelves had served other purposes before being used to display model airplanes, and there was a bulletin board beside the glass front door, advertising El club Teledirigido del Vuelo de Madrid would be hosting a model airplane show and meet in April. "Hola," said Tessy in Spanish, walking in out of the blustery wind and smiling at a gray haired man in his middle fifties.

"We saw the sign for El club Teledirigido del Vuelo de Madrid, and we were wondering if you could tell us anything about it?"

"I could," admitted the man, rubbing the end of his nose with a fingernail. "I'm the treasurer. Was there something specific you wanted to know?" He looked around the store and back at them. "I've got the time. There are no customers here."

"Well, we're looking for a member, a Señor Aquilino Carrión de la Peña. Do you know him?"

"Our president. He's in the phone book."

"With fifteen other men of the same name."

"True. Could you tell me why you want to reach him?" the man sat down on a stool. "After all, he's my friend, and you are, well, four tough looking foreigners. You could be planning to hurt him. I'd be a poor friend if I told you how to find him without checking."

Tessy looked at Don, and Don nodded. "If you doubt us, you could check with Comandante Roberto Lorca Guerrero of the Benemérita. He's the man who told us how to look for Señor Carrión."

The man hesitated. "The Benemérita. They are not to be played with."

"We know."

"Has my friend done something wrong?"

"We don't know. A while back you sponsored a meet in Mexico. There was a boy there with a plane that had been given to him by his uncle. Unfortunately, the uncle had included something in the plane that he should not have put there. Señor Carrión thought the boy was breaking the rules and confiscated the airplane and evidently brought it back to Spain. We're looking for that plane, a Messerschmidt Bf 109. It's about one meter by point nine meters, and maybe twenty-five centimeters tall."

"Like that one over there?" All four officers turned and looked at the airplane hanging from the ceiling.

"Is that it?" asked Don in his halting Spanish.

"Yes, though the piece of sponge you're looking for is not there." They all turned back to the man behind the counter. "We flew it a half dozen times trying to figure out what made it go so fast, and then we found that if we didn't even turn on the engine it would still fly if electricity were applied to the sponge."

"And what happened to the sponge?"

"We sold it," said the man after a moment's hesitation. "To a biologist, at the university."

Chapter 40

"How could you possibly sell something that never belonged to you in the first place?" asked Anna.

"What ever gave Señor Carrión the right to confiscate the airplane?" asked Tessy.

"Guys!" snapped Don. "It's done." Switching to his fumbling Spanish he asked, "Señor, who did you sell it to?"

"Get out of my shop before I call the police!" the man snarled, but the four didn't move. Don caught Anna's arm and squeezed it, caught Tessy's eye and nodded.

"If you wish to call the police, be my guest," said Tessy, deliberately keeping her voice calm. "I suppose the charges will be theft, transportation of stolen goods across an international border, and espionage. That would be good publicity for your little shop, wouldn't it?"

The man stared at them for a long moment. "Espionage? How could we be charged with espionage?"

Tessy looked at him like he was an idiot. "Well, you send someone to Mexico to steal something that happens to be top secret, in both Mexico and Spain, and then you sell it to the highest bidder. That's how."

"And you're investigating this?"

"Yes! Like we said before, in conjunction with the Benemérita. Actually, Comandante Roberto Lorca Guerrero is helping us. We could have worked through Interpol, but we thought this would be more, well, discrete, but Señor, people have died because of that sponge! We need the name of the man you sold it to, and when, and we need that information now!"

The shopkeeper looked horrified, but nodded, took a pencil from his counter and wrote down a name and address on the back of a business card. "Professor Benedetto Delgado y Aguilar. He's a biologist at Universidad Complutense. He was at a match. We sold him the sponge over a year ago."

"Thank you," said Tessy. "You may hear from the Benemérita, but for your sake, I hope not."

Outside, they checked their map of Madrid, quickly finding the address listed. It was just outside the university grounds. Don checked his watch. "It's close to lunch. Let's grab a bite and then head over there."

"I have a suggestion," said Anna, over a quick lunch of Tacos bought from a street vendor and eaten in a park. "We think this address is Aguilar's home. It's possible he's there, but he could be at work. Why don't Rob and I head off to the university and see if we can locate him, while you two hit this street address? We'll cover twice as much ground."

"All right," said Don. "Check in with me every hour, call me ASAP if you find him." His phone rang and he answered it as they left. It was Comandante Lorca.

"Lieutenant. We have discovered a link between Roberto De Borbon and Señor Tusk, and we are glad that you brought it to our attention. It seems that De Borbon has links to an organized crime ring that we never suspected. How are you doing?"

"Well, sir, it seems the men who brought the plane to Spain sold the secret to a university Professor, a man named Benedetto Delgado y Aguilar. He's a biologist. Rob and Anna are going to try and snoop around the university. I'm taking Tessy and we're going to his home address," Don said.

"Good," said Lorca. "Keep me informed."

"Yes sir."

On the metro ride towards the Professor's address Tessy looked troubled, and Don asked her about it. "Tess, are you all right? You're looking kind of worried about something."

She gave him a half smile. "I don't usually let people call me Tess, sir, but it sounds all right coming from you." She paused. "Sir, I don't know you very well, and I don't think you know me that well either, but Anna and Pat and Jez and I, well, Anna and Rob took off because I asked them to. We sorta took a vote and I got elected to tell you, but I don't want you to think I'm telling stories out of school."

Don closed his eyes and shook his head, rubbed his forehead, and then his neck, opened his eyes. "It's about Hitomi, isn't it?"

"Yes, sir, it is." Tessy seemed to shrink inside herself a bit, but it didn't stop her. "Sir, she's been going around claiming that the two of you, well, not that you're a couple, but that the rest of us should stand back, because she's going to *take* you.

"Sir? It seems, well, disrespectful, sir. I know, we all saw that dress she wore in Vegas. It was designed with only one intention in mind. Sir. We know, or, well we really don't know, but we're trying to understand what you've gone through lately, and, well, we're concerned about you. Sir."

Don grimaced, tried to think of what to say, failed. "Tess, you don't need to call me sir all the time.

"It is true Hitomi has tried to seduce me, well at least seven times, by my count. She has not succeeded and I'm determined she won't. I know that it's throwing a division into the crew, and I don't quite know what to do about it. Personally, I find it more than annoying. I don't know what your childhood was like, but I was the guy who never fit in. Everybody else in my school, in my life, had little slots they could fit into, I didn't. I didn't have many friends my age, though some kids tried, and I tried. It just didn't work out. I never had a girlfriend until Juanita came along. Suddenly here was a girl who thought like me, had the same experiences like me, and she had suffered the same way I had. From the beginning we had everything in common."

"Subsequently, Juanita was shot, and I thought my world had turned to sand beneath my feet. But, by then I had several friends who had also gone through what I had gone through, people who understood me. I hope I can count you as one of those. Then, wham, Hitomi came into my life and made it strange! First she wanted to dominate me one way, and now she wants to dominate me another, but I'm not going to let her. You have no idea how angry I am with her, and yet I have to let her be for a while. I've ordered her to stop, but she won't, saying it's a matter of personal honor. Hopefully, it will lead to someone from Japan who is connected to the people who are fighting us here."

"That's what was supposed to happen on the trip to Las Vegas, though it didn't." He looked up as the train pulled into a station. "Our stop."

The address they had led to a narrow, picturesque side street and a second story apartment, reached by a wrought iron spiral stair. "Doesn't seem to be anybody home," said Don, after they had knocked twice. He tried calling the number on his cell. Inside they could hear a radio playing, and the phone ring, but nobody answered it. Don cut the connection and called Rob.

"The university says he stopped showing up to teach classes about six months ago," Rob reported when the call went through. "He was all excited, and claimed he was about to reap millions, and then he disappeared. They sent people around to his house when he stopped coming in, but there was no answer."

"See if you can find out if he had a buyer for his discovery."

"No joy boss, we already tried that."

"Ok, meet me at the house. It's closed and locked, but I've got a bad feeling about this. I think I'm going to ask Lorca to call in the troops."

After he hung up the phone, Don made a quick call to Lorca, and five minutes later there were two very grim police constables climbing the stair. Don introduced himself and the heavier of the two men nodded. "We have been briefed," he said, and taking a lock pick from his pocket he proceeded to unlock the door. Neither Don, nor Tessy had to ask what happened when the door was opened. The smell told them everything they needed to know.

Chapter 41

"So he was dead?" Will asked, sipping his coffee from a covered steel mug. The Intrepid was drifting along at ten thousand kilometers an hour as Don held a debriefing in the main control room.

"Had been for several days," Tessy said. "The smell was so strong I was surprised that the neighbors hadn't complained. Fortunately, the police let us go after only a few questions. They didn't even ask to see our passports." He took a breath. "Probably the Comandante had something to do with that."

"So, where does that leave us?" asked Pam. "I think it lets us conclude that the opposition we're facing is highly organized, will stop at nothing, including murder and espionage, uses, but may not include, Bali's people and Tusk, and that they have a working prototype saucer that may be as functional as our own."

"I think that goes a little far," said Don. "They may have the sponge, but I don't think they have anything else, especially the Nano technology to build the saucer. As a matter of fact, I really doubt they have a saucer like we do. My money is on they don't, but the safest way for us to proceed is to assume they do.

"Therefore, Hitomi, I want you, Jean-Paul and Lucky to

collaborate on six, no eight, evasive programs. If I give you a number from one to eight you will have one of these programs assigned to each one of the eight programmable keys on your console. I want to be able to go through a complete set of evasive maneuvers with the touch of one key.

"Rob, somebody stays at the engineering console twenty-four seven. I want to be able to go from zero to top speed in an instant. I know our top speed is fast, but theirs could be just as fast, though I don't know their power source. Hopefully they can't react with our speed.

"Anna, I need a variety of missiles ready in each launcher. They may have the same capabilities we have to absorb radiation and heat, they may not. The first missile we launch will be a heat seeker, but we've got to modify it to run by radio signal as well. As soon as we spot them then we can teach the missiles to recognize the shape of their ship, or ships. At the same time we'll need anti-missile missiles. Give me something along with the phalanx to knock out their missiles. You have flares and chaff loaded?"

"We have ten flare launchers and ten chaff launchers, each set on auto to fire three rounds. If I trigger them twice, that will give us sixty flares and sixty rounds of chaff. Hopefully that will be enough. Each launcher has a magazine of ten. I've also modified some of the missiles with scraps of sponge from the tank at base. When we fire a missile, it's going to *move*, and have an incredible kinetic force when it contacts. Of course, we've got electronic measures too, but I don't want to deploy them until we're detected."

"Good. Sacks, you'll have to be ready to treat both crew and prisoners alike, for all kinds of injuries, including partial explosive decompression."

"Low pressure we might be able to deal with boss, extremes, well, the victims of complete decompression will be dead before we even get them aboard. I do have plasma supplies, and I can treat any blood type. A reminder to all crew to stop in so I can take another half liter of their blood for their own store might be in order."

"As long as it won't inhibit their ability to fight in the next twenty four hours," Don replied.

"Will, I want you to program me a low level search grid for the far side of the moon, passive receptors only, I don't want to advertise our presence."

"Pam, I want someone on communications twenty-four seven. I want you to search every band, constantly."

"No problem boss," said the suave black woman. "I've already got all receivers sweeping their bands, and programmed to notify me if they pick up any signals coming from the vicinity of the moon, or directed from Earth towards the moon, with an automatic recording of course.

"Jez, I know this is a lousy time to ask, but will the chances of action traumatize our computers? I never even thought of it before, but I don't want them seizing up when they should be acting to save our lives."

"Should be no problem boss," the English woman said, with a brief smile. "I asked them, and they seem to be able to understand what's going on and it doesn't bother them."

"Fine. How about everybody else? Does the prospect of having to fire on real people bother you to the point where you don't think you'll be able to do your jobs? Rob? Anna? Pam? Sacks? Jez? Will? Jean-Paul? Tessy? Hitomi? Lucky?

"No? Good." Don glanced at his watch. "I've got 08:00. Pam, I need you at your station, everybody else please work on the projects I've given you. If you don't have anything to do, we'll need two good meals in the next eight hours, with two sittings at each. I'll be circulating between stations, checking on your progress. At 16:00 I'm turning the ship toward the moon. From this point, all airtight doors are to be kept closed except when in use, all personal items are to be kept secured at all times. There will be strict radio silence observed at all times."

At 15:45 everyone was sitting at general quarters, each in their place, each fastened down in case they lost gravity compensation. No one spoke and instead of the usual good-hearted banter, an eerie quietness filled the ship, a quietness that came from the realization that they were about to go to war. Don pressed the talk button on his mike. "Attention all crew. I see you're at your stations, and I see no reason to prolong the suspense. Hitomi, rotate ship."

"Aye sir." With the push of a single pre-programmed button, the Japanese girl caused the ship to rotate almost ninety degrees, though no one inside felt any movement. The stars seemed to slide away to the bottom of the screens and a full moon slid into place to fill the two forward screens.

"Rob, give me two full rods of power."

Instantly the power display on the engineering panel snapped upward before Tessy turned up an attenuation control on the display, switching to a wider format. "Two rods of power," came the disembodied voice in his ear.

"Full forward thrust," said Don, and Tessy pushed forward a lever on her panel, causing the picture on the forward screens to bulge over the next hour, and then overflow both screens on to the adjacent displays.

"Attenuate the magnification factor to normal sight please," Don ordered eventually, and the size of the moon diminished, but only by about half. "Will, you have laid in a course for us?"

"Aye sir. We'll skim the west side of the moon by a couple of thousand kilometers, and then we'll drop most of our speed and pull down to a thousand meters on the far side, taking videos and photographs as we go. All sensors are in passive mode, but if there's some sort of ship, or base there, we'll spot it."

"Speaking of spotting it, what's that there?" Hitomi pointed to the side of the moon as it enlarged on the screens.

"Mare Orientale," said Will. "These mountains here are the Montes Rook. The outer ones are Montes Cordillera. You can barely see the mountains from Earth, and only at certain times of the month. They're all part of a massive impact basin."

"How big is that?" Jean-Paul wanted to know.

Will had to check his computer screen to answer that. "About eight hundred k, a little less."

"Wow," said Tessy. "The other side has impacts, this side looks like it has acne!"

"Listen up people," interjected Don. "We've got to keep focused. Silence on the deck." Startled, everybody looked at him, and then back to their sensors and controls. Don knew that for a moment they had forgotten what they were out there to do, but it had been his job to remind them. They were here to kill, or be killed. An hour later the magnetometer let out a plaintive beep.

"Silence that sensor," Don ordered in a snapped whisper. Jez was sitting at the scanning console and she quickly moved to obey, though she didn't dim the slowly flashing red led that accompanied it. "Helm, take us down to the deck and reduce our speed to a crawl. Engineering, give me a quarter rod maximum. Jez is there any indication of the quantity of metal detected and it's direction?" the magnetometer had indicated several meteors, but this was it's strongest reaction yet.

"Direction is about twenty degrees to the starboard of our course, twenty five, thirty. We have a fairly substantial mass of iron here Captain." The English woman kept her voice steady, but they could all tell the excitement in her voice. "If we compensate for the mountains between us, there would be ten or twelve tons of iron, concentrated in one spot."

"Is there any movement, or activity around it?"

"None of the other sensors is showing any movement," Jez said.

"Helm, full stop," Don ordered. "Better yet, pull into the shadow of those mountains to starboard, and bring the ship to rest. Guns, phalanx on full automatic." He glanced around the screens and saw no visible threats. "Then come to the control room, please."

It took only a moment for the weapons officer to arrive. "What do you need Captain?" she asked, ducking through the hatch.

"You showed me a small missile back on Earth. You called it your eye in the sky?"

"Sure," she said, "but if we shoot one of those over their location they'll spot it and shoot it down."

"Then I suggest we take a page from Professor Julio Romero y Lopez. Grab an eye, and pull out the rocket motor. Then I want you to put in a chunk of sponge, a battery, a remote control and a bomb. We fly the eye up to the hills above the iron deposit and take a look. If there's nothing there we bring it back and go back on search. If there is something there, well then at least we're forearmed."

Anna grinned. "Two steps ahead of you boss. Your silent eye is ready to launch. I've just got to test it first."

"You," he said, "are an Ace!"

Chapter 42

When they tested it in the hydroponics lab, admittedly the largest room on the ship, the first few moves the modified eye made were stumbling and uncertain, the tail hanging far below the level of the nose. "Oops," said Anna. "The sensors are in the nose, and calibrated for level flight. That's not going to work."

"Is it just the location of the sponge that's wrong?" Rob asked her.

"It shouldn't be. We weighed the missile, and found the center of balance before we taped in the sponge."

"I've got an idea," said Rob, picking up the missile and carrying it back to the workbench. Quickly he used a dime from his pocket to undo the four large screws holding the engine access plate down and lifted it off the body. "Aha!" he shouted, and Don had to remind them to hold it down.

"What do you see?" demanded Anna, and Rob grinned at her.

"The electrodes to the sponge. Look, this pair is too far forward, so the upward thrust is three inches towards the nose. No wonder the missile is unstable!"

"Easy fix then," said Anna, unfastening the alligator clips that held the wires to the sponge and moving them back wards down the body of the sponge closer to where they had marked a pencil line showing the center of gravity for the missile. "And that," she said, "Should do it!"

Don gestured at the controls. "Prove it."

Anna took the controls with a grin, sitting down before the monitor that showed the view from the camera in the nose. First she slid forward the lever that caused the missile to glide up towards the ceiling, and then she let it hover there, perfectly balanced. Then she nudged the forward control and let the machine glide gracefully halfway across the room before she slid a third control to the right, causing the missile to turn in a large circle and float back to where it had started from. Then she gently lowered the machine to the floor and took a bow.

"Well done," said Don, and he grabbed the missile as Rob picked up the control station, Don carrying his burden to the armory, while Rob carried his to the control room, plugging it in near the engineering console.

In the armory, Anna opened the inner door on a launch tube and Don slid in the modified missile. Then she closed the inner door, drained out the air and opened the exterior door. When they had satisfied themselves that there were no leaks, they both moved to the console in the control room. Using just enough lift so that the missile didn't plunge down when it left the launch tube, Anna gently pushed it out into space, using a controlled burst of compressed air.

Don ordered Pam to patch the feed from the missile to one of the main screens and then pointed at a notch in the mountains above them, about ten k away. "Give me a look through there."

With a nod, Anna lifted the missile a dozen feet from the crater floor and gave it some forward momentum, climbing up to the thousand meter height of the notch, and then slowing it down again as she inched it forward. To everyone's great disappointment, there was nothing there but rock.

"Good enough," said Don. "Anna, I understand your baby has a limited battery, so bring it back and let her rest on the roof until we find another large reading. Well done to you and Rob. Jean-Paul, please resume the patrol."

Three hours later they hit another large reading, and this time it was huge.

"Call it a hundred tons, give or take twenty percent," said Jez, tweaking the display at her console. "I'm afraid I can't be more accurate than that."

"It'll do," said Don. Don and Sacks had relieved Hitomi and Jean-Paul at the controls so Don brought the ship down to a soft landing deep in the shadow of a mountain peak. "Anna to the control room, Lucky, please take over guns. Somebody make some coffee!" Ten minutes later they had the drone flying again, this time sliding through a valley that reached just less than three kilometers high.

"What's that?" Tessy said, pointing to a smooth rounded shape. "It's a geodesic dome," she answered her own question, "And a big one too. It's colored to blend in with the rocks, but it's a dome for sure.

"And there's another one. It looks like it's connected to the first one by, wow, there's a whole network of buildings and tunnels down there."

"I wish," said Anna, "That we could just pull over this ridge, drop down and say hello. Maybe just drop in for a cup of coffee. You know, hi, how are you? We were just in the neighborhood, that sort of thing."

"You and me two," said Rob.

"You and me three," said Don, stealing Rob's favorite joke. "You and me three. Anna, forward just a trifle. Everybody sit back for a moment. We've found people living on the moon."

"We don't know who they are, we don't know why they're here. All we know is that someone, probably human, has an advance base on the moon. Everybody take a break and scan your sensors." He kept an eye on the control screen for the missile as Anna inched it forward. "I can see pretty much the main camp now, and I don't see anything that looks like a ship. Anna, switch to infrared."

Anna flipped a switch on her console and most of the screen went dark, with three dull red spots showing the location of the main buildings. "It looks like they're too well insulated boss," she said, her voice tinged with the tension they were all feeling. She switched the screen back.

"Ok. Will, do you see anything on your telescopes and sensors that indicates another ship in the vicinity?"

The navigator quickly flicked through his readouts. "All is calm, all is bright boss."

"And I forgot the mistletoe at home," said Jean-Paul.

"I understand that mistletoe is a parasitic shrub," said Tessy a little tensely, and Don reminded himself to have a talk with Jean-Paul.

"Focus people," he snapped. "What do we do about the colony down there?"

"Sorry, Boss," said Tessy.

"Don?" Pam's voice was quiet, but firm.

"You have an idea?" Don asked.

"I think so. If we have one missile with cameras, how about we send out another missile with relay equipment to the east, call it a thousand kilometers, and then shoot it up to look like a satellite coming from earth. We can send a message through it, using a laser uplink and a radio downlink, pretending to have just spotted the settlement, and then see what happens. We won't even have to use sponge to power it, since a normal missile will look better on their screens. If we get an answer, we go from there, and if we don't get an answer we can work from that angle too."

"Good thinking. Anna, Tess, you're on it. Jean-Paul, you've got the watch. Keep an eye on the base and on Will's sensors. Pam, you've been on the radios for several hours, Will, you've been steady at your station for just as long. Both of you take an hour of down time."

"Hitomi?"

"Need food, Hitomi make."

"Good thinking. Jez, can you give her a hand? I'm not in the mood for rice balls and squid. Sacks, can you handle communications for an hour?"

Chapter 43

They had to move the Intrepid out into space to launch the missile, so they set it to completely orbit the moon once before it would be in position to contact the moon station, and then crept back to their hiding place and used the time left to send their first probe in a complete circle around the station, checking to see if there were any signs of habitation in the surrounding hills. "Nothing there," Anna reported, having completed the task and moving her surveillance missile back to it's original watch station. They were in the tiny lounge, eating the lunch Hitomi had whipped up, steamed salmon, bamboo sprouts and saffron rice. "Either they're very good at hiding their tracks, which it looks like they are, or they're just not interested in exploring outside their little crater. Either way, it doesn't look like there's anybody home, just three low power heat sources, that's all."

"Is there anything to indicate why they are there?" Don asked.

"Questions, questions, questions," Rob said. "Why does anybody go to the moon?"

"Because it's there," Tessy said.

"To search for minerals?" Anna suggested.

"To prepare to go further," said Jez. "It's the first step to the next planet."

"Type it into your Internet browser and you're likely to get a dozen good answers," Rob said, "But why are these people on the moon? What's their rationale for being here?"

"I think they're here to hide," said Tessy.

"Bingo," said Rob. "Keep talking."

"Well, we know that the people we've encountered so far have been pretty skuzzy. Is that a word? I think it is. Anyway, they're bad guys, they're thieves, spies, kidnappers, slave traders, drug pushers, murderers, and who knows what else. Is that base over there legitimate, or is it some sort of treasure cache? Should we be popping over and saying the magic words to get at Ali Baba's treasure? And even if it is stolen on Earth, do we have the right to steal it back on the moon?"

"Tessy!" said Rob, dramatically rubbing his temples and then holding up his hands as if in protest. "It was so simple, and you had to bring the law into it! Wait a minute, isn't the idea of countries on Earth passing laws in space a lot like the Pope dividing the Earth between Portugal and Spain? Seems to me England put the kibosh on that one."

"England, and the Netherlands, and France and anybody else that went out and claimed one of those territories for their own."

"People who own country before Pope, have say," Hitomi interjected. "Like Nippon."

"Enough," said Don. "Yes, I know it's complicated, and we don't just represent ourselves, we represent, what, twenty-seven different nations around the world?"

"Thirty-one," said Anna. "Saint Lucia is the latest signatory to the pact. But at any given time there are about a hundred and ninety two members of the United Nations, not counting the Vatican, Kosovo and Taiwan. So, right now I think we represent one hundred and ninety five nations."

"We have a politician among us," said Rob, "but like the boss said, enough. We could go on forever. Question, do we have the right to take action on the moon?"

"I say we do," said Don. "There are written laws, and there are moral laws." He shook his head to clear out some of the hate and anger that was bubbling up inside him. "It's possible, even probable, that these are the people that killed Juanita, that attacked us over British Columbia, that kidnapped Anna and Jean-Paul in Rio, and I'd love to do nothing but rain down a dozen explosive missiles on those domes. But, the people on the other side of this mountain may be innocent victims, as innocent as our friends. We have to find out who they are, and why they're here.

"Enough talking. Pam, do you have your conversation prepared?"

"Ready." The South African held up a clipboard. "I feel like a telemarketer getting ready to call people at supper, but I'm ready."

"Then let's do it."

"Mountain Bluebird 1899 calling unknown moon colony, come in please." Pam waited for a moment and then repeated her call.

"Do you mean us?" came a female voice from the speaker overhead. "Mountain Bluebird, whoever you are, can you help us? Please?"

Pam waited long enough to simulate the delay caused by the distance from Earth. "Who are you please, and what help do you need?"

"We're prisoners, twelve of us. We are hungry, we have no food! We need to get out of here!"

Pam waited again. "Who's holding you prisoner?"
"We don't know who they are! I don't know their names! I don't even know where we are, though it is strange! Can you help us?"

"Stand by moon colony." Pam released the mike switch and looked over at Don. "Captain?"

"I guess it's time we took the initiative."

It was actually a very simple thing to do. Hitomi, at the controls, lifted the Intrepid high enough off the moon's surface to glide quietly through the mountain pass where their surveillance missile waited, and then she brought it down to a gentle landing right beside an air lock. Xiang Wu and Will put on their armor, and going out through the Intrepid's airlock managed to arrange for the two surfaces to mate, and then Anna led Jean-Paul and Jezebel through the airlock and into the dome. Xiang Wu and Will, on the outside, circled the dome and entered from an airlock on the far side. All five were well armed, with P-90s and Glocks that used ammunition that had been modified to work in a vacuum. They found eleven live women inside, all suffering from obvious malnutrition, and one dead body, a young Asian woman who looked like she had simply given up living. Anna and her crew led the living back aboard the Intrepid and locked them into one of the two main holds on the first level, putting the body in the second hold, along with several unopened cases that they found in a locked storeroom. Meanwhile, Lucky and Will searched the rest of the complex, but found nothing of value. Then they too returned to the Intrepid, and Don had Hitomi return to Earth.

Chapter 44

"You sent for us, Sir?" Don and Rob stood at attention before the General's desk and saluted.

"Stand easy, Lieutenants," Hines said. "Doctor Shackle tells me that ten of your prisoners will live, and that the last young lady will not. He's not too happy about it, but admits there's nothing he could do. He takes his patients seriously, and feels it personally when one dies. It's something I like in a doctor, it shows he's not yet jaded, but it's also very hard on a man."

"Yes sir. Do we know who they are yet?"

"Yes. Seven are from Nepal, the rest were from India. We're looking at about five different languages here, and we were very lucky that one of the Indian girls spoke limited English. Several of the others speak some Hindi, so they could communicate a little, not a lot.

"We're assuming that they were intended to be comfort girls for the crew of the Navarra whenever they were on the moon."

"But why the moon sir?" Don asked. "It's so far! Why not just a base here on Earth? It would be a lot easier to build, and maintain, and why leave the girls to starve to death? It's insane!"

"Insanity is only obvious to the sane young man, and you would do well to remember that," said Hines, but without rancor. "About the only answer I can offer is one you postulated yourself in your report. 'Nobody can hear you in a vacuum.' On the moon there's nobody there to stop them, and like you, there's no restriction on their travels. If they have the sponge, and from the girls stories it seems they do, then they can have their base anywhere they want it."

"Now, from what we've seen on the photographs you've taken of their base, they don't have a reactor, so their ship is working from batteries and solar cells, but it seems pretty well put together all the same." He looked down at the papers on his desk, shuffled through them for a moment and pulled out one, handing it over. "This is your authorization to shoot them out of the sky. It's signed by the President, your Prime Minister, and the President of Spain. If you meet them on Earth you've got to get them out to sea, out of the twelve-mile limit unless you're over one of these three countries. If you're over the US, Spain or Canada, just blow the sucker out of the sky, understood?"

"Sir, yes sir."

"Of course, we have no idea what their ship looks like. We have no idea what it's made of, though we doubt it's a Nano extrusion."

"Well at least that's good news, sir."

"I'm full of good news son. Haven't you been listening to me? You saved ten women from death by starvation, you've dealt a heavy blow to our foes, whoever they may be, you have authorization to blow them out of the sky and," he flipped open the intercom on his desk. "Sergeant, send in Miss Kushnir."

A moment later a pretty blond girl in an unusual uniform walked through the door. "Meet Lieutenant Alina Kushnir, your new exec."

Don stiffened, his world dropping out beneath his feet. "Sir, Rob, that is, Lieutenant White has been doing an excellent job as my exec. There's no way he should be replaced at this time. I depend on him doing his job, and he does it well!"

"Would you hold him back so he can be your exec?" Hines asked, a glint of laughter in his eye.

"No, sir, never!"

"Fine. Next week we're beginning to extrude the ES Resolute. I expect him to train Lieutenant Kushnir, and then take over the prep on his new command."

"Congratulations, Lieutenant White." Hines held out his hand and Rob took it, the grin on his face unmistakable.

"Thank you sir. I appreciate your confidence in me, sir."

"Mister Fields, half of your crew will be moving over with Lieutenant White, including Lieutenants Fleet, Post and Golden. Meanwhile, you will train Lieutenant Kushnir to replace Lieutenant Golden as a pilot. I will be assigning replacement crewmembers to you over then next few weeks. You will also maintain command over the fleet."

"Fleet, sir?"

"Fleet son. We're also taking Captain Tanaka and Lieutenant Lyondell immediately, moving them to fleet tactical until we can extrude the support ship ES Juanita Hernandez. Meanwhile, Tanaka will act as Lieutenant White's executive officer. I hope you don't mind us using the name."

Don felt stunned, with over half his crew suddenly gone, but he quickly found himself. "Sir, no sir, Juanita would have loved the idea, sir."

"Now, your next assignment. In a couple of weeks I'll need you to transport a crew of marines to take over the moon base and hold it. Your job will be to provide logistical and long-range support, which means you will have to be ready for at least two weeks continuous patrol, with the possibility of up to three months. Lieutenant White will go with you until then, but I need him back here on the fourteenth to take command of the Resolute project." He picked up a bundle of envelopes from his desk. "Orders for you and your crew. You have fourteen days. Get Lieutenant Kushnir trained and let her fly the ship a bit, work her into the crew."

Outside, Don gave Rob a high five. "Yo, a ship of your own! Man, it couldn't happen to a better guy!"

"Oh, my life is complete," Rob shouted. "The Resolute, yes!"

"I take it you two are good friends?" Kushnir asked, a touch of sarcasm edging her voice.

"Oh, you bet," said Don, still high on excitement for his friend. "Rob was my exec. We've fought together, wrestled on the floor together, been under fire together. Like I said, couldn't happen to a better guy! Pizza on me tonight, bro! Lets go tell the crew. Alina, we gonna have us a party, and you better come, cus when we has ourselves a par-tee, the more the merrier!"

Hitomi was not happy with the news. "Disappointed, Hitomi?" she asked Don.

"No, I'm proud of you, like I'm proud of every member of my crew! Hitomi, you're getting your own ship! Isn't that what you've always wanted, to be in command?" Don couldn't understand, though he tried. "You're going to be the executive officer on one of Earth's primary defenses! Doesn't that excite you? I swear, there's not a man or woman in the crew that wouldn't give everything they've got to be in your shoes! If this isn't what you want, tell me and I'll see if I can fix it."

"Iiya," she said, "Not fix. Not give Hitomi what want." The Japanese woman got up from the chair and left, stiff-backed, oblivious to the stares of Rob, Don and Alina.

"Women," said Rob with disgust.

"Men," said Alina.

Both Rob and Don turned to stare at her.

"What?" she asked. "Can't you see? The woman has fallen for the Captain. She would be willing to give up her chance at command to be with him!"

"And that," said Don, flatly, "Is precisely why I want her out of here and off my ship!"

"Oh, it is, is it? Well if I'm going to be your exec you better tell me about it, because I'm willing to fight with you, I'm willing to be under fire with you, but I'm not willing to help you break that woman's heart."

"Listen," snapped Don, "If it were…"

Rob cut him off with a hand on his arm. "Buddy, she don't know. You've got hours worth of reports and requisitions to go through, you siddown and go through them. Me and Miss. Alina, we is gonna go for a pre-amble. You don't knows you like ah knows you, so yous just re-lax, ok? Good boy, down. Maybe you good, we gits you a nice strong caffeine afore we come back, ok?"

Don sat, and Rob took Alina by the arm, leading her out of the office. Before the door closed behind them he heard Rob say, "Miss, maybe you don't know it, but this traditional deep water sailor has some really sad news for you. You just stepped right on a rotting squid." But then the door swung shut and Don put his head down on his hands and wept.

The pizza was good. There was an outlet on the base that actually had a very good thick crust pizza, and Rob, as efficient as ever, had ordered several. But the mood was somber, the guests quiet. They all knew that it was their last night together as a complete crew. Hitomi was going, which was not so bad. She had been a precise and efficient crew member, but wouldn't be missed much since she had remained aloof from most of the crew, but Jezebel had been a courteous and friendly crewmate, always ready with a smile or to laugh at another's joke, no matter how poor, and they all knew they would miss her. And in two weeks the crew would be totally torn apart. That sobered everyone, even more than the fact that Hitomi had chosen not to attend.

Chapter 45

"Sir, fifty percent rod available." Tessy turned from her screen and nodded to Don, who was sitting in the left hand seat at the main console. Don looked over at Will and nodded.

"Mr. Post, do sensors show us a clear sky?" Don asked.

"Clear sky, sir."

"Miss. Kushnir," Don said to the young Ukrainian sitting beside him. "You may lift the ship."

"Yes, sir." Alina pushed the slider control along its track, and the circle of screens showing the exterior of the ship showed a flash of mountain, clear blue sky, and then the black of space.

"I thought your jaw was going to drop through the console," Tessy laughed. "Now, is that unbelievable, or what?"

"And you just let me push the throttle to maximum!" Alina turned on Don. "How could you do that?"

"And how else would you want to learn?" Don asked in response. "They tried to teach us to fly every plane that could fly, but nothing prepared us for this." He reached over and twisted the control that altered the thrust from vertical to horizontal. Then he adjusted the ship into Earth orbit. "This isn't like flying an airplane. When we want to land we point at a spot and Will tells Junior that we want to land over there. Junior has more control than you do, and he knows how far away the Earth is, or the moon, and he brings us into a soft landing." He looked at the speed control under her fingers and shook his head. "If you want to manually control the ship, you have to take main power down to ten percent of one rod and then never move your directional slider more than an inch at a time."

"You're serious?"

"I'm serious. When flying the Intrepid, or any of the ships in this class, your slider gives you a percentage of the available power. If you are showing fifty percent rod on the engineering console, to push the slider halfway gives you a quarter rod's worth of power, and twenty percent rod's worth of power is more than enough to launch you into space. If you turn your right hand grip left or right, the ship will turn that direction. If you push it forward the nose will go down, if you pull it back the nose will go up. If you let go, the power to the goop will stop and you'll just coast, unless you're on autopilot of course. This control here changes the direction of thrust, up, down, forward, back, or sideways."

"You're telling me we can go full speed in reverse, while turning the ship around to face in the right direction?"

"While flying upside down. If you wanted to fly upside down that is. And, frankly, it doesn't matter which way is up when you're in space. And you can do it all without feeling almost any motion inside the ship. When we're on Earth, or very close to it, gravity is normal, when we're in space it drops to approximately Moon normal. I don't know why, we have physicists trying to figure it out. The kicker however, is the rods. You can only control the speed in relationship to the number of rods retracted, and you can't shut down with more than ten percent of one rod exposed. If you have a lot of power being generated that that power will be directed to the engine goop, and that means speed."

"How fast can this ship go, sir?"

"We don't know. We built it with five rods, but experience has shown us that the more rod we show, the speed increases exponentially. The math says three rods is about the speed of light. Therefore, this ship is limited to two rods, plus an emergency eighty percent, simply because we don't know what will happen if we cross that threshold."

"Captain?"

"What have you got, Pam?"

"Admiral Hines, for you sir. He says it's private."

"Understood." Don stood up and Jean-Paul slipped into his seat. "I'll take the call in the office." The office was a small cubicle opposite the armory, only a dozen feet down the corridor, a room big enough for only a desk, a chair, a telephone, and Hitomi. She was sad eyed, kneeling on the floor, wearing the seduction dress, and a bomb. There was a paper in front of her on the desk covered with careful Japanese calligraphy, a switch in her left hand, and a long knife in her right.

"Hitomi," he said when he opened the door and saw her, "What are you doing here?"

"Captain," she leaned forward in a formal bow. "Wish to apologize for all trouble have caused. Will cause no more." She shifted her grip on the knife and Don could see that she held it by a piece of white silk wrapped about the blade, the sharp side turned toward her stomach.

"Hitomi, why don't you put the knife down? We can talk." He carefully lowered himself to his knees, conscious of the nearness of the woman, her light scent of talcum powder, and incongruously, the ringing of the telephone.

"No," she said. "Need tantō. Old, Yoshimitsu make, during Kamakura age. Very good blade. Hitomi must cleanse name of Tanaka."

"Hitomi, you don't need to do anything of the sort. There is no stain on the name of Tanaka." Don didn't know what to do. Degrees in math and physics, training in leading men had not prepared him to face a woman who's wound was to the heart.

"And if there is, something you can see but I can not, will your death cleanse that stain? No. You can only cleanse your stains by living." The phone rang again and Don wanted to get up from his knees and answer it, to pass the responsibility on to General Hines, but he couldn't.

"Gaijin not understand. House of Tanaka ordered to take control of ship. Hitomi fail, Hitomi die."

Don rubbed his eyes, but when he opened them again she was still there, her eyes pleading with him to understand, and he did not. The phone rang again. "Hitomi, I've asked you before who ordered you to do this, but you've refused to tell me. Who has ordered you to do this?"

"Friend of family."

"He's no friend of yours!" The phone cut off in mid ring and a moment later Tessy came down the hall to investigate. She took in the scene in a glance, but instead of running back to the control room, knelt on the floor beside Don and bowed low to Hitomi. She said nothing, a look of grim patience on her face. Don glanced at her, angry that she had put herself in danger as well, and then realized that there was nothing either of them could do if Hitomi pulled the trigger on her bomb. The ship would be destroyed and they would all die, whether she was there or not.

"Tessy," said Hitomi, returning the bow. "You stand by your man."

"I stand by my captain," said Tessy. "I am an officer, and my duty is to my commander above all else. I came here to tell my captain that a ship has been spotted near the western edge of the moon, most likely the men who were holding those twelve girls captive. Our mission has been changed from training to seek and destroy."

"Can not allow that," said Hitomi.

"And you will kill yourself and your friends to stop us?" Anna had opened the door to the armory and crossed the hall, and recognizing the danger, knelt down on Don's other side, her hands in her lap, her face neutral. "Look me in the face Captain Hitomi Tanaka. Tell me what kind of honor requires you to kill your friends."

For the first time, Don thought he saw Hitomi waver, but he wasn't sure. "Hitomi, beautiful eyes," he said, "Here are three of your friends, people you plan on murdering in cold blood." He shook his head slowly. "I forgive you, Hitomi Tanaka, and I am glad that when I die I will have three close friends with me, but I still want to know who ordered my death."

Hitomi looked from one to the other, her hands visibly shaking. Finally, she whispered the word, "Tennō."

"Tennō?" Don asked.

"The Emperor," said Tessy. "She believes she was ordered to stop us by the Emperor."

At the mention of the name, Hitomi flicked her eyes to the side, and Anna leapt forward, ripping loose the wire that had connected the plunger in Hitomi's left hand to the belt of explosives about her waist. Don, lunging at the same moment he felt Anna moving was able to grab the Tantō before Hitomi had a chance to plunge it into her belly. Tessy, leaping forward, grabbed Hitomi's forearm and helped Don wrestle the knife from her hand. Then the pair of them held her down while Anna stripped the belt of plastic explosives from her and threw it into the hall. Finally, they sat back and let her go. There was no longer any danger, Hitomi was going nowhere. Weeping, Tessy held out her arms and Hitomi crawled into them and wept with her.

"Pam, get the general on the line please. Sir, yes, there was an unforeseen difficulty. Yes sir, Captain Tanaka was on the ship with a bomb, sir. However, the situation is under control.

"Sir, Lieutenants Thewes and Fields acted with intelligence and calm bravery in the face of extreme danger sir, I will be mentioning them in my report."

Chapter 46

"Doctor Wright, sound general quarters please." Don sat down on the command chair and looked around the bridge as the surprisingly musical gong sounded the alarm. His crew was here, they were all in place, and they had been for the last three hours. The only possible weak link he could see was Alina Kushnir; sitting second seat beside Jean-Paul Golden. The only bridge officer missing was Tessy Thewes, who was guarding Hitomi. Arresting her and locking her up was an order he hadn't wanted to give, but it had been necessary. He wished Hitomi could be sitting beside Jean-Paul, but he knew it wasn't to be, and thinking of Hitomi, he wished he had that Marine guard on board, but they weren't due for another three days. He pushed the button on his console that opened the ship wide address system.

"People, you have no idea how proud I am to be in command of this crew today. You know every one of you has been handpicked to be the best, and I for one believe it. There is someone out there who has stolen some of the technology that created this ship, and while they did it they killed Juanita, they killed Sarah Franks, they killed Andre Dupuis, and they killed Professor Delgado. And they tried to kill many of you."

"Those that have been killed aren't the only casualties. Some of us lost friends and loved ones; many people were harmed in Las Vegas and in the other schemes our enemies have promoted."

"They have declared war on us, and we're going to finish it, now."

"Captain," said Lieutenant Wu. "I have a fast moving blip on radar."

"Where, at what speed?"

"Three oh five degrees, about ten down on the elliptic. A laser bounce gives me fifteen thousand kilometers per hour, about five thousand kilometers distant. Course is diverging at about five degrees."

"Passive sensors only. Do you think they've spotted us?"

"No sir, there's no deviation in course."

"What are the chances they're faking?"

Wu stared into space for a moment and Don let him, knowing that the man was as smart as he was, and trusting him. Finally he said, "If it was me, I would have picked up our radar scan."

"That's what I thought. Pam, any traffic on the radios?"

"Nothing I can detect, sir."

"Guns?" Don spoke into the mike attached to his headset.

"Yes, sir?" Anna replied.

"Do we have a communications missile ready to shoot?" After their experience on the moon they had decided that a communications missile was a handy thing to have along and Don had ordered three prepared.

"Laser intercept? Yes sir."

"Will, give Anna the co-ordinates to intercept any laser traffic between our friends and Earth. Anna, fire your missile now at three oh five degrees, down ten from our present course. Will is going to update your course in two minutes."

A moment later came the thump of a missile being fired from the rear battery. "Helm, please bring us to all stop."

"All stop, sir."

"They've run an active radar scan, sir. Enemy course is unchanged."

"Our missile has intercepted activity on the communications band sir," Pam announced a few moments later. "It seems to be in Spanish, sir, transmitted by laser."

Don cursed his stupidity under his breath. It was something else he should have prepared for. "Right. Recording?"

"Yes sir."

"Alina, get upstairs to quarters and relieve Lieutenant Thewes ASAP. Tell her I need her here, now."

"Yes, sir," the Ukrainian said, jumping to her feet and out the door, but there was resentment in her eyes. Don knew he was going to have to deal with that sooner or later, hopefully later. Leaving his seat he slid in beside Jean-Paul at the helm. It was no more than thirty seconds before Tessy came running through the door.

"Communications!" Don snapped. "Translate that conversation."

"Yes, sir." Tessy grabbed a spare set of earphones from the communications console, dropped into a seat and closed her eyes. Pam flipped a switch to start playing back the recording. "Who do you think you're kidding?" Tessy said. "I'm not a fool. Station one has been compromised; we can't use it any more."

"No, most of the stuff was where we left it, but the girls were gone."

"No, Chechu is moving what's left to station two."

"Are you kidding me? I can barely find it, and I know where it is!"

"I'm almost halfway back. I'll give you a full report when I get there."

"What? I'm not going to kill Chechu! He's my cousin! There's a lot of swearing in Spanish. Yes, I'll go back and keep an eye on him, but he's family, and family keeps together, understand?"

"Ship is turning around Captain. He's coming our way," Will said.

"Thank you, Lieutenant Post."

"Transmission lost sir," Pam turned from her console. "Either the missile has moved past the laser beam, or the beam's vector has changed."

"Lieutenant Thewes, analysis of what you heard?"

Tessy opened her eyes. "I only got one half of the conversation sir, but it sounds like they have at least two ships sir, the one in front of us, and another one on the moon."

"Lieutenant Wu, did you run an analysis of the radar returns Navigation had before I ordered passive surveillance?" Don asked.

"I think their hull is titanium, sir. I also detected a heat signature and radiation leakage from passive sensors. He may have a reactor sir, but it's not shielded as well as ours. If he's not using the same power conversion technology we are, I suggest that his ship is far less efficient. I also think he's less agile, since he's consistently made large turns instead of tight ones."

"Noted. Helm, hold steady until he passes us, and then fall in behind at about two thousand kilometers, building speed slowly. Lieutenant Wu, give us ten percent of one rod."

"Ten percent, Sir."

Moments later, Jean-Paul gently slid the throttle forward to seventy-five percent. "In pursuit, sir."

"Very good Mister Golden. Why don't you take ten minutes while I hold down the shop?"

"Captain!" shouted Wu. "Five rods! We've got all five rods retracted!"

Don grabbed his mike. "Rob, scram that reactor! Now!"

"Captain, speed is increasing."

"Rob!"

"One million miles per second. Ten..." Don didn't wait, but

plunged out of the control room door, raced along the corridor to the ladder, jumped down and ran to the end of the hall, sliding around the corner and charging toward the reactor room. Suddenly the ship shuddered, knocking him off of his feet. Pulling himself up by the handle on the reactor room door he shook it and realized it was locked. It took several seconds for him to punch in his over-ride code and swing the heavy door open.

"Rob!" he shouted, seeing his friend lying motionless on the floor. He wanted to go to him, make sure he was all right, but could not. Jumping over to the reactor control he flipped up the cover and then slammed his fist down on the big red scram button on the board, cutting the power to the electromagnets holding the control rods out. Instantly the magnets released their hold and the five rods crashed home with an audible thump, driven by huge emergency springs. Then the lights went out, followed a few moments later by the red lights of the emergency battery backup switching on. Don grabbed a spare headset from the control board, flicked the switch to emergency intercom. "Medic to engineering!" he was saying, even as Sacks came running through the door and dropped to his knees beside Rob's still body.

"I've got a pulse, and he's breathing. His pupils dilate."

"What happened?" Don snapped, even though he was sure he already knew the answer.

"There's bruising on his neck," said Sacks. "I'd say he was held in a choke hold from behind."

"How long will he be out, and will there be any permanent damage?" Worry for his friend was the only thing that kept Don from rushing out and looking for Hitomi, though his fingers itched to be around her neck.

"Anywhere from a few minutes to half an hour, depending on how long the blood was shut off to his brain. I think he'll be fine, but I can't tell until I do a complete exam."

"Oh my head!" Rob struggled up to a sitting position a few minutes later. "That madwoman, I'll kill her!"

"Who?" Sacks demanded.

"Hitomi! How'd she get loose? I thought Tessy was guarding her?"

"I needed her in the control room, but I sent Alina to cover for her." Don keyed the mike on his headset. "Lieutenant Kushnir to engineering, now!"

"Rob, I need power, now."

"Hold it," interjected Sacks. "He's off the duty roster till I check him out."

"Lieutenant Wu to engineering, on the double," Don barked into his mike. "Attention all hands, Lieutenant White has been attacked. He's all right, but we think it was Hitomi that attacked him. Be on the lookout for her, and if you spot her, be careful." He started to set the reactor board for restart, and a couple of moments later Wu burst through the door and started working quickly beside him. Since it was a relatively simple matter to reattach the magnetic couplings, they had twenty percent of a single bar in no more than five minutes.

The intercom buzzed in his ear, the signal coming on his private channel. "Fields."

"Golden. Sir, Will tells me we're well out past the orbit of Mars, a couple of dozen degrees below the elliptic. Request permission to try and bring the ship to a halt using two and a half rods."

"Granted."

"Sir, Lieutenant Thewes would like to speak to you."

"Put her on."

"Sir, she requests to meet you in the office."

Don bit his lip and said, "I'll be there in a few moments."

Chapter 47

Tessy was already there when he walked in. "Sir, please close the door behind you."

Don did, a sinking feeling in his gut.

"It's my unfortunate duty to report that when the ship went into massive acceleration, and you left the bridge to deal with it, I went to check on the prisoner. Somehow, Captain Tanaka escaped custody. From the evidence, I believe Captain Tanaka convinced Lieutenant Kushnir to set her free. Possibly to use the facilities, I don't know. It looks as if the Lieutenant was attacked from behind at approximately 14:30 hours and died almost instantly with a knife thrust to her throat. At 14:38, airlock A blew open with a massive decompression. I have scanned the video footage of the incident and Captain Tanaka was in the airlock when it blew."

Two more crewmembers dead. Don had to bite his lip for a moment before he could allow himself to speak. "You think Kushnir set her free?"

"Sir, there was no sign of a struggle at all, and, I'm not trying to speak ill of the dead sir, but the Lieutenant was, ah, inexperienced. She believed that the Captain had a point, and I don't think she took guarding the prisoner seriously. I don't think she believed that the Captain was a serious threat."

Don gestured to the computer on the desk. "Can you show me the footage from the airlock?"

"Yes, sir." The officer sat down at the computer terminal and typed in several commands. A few moments later a picture appeared on the screen, showing the inside of the airlock. While they watched, the inner door cycled and Hitomi ran into the small room, her hair disheveled and her gown marked with a large bloodstain. Sealing the door behind her she lifted tear filled eyes to the camera and then pushed the lever that opened the outer door. Then she was gone, and the ship automatically closed the door and recycled the airlock.

"It doesn't get any easier, does it?" Don asked, more to himself than to Tessy. The shock of what he had just seen made him tired, made him just want to sit down and stop being. Period.

The sound of Tessy's voice pulled him back. Watching the screen he had almost forgotten that she was there. "No sir, it doesn't."

Don picked up Hitomi's death poem from the desk beside the computer screen; it's careful calligraphy defying his ability to translate. "And there's two more lives I've lost, because I sent the wrong person to guard a dangerous killer. How can supposedly smart people be so stupid? How could I be so stupid? Do you know the answer to that Tess? I don't."

Tessy looked up at him and shook her head. "Don, people, even the smartest people, are ruled by their emotions more than by their minds. It doesn't matter who you sent to guard her, Hitomi was going to escape, and she was going to die. It was her choice, not yours. You sent Alina because until she was fully trained, she was useless on the bridge. I would have done the same. Even you can't lay these deaths at your door. That really would be stupidity, and no, you aren't stupid."

"People have died, yes, but ours is an inherently dangerous

profession. It's our job to put ourselves in danger so that others may live. Those ten girls we saved on the moon are free today because we were willing to risk death to save them. Don't ever forget that. And we're going to save others, you, me and the rest of this crew."

Don looked down at her and tried a half smile. "Now you're sounding like Rob," he said, shaking his head, "but you're much prettier than he is." The words just slipped out, and he instantly blushed and turned away, opening the hatch and stepping through, leaving an astonished Tessy as the sole occupant of the office.

On the bridge he was far more professional. "Mister Post, report!"

"Sir. I believe we're about seventy four million kilometers from Earth. It took you about six minutes to shut down the reactor. Taking into account the rate of acceleration, a guesstimate would put our maximum speed at one point one."

"One point one what?" Don sank down into his chair, knowing the answer, but having to ask the question anyway.

"C. The speed of light."

"That's impossible."

"The difficult we do immediately; the impossible takes a little longer."

"The Air Force motto, I know. Helm, have you brought us to a halt yet?"

"About another two minutes sir."

Don picked up a headset and connected to the infirmary. "Sacks, how's our patient doing?"

"I'm fine," Rob answered from the door behind him. "He wanted to make me rest for a day, but I told him I wasn't having any of it."

"I can't guarantee his efficiency," said Sacks, "but I'll return him to duty if you want him. I know how short staffed we are."

"I knew there was a reason I liked you," Rob said. "I'll be in engineering if you need me boss."

"Hold it," Don said. "Take the engineering station here. Lucky's got the reactor room up and running, and I'm not letting you out of my sight till I'm one hundred percent sure you're ok."

"Mister Post, do we have a return solution for the moon yet?"

"Yes sir, Junior has the numbers, and we're ready to launch on your order."

"Time frame?"

"About an hour and a half, sir."

"Lets do it."

They parked the Intrepid a thousand kilometers from the moon, high above the dark side and again began their search for signs of life. Two weeks later, Don was just about to order Jean-Paul to return them to Earth to drop off Rob and pick up the marines, when Pam spotted movement on the scanners. "We have a vehicle launching from the surface," she said, and everyone leapt to their battle stations.

Will checked his instruments. "Sighting confirmed," he said, recording the co-ordinates.

"Everyone play it easy," Don ordered, slipping into the co-pilot's seat. "We've waited two weeks, let's not spook them now. Guns, launch a surveillance missile to the launch co-ordinates. Pilot, I want you to follow them, but first duck under the horizon so nobody on the ground sees us going in their direction."

"Missile away," said Anna in his earphones.

"Tracking," said Jean Paul. "Engine room, I need a half rod please."

"One half rod," repeated Rob. "Acknowledged."

"Increasing speed," said Jean-Paul, sliding at right angles to the path of the other ship.

"Bring her about," said Don, as soon as the mountains had cut off direct sight of the moon base. "But keep about five hundred klicks back." He used the co-pilot's main screen to pull up photos of the launch site. "Look at this, wow. If I didn't know for sure that a ship had just launched from that site, I would never imagine that there might be a base there."

"They did an amazing job of hiding it boss," said Tessy, leaning over for a look. "What's that over there?"

"Looks like a cave," said Pam, who had moved back to her station. "But I doubt it's natural. I think they must have carved it out of the side of the mountain. Look, this over here looks like a slag dump."

"Captain, target one has cleared the eastern edge of the moon and is on a trajectory for Earth," Jean-Paul reported.

"Track him till we know where he's going."

"Yes sir," said Jean-Paul, and for the next half hour everything was quiet on the bridge.

"Target two has launched," Anna said. "He's accelerating quickly."

"Can you follow him with the missile?"

"Negative sir, he's moving too fast. Also, we're losing telemetry from the drone."

"Park it if you can, we'll pick it up when we come back."

"Captain, it looks like target two has pulled in behind us, about five hundred K back. I think we've been made, sir."

"I concur. Pam, set a radio on the frequency we heard them talking on before."

Pam worked her console for a minute and announced. "Frequency set. Reception and transmission available at your station, sir."

"Mountain Bluebird 1899, calling unidentified ship entering Earth Orbit, identify yourself," Don demanded, but there was only a burst of static in response.

"Unidentified ship, we have designated you as target one. If you do not identify yourself we will shoot you out of the sky. Do you understand?"

In response the unidentified ship put on a burst of speed, but it was speed that the Intrepid easily matched. "Helm, bring us up beside them, about a kilometer out. Match speed and course. Guns, I want the phalanx on full automatic. If either of these Bozos starts shooting missiles I want something between them and me. I want missiles ready forward and aft, both active and kinetic. And I want that rail gun you've got hidden downstairs ready to shoot, do you understand?"

"What rail gun?" Anna asked.

"Yeah, don't get cute with me sister. I've got the plans for this ship memorized and I know what's hidden between the decks, so just power it up."

"Tess, I want you on counter measures. If anything gets past the phalanx, I want it confused by flares and chaff, got it?"

Don pressed the button on his handset. "Unidentified ship, this is the Earth Ship Intrepid. This is your final warning. I will kill you if you do not identify yourself."

"Sir, they have a firing lock on us," said Tessy.

"Anna, rail gun, aim to kill, fire at will, five shots."

"Sir, they have fired a missile and are taking evasive action," said Tessy.

"Helm, give me a barrel roll to the left, and bring me in behind target one." Distantly, Don heard the port phalanx start its firing rattle, followed moments later by the starboard gun and after that the third machine gun lit up. A long moment later there was a bright explosion to starboard and the three machine guns automatically shut down. Then there were five quick coughs from below their feet and suddenly the ship in front of them was spinning out of control, gas of some type leaking into space and instantly freezing to form a cloud. "Helm, give me vertical thrust now!"

Jean-Paul had been waiting for the order, and instantly the Intrepid changed course, flying at ninety degrees to their original route, straight up. "You want a loop over, boss?" Jean-Paul asked.

"You got it," snapped Don. "Bring me right up target two's butt."

Jean-Paul pulled back on the right hand joystick and flipped the Intrepid over, completing the maneuver as they passed the opposing ship going the opposite direction, landing them a hundred kilometers to target two's rear. Don switched on his microphone. "Target two, I demand you identify yourself now! If you do not identify yourself, I will kill you. Do you understand?"

"Sir, he's taking evasive action," Tessy said.

"Follow him, helm," Don ordered.

"Yes sir, but it's some very erratic flying he's doing."

Don leaned over and studied the pilot's screen and had to agree. "It looks like he's trying to draw us away from target one, doesn't it?" he asked.

"It does, sir," Jean-Paul answered.

"Target one has regained some mobility sir," said Tessy. "And it looks like he's stopped leaking gas."

"If we circle back to finish off target one, this one will escape, Captain," said Anna over his headphones. "And if we pursue this guy, target one has a chance to elude us while we run him down."

"But target one is injured," Don reasoned out loud. "This guy has the most potential to do harm. Guns, toss a couple of long range missiles at target one, and then bring everything you have to bear against target two."

The ship coughed beneath their feet twice and Anna said. "Two long range heat seekers on course for target one." The ship coughed three more times and Anna announced, "Three missiles on track for target two."

"Captain, both target one and target two have fired a wide spread of missiles."

"Guns, use your rail gun on target two. Helm, hard left side, increase thrust to two full rods," there were five quick coughs from below decks, "Now, now, now!"

Instantly the Intrepid shot sideways, rolling on it's left side and then shooting forward towards the Earth, passing target two by a hundred kilometers and then spinning back to once again face her enemies. "Careful we don't get nicked by our own shots," said Don. Ahead of them, target two disappeared into a cloud of debris. "Helm, up and over, take us back to target one."

"Captain, target one has disappeared into the atmosphere," said Tessy. "We've got to get a lot closer in order to track them."

"Lets go then," Don said, "But we have to be a lot more careful with shooting missiles. One of those things could take out a complete village somewhere."

"And the ones we shot in space?" Jean Paul asked, looking worried.

"Will explode about twenty K up," said Anna. "Not only am I smart, but I'm awful careful."

"There he is," said Will, pointing to a screen, and Jean-Paul dove the Intrepid in pursuit.

"Where are we?" demanded Don.

"Over China, deep south east," Will said.

"Guangdong province," said Xiang Wu, "close to Zhaoquing, north west of Hong Kong."

"What's he doing here?" Don demanded of nobody in particular, though Xiang took it upon himself to answer.

"We know many of them speak Spanish. Well, there is a Spanish element in the Philippines. That's just past Hong Kong."

"Sir, target has turned to course one thirty-five degrees, true," said Tessy.

"Follow him Lieutenant Golden. Don't let that schmuck out of your sight!"

"I'm on him, sir."

"Captain, we are being challenged by the People's Liberation Army Air Force. They are sending fighters to intercept," said Pam.

"Are they in front of us, or behind us?" Don demanded.

"Port, about one thirty degrees," said Tessy.

"What's our speed?"

"About mach three, sir," responded Jean Paul.

"Then they can't catch us."

"They could be equipped with the PL-12 missile sir," said Wu. "It has a top speed of about mach four."

"Passing the Chinese coast," Will said.

"Target has reduced speed to mach two, sir," said Tessy. "We have two jet fighters to our rear sir, they have launched missiles."

"Jean-Paul, put target one between us and the missiles please."

The Israeli made an adjustment on his board. "Yes sir. Three hundred kilometers. Two hundred kilometers..."

"Sir, the PL-12 only has a range of about one hundred and fifty kilometers. If that's what they are, they'll run out of fuel and drop into the sea long before they reach us," said Wu.

"Understood," said Don. "Continue, Lieutenant Golden."

"Yes sir, we have passed target two. He is turning away, going back the way we came, but he's not speeding up."

"He has serious marks of damage on his hull, sir," said Tessy.

"On his tail helm." Don flicked the switch on his headgear that gave him access to the radio. "Target one, this is your last warning! Are you ready to die, or are you going to surrender to me?"

"Espero que usted se estrangule en su propio vómito y se muera!"

"Don't bother translating Tess, I get the idea. Guns?"

"Yes, sir?"

"Splash him."

"Yes sir." Three ominous coughs came from below decks and the gleaming spaceship on the screens burst into a thousand pieces, and then disappeared.

"Navigation," Don said, not taking his eyes from the deaths he had ordered. "Plot us a quick route home."

48 Epilogue

Don looked at the three members of his crew and sighed. He picked up his coffee mug from the table and stirred in another spoonful of sugar. He liked sugar, but not this much and he realized he was just trying to find something to do with his hands. He forced himself to put the mug down and relax. In the distance he heard the whistle of the Southwest Chief, coming in from Los Angeles. It was nearly 03:00 and the train was due any moment. "Sacks, Will, I know I can count on you two to sort out the new troops and keep them busy. I've spoken to Rob, and he's going to need all the help he can get to outfit his new ship, so be sure to divide the people with him accordingly. Actually, you should make sure everybody gets several shifts working on the Resolute. The more experience they get with the guts of the ships the more they'll relate to them." Don picked up his spoon again and Tess reached over, and taking it from his hand, put it right back down on the table.

"We shouldn't be more than a week or so at the most, and I sure wish all of you were coming with me."

"Don, relax," said Will. "We know you've got a lot on your mind, but s'all right boss, don't you worry yourself about the kiddies, they'll be all right with us." He grinned evilly. "Green troops we can handle, but it's those folk in Washington you've got to watch out for."

"Which ones," Don asked. He knew the answer, and yet he knew he was expected to ask the question. "The CIA? The FBI? The NSA?"

"Nah," said Sacks, grinning. "The nasty ones, you know, the presidents, the prime ministers, the ambassadors, them kinda folk."

"Oh, like the ones that pay our salaries? Them kinda folk?"

"You got it pawdnah." The doctor seemed to accentuate his Australian accent even as he spoke with a western drawl. To Don's ear it sounded awful, but then, he reflected, it was supposed to. "They say one thing with their mouths, but their actions speak much louder than their words."

With a loud growl and the shriek of steel wheels on track, the train rumbled into the station and a dozen young men and women in various military uniforms detrained from the coach cars, some of them staring around at the night, some looking for their baggage, one or two staring at the officers in the gray uniforms sitting in the terminal coffee shop, wondering if they were the reception committee, wondering what they were doing here. The four officers pushed themselves to their feet and walked out onto the platform and shook hands.

"Look guys," Tess said, "There are so many unanswered questions out there, and I don't even know which ones to ask first. But I do know this; there are no better people to find the answers than us.

"We *will* find out who the Spaniards are. We *will* establish Earth Space as a viable military unit, we *will* find out who these Aliens are, and whether they are good news, or bad, and if they're bad, we *will* protect the Earth from them!" She turned to look at the newcomers and then back at her friends. "We will do it, you, me," and then she grinned, and jerked her head towards the newcomers. "And them."

With a laugh Will and Sacks turned to the disorganized group of men and women by the train while Don and Tessy boarded the first class compartment.

"Chicago here we come," said Tess with a smile. "And then Washington, a medal for me and a medal for you, and then a Unit citation, presented by the big man himself. Pretty classy way to treat some foreigners."

"Not bad," said Don, and smiled back. "I'm just glad I was able to bring my exec, or at least the new one. She's a lot prettier than the first one."

And Tess said nothing, she just smiled.

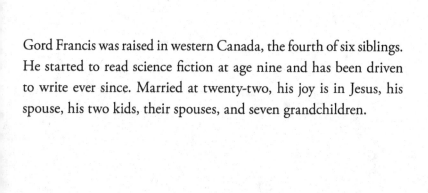

Gord Francis was raised in western Canada, the fourth of six siblings. He started to read science fiction at age nine and has been driven to write ever since. Married at twenty-two, his joy is in Jesus, his spouse, his two kids, their spouses, and seven grandchildren.